D1525330

BAD
SEED

First published 2015 by
FREMANTLE PRESS
25 Quarry Street, Fremantle 6160
(PO Box 158, North Fremantle 6159)
Western Australia
www.fremantlepress.com.au

Also available as an ebook.

Consultant editor Georgia Richter
Cover design Ally Crimp
Cover photograph Getty Images: Shanghai Skyline
Printed by Everbest Printing Company, China

National Library of Australia
Cataloguing-in-Publication entry

Carter, Alan, author, 1959 –
Bad Seed
ISBN 9781925162257 (paperback)

A823.4
Detective and mystery stories

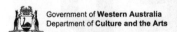

Fremantle Press is supported by the State Government through the Department of Culture and the Arts. Publication of this title was assisted by the Commonwealth Government through the Australia Council, its arts funding and advisory body.

ALAN CARTER

BAD
SEED

 FREMANTLE PRESS

For Vilya, Isaac, Grace and Liam

PROLOGUE

Shanghai, Songjiang District, Sunday, March 9th, 2013.

Zhou hadn't slept well. He was still sick; a bug that he couldn't shake off. Once again he'd spent most of the night squatting in the toilet, emitting a foul liquid stream. He took a swig from his flask of tea, hoping it would stay in his stomach for a while. The kids were down with the bug too, complaining the whole time, but the hospital was full and the drugs were too expensive. The kids just needed to finish their education and get a job with computers so they wouldn't end up a city sanitation worker like him, clearing up everyone else's shit. The boy was a worry though, fifteen and already flirting with the local gang. Another cramp gripped Zhou's guts, he wanted to fart but he didn't dare. He stood on the river shore among the debris of plastic and aluminium and surveyed the earthmovers rumbling across the mud on the far side. Maybe one day they would live in one of those fancy clean skyscrapers and have their own yokel servant to bully. He lit a Double Happiness cigarette and drew deeply, gazing at the Huangpu River and the yellow-grey smog hovering over his life.

The river was brown and sluggish today, like nearly every day. The gulls flew low, squawking half-heartedly. A sand barge chugged by, low in the water, filthy smoke curling out of its funnel. Around him people went about their business of scraping a living. Zhou shivered and pulled his jacket tighter, wondering when spring might arrive to drive away the sickness and misery. He took a final gulp of tea. A full and stinking communal bin awaited his attention, a builder's skip brimful of grease and oil, rotting food, cans and bottles. He readied his shovel and hose and flicked his cigarette into the river. That's when he noticed the dark shape bobbing in the water.

Was it a body? He couldn't tell. Then there were more. Many more. The river seemed to change colour: brown, rust, red. He tried to count the shapes but it was impossible, there must be hundreds. It was like the stories his grandfather told him of the Japanese occupation – the massacres, the rivers of blood. He could see flesh now, pinky-brown torsos rolling in the current. As one edged close to the shore he could finally make out clearly what it was.

'It's a fucking pig,' he said.

Thousands of swine floating down the Huangpu River on a chill morning in March. It had to be an omen for something terrible. Others had seen them now; pointing, chattering, cursing, even laughing. He too started to laugh.

'Shanghai Pork Soup! Throw in some dumplings. It's breakfast for those rich bastards down in Pudong.'

He cackled. He couldn't help himself. If he didn't laugh he would surely cry.

PART 1

1

Coogee, Western Australia, Monday, August 5th. Dawn.

Cato Kwong wondered how long it had been since the goldfish was fed. He sprinkled a couple of flakes in the tank and the fish lazily vacuumed the surface. Rain lashed the windows and another southerly gust shook the walls. Across the road the ocean was churned milky green-grey. Foaming rollers pounded the limestone groyne of the marina. Several million dollars worth of pleasure craft bounced around like corks in a washing machine. Cato looked out across the luxury development they'd called Port Coogee. It was one of several coastal confections that had emerged from the undergrowth south of Fremantle, like dieback in a national park. It had been built on industrial wasteland and offered sparkling ocean views and the chance to live the dream. The blocks alone were priced anything up to three-quarters of a million. But here in Coogee the property boom seemed to have faltered. Cato glanced out of the rain-spattered window. Sand from the many unsold lots wind-whipped and swirling across the deserted streets; half-built McMansions abandoned with flapping tarps; a security guard patrolling in a Hyundai runabout to scare away undesirables. The guard had failed miserably today.

The master of the house, Francis Tan, had been the first to die – and the quickest. Cato turned to the sound of bootie-muffled steps on the metal footplates. It was DI Mick Hutchens, phone glued to his ear, tiptoeing across the blood in a blue paper suit.

'Yes sir, I will still be at the hearing as arranged and on time.' He frowned at Cato, rolled his eyes, and mouthed 'fuckwit'. 'I appreciate that, sir. Look it's a bit of an abattoir down here so I'd better get back to it. I'll keep you posted throughout the day. Cheers.'

One of Duncan Goldflam's forensics boffins shuffled by, taking in the wretched scene on a video camera and murmuring her commentary along the way. Hutchens waited until she'd moved on.

'Okay, lead me through it.'

Cato took a deep breath and waded in. He pointed towards the front door. 'The mains power switch was either manually flicked off or triggered by a short circuit or power cut in the storm. We'll know later. Either way the result's the same, darkness.'

Technicians measured, cameras flashed, shadows played on walls. Outside, the weather got worse. Cato led Hutchens up the wide polished jarrah staircase past a large gilt-framed family portrait. Their steps echoed dully on the footplates; along the way there were numbered markers on blood splashes, prints, and smudges. 'No signs of forced entry. Our killer heads straight to the master bedroom.'

The room was tasteful and subdued in its decoration: a large picture window overlooked the frothing Indian Ocean, thick cream-coloured carpet, en suite bathroom, and walk-in robes. A Nellie Crawford still-life needed straightening. They stood on the threshold and surveyed the sprays of blood on the walls and sticky dark puddles on the bed. A naked man, face down, with the back of his head caved in.

'Victim one: Francis Tan, age forty-three. No struggle. He never even got to wake up.'

Next to him, a naked woman lay sprawled on her back, half out of the bed, a bruised and bloodied left arm hanging down and shattered wrist grazing the carpet. Face gone.

'Victim two: Genevieve Tan, age thirty-nine. She probably woke up as her husband was being attacked. Tried to do something. Failed. Some defence wounds on the arms and hands.'

The boss didn't ask Cato how he knew it was her for sure with the face obliterated. Just as well, this wasn't the time to tell everybody he recognised the birthmark low on her hip. He knew everyone in this house, at one time they had been as close as family. Closer. He was used to wading through other people's bloody nightmares. Now he'd taken a wrong turn, got lost, found himself back up his own street. Inside his own bad dream.

Hutchens nodded, businesslike: tick, move on. Cato felt the strong need for a hot shower and a long sleep; he was ready to tear adrift, like those boats rocking in the gale. They followed the sad trail down the hall to the next bedroom: a Bob Marley poster on the wall, clothes erupting from drawers and scattered on the floor, an acoustic guitar and a Fender Strat leaning against a bookcase. A desk cluttered with files and a laptop, an unmade bed. Just inside the door, a body curled foetus-like on a blood-soaked sheepskin rug. Jocks. A T-shirt. Eyes wide open.

'Joshua Tan. Fourteen. Must have heard the commotion and was on his way to find out what was going on. Again, defence wounds, he tried to put up a fight.'

There was one more bedroom. Duncan Goldflam, forensic honcho, just coming out as they were going in.

'Dunc?' said Hutchens.

A shake of the head. 'This might be the one that finishes me, boss.'

Kanye on the walls: a double bed, dressing table with make-up, tampons, pills. A framed happy snap of a couple, the young man with tickets on himself. No body here, just an awful lot of blood. Cato swallowed the metallic taste of nausea.

'Victim four: Emily Tan, sixteen. Still alive until about half an hour ago. She died on her way to hospital. She was the last.'

Then the killer had left. A bloody smear of size nine sock footprints down the stairs and out the front door, disappearing where he'd have put his shoes back on and went his merry way.

Hutchens thumbed over his shoulder. 'Coming up the stairs we passed a family photo. Five people. Where's the other one?'

'Matthew Tan. Nineteen. We haven't managed to locate him yet.'

'And no forced entry, so we assume either the door was unlocked or the killer was welcomed over the threshold. Or he had a key.'

'Fair bet,' said Cato. He could see that even surrounded by all this carnage, the DI seemed to be distracted, somewhere else. Hutchens still hadn't asked Cato how he knew so much about the family, so soon.

A call came in on Hutchens' mobile. 'Hold on a sec,' his hand covered the mouthpiece. 'Matthew Tan sounds like a good place to start, do you reckon?'

Another strong gust shook the walls. Cato couldn't disagree. He knew the boy, and if anybody was capable of this, he was.

2

Lara Sumich was hunched over the toilet bowl, naked and spewing. It felt wonderful.

'You did this to me, you bastard,' she said to the man brushing his teeth behind her.

His reflection grinned in the bathroom mirror. 'Love you,' he said, through a mouthful of froth.

Lara wiped her face with the back of her hand and stood up. She nudged him aside from the washbasin and gargled some water. Then she pressed her lips to his broad back and wrapped her arms around his front, hands rippling over the belly hair, creeping lower.

'How about John?' she said.

He spat some toothpaste into the sink and rinsed. 'Terrible name. He'll end up working in a library, or a ballet dancer or something; overcompensating. Tyson, I reckon.'

She felt him growing under her touch. 'Is that what you're doing?' she murmured. 'Overcompensating?'

'Always.'

Her mobile trilled. 'Fuck.'

'Leave it.'

But she couldn't. It was her boss from Major Crime, DI Pavlou. 'Put him down, dearie, and get yourself into the office, quick sharp.'

'Something up?' said Lara giving John a last regretful tug.

'A nice juicy murder, back in your old patch. The name's triggered all sorts of bells and whistles in the system.'

'Be right in, boss.' She terminated the call and quickly threw some clothes on.

John was flushed and still proudly erect. 'And what am I supposed to do with this?'

Lara gave him a chaste kiss on the cheek. 'Later, sweetie.'

'What if it turns out to be a girl?' he said, wrapping a towel around himself and patting her tummy. 'A little you, running around the place.'

'Heaven forbid,' said Lara, closing the door behind her.

*

'So how come you know so much about them?'

DI Hutchens was on his way out of the office. There was a whiff of aftershave and a sharp trim to his greying forward comb. He was dressed to impress and seemed to have shed a couple of kilos in preparation for his summons before the court of public opinion. Cato had hoped the hostel inquiry would keep his boss distracted for quite a few more weeks but was reminded, once again, never to underestimate the man's ability to concentrate when you least expected it.

'I went to school and uni with Francis Tan. We were mates back then.'

Hutchens nodded. He liked proving himself right. 'And the wife, face all bashed in, but you still knew it was her.'

'Yes.'

'Stayed in touch, did you, after school and that?'

'Off and on.'

'Okay.' Hutchens checked his watch. 'Fill me in later. Found the son yet?'

'No.'

'You happy to front the hyenas?'

'Police Media have got their golden girl doing the honours. I'll be standing next to her looking serious and capable.'

'Okay, keep me posted. Squad meet at five.'

And Hutchens was gone.

'Sarge?'

Cato sat at his desk and logged on.

'Sarge?'

Cato realised somebody was talking to him. He was still getting used to the new rank, he'd only had it a week. To be precise he was still only Acting Detective Sergeant Kwong; it all depended on whether his predecessor, DS Meldrum, returned from his triple bypass operation. It seemed unlikely. 'Yep?'

It was DC Chris Thornton, a Sydneysider with ambitions beyond his abilities but, his saving grace, a keen eye for detail and order when pressed. He'd make a really good warehouse manager one day. 'Call for you on line two. Some woman.'

'Name?'

'Didn't give one. Said it was … personal.' The last word accompanied by finger quotes and the kind of smirk that invites a headbutt.

Cato picked up the phone. After a few seconds he closed his eyes and pinched the bridge of his nose. This was the last thing he needed right now.

*

'So, over the course of nearly two years at Hillsview, during nineteen ninety-six and nineteen ninety-seven, you were regularly sexually abused by the warden Peter Sinclair?'

Counsel Assisting the Inquiry, Andrew Burke QC, looked like he rowed for Guildford Grammar old boys. Fit, lean, grey and rich. And a chip on his shoulder – probably bullied at school. Hutchens had his phone on silent: he checked for any messages. Lots.

'Yes.' The witness was David Mundine, a nervous pudgy man in his late twenties who, judging by his yellowed fingers and twitches, was itching for a cigarette break. Hutchens glanced at the rap sheet in his file: drink, drug, property damage and burglary convictions and a restraining order taken out by the de facto. A gust from outside seemed to sway the whole building. Horizontal rain flayed the windows.

'Did you tell anyone what was going on during that time, David?'

'Yes, I told the police.'

Burke QC raised an eyebrow in apparent surprise. 'You told the police?'

'Yes.'

'Can you remember the name of the officer you spoke to?'

'Yeah, Michael Hutchens, like the bloke from INXS.' He pointed in the general direction. 'Him over there.'

Just about everybody in the bland overcrowded room on the fourteenth floor of the St Georges Terrace tower block turned to get a good look at the man sitting three rows back. Hutchens ignored them and played Zen. So it was his turn to be the dancing bear in this seedy little sideshow. The judicial inquiry into sexual and physical abuse at state-run institutions was the gift that kept on giving for the tabloid media: lurid allegations, sex and violence, dastardly villains, and pitiful victims. Hutchens had already worked out that it was his role to prance across the stage in a humiliating costume while they prodded him with spears. Fine. All he had to do was get to the other side in one piece.

Burke QC sniffed like he'd become aware of something unpleasant on the soles of his expensive shoes. 'And what response did you get, David?'

David looked down and took a sip of water. 'He told me to piss off and stop wasting his time.'

Cue audience boos and hisses.

*

Cato was on Leach Highway in a pool Commodore driven by DC Deb Hassan. She'd been assigned the job of family liaison. In recent months she'd shown herself adept at prising nuggets of information and evidence from grieving relatives under the guise of being caring and concerned. They were headed to a riverside address in Shelley, a girlfriend of Matthew Tan's. Cato's mobile sounded. It was a voice he recognised: DSC Lara Sumich, one-time colleague now on secondment to Major Crime. They'd had a problematic relationship over the years. A one-night stand, quickly followed by a falling out as Cato stymied her efforts to frame a man for murder. Then a truce of sorts with Lara saving his life two years ago. They'd developed a mutual grudging respect but since her transfer to Major Crime they'd had little contact.

'How's the job going?' said Cato.

'Good, mate. Saw you on News 24 this morning next to Headline Hannah. How's the new rank?'

'Easy come, easy go. I've learnt not to get too attached to these fripperies. What can I do for you?'

'We're offering our support and expertise to your Tan inquiry.'

Whether we like it or not, thought Cato. 'Thank you, why so soon?'

Usually it was seventy-two hours before Major Crime stepped in on a murder inquiry, the theory being that most homicides were three-day jobs: domestics and the like, devoid of any subtlety, forethought, or even a compelling motive. If they remained unsolved after three days then the shiny suits might either offer their expertise to the local office as required or even take over the whole show. But sometimes they wanted in from day one.

'Lots of bodies, looks nasty, they're a well-known family. It's going to be bigger than Ben Hur.'

'Talked to the boss about this?' said Cato.

'His phone's turned off. I've been asked to start the ball rolling.'

Cato wasn't surprised by the early move. She was right: it would be big but was it complex yet? Maybe all they had to do was bring in Matthew Tan and it would still be a three-day job. He could see no real harm in Lara attending the squad meeting later that day but he knew that his boss was as territorial as they come. He gave it a moment's thought then invited her to the meeting. At worst he would suffer a bollocking from Hutchens and that wouldn't be the first time.

'Beauty,' said Lara. 'We'll see you at five.'

Wind buffeted the car and the windscreen wipers struggled with the deluge. Power lines swayed and bits of trees bounced down the road. Cato's mind returned to the call he'd taken just before he left the office: his sister, in tears, and all Cato could do was to promise he'd really try his best to be there.

Deb Hassan signalled a right off Leach Highway just before Shelley Bridge. A few minutes later they pulled up in front of a Louisiana plantation–style mansion with frontage to a black, storm-whipped Canning River. Cato and his colleague hurried up the path and rang the doorbell. It was only a few steps but still enough for them to get drenched. There was a yap and the door opened. Both poodle and girl had matching yellow bows. The girl was in a blue silk kimono and had a recently bedded look. According to the file, she was Lily Soong, a family friend, eighteen.

'Yeah?'

Cato showed his ID. 'Seen Matthew, Lily?'

She turned her head and yelled. 'Matt!' A grunt from up the stairs. 'It's the pigs. For you.'

3

Cato could recall exactly the moment he no longer wanted to be Matthew Tan's godfather. It was a warm Sunday afternoon in late spring: the Swan River sparkled, boats rounded the spit at Point Walter, and Cato was already acutely aware of the difference in earning power between him and his old school buddy, Francis. They were drinking on the Tans' back deck while the barbecue sizzled and the view dazzled. Jane was sticking to mineral water while six-month-old Jake nuzzled her breast. In those days her smiles and bright eyes were still for Cato. The Tan kids raced around the backyard: four-year-old Emily shepherding the chubby toddler Josh away from the careless exuberance of his big brother.

'Matthew, darling, careful with your little brother, sweetie.' The mother's words floated past the boy unheard and unacknowledged. Genevieve Tan's gaze had drifted back to the immediate company on the patio, resting briefly on Cato. It was an unsettling nanosecond of intimacy from days of yore. Uni days. A semester of unforgettable sex before Genevieve moved on and found her future husband. Francis, as usual, was in full flow about himself.

'I was such a lazy bastard at school. If I ever got a mark back saying fifty-one percent I felt dudded, I'd obviously done one percent too much work.' Francis fixed Cato with a sly grin. 'Phil was the swotty arse; anything less than an A was an epic tragedy. He never went out anywhere.' Francis swung his beam on Jane just as she was detaching the baby from her nipple. 'Surprised he ever managed to get a girlfriend at all.'

Cato ignored Genevieve Tan's mischievous half-smile while Jane excused herself and took baby Jake out to a shady spot under a fig tree. She side-footed a couple of steel bocce balls from their earlier game and sat in the cleared space, burping Jake over her shoulder, Matthew and his siblings circling mother and son like injuns around a wagon train.

'Looks like you proved us all wrong, Franco.' Cato gestured towards the multi-million-dollar river view. 'You might not have done that well on trig but you know how to crunch the numbers.'

'True, but I suspect that high-achieving brain of yours won't be wasted in your new job, *Detective*.' Francis lifted his glass in salute. 'To us.'

There was a dull thud followed by a moment's silence. It was shattered by a high-pitched wail from baby Jake.

Jane had a look of horror on her face. 'Oh god,' she said. 'Oh god, oh god.'

Cato looked around, trying to catch up with what had happened, what he'd missed. A bright trickle of blood ran down the front of his baby son's head. Sunlight glinted off a rolling bocce ball. Six-year-old Matthew Tan staring at the blood, fascinated.

The barbecue never happened. Cato remembered children crying. Excuses and admonishments. You didn't mean to do that, did you, Matthew darling? Say you're sorry. He remembered that feeling of cold dread on a warm sunny day, a dread he'd never known before becoming a parent. A blurred rush to the hospital with time standing still. The bewildered wailing of a baby introduced to real pain before it was time. Jane's wet, red accusing eyes: your friends, their fucking psychotic child. Tests. No sign of concussion or brain damage: probably the fact that it had been a glancing blow and Jake's baby skull was still soft, still forming, still pliable, was what saved him from serious damage. Keep an eye on him for the next few days, said the doctor. Cato remembered those snapshots from that day, clicking into focus like Dad's old holiday slides on the carousel projector.

Say you're sorry, Matthew.

He's only six, for goodness sake.

Cato had known from that day that he no longer wanted to be godparent to his best friend's first-born. They'd made the effort over subsequent months: a couple of dinner invitations on neutral ground in a restaurant, stalled conversations, taboo topics. Matthew never did say sorry; it seemed like a point of honour for him. Cato found himself in a succession of staring matches with the boy during those dwindling encounters. Willing him to give in, to acknowledge what he'd done, to do the right thing. They all ended with Matthew's look of triumph. Then, last minute cancellations, work and that, or sick kids. Christmas cards, the odd short phone call, bi-annual email updates to a mass mailout. Within three years, if their paths crossed, it was usually by accident. No specific falling out, just continental drift. Ten years later, for Cato, the Tans were faded photos in an album he couldn't bring himself to toss out. At least they were until this morning.

*

Matthew Tan seemed genuinely surprised to find the police waiting for him at the bottom of the stairs in his girlfriend's house – or rather his girlfriend's parents' house. He finished buttoning his jeans and tugged his T-shirt out over the waistband. He'd let his hair grow since Cato had last encountered him, a chance meeting at a bowling alley. Jake would have been ten, Matthew fifteen or sixteen. He and his mates had the adjacent lane. After greetings and handshakes they'd got on with their own thing. Cato had noticed Matt talking to his mates, looking their way, sharing a laugh at their expense. Jake wondering why his dad's mood had sunk, their evening poisoned. Now Matt had a Celtic-style band tattooed around his upper left arm. He still had traces of chub around his cheeks but he'd lost a lot of weight and what remained seemed harder.

'Uncle Phil?' Matthew stuck out his hand and Cato shook it. DC Hassan offered hers too but was ignored. If Hassan was surprised by her colleague's apparent family relationship to the prime suspect, she kept it to herself.

Cato decided this was not the time to be pedantic about the true nature of their connection. 'Matt, is there somewhere we can all sit down?'

'Sure.' Matt loaded himself up with a cigarette, dispatched Lily to make coffee, and they adjourned to the lounge room. 'What's up?'

Cato had done this sort of thing enough times in his career. It never got any easier, but this was the first time he'd ever had to do it with somebody he knew.

'I've got some very bad news. Your mum and dad, Emily, Josh. They died this morning.'

Matt blinked rapidly, took a long shaky drag on his cigarette. 'What? No! How?'

Cato told him. As Matt listened, tears rolled down his face and he kept wiping them away with the back of his wrists. Lily arrived with the coffees. She caught up with the news, sobbed and hugged Matt who seemed to stiffen and try to shrug her off. Cigarette smoke hung in the air. The coffees went cold. In the silences Cato studied the body language, looking for inconsistencies, for anything that didn't fit. There was nothing.

'We'll need you to come and formally identify them, Matt.'

He nodded dully. 'When?'

'We'll call you, probably a bit later today or this evening.'

'Right.' He gave them two mobile numbers, his and Lily's.

'So Matt,' Cato glanced at DC Hassan who clicked her biro. 'Could you tell us where you've been during the last twenty-four hours?'

*

The Hillsview Hostel hearing was adjourned until the following day. Hutchens had listened calmly and made occasional notes as Burke QC continued to probe David Mundine about the nature, extent, and frequency of the sex abuse at the grubby hands of the warden, Peter Sinclair. It wasn't pleasant and there had been several breaks for drinks of water and wiping of tears. Mundine had failed to meet Hutchens' eyes any more since the first pointing of the finger that morning but Burke QC hadn't been so shy. The man was obviously relishing the upcoming confrontation over the next few days and the acres of media coverage that would ensue. Hutchens packed his papers into his briefcase and checked his mobile again. He had an hour to get back down to Fremantle for the squad meeting on the Tan case. He felt a presence at his shoulder.

'You're toast, mate.'

It was Andy Crouch, retired long-time colleague, sometime mentor, but never quite friend.

'Crouchy, you old bastard. How's it going?'

'Fair to middling.' Crouch nodded towards the departing Burke QC entourage. 'Good day for a hanging.'

'Surprised you didn't bring your knitting.' Hutchens' mobile beeped with some waiting messages. 'Let's catch up soon if you're going to be around. Beer or something.' He waggled his phone. 'Duty calls.'

Crouch smiled. 'Yeah, good, sure. I'll be around. Wouldn't miss this for the world.'

*

'He says he was in bed with his girlfriend.'

'Bugger, thought for a moment there we might have had him.' There were a few dutiful snorts and chuckles. Hutchens gave the floor back to Cato.

The Incident Room was full. It was bigger than the old one in the colonial-era building they'd recently abandoned after an asbestos scare. Now they were in a converted bank on High Street, with a bookshop a few doors down, a record shop over the road, more cafes than you could poke a stick at, and room enough to swing a cat burglar. But parking was a pain in the arse. Rain spattered the windows and daylight was long gone. Whiteboards marked up with names, circles, joining lines and grisly photos. A sea of faces watching Cato on his first major case as a sergeant: some possibly waiting and hoping for him to fall flat on his face, again. 'We'll bring Matthew in for the identification this evening. See how he reacts. Film it. Meantime maybe you can fill us in on some of the science, Duncan?'

Goldflam looked more tired and somehow less tall with every passing day. There were dark circles under his eyes and a grey tinge to his skin. He seemed to have finally had enough. 'Size nine feet, right-handed, using a large spanner or pipe wrench or some such. Pretty angry, very thorough, probably alone but not necessarily, too early to say. No forced entry. Several messy and complicated crime scenes, a lot of trace to work through, we'll keep you posted.'

'Anything missing?' It was Lara Sumich, accompanied by another Major Crime suit, male and older.

'Too early,' said Goldflam.

Lara's eyes on Cato now. 'Known associates, enemies, suspects – apart from the son?'

'Too early,' said Cato.

'We have a few suggestions,' said Lara.

'Too early,' said DI Hutchens.

*

It was nearly 9 p.m. by the time Cato landed at his sister's front door, having been dropped off by DC Thornton. Cato's old Volvo station wagon had failed to start and he'd abandoned it in the car park at Charlie Gairdner's, leaving a terse note on the windscreen to ward off the zealous hospital parking rangers. The identification of victims in the morgue had been largely uneventful – Matthew Tan had cried in all the right places, more so when with his siblings. A body language expert would review the video footage in due course but so far the surviving Tan hadn't put a foot wrong. Too early. Lara Sumich had tried to invite herself along to the mortuary but this had been stamped on by DI Hutchens. She had made thinly veiled threats about her superiors taking up the cudgel, but Hutchens had shrugged in a bring-it-on manner. He was obviously shaping up for a combative week. The door opened.

Cato looked up and found a smile for his big sister. 'Mand.'

'Took your time.'

'Yeah, work, sorry.'

'The Tans?' she said. Cato nodded. 'It was on the news, horrible.'

'Very.' He stamped his wet boots on the mat and Mandy shushed him. 'Sorry. Kids in bed?'

She nodded and led him down the hall along polished jarrah floorboards and out into the open-plan kitchen and dining area. The committee was waiting: his younger sister, Susan, along with Mandy's husband, Kenneth. They were gathered around the kitchen table nursing mugs of tea. Susan looked like she'd been crying. Cato gave her a hug.

'Pip,' said Susan.

'Susie.'

'Phil,' said Kenneth.

Cato shook his hand. 'Ken. How's the orthodontics going, business good?' A nod and a wink in reply. A plant pot blew over on the back patio, a plastic garden chair rolled against the French windows, the lights flickered.

'Tea?' said Mandy.

'Great.'

They all sat and got down to business.

'Dad?' Cato blew on his tea.

'Asleep,' said Mandy. 'Brain tumour. The doctor reckons three to six months.'

Cato felt like he'd been slapped. 'That's quick.'

Susan sniffled and welled up.

'The Parkinson's helped disguise the cancer symptoms until it was too late. There's an inoperable lump and secondaries in the lymph glands.' Mandy swallowed back some tears and Kenneth patted and rubbed her shoulder. 'The best he can manage these days is a two-star Sudoku. And even that takes all day.'

And so it went around the table: preparations for a death in the family, the merits of home versus hospice. What ifs. Cato excused himself, ostensibly for a toilet visit, and went to his dad's room. The door was ajar. He looked through the gap. The old man was dozing, the bedside lamp was on. He didn't look any different, didn't look like he only had a few months left. A lock of grey hair hung down over the lined forehead. Cato felt a tightness, a pounding in his ribs.

Susan stood behind Cato. Put her arms around him, hands on his chest, rested her head against his back, let her tears dampen his shirt. 'What are we going to do without him, Pip?'

'I don't know, Susie.'

Cato realised he was crying too.

4

Tuesday, August 6th.

The power was out further south in parts of Bunbury and Busselton, and in some of the northern metro suburbs. Trees across roads, the roof lifted on a new school library in Palmyra, and flash flooding in low-lying areas. The SES had about three days to try to clean up the worst of it before the next front came through. A blown-over wheelie bin in nearby White Gum Valley had disgorged pizza cartons, cat cans, disposable nappies, and a large adjustable spanner covered in what appeared to be blood. The owner of the wheelie bin didn't remember putting a bloody spanner in there and didn't fancy getting the blame for anything, so he'd phoned it in. He had no criminal convictions but there was an outstanding speeding fine listed under his wife's name. The spanner was now with the scientists.

For Cato it was a good start to the new day. Or it would have been except for the ticket on the windscreen when he'd retrieved his Volvo earlier from the mortuary car park. At least the car started this time so he decided to try and be philosophical about it. Cato sipped on a takeaway coffee and glanced down the hill towards the Port Coogee marina as a strong breeze riffled the surface of the ocean and snapped at the crime scene tape. With the improvement in the weather, a shrine had appeared against the first tree outside the cordon on the corner of Leonidas Road: teddy bears, flowers, photos, messages of condolence. Leonidas, Cato recalled from his student days, had been king of the Spartans and sacrificial hero of the '300' Battle of Thermopylae. And now here he was, immortalised in Port Coogee. Leonidas had drawn his stubborn line in the sand and been swept away by the relentless forces of history. Maybe that was the lesson of Port Coogee, mused Cato. Resistance is futile.

A temporary CCTV camera had been positioned to record those paying their respects, just in case one of them turned out to be the killer. Before he'd left the office, Cato's attention had been drawn to a Facebook tribute page for the daughter, Emily. The tech geeks at HQ were watching that too. Cato could see by his expression that Duncan Goldflam had some news.

'Duncan?'

'We're still wading through the soup: there's blood, fibres, bodily fluids of at least half-a-dozen people sloshing around in there. It's not going to be quick or easy.'

'So?'

'So I'm wondering why there are no significant traces around the spare bedroom.'

'Show me.'

They went inside.

Matthew Tan's old bedroom had been converted to a guest room but still carried echoes of his presence. The perceptible tang of old cigarettes not completely erased by opened windows or a spray of air freshener. A fist-shaped dent in the wall beside the door where his temper had got the better of him. A gouge on the paintwork of the skirting boards below the window and the initials *MT* carved there with something sharp.

'No sign that the killer even bothered opening the door,' said Goldflam. 'No trail of footprints to the threshold. Nothing fresh on the handle.'

'Because he knew there was nobody in here. Knew there was no point,' said Cato.

'No wonder they promoted you.'

Cato's mobile tinkled.

'Latest?' It was DI Hutchens, in a car, presumably on his way to another day at the Inquiry. This was his version of operational leadership.

'Probably worth having another chat with Matthew, on the record and under caution this time.' Cato told him why.

'Good enough for me. See if you can batter a confession out of him and wrap it all up before tea-time. That'll keep the hyenas yakking.'

'Will do.'

'And if Major Crime ring again, tell them fuck off from me.'

'Yes, boss.'

'When's the PM?'

'Later this morning. Ten. I'll call in for a while but best let them get on with it given there's four bodies to work on.'

'Fair enough. While you're up in town, let's meet. This circus usually wraps up around four. You still haven't told me about your relationship with the victims.'

'Right.'

'There's nothing for me to worry about here, is there? No conflicts of interest or anything?'

'No.'

'Good. There's a Dome over the road in the Trinity Arcade. See you there at four fifteen. Flat white, one sugar, your shout. Maybe a bikkie as well.'

Cato left Duncan Goldflam and his mob to continue sifting through the forensic broth in the Tan home and headed back to the office. A team of detectives and uniforms was doorknocking the area. That was expected to take most of the day. The boffins had taken away the array of family PCs, Macs, iPads, smartphones and such, and were picking the bones out of them. The telcos were also doing their bit: logging calls received and made, durations and locations in the preceding week, timeline to be expanded as required. DC Thornton hovered by Cato's desk.

'You invited Matthew Tan in for a chat, yet?' said Cato.

'He's just checking the availability of his lawyer, says he'll get back to us.'

'Get back to him. Tell him I'm just checking the availability of the Tactical Response Group. If he's not in here by midday we're going to come knocking. But keep it nice and polite, he's in mourning.'

Thornton seemed pleased with that.

*

'And you had no further contact with Mr Sinclair from that day?'

'That's right.'

Burke QC checked his notes. 'October twenty-second, nineteen ninety-seven. A Wednesday.'

'I'll take your word for it.' Carol Ransley, a farm girl if ever there was one, had been the office manager at Hillsview Hostel between 1992 and 1998. She'd retired early to care for an ailing husband who had since died. Fifteen years on, and pushing seventy, she presented as remarkably fit and mentally sharp. Hutchens had hoped she might have gone to seed, at least mentally. No such luck.

Burke QC paused for a sip of water and enquired after Mrs Ransley's welfare. She curtly let him know she was fine and keen to proceed.

'At what point did you alert the authorities to Mr Sinclair's disappearance?'

'I gave it a couple of days.'

'A couple of days?'

'Look, to be honest he wasn't the most pleasant fella to work for. We were a bit relieved to have a break from him.'

'Really? Why?'

'He was a creep.' A titter in the public gallery. Hutchens saw Andy Crouch glance his way, grimly amused.

'And how did that manifest?'

'Manifest? He ogled the boys, bullied the female staff, and smelt funny. Don't know how he got the job in the first place. He wasn't right.'

'We'll return to that in due course but for the moment perhaps you can tell us what eventuated after those couple of days.'

'Eventuated?'

'Happened.' Burke QC's manner was becoming more clipped by the minute. He didn't seem comfortable with ordinary folk who answered back. Hutchens stored that away.

'Right. Well what eventually eventuated was that I called the cops.'

'You called the police?'

'That's right. And they sent a couple of blokes along to look into it.'

'What did they conclude?'

'Nothing. Thin air. Big mystery. After about a week they reckoned we should advertise for a new warden.'

'Do you remember the names of the two police officers?'

'Nah, not both, just the main one that did all the talking.'

'Yes?'

A liver-spotted hand pointed to the back of the room. 'Him over there, that Hutchens bloke.'

Hutchens could swear he heard Andy Crouch chuckle.

*

Cato's file on Matthew Tan was shaping up nicely and he hadn't even formally cautioned him yet. There was the matter of the young man's violent criminal record, assaults on previous girlfriends and a restraining order against him, along with some early results from the doorknock and from the examination of computers from the Tan household. It was a good starting point and Cato should have been feeling fairly cocky. But while Matthew himself was a blank, there was a pre-emptive smugness oozing from the lawyer, 'Hooray' Henry Hurley – or was that just Hurley's permanent expression? Cato had crossed paths with him before, he was the lawyer of choice for those that could afford him. Cato feared an ambush. He decided to send DC Thornton out from the trenches first, just in case.

'What kind of car do you drive, Mr Tan?' asked Thornton.

'BMW 3 Series, black, new.'

'Nice,' said Thornton. 'It was parked outside your parents' home on Sunday night. The night of the murders.'

Matthew blinked at the final word. 'They're my family. I told you already. I visited them that night.'

Thornton looked at his notebook. 'And you told my colleagues you left by about nine p.m.?'

'Yes.'

'But your car was still there at midnight.'

'I'd had a couple too many glasses of wine over dinner. I got Lily to pick me up. We were meeting some people in Freo.'

'Hers is a Hyundai i30, silver, right?' A nod that turned into a 'yes' for the benefit of the recording. 'And when did you return to get your car?'

A show of thinking. 'Midnight, one-ish? I'm not sure. The grog had worn off by then.'

'Did you notice anything unusual when you returned?'

'Like what?'

'Cars parked nearby, lights on in the house, anybody around on the street. That kind of thing.'

'No. The lights were off. I assumed everybody was asleep.' A choking sob on the last word. Henry Hurley patted his client's arm consolingly.

'Mr Tan is clearly very upset. Is this really necessary right now?'

'Yeah, sorry,' said Thornton. Back to Tan. 'Do you remember the routes you took returning for your car and then heading back to your girlfriend's house?'

Matthew told them. Any CCTV along the way would be checked for corroboration. Cato cleared his throat as a signal that he was incoming. Thornton gave way.

'Tell me about your folks. How do you get on with them?'

Matthew had been staring at the tabletop. He lifted his eyes to Cato's. 'Did.'

'Yes, of course.'

A shrug. 'Not real close to Dad. I think I was a bit of a disappointment to him.'

'In what way?'

'You must know all this already, Uncle Phil.' DC Thornton shifting in his seat and a sideways glance; an amused curl of the lips from Hurley. That would be one of their angles of attack when it came.

'For the record, Matthew.'

'Sure, of course. As you know, Dad's got, had, a strong work ethic: successful businessman, pots of money, good provider. He saw me as a lazy, spoilt, useless bludger.'

'Are you?'

'I'm only nineteen. Bit early to write me off, don't you think?'

Cato thought about his own parents and their disapproval of his career choice when the expectation was medicine or law: the lawyer kind of law, not cop. 'Fair enough. How about your mum?'

A smile and a filling of the eyes. 'We were really close. She understood me, defended me whenever Dad was having a go. Didn't judge. She was ... warm.' The tears rolled down his face.

Cato nodded. 'So why did you send her an email last Friday calling her a "fucking bitch"?'

*

En route to the post-mortem, Cato picked up a chicken roll and a Mars bar. He had just polished off the former and was about to unwrap the latter when his mobile went. He slotted it into the hands-free cradle.

'Lara. Hi.'

If she was still feeling tetchy about Hutchens putting up the barricades, her voice didn't show it. 'Thirty hours and counting. How's the investigation going?' She made the word 'investigation' sound like some hobby of Cato's.

'Fantastic.'

'Great. Had the PM yet?'

'Heading there now.'

'Need company? Somebody to hold your hand in case you spew?'

'No, I'm good, thanks.'

'Cool, no sweat, we'll take a look at the professor's report when it's ready.'

'Look, I have no issue with you guys coming in as soon as you like.' That glance of Henry Hurley's, the personal interest angle of attack they would take. Once Cato brought up the abusive email from son to mother it had gone 'No Comment' after that. At the end of the session Hurley had a 'gloves are off' demeanour about him as he guided his apparently distressed client out of the interview room. Some objective, expert, arms-length overseeing from Major Crime was probably a good idea and sooner rather than later. 'But you know the boss as well as I do.'

Cato had his own misgivings about Hutchens being distracted

by the hostel inquiry right at the time he needed to be focused on a major murder investigation. Headline Hannah from Police Media was doing a fair job of feeding the ravenous press pack but already the seasoned hacks were wondering aloud why their favourite Major Crime hotshots weren't in on it yet. Hutchens couldn't have it both ways. If he was out of the game then some other big boys, or girls, needed to be in.

Lara stayed as bright and bouncy as Tigger. 'Sure, mate. My boss is pretty relaxed for the moment. She knows DI Hutchens has a lot on his plate with the Inquiry. Doesn't want to add to the poor bloke's burden.' Code for kick him while he's down. 'In the end we're all on the same team, good versus evil.'

Somehow she made it sound like a threat. 'Right,' said Cato.

'Meantime you might want to take a look at some of Francis Tan's business deals. He's been keeping some interesting company.'

'Really?'

'I'll send you an email. Regards to the professor.'

Cato pulled into the hospital car park. It reminded him he had a bone to pick with the parking ranger. He gobbled down his Mars bar and headed for the mortuary.

*

Professor Mackenzie, a petite Glaswegian with rosy cheeks and an accent right out of *Braveheart*, pointed Cato to a bulky A4 envelope on a nearby desk as she finished zipping young Joshua Tan back into his body bag.

'A hard copy of the reports on the mum and dad plus photos, toxicology, et cetera: the rest to follow later today by email. Time of death estimated at somewhere between ten p.m. and about two a.m. If I can narrow it down any further from subsequent tests, I'll let you know. Indications are that Mrs Tan had sex that day but so far nothing suggesting any of it was improper. In summary it looks like they both died from being hit with that spanner you found in the wheelie bin; the blood traces, indentations and wounds correspond.' She slid Joshua Tan back into his drawer. 'Same with the young lad. Mother and son had defence injuries. Particular ferocity applied to the mother, especially the face. Obliterated. Mr Tan didn't even get to wake up, luckiest of the lot I suppose.'

Cato found himself thinking about Genevieve Tan, about the birthmark on her hip, about college days and happier times. About how infatuated he had been with her. He also thought about the savagery applied to her and about the anger in Matthew Tan's email. Matthew, bouncing a solid steel ball off baby Jake's head and never saying sorry.

'What about the daughter, Emily?'

'Next cab off the rank.'

The professor opened a body drawer and got to work. Cato retired to the gallery and checked phone messages while the preliminaries were done. The Y-incision, the snapping of ribs, the cranial saw, the peeling and cutting and weighing were all things he was happy not to witness.

'This might be of interest to you, Philip.'

Cato looked up from the square metre of floor tiling he'd been examining for the last ten minutes. 'Yes?'

'The young lady was pregnant. I'd estimate two months.'

5

'No confession yet, then?' Hutchens blew on his coffee and munched absent-mindedly on a king-sized Anzac dotted with Smarties.

'Not as such.' They were in a city-centre Dome: kids with silly hats serving so-so coffee. Outside in gloomy bus shelters, commuters braced against the wind tunnel of St Georges Terrace. Cato had left his car near a station on the Fremantle line rather than try to park in the city; life was too short and pay too meagre. Cato filled his boss in on the day's developments, starting with the doorknock.

'So his Beemer's still parked there within the murder timeframe?'

'Yep,' said Cato.

'And he's come up with a story and you're checking it.'

'Yep.'

'What's a nineteen year old layabout doing with a car like that?'

'Good question. Probably paid for by the parents. We need to look at the money thing: it's come up in emails between Matthew and his mum, and Major Crime think Francis is a bit iffy in his business dealings.'

'Still sniffing around are they? They should mind their own fucking business. Go and buy a nice set of matching ties or something.' A bite of the bikkie.

'It makes sense. You're otherwise engaged, they've got the experience. I haven't.'

'Bullshit. You know your stuff. You've taken a few scalps. You might take a while, go round the houses, sniff the daisies, but you get there.'

Cato realised there was probably a compliment in there some-where if he went looking.

Hutchens picked a blue Smartie off his Anzac and put it to one side. 'Neighbours heard nothing?'

'What neighbours? You've seen it. Most of that part of the suburb is still a building site. The lot next door on one side is only half-built, across the road it's just sand, and the other neighbour is semi-retired and didn't have his hearing aid in. His wife was off visiting the rellies down south.'

'Port Coogee.' Hutchens snorted. 'Why are the Tans living there anyway?'

'They like it?'

'But I thought they were filthy rich. Why take up residence in Legoland?'

Cato hadn't got around to thinking about that but, on reflection, Hutchens had a point. The suburb aspired to be exclusive and, in terms of value for money, it was certainly expensive: a cramped collection of off-the-peg McMansions. Okay, if you liked that sort of thing, but compared to the Tans' previous residences this was indeed, well, not Bicton.

'I grew up down that way,' Hutchens said. 'Used to fish and swim along that beach before it became private property. It was fine as long as you stayed away from the PCBs they dumped from the power station.' Hutchens fiddled with his teaspoon. 'Up and down the coast, everywhere you look it's Samesville. They should ban those fucking white-shoe tossers from building those crappy plastic shitholes.'

Cato suspected an element of anger displacement. 'So how's the Inquiry going?'

'Shit. There's something brewing, some trap they're getting ready.'

'When are you up?'

'Tomorrow or the day after; they're behind schedule. Who knows?'

Cato studied his boss. He seemed taut, on the verge of snapping. Cato almost felt sorry for him. He finished off his report with the preliminaries from the post-mortem confirming the ferocity of the attack on the mum, Matthew's email, and Emily being pregnant.

'Thoughts?' said Hutchens.

'We'll take a look at Emily's boyfriend, see if he knew she was expecting, and how he felt about it. The violence on Genevieve Tan still makes me think it's Matthew.'

'Sure, he definitely warrants a look, but chucking an email tantie with your mum is a big step from slaughtering your family.' Hutchens finished his coffee. 'Tell me where you fit into all this.'

Cato did.

Hutchens yawned and checked the time on his mobile. 'So you and her had a thing going at uni but she ended up with your best mate?'

The man had a way with words. 'Yes,' said Cato.

'And you reckon Matt's a little psycho because at the age of six he chucked a bocce ball at your baby boy and didn't say sorry?'

'Yes.'

Hutchens frowned, popped that last blue Smartie in his mouth. 'You really need to build a bridge, mate.'

*

Cato collected his car at Karrakatta station. His mobile went off just as he was coughing the Volvo into action.

'Clock's ticking,' said Lara Sumich. 'Checked your emails recently?'

'I'm trying to maintain a healthy work–life balance. Thought I'd do it back at the office.'

'We'll be moving in first thing tomorrow.'

'Says who?'

'My boss.'

'Has she talked to my boss about this?'

'Doesn't need to. She's bigger than him. But yes, she has anyway.'

'What'd he say?'

'Fuck this, that and the other. My boss reckons he needs a new dictionary.'

'So what's the point of this call?'

'Courtesy. I sent through some info about Tan's business dealings that has come to the attention of the ACC.' Australian Crime

Commission. 'One associate in particular is booked on a flight out of Perth tonight that will have him in Shanghai by morning.'

'Shanghai?'

'It's in China. Thought you'd know that.'

'That expensive education of yours wasn't wasted. What about him?'

'He's a really bad guy and we need to stop him getting on that flight before we've had a word.'

'Do we have just cause?'

'Murder good enough for you?'

*

Cato read up on Francis Tan's business dealings on the way out to the airport. He was in the back of a Commodore squeezed between Lara Sumich and a muscled blond called James who didn't like talking. The driver could have been James's twin: they had a lot in common – blond, dumb. In the front passenger seat was Lara's boss, Detective Inspector Sandra Pavlou. She had cropped dark hair and the physique of a runner. Cato recalled her from the Academy, a year ahead of him. They'd recognised each other as that year's over-achievers. Somehow Cato had since got waylaid on the road to success.

Tan Enterprises had signed up to a joint venture with Golden Endeavour Holdings which had offices in Shanghai, Macau and Perth and was registered in Nauru. Francis Tan was the front for a number of major land acquisitions in the state's South-West and Great Southern, along with strategic investments in smaller iron ore mining ventures in the Mid- and North-West and some luxury developments along Perth's urban sprawl. So far, so good – Properties R Us. The main mover behind Golden Endeavour was Li Tonggui, or Thomas Li as he was also known. The ACC thumbnail was big on innuendo, small on detail.

'Are you guys serious?' said Cato.

DI Pavlou twisted her head to acknowledge his presence. 'Meaning?'

'Li comes over as a cross between Alan Bond and Fu Manchu.'

'Yeah?'

'But he has no criminal history, no convictions, no dodgy paper trail, and the company he keeps seems to be respectable enough, as business empires go.'

'So?'

'So what's our reason for stopping him going about his apparently lawful business?'

'He's on a watch list.'

'Whose list? Why?'

'Have you been taking anything in from the intelligence brief? ACC says he's bad.'

'Is there something I'm missing, something I'm not being told?'

'Yes,' said DI Pavlou.

The driver dropped them outside the international terminal and they marched in while he parked up.

*

They caught up with Li in the Kris Lounge waiting to board a flight to Singapore. They'd had a bit of trouble getting past the woman at the door given that they didn't have boarding passes or Kris Lounge memberships. Li was medium height, tubby and affable, and seemed bemused by DI Pavlou and her entourage. He gave Cato a funny look too. He conferred in Mandarin with his PA, a striking Chinese woman of indeterminate age, and agreed to assist DI Pavlou with her enquiries and catch the next flight. The PA went off to make alternative arrangements and they all adjourned to a private room in the Kris Lounge.

As they were settling into their chairs, DI Pavlou took a call on her mobile.

'Your PA was quick off the mark, Mr Li,' she said after she hung up.

'Really?'

'Your lawyer will be here in thirty minutes. Wonders if we'd mind waiting.'

'Do you?'

'Not at all.' A door opened and a tray of coffee, sandwiches and nibblies was brought in. 'If your PA ever decides to leave maybe you could send her my way,' said DI Pavlou, munching on a smoked salmon canape.

'I doubt you could afford her.' He reached for the coffee pot. 'Shall I be mother?'

*

The lawyer actually took forty minutes. Maybe he needed the extra ten to check himself in the mirror. He arrived looking immaculate and smelling a little of man make-up. His name was Damien and Lara seemed to already know him.

'This had better be good,' he said briskly, checking his watch. 'Mr Li's flight is boarding now. He should have been on it.'

The time had passed amiably enough. Li had been engaging and entertaining in his small talk, commenting on everything from the weather, to the upcoming Federal election, the prospects for the Dockers in the footy finals, and fishing. He enjoyed fishing out deep and pulling in the big ones. DI Pavlou had nodded, she liked doing that too.

'Glad you could join us, Damien.' DI Pavlou turned back to the client. 'We really do appreciate you sparing us a few moments, Mr Li.'

'My pleasure.'

Cato wasn't sure what he was doing here. The show was DI Pavlou's. Lara Sumich had adopted the role of protégé. James Blond and his driver twin had retired to the other side of the door to chew on sausage rolls and watch some sport. Cato really wasn't needed and he certainly, at this stage anyway, had no issue with the product.

'We're investigating the murders of the Tan family. Of course you'll know Francis Tan, your business partner.' Pavlou took a sip of coffee.

'Terrible business. Yes, terrible.'

'How well did you know Mr Tan, beyond your business dealings?'

'Not very well. I have joint venture partners all over the world.

Francis was one of many. We had dinner or lunch together sometimes. We did business trips together down south and up to Geraldton. He was a very professional but also a very private man.' Li's English was confident and fluent. He also spoke Cantonese, Mandarin, German, Spanish, Portuguese and French. The ACC thumbnail mentioned an education at London School of Economics and six years in a private equity bank in Hong Kong before returning to his home base in Shanghai.

'How did you come to be business partners?'

Damien leaned in. 'Is this relevant to your inquiry, Inspector?'

'Of course. We're trying to build a picture of Mr Tan so we can work out who killed him and his family and why.'

'I'd be looking at Mad Matt, the son,' said Damien.

'You seem very familiar with the case and the family?'

'Perth's a small town. Am I a suspect now too?' Damien earned himself a sharp look from Li and pulled his head in.

Pavlou enjoyed the moment. 'Not yet, but we're following several lines of inquiry.' Back to Li. 'So how did you become acquainted with Mr Tan?'

Li thought about it. 'A mutual friend, I believe. An associate in Shanghai.'

'Name?' said Pavlou.

Li gave it, along with contact details.

'And what made Tan a good fit for your business, Mr Li?'

'He was well connected, honest, reliable. And he had a history of delivering good results.'

'Until recently,' said Pavlou.

'Sorry?'

'He failed on the land acquisition deal in the Great Southern. He's been haemorrhaging his own capital for the last couple of years. He's gone off the boil, hasn't he?'

Clearly Major Crime had already been doing some digging over the last forty-eight hours while Cato plodded along with small picture stuff and DI Hutchens dealt with baggage from his past. Pavlou's crew should have been in from day one, Cato conceded. And maybe this was why he was along, to watch and learn.

'Mr Tan was having some liquidity issues, yes,' said Li. 'And he had some bad luck with the FIRB.'

'The what?' said Cato.

'Foreign Investment Review Board,' drawled Damien helpfully.

Pavlou cast Cato a glare and he got back in his box.

'Cost you a packet too, didn't it?' said Pavlou.

'That's a matter of commercial confidence.' Li smiled and checked his watch.

'Mr Li's next flight is due to board soon,' said Damien. 'Anything else?'

'Plenty, but we won't delay you any further. When are you due to visit us again, Mr Li?'

'I'm usually over this way every fortnight or so. Contact my PA, Celia, in the Perth office if you'd like to make a further appointment.' He shook hands. 'But promise you won't try to poach her.'

Pavlou grinned. 'Wouldn't dream of it.'

*

'So what were they trying to prove?'

Hutchens' voice was slurred. A red wine too many? Cato didn't blame him under the circumstances. He'd just updated his boss about the evening run with Major Crime. On the way back from the airport DI Sandra Pavlou had professed concern for the level of pressure Hutchens must be under.

'If nothing else, that it's bigger than we can handle alone, boss,' said Cato. 'Just looking into Tommy Li would be an industry in itself.'

'They've got nothing on him. They interviewed him, wasted everybody's time, and let him bugger off to China anyway. What's their grand plan if he decides not to come back now he's been tipped off that the authorities are looking at him? Smart as.'

'Maybe, but they're in as from tomorrow, apparently.'

'Sounds like they've been in all along; and they've got such an exemplary record with all the big cases haven't they? Not.' A rustle and scrape on the phone and the clink of bottle against glass. 'Who's running the overnight?'

'Deb Hassan.'

'Good. She's worth ten of the Armani Brigade any time. Keep me posted.'

It was close to midnight by the time Cato made it to bed. The good thing about the wintry weather was that next door tended to keep their Jack Russell, Madge, indoors. He knew he owed the dog his life after its incessant yapping once warned him of an intruder but it wasn't easy holding the truce. Except in winter. His phone went.

'Are you on Facebook?' Deb Hassan.

'Yeah, I'd been counting all my friends and I was just falling asleep.'

'Sorry. Check out Emily Tan's tribute page.' She gave him the directions to it. His laptop was snoozing on the kitchen table. He would have liked to be doing the same.

'Found it.' He could see immediately what she was on about. 'Trolls.'

'The techs are on to it so no need for us to wade through the sewer, not tonight anyway. Still, I thought you might want to know and I can put somebody on to follow it up in the morning. '

'DC Thornton's your man. It's right up his street.'

She chuckled. 'Sleep tight.'

But Cato knew he wouldn't. Sewers were right up his street too.

6

Wednesday, August 7th.

The Incident Room at Freo cop shop was standing room only. Hutchens' crew were there plus Major Crime, Forensics, some specialist IT techies, a couple of accountants from Fraud, and a bookish-looking man who didn't introduce himself but stuck close to DI Pavlou. Cato guessed he was Australian Crime Commission. Even Headline Hannah was there, oblivious to her surroundings and talking into her phone headset – an air traffic controller without a tower. DI Hutchens still ostensibly ran the show but he had a faraway look and DI Pavlou was itching to get on with things.

'We're blessed,' said Hutchens, with a desultory sweep of an arm. 'Resources and expertise coming out of our ears. And we have a number of lines of inquiry.' He prodded the photo of Matthew on the whiteboard. 'Matthew: spoilt son with a bad temper.' A glance towards DI Pavlou and a finger to another name on the board. 'Thomas Li: shady business partner. He took a big hit when Tan senior blew a deal. Not happy apparently.' And a new one from overnight. 'Zac Harvey: boyfriend of the daughter, Emily, and probable cause of her pregnancy. He trolls for Australia.' Hutchens turned from the whiteboard to face his fans. 'Thank goodness for Facebook, best crime-detection tool since fingerprint powder. Dickheads used to boast about their deeds to a few mates in the pub, now they put it on the internet with a photo and a signature. Sweet.'

DC Thornton put up a tentative hand. He'd briefed Cato earlier and been given the go-ahead to raise the matter. 'Something else has emerged, boss.'

'Yeah?' said Hutchens.

'A bloke round the corner from the Tans' house woke up that morning after the murder and found his jet ski had been vandalised.'

'In what way?'

'Somebody had spray-painted "WANKER" on it in orange fluoro.'

'What's his point?' A low titter around the room.

'Well I checked with the Neighbourhood Watch team and there's been a handful of incidents in the same area over the last month.'

Thornton listed them. An advertising billboard had been smeared with faeces, possibly human. An architect's sign had been defaced with the words "HOW HARD IS IT TO DRAW A BOX?" and a wall beside one of the main entry roads to the development had been graffitied with "ABANDON HOPE ALL YE WHO ENTER HERE". Clearly somebody had a grudge against the place; maybe it was DI Hutchens?

'So what's the theory?' said Hutchens. 'Is our man escalating from petty vandalism to wholesale slaughter?' Another titter.

'No,' said Thornton. 'But he, or she, might have been loitering with a can of spray paint around the time of the murders but feels unable to come forward in case we bust them.'

'Good point,' conceded Hutchens. 'Check the CCTV for any anarchists. Failing that maybe an early morning raid on Murdoch Uni? Ten a.m. should be fine.'

More mirth. Even Duncan Goldflam was grinning. 'We could get some DNA from the faeces. We might get a hit on the shit.'

Hutchens restored order before things got too out of hand but gave Chris Thornton a passing thumbs up. Hutchens, Pavlou, and the ACC Mystery Man had been locked up in the DI's office since dawn. Cato, as 2IC Investigating Officer, hadn't been invited. He suspected a carve-up of Yalta proportions. Hutchens introduced DI Pavlou to the throng even though everybody knew who she was.

'As some of you may already know, I have a pressing previous commitment with the judicial process so it's in the best interests of this case that it's handled by a focused and experienced leader with plenty of time on her hands.' Hutchens thumbed in Pavlou's direction. 'Here she is.'

'Thanks, Mick,' said DI Pavlou, checking her watch. 'You should be able to make the eight forty-seven. Don't let those bastards grind you down, mate.' Hutchens left in a new huff. An exchange of winks between Pavlou and Headline Hannah. The A-Team was now in charge.

Pavlou then announced the results of the carve-up. Major Crime and ACC would follow the Thomas Li thread exclusively. Got that? The domestics, Matthew the Bad Son and Zac the Troll, would be pursued by Fremantle with a Major Crime finger in each pie. The fingers were DSC Lara Sumich and DC James 'Blond' Maloney. Forensics and the techies would continue to do their specialist boffin thing. DC Chris Thornton would collate everything into the system with the assistance of some civilians: a dream job for a budding warehouse manager. DI Pavlou was in charge and no initiatives were to be taken without her blessing. Her eyes rested on Cato as she said that. So did Lara Sumich's. They'd been talking.

The meeting broke up and Pavlou summoned Cato, Lara, and James Blond into her office. She'd set up camp at Hutchens' desk, the photo of Mrs Hutchens now blocked by a bigger one of Pavlou's husband and kids.

'All of that sit well with you, Philip?'

'Sure,' said Cato.

'Everybody seems to still call you Cato around here.'

'Yeah, it stuck.' She would know. She was at the Academy when it kicked off. He seemed to recall her nickname then was The Velvet Hammer. It too had stuck.

'Do you mind?'

'No,' he said.

'I'll go with Philip, or your rank, as the situation demands. You can call me Boss.'

'Right. Thanks. Boss.'

*

ALAN CARTER

'Here be Dragons.'

'What?' said Deb Hassan.

'It's what they used to say on the maps when they didn't know what was over the horizon,' said Cato.

'Who? When?'

'Explorers. A long time ago.' They were driving around a new-build suburb at the southern end of the freeway. According to the street directory it didn't exist yet. The satnav had never heard of it either.

'Good place for a troll to hide,' said Hassan. 'Maybe there's a whole community of them out here. Waiting. Watching.' She crossed her eyes and stuck out her tongue. 'Trolling.' She pulled over to the kerb and Cato rolled his window down to speak to a passing mum with stroller. The wind whipped up dust and sand, black clouds loomed.

'Endeavour Boulevard?' he said hopefully.

'Second left,' said the woman without stopping.

'Thanks,' said Cato.

'Where do you reckon she was going?'

'Mmm?'

Hassan nodded her head back at the mum. 'No bus stops. No shops. Nothing.'

'Friend? Fresh air?'

'She might have been a troll. Off to a meeting.'

'Next left,' said Cato.

Zac Harvey's house was one of just four completed in the street. An off-the-peg Tuscan villa with a boat on a trailer in the driveway, blocked in by a powder-blue turbo ute. The doorbell went ding-dong. A dog barked. A woman answered the door.

'Yes?' She was somewhere in her forties and dressed for the gym.

'Mrs Harvey?' said Cato.

'Yes?' Her face didn't move. Maybe it couldn't.

Cato showed his ID and introduced his colleague. 'Is Isaac home?'

'Why?'

'We'd like to talk to him.'

'What's he done?'

'Is he home or not?' said Deb Hassan. 'We need to talk to him, either here or at the police station. We're investigating the murder of his girlfriend.'

'Ex-girlfriend,' said Mrs Harvey, turning her head. 'Isaac, sweetie. Visitors.' She walked back down the hall. 'You'd better come in then,' she said over her lycra'd shoulder.

They sat in the lounge room: lots of glass, straight edges, gadgets, and a view of a bleak, recently turfed backyard. The dog, a tan staffy, was shivering against the wind and scratching to be let back in, leaving muddy paw prints on the glass.

'Bernice! Stop!' snarled Mrs Harvey. The dog stopped and looked sad.

Zac Harvey made his appearance. The boy from the framed photograph on Emily Tan's wall. He was a good-looking kid. He yawned a lot and kept tossing his head to keep the blond frullet out of his eyes.

'No school today?' said Cato.

'Don't go to school. Go to TAFE.'

'Right. No TAFE today?'

'I'm sick.'

'Sorry to hear that. You'll have heard the news about Emily Tan then?'

'Yes.'

'You don't seem very upset that your girlfriend died a violent death.'

'Ex-girlfriend,' said Mum.

'Is that right, Zac?' said Cato.

'Yeah.'

'Since when?'

'Last week.'

'When last week?' said Deb Hassan.

'Thursday, Friday.' A shrug.

'Why'd you finish?'

Another shrug and a yawn. 'Got boring.'

'Who finished it?'

'Me.'

'Fair enough,' said Cato. 'Still it must be a bit of a shock even if you weren't an item anymore.'

'A what?'

'An item.' Cato glanced at Mum who was playing with her smartphone. 'I'll try a direct question. Are you sad or shocked by Emily's murder?'

Zac flinched at the word. 'S'pose. Yeah. Sucks.'

Try to contain your grief, thought Cato. 'What are your feelings for Emily?'

'Nuthin. She's dead now isn't she?'

'Do you hate her, Zac?' asked Deb Hassan.

Another shrug. 'Nah.'

Hassan unfolded a piece of paper and showed it to him: a printout from last night's Facebook tribute page. 'So why did you say, among other things, "U got yours fucking slut"?'

A smirk. Charming.

'She was pregnant. Was the baby yours, Zac?' asked Cato.

That wiped the smirk off his face. Even Mrs Harvey bothered to look up from her phone.

7

Cato found Lara Sumich sitting at his desk and Deb Hassan found James Blond sitting at hers. They all adjourned to a meeting room down the corridor.

'How'd it go with the boyfriend?' said Lara.

'We've invited him and his mum in for another chat first thing tomorrow. They'll probably be lawyered up.' Cato sipped from a water bottle.

'Reckon he did it?'

'He's a self-absorbed little prick like most teenagers but, first impressions, he seems a bit puny and low energy. Mass murder requires a bit too much effort for this kid. He gets his aggro out on the internet, doesn't even have to leave his bedroom.'

'Amen to that,' said Deb Hassan, who had a fourteen year old.

'Meantime, what've you been doing?' said Cato. 'Any progress?'

'Been trawling Matthew's phone and financial records and internet use.'

Cato had already done that. Yesterday. 'Anything new?'

'Well, in addition to calling her nasty names by text last Friday ...'

'Which he reckons was just a little tantrum, nothing to worry about. He wanted an advance on his allowance.'

'Not surprised. He's living way beyond his means and has debts left, right and centre.'

'Yeah?'

'Yep. One name in particular stands out. Not known for his patience and understanding.'

'Go on then, dazzle me.'

She did, and Cato was duly dazzled.

The Inquiry was winding up for another day. Another day of pale, angry, shattered young men who'd suffered as boys at the hands of the missing warden Peter Sinclair. The man was a beast, no doubt about it. Another day of accusations of cover-ups and whitewash, of finger-pointing at local school principals, social workers, councillors, and police officers. Hutchens' name kept popping up. Another day of Burke QC harrumphing.

Hutchens had been slipped a note from the young woman assistant to the ex-judge presiding over the Inquiry. *You're on tomorrow morning.*

'About time,' he muttered under his breath.

He wanted this over and done with.

Hutchens shoved the note in his pocket and took the lift down to the foyer. He checked his phone messages: Cato wanting to give him an update, DI Pavlou wanting to keep him in the loop, Mrs Hutchens checking his availability for a dinner date. Various brass, or their minions, looking for reports, budget estimates, policy feedback, stats, agenda items for upcoming meetings. The tightness was there again in his chest. Hutchens reached into his briefcase, found what he was looking for, and shoved the angina spray up his nostril.

'Stressful times?'

Andy Fucking Crouch.

'Still here, Andy? Bowling club shut for repairs?'

Crouch tittered. 'Won't be long now. Better get home and iron my shirt. I'm up tomorrow. Just before you, apparently.'

Hutchens realised now what lay behind the smirk. 'Surprised you can remember that far back, Andy.'

'Don't need to, mate. I kept a diary.'

*

Matthew Tan owed money to GFC Loan & Savings Pty Ltd, a company owned by prominent Northbridge identity Guy 'Guido' Caletti. The 'F' in GFC stood for 'Federico' apparently. Lara, James and Cato paid him a visit. As ever, Northbridge had a Jekyll and Hyde personality. On a hot summer weekend night you could be forgiven for thinking you'd just wandered into Dante's inferno, but on a winter's day, if you managed not to see the junkie whores scratching their goosebumped arms and nursing Coke Zeros at a recently hosed kerbside table, the place had a soiled normality about it. Like a vicar harbouring a secret.

Guido was sipping Turkish coffee in a little place called The Cazbar down a side street near Cinema Paradiso, a couple of henchmen at a table nearby. An immaculate white polo shirt stretched across his broad chest, his black leather jacket was draped across an adjacent chair. The *West* was open on the table in front of him – election news. Caletti tutted and shook his greying ponytail disapprovingly.

'I thought we were better than this.'

Lara signalled for extra coffees, flashed her ID to anybody who was interested, and pulled up a chair. 'Something bothering you, Mr Caletti?'

He flicked a finger at the newspaper. 'This race to the bottom. Competing to see how badly we can treat asylum seekers. Tents on Castaway Island for fuck's sake. They'll be promising to spit in their food next. Pathetic.'

A Perth gangster with more humanity and political insight than a Federal political leader; it gave you pause for thought. Cato sat back, happy to let Lara run this show. A few minutes of introductions and small talk followed. Then Caletti said, 'What can I do for you?'

'Matthew Tan,' said Lara. 'A client of yours.'

'What kind of client? I have diverse business interests.'

'He owes you money. Eighteen grand.'

'And?'

'Are you seeking redress?'

'I'm always diligent in my business dealings.'

The coffees arrived. Lara ignored hers. 'Are you pursuing him?'

'I probably am but I'm not the micro-managing type unless it's really necessary. I have highly trained and very competent staff to deal with that.' He nodded in the direction of his henchmen. 'In the scheme of things, eighteen grand is not a huge amount. We'll probably pursue the usual legal channels if and when the default clause kicks in.'

'I think that was some time last week,' said Lara.

Caletti smiled. 'No concrete boots around here, officer. I keep paperwork, receipts, all of that. I file my tax returns and pay up on the due date.' He nodded towards the newspaper again. 'This nation needs to grow up and move beyond stereotypes.'

Lara appraised him for a moment before standing to go. She patted the chair beside him on the way out. 'Nice jacket, Guido.'

His eyes were back on the newspaper. 'This about that nasty murder then?'

'Yes.'

'Hoping I'm your man, eh?'

'Enquiries are continuing.'

'Don't waste your precious time and resources on me. I'm not worth it.' He turned a page.

'Thanks for the advice,' said Lara.

Cato decided to speak up. 'The crossword.' He pointed at Guido's paper. 'Are you keeping that?'

*

Bad story leaves uncle wanting more. Cato was halfway through Guido's donated cryptic when he took a call on his mobile on the way back to Freo. He was in the back seat, James and Lara in front. They'd opted for Stirling Highway, the freeway would be chockers at this time of day. Passing the old Swan Brewery, the river was chopped by the wind and a bank of clouds hung over the western sky. It was his sister Mandy phoning, wanting him to drop by.

'Dad's asking for you.'

'Me?' Cato wasn't used to specific attention from his father. Mandy usually got that. 'Is he okay?'

'Yes, you're his son, remember?'

'Any idea what it's about?'

'Dunno. Maybe he wants to give you that birds and bees talk you missed out on.'

They agreed a time about an hour hence, traffic permitting. Cato tapped the biro on his teeth. *Bad story leaves uncle wanting more.* Four and eight. Poor relation.

'Much as I'd like to, I can't see Guido being involved in this,' said Lara from the front seat.

'No,' said Cato.

'But Matthew's still a bit on the nose, no doubt about that.'

'Yep.'

'We need to find a way into him. I'll check with the DI, see if she's got any ideas.'

'If you like,' said Cato.

'Everything okay with you?' Part challenge, part genuine inquiry.

'Yep, all good.'

But it wasn't. Plenty bothered him. The investigation had already become unfocused, swampy. The tail was wagging the dog. Lara seemed to have promoted herself to his equal. That was probably his fault because he'd let her. And strangely he already missed DI Hutchens. There was something about his prodding and goading and mind games that helped keep Cato on his toes. Under DI Pavlou and Major Crime he felt like he was being jerked along on a leash just to show him who was in charge. Stuff that. If they wanted division of labour and demarcation lines, they could have them.

They pulled up in High Street outside the cop shop and Cato headed down the road for his Volvo. 'Freo Squad meeting, tomorrow at eight,' he said. 'See you both then.'

*

When Cato arrived at Mandy's house he was surprised to find his father sitting up in an armchair in the lounge room sipping at a cuppa and tackling what looked suspiciously like a crossword. In his mind, since the news of his dad's death sentence, Cato had consigned the man to seeing out his last days in bed and communicating by hand taps from the depths of a coma.

'Dad,' said Cato. 'Good to see you up and about.'

Jack Kwong looked up. 'Eight across, "postman's sack".'

'How many letters?' said Cato, knowing the answer already.

'Hundreds!'

Cato grinned on cue. 'How's your day been?'

'Had worse. Did your sister mention I'm going to die soon?'

'Yeah. Bugger.'

'That's what I thought. Did you hear the one about the two Aussie soldiers in the trenches?'

'Go on,' said Cato.

'One's been there for months, haunted look, shell shock and that. He says to the new bloke, "Did you come here to die?" The newcomer shakes his head. "Nah mate, I came here yesterdie".'

Mandy delivered a cuppa to Cato, rolled her eyes at Jack and retreated.

'You were asking after me,' said Cato.

'Was I?'

'Mand reckons.'

The old man studied the crossword for a moment, frowning in concentration, panic flitted across his face. He looked up and smiled. 'Buggered if I know what that was about.'

'You were probably wanting to let me know you'd be leaving everything to me.'

'Nah, I said that to Susie earlier.'

Jack put his head back and closed his eyes. Cato leaned over and took the cup out of his hands. The old man was whispering something. Cato leaned in closer to hear. For all he knew these could be his father's dying words.

'Champagne,' he said. 'Champagne.'

8

Thursday, August 8th.

It was a poorly attended squad meeting. Lara and James, although notionally attached to the Freo office and obliged to show up, had been called out somewhere. DI Pavlou was at a meeting at HQ, and DI Hutchens was off prepping for another big day at the Inquiry. Two others had called in sick; winter flu was working its way through the squad. That left Cato, Deb Hassan, Duncan Goldflam, Chris Thornton, and a couple of civilian data wranglers. There was plenty of yawning, fidgeting, sniffles, coughs and phone-checking going on. Deb Hassan reported that Zac Harvey's mum had declared herself a responsible adult even though her son was already eighteen. They would be in later that morning with their lawyer. Apparently Mrs Harvey was not happy. Bring it on, thought Cato. Deb also reported that the Emily Tan Facebook tribute page had been taken down overnight.

'Trolled into oblivion,' said Deb. 'A new one has sprung up, though. "Zac Harvey Is Innosent" – with an "s" instead of a "c".'

'Lovely,' said Cato.

Next up, Chris Thornton summarised the sitrep on the door-to-doors. In short, everyone was asleep and didn't hear a thing. CCTV and traffic cameras were still being trawled to confirm or deny Matthew Tan's account of his movements and so far his story stacked up. His and his girlfriend's cars were spotted in various places within the timeframe stipulated. It looked like she had indeed dropped him off at Port Coogee not long after midnight to pick up his BMW and they'd driven in loose convoy back to her place in Shelley. There was still no sign of the phantom vandal and architecture critic.

Duncan Goldflam stepped up. 'We're gradually thinning out the forensic soup. About half of the trace samples we took can be attributed to the key family members including Matthew, who has already confirmed he was there that day. So far we can't put him in any of the bedroom murder scenes.'

Cato looked down at his notepad. His action list looked pitiful. He was meant to come up with something at the end of this meeting to rally the troops, renew their focus, pump energy into the investigation. All he could think of so far was: *keep at it, the truth is out there somewhere. Rah, rah, rah.*

'There are about half a dozen other significant – as in probably recent and strong – traces which we now need to investigate and eliminate,' said Duncan.

That was more like it. 'Any of those in the bedrooms?'

'Yes. One cluster in the master bedroom.'

Cato felt a quickening in his blood. 'A recent, strong trace of someone, not a family member, in the master bedroom?'

'Yes,' said Goldflam. 'And, as far as I know, they don't have a cleaner. Maybe a tradie or something? Or maybe the killer.'

Cato's list now had an excited little asterisk on it.

*

Zac Harvey was wearing the same shirt as yesterday. Mrs Harvey was dressed for success and domination in a dark, conservative contour-hugging office suit and killer heels. Their lawyer was some bloke from Armadale with a nervous squint, a nondescript man who seemed to merge into the background of the grey-painted interview room. Cato figured Mrs Harvey intended to do most of the talking. He decided to set her straight.

'Thank you for coming in, Isaac. You're welcome to stay too, Mrs Harvey, as an observer, but this interview is with Isaac and his official legal representative.'

'Whatever,' said Mrs Harvey.

Deb Hassan was busy checking the recording equipment. She

announced the usual preliminaries and nodded for Cato to kick off.

'So Isaac, we'd like to go through those matters we discussed with you yesterday and have it all on record. Okay?'

'Does he have a choice?' said Mrs Harvey.

Cato ignored her. 'Is that okay and clear with you, Isaac?'

'S'pose.'

'Is that a yes?'

'Yep.'

'Great. Mr...' Cato checked his notes. 'Terhorst. You've had enough time to consult with your client? You're comfortable with proceeding?'

There was a clipped and timid 'Yes'. Cato didn't think he'd ever come across a nervous South African before.

'I'm not,' said Mrs Harvey.

'Then feel free to wait in reception,' growled Cato.

Mrs Harvey pursed her lips and shot Cato a glare. She would have been one of those mothers that teachers hate. Cato took Zac Harvey through the last week or so: the break-up – acrimonious and one-sided he reckoned; the last time he saw Emily – just all this crying and shit; and finally his comments on the Facebook page – another smirk. Cato presented Zac and the lawyer with another printout just to remind them it was all on record.

'Not a nice thing to say about somebody who's just been murdered. Why did you do it, Isaac?'

'Joke. Didn't mean anything.'

'That's your idea of funny?'

A shrug. 'So you don't like my sense of humour. No law against it.'

Mrs Harvey smiled. Her son was holding his own. The lawyer looked like he'd found a nasty piece of gristle in a favourite pie.

'Were you aware that she was pregnant?'

'Nah. Any idea whose it is?'

'We'll be seeking a DNA sample from you to try and answer that question.'

'Not without permission, you won't.' Mum sniffed.

Cato turned to the lawyer. 'Your client has admitted leaving those abusive and threatening comments on the Facebook page. In fact there *are* laws against that for which I am willing here and now to arrest him. At that point he can be required, by force if necessary, to provide a DNA sample. Alternatively he can continue to cooperate and assist us in our investigation into this dreadful crime. Would you like some time to consult further?'

'Don't bother,' said Zac. 'I get it.'

*

Andy Crouch had put on a suit and tie, shaved, and brought some kind of order to his wispy white hair. He still had the look of a coffin-dodger though, his skull almost visible through his semi-transparent skin. He managed not to meet Hutchens' steady gaze. So what's he got in that fucking diary of his? thought Hutchens.

'Can you state your name and occupation, please?'

'Andrew Martin Crouch, police officer, retired.'

They went through his CV, how long he'd served, in what capacities, any awards and commendations: establishing his authority, credentials, and utter trustworthiness. Crouchie had been in Kalgoorlie when Hutchens took the posting in Mundaring. What the hell would he know?

Burke QC was so excited he seemed to be standing on tippy-toes. 'You were a close friend and colleague of Detective Inspector Michael Hutchens, were you not?'

'In some ways I considered myself his mentor. I took him under my wing. We worked very well together, particularly in the Armed Robbery Squad.' Burke QC checked the dates and confirmed them with Crouch. 'And then that squad was disbanded and you transferred to Kalgoorlie while Mr Hutchens went to Mundaring. Correct?'

'Correct.'

'Why was the squad disbanded?'

'Restructuring, happens all the time. Some of the top brass go off to do a management course one weekend at a country retreat and they come back and change the names of everything and move a few people around.'

A chuckle of recognition went around the room like a polite

Mexican wave. Burke QC allowed himself a smile to show he was human after all. 'But the Armed Robbery Squad had been together a long time, getting results, knocking heads. If it ain't broke, why fix it?'

'That's a question for higher powers than me, mate.'

Burke's smile faltered. This was harder work than he'd imagined. He didn't know Crouchie. Crouchie was his own man, would say what he wanted when he wanted, and have his bit of fun in the meantime. Hutchens sympathised with the QC on this one, he just wanted the tedious old fucker to get to the point.

'Do you know of any other reason, apart from internal management processes, why the Armed Robbery Squad was disbanded?'

'Yes,' said Crouch, enjoying a leisurely sip of water.

Burke took a big impatient breath. 'Then please do tell us.'

'Okay.' And he did. He told the inquiry all about the wheeling and dealing and consorting they had to do with scumbags to get intelligence, the pay-offs, the tip-offs, the biffo in the interview rooms, the fuck-ups, the protection of low-life informants to the detriment of public safety.

'That's appalling,' said Burke QC, 'How did you become aware of such things?'

'I had a leadership role in the Squad,' confessed Crouch. 'I couldn't help but be aware of some of it.' Because you were doing your fair share, you hypocritical old git, thought Hutchens. 'My only regret is that I didn't do more to prevent it. It brings the whole service into disrepute. But peer pressure is a powerful thing.'

'So you and Mr Hutchens parted company at that point, having had a successful partnership for nearly six years.'

'Mick Hutchens was a rising star. I didn't want to hold him back. My way of doing things wasn't his.'

'What do you mean by that?'

'What I said. Different temperaments.' For the first time Crouch allowed his eyes to meet Hutchens'. 'Out with the old, in with the new.'

No matter how much Burke QC pushed him to elaborate, he wouldn't, but the damage was done. Crouch had said nothing and said everything. DI Mick Hutchens was a corrupt, corner-cutting thug. Hutchens felt his chest tighten again but he wasn't going to let that sly old bastard see him reaching for the angina spray.

*

Zac Harvey was swabbed and sent on his way with mother clicking along beside him in her heels. DC Thornton admired her departing figure.

'I would,' he said.

'She wouldn't,' said Deb Hassan. 'You're too short for her.'

Cato smothered a smile. 'Make yourself useful, Chris. Get Harvey's spit sent off to the lab.' He saw DI Pavlou emerge from her office and head for the kettle. He joined her. 'All well at HQ?'

She spooned some coffee into a plunger. 'Yes. Anything I need to know about?' Cato brought her up to date. 'The Harvey boy is obviously a waste of time,' she said. 'The priority remains the son and the business associate.'

'So how is the Li inquiry progressing?'

For a moment he thought she was about to tell him to mind his own business, but she didn't. 'Lara and James are following up on some matters now with Mike.'

'Mike?'

'Our man from the ACC.'

Ah, Mystery Mike. 'What are they up to then?'

'Classified.'

'Even for the 2IC on the investigation?'

A thin smile. 'I'm afraid so.'

Cato could feel one of his reckless surges coming on. 'So Sumich and Maloney continue to do their own thing and report to you, even though they're also seconded to my side of the investigation?'

'Yes.'

'Makes for a blurred chain of command doesn't it?'

'Are you questioning my management of this operation?'

'Just seeking clarity.'

'Everything clear now?'

'Not yet but I'll play it by ear.'

'You do that.' She poured some scalding water into the coffee pot and didn't offer Cato any.

*

'So when did you first become aware of Peter Sinclair and the allegations of abuse at the Hillsview Hostel, Mr Crouch?'

'October twenty-first, nineteen ninety-seven.'

'That's very precise. How can you be so sure of that?'

'It's in my diary. Do you mind if I consult it?'

Burke QC addressed the Inquiry chair. 'Your honour I've taken the liberty of copying the salient entries from Mr Crouch's diary. Are you happy for me to distribute these to the relevant parties? The original diary will of course be entered officially into the record.'

The judge nodded his assent and copies were given out. Hutchens got one too.

'Now Mr Crouch, can you read the entry you have for that day, Tuesday, October twenty-first, nineteen ninety-seven. The day before Mrs Ransley recalls that the warden, Peter Sinclair, went missing.'

'Really?' said Crouch. 'Well there you go.' He slipped on a pair of half-moon glasses. 'Here it is. "Ten p.m.-ish. Call from MH. Pissed as usual. Reckons he's killed some kiddie-fiddler from the Hills. Bullshit".'

Eyes turned Hutchens' way.

'Anything else?'

'No.'

'What was the purpose of you recording that particular diary entry, Mr Crouch?'

A rueful shrug. 'I was thinking of writing me memoirs. I was in the middle of a first draft. I'd taken to keeping a diary of my thoughts at the time. Nothing ever came of it, though.'

'Never say die, it might have just assumed a new lease of life.' Burke QC chortled, enjoying himself immensely. 'And who do the initials "MH" refer to?'

'Mick Hutchens. Him over there.'

A few journos made hasty exits and the crowd did a dramatic hubbub.

The judge adjourned the hearing and summoned Hutchens into his anteroom. 'At this juncture you might want to consider legal representation, inspector.'

'Fucking right, your honour,' said Hutchens, shoving the angina spray up his nostril.

9

Cato took a call from Jane, his ex-wife and mother of their son, Jake, who had survived having a bocce ball bounced off his head at a very young age to develop into a handsome, confident fourteen year old halfway through year nine at John Curtin Senior High in Fremantle.

'He doesn't want to come over to yours this weekend.'

'Oh. Something on?'

'Nothing special. He just, quote, doesn't feel like it, unquote.'

Cato tried to keep the hurt out of his voice. 'Fair enough. He didn't feel able to call me himself, then?'

'He's fourteen. He wants us all to stop treating him like a kid except when it suits him. Put it down to hormones, I don't think it's personal or terminal.'

'Yeah,' said Cato. 'Probably right.'

'I've got a bit of news. I thought you should hear it from me, first.'

Uh-oh. Cato steeled himself. 'Yeah?'

'Simon and I are getting married.' Simon, the hippy musician boyfriend.

'Great,' said Cato. 'When's the happy day?'

'September fourteenth.'

'Wow, that's near. Keen, eh?'

'There's a reason. I'm pregnant.' She laughed softly. 'I'd like to do it before I start to show too much. Old-fashioned girl that I am.'

'Congratulations,' said Cato. 'Really.'

'Thanks. There'll be an invite in the post. Plus a friend if you want.'

'Cheers.'

'I'll keep you updated about Jake, okay?'

'Yeah. Cheers.'

The call ended. Duration: one minute and fifty seconds. It had taken less than two minutes to turn his world upside down and leave him wondering if there was any point to this existence of his. Any fucking point at all.

*

Hutchens got the Police Union lawyer to persuade the judge to adjourn for a week. Burke QC wasn't too happy but to hell with him. The Police Union solicitor, a short motherly woman called Joan Peters, would read up on the story so far and have him in for a chat tomorrow. At this stage she had only two questions: did you phone Andy Crouch and did you kill the kiddie-fiddler?

'Fucked if I know,' he said.

The truth was that both were a complete blank. In those years he was hitting the Jim Beam and Prozac pretty hard and he'd had a number of memory lapses and blackouts. He could have done anything. Maybe he should have kept a friggin' diary like Crouch and his bastard 'memoirs'.

What he did remember, and what he knew was on record because he'd checked in preparation for this hearing, was that on Tuesday, October 21st, 1997 he'd been called out to an assault at the Mundaring Weir Hotel that early evening towards the end of his shift. He probably could have flick-passed it to someone else but he'd taken it. Some bloke had a broken stubby shoved in his face and the perp had legged it. It was all on CCTV and the barman knew who'd done it. They'd arrested the little prick at his mum's place in Chidlow the following morning. But that Tuesday evening, after taking the statements and viewing the security footage, was a blank. His partner that night was a detective constable called Vesna who'd given the job up two years later to have kids and then subsequently died of breast cancer at the age of thirty-nine. He remembered he'd quite fancied her and possibly had made a clumsy drunken pass at her one time at a work do. He must have decided to stay on at the Mundaring hotel for a drink or two. In those days that would have extended to half a dozen more. There'd be no CCTV to prove it now but maybe the barman remembered him? Then Hutchens remembered something about the barman. He was a Pommie backpacker, long gone.

Maybe if he thought about something else completely for a while, then some nugget might return. He had an adjournment for a week and could get stuck back into the nitty-gritty of the job. He took out his mobile and rang Cato.

'Got a bit of blue sky in my schedule, mate. Anything I need to know?'

Cato gave him the update but Hutchens found his attention wandering.

Driving back down the freeway he switched on the radio, Classic Hits, to try and take his mind off things. It was Barbara Streisand, 'The Way We Were'. Could it be that it was all so simple then? Before 9/11 and Tampa, before Facebook and fucking Twitter. In 1997 Howard was in, Keating was out. Keating: now there was a man who knew how to wield a good insult and still keep his eyes on the big picture; a professorial intellect with the pugilistic instincts of a street fighter. These days it was all the bloody flag; he said – she said; dumb and dumber. Kids in the playground

That next morning, arresting the prick in Chidlow. Why hadn't they arrested him the previous night, straight away? By the time they finished with the statements they'd gone two hours over shift's end. He'd probably had enough. Pass it over to the night crew, he'd have thought, get a few JBs down and unwind. And the night crew had failed to find the kid. That was it – he remembered now: next morning Hutchens showed up to work clean and without a hangover, he must have, otherwise Vesna would have got stuck into him and she didn't. So he must have got home that previous night; slept, showered, shaved, brushed his teeth. He couldn't check with Marjorie, they'd been going through a bad patch then and she often took the kids and stayed for weeks at her mum's. The grog, the attitude, it gave her the shits. The disbanding of Armed Robbery had hit him hard, it was his niche, his reason for getting out of bed in the morning. It took him a year and a marriage ultimatum to get over it.

Scattered pictures. So he'd turned up to work that day clean and sober for a change. In some ways that was even more of a worry. Something must have shaken him into caring about how he presented to others. What was it?

Vesna had noticed something. Scraped raw knuckles and a graze on his chin. 'Been fighting again?'

'Nah. Ever tried opening one of those little plastic thimbles of milk?'

'I'd stick to black coffee if I were you.'

'I did, in the end.'

What's too painful to remember we simply smother with pills and booze. The song was getting to him, blurring his eyes, tightening his chest. He needed to get a grip and stop getting sentimental and soft. If he didn't watch it he'd end up like Cato.

Cato!

Now there was a bloke with a brain. A lateral thinker, a left-field sort of bloke. All those cryptic crosswords and tinkling on the Joanna. A Keating without the uppercut. He'd definitely come up with something to get Hutchens out of this basket of shit. He wouldn't be able to order Cato to do it though, like usual. It would have to be a favour. He'd have to ask him nicely. Woo the fucker.

*

Perspective. Cato needed to put it all in perspective. His ex-wife was just getting on with her life and Jake was just being a selfish teenager. They weren't doing this especially to make Cato feel bad, the world didn't revolve around him. There. Better? Not really, he thought, but probably nearer the truth. He wasn't sure which hurt more: Jane getting pregnant and remarrying, or Jake deciding he couldn't be bothered to come over for the weekend. Maybe the fact that they hurt at all was evidence that he really needed to get a life. Yet another year had slipped by and he was still single, still alone. No surprises there. All he did was work or stay at home. He never went to the places nor did the things that might help him meet normal people. Why? Maybe it was fear of failure. Maybe it was denial, an unreal hope that magically he, Jane and Jake might one day be a family again.

'Cato, mate. I want to invite you to dinner.' Hutchens barged through Cato's office door and plonked himself down in a spare chair, breathless and flushed.

'What? Me? Dinner?' Cato's day was going from bad to catastrophic. He wondered what he'd done wrong this time. He racked his brain for a recent misdemeanour that might have been sackable.

'Yeah. Curry or something? What do people like you eat?'

'Chinese people?' said Cato, bristling, wanting a fight with someone, anyone.

'Nah, fuck that. Sensitive, thinking people.'

This was too much. It really was. 'Well, normal food I guess, like everybody else.'

'Really?'

'Yeah.'

'Good steak, then?'

'Fine. Sure. Whatever.'

'Great. When suits?' Hutchens seemed oblivious to Cato's state of emotional turmoil.

'Tomorrow?'

'It's a date. The Dav okay with you?'

'Sure.' Cato wouldn't have sworn to it but he had the unnerving impression that Hutchens was thinking about giving him a hug. He changed the subject. Work. That was it, bury it all in work. 'You'll be after an update.'

'The Tans?' said Hutchens, frowning in a show of concentration.

Cato outlined the story so far. The most promising bit seemed to be the rogue DNA in the master bedroom. Hutchens nodded in all the right places. Cato wanted to know why his boss was back in the game. 'You mentioned blue sky in your schedule. Something happen at the Inquiry?'

Hutchens clapped him on the shoulder. 'I'll tell you all about it over a nice piece of Scotch fillet tomorrow, mate.'

Cato couldn't wait.

10

Friday, August 9th.

Lara looked at the screen. The pulsing shifting shape. The life that was growing inside her. Mesmerising. She gripped John's hand tighter as the ultrasound glided over her belly. The beeps and beats and the muffled roar. John seemed hypnotised too, eyes full with emotion even though he had been here before – he already had two kids from his first marriage. The one she broke up.

'Do you want to know the sex?' The technician seemed as excited as them, maybe it was part of her training.

'No,' said John.

'Yes,' said Lara.

'So?' said the technician, hand monitor hovering over the goo on Lara's tummy.

'I want to know,' said Lara. 'It just seems right.' Her eyes searched John's face. Farmer John. He'd given his gorgeous bulk over to her on demand that first night they met for a quiet drink. He'd taught her things, about the job. She'd taught him a few things too. But what surprised her was how quickly it had moved from just another conquest to something deeper. She loved him and it was mutual. They were head over heels, still, two years on, through the ugliness of his divorce, through the long antisocial hours of the job. He was a keeper. He'd given up on the undercover spook stuff and moved up the food chain. He was a nine-to-five desk jockey at Police HQ. He got his adrenalin from her now, he said, and he didn't need the heroics anymore. She was the one keeping the shit hours and it was beginning to scare her. Could she have it all? The job she had coveted for so long, this man, this child? A family?

'Okay.' A nervous smile drifted across his face. They locked on the screen again.

'It's a girl, isn't it?' Lara felt she might crush John's big hand.

'Yes,' said the technician.

'Our little girl.' Lara smiled through her tears. 'Our beautiful baby.'

*

Cato woke with a hangover. He'd sulked his way through a full bottle of Shiraz before falling into bed and dreaming he and Jane were still together and about to have a baby. He'd woken up happy for a moment or two before he realised. He doused himself under the shower and padded to the kitchen to make a plunger of coffee and some toast. On the way he stubbed his toe on the piano. No wonder, it was so long since he'd played it, why would he remember it was still there? There was the half-done Guido crossword left over from earlier in the week. *Match token.* Seven and four. Wedding ring. Very funny.

Cato smeared some vegemite onto his toast and chewed without enthusiasm, flicking on the radio to distract him from his evil self-centred thoughts. The Tan family massacre was still up there but getting vaguer by the day; police were following various leads and appealing for anybody who knew anything to come forward. On the hustings, the politicians had taken a break from bashing asylum seekers and finding black holes in each other's costings to ruminate on whether selling the ailing family farm to the Chinese was really in the national interest. Nothing meant by it, you understand, just a thought. Dog-whistle politics, almost subtle compared to the baying three-word slogans dominating the rest of the election campaign. His phone rang, he silenced the radio.

'We've found our Port Coogee vandal.' Chris Thornton's voice had risen in pitch. He could barely contain himself.

'Where is he now?'

'She. Her name is Ocean Mantra. Freo girl. Walked in off the street to volunteer her services. She's in reception jangling her piercings. Ready when you are.'

The name seemed familiar but Cato couldn't think why. 'Be there in fifteen.'

Ocean Mantra took a seat in the interview room and declined the offer of a hot beverage. Her outfit was a baggy mix of ex-army cast offs and tie-dye, topped off with piercings and blonde dreadlocks. Underneath the metal was the pixie face of a twelve year old and a heart-melting smile. She'd got word that people were asking after her, knew about the murders from the news, and joined the dots. She identified herself. Her full name was Ocean Mantra Davies, she was twenty, and studying Architecture at UWA. Cato recognised her from a poster he'd seen one time in X-Wray Café, she was a singer-songwriter he seemed to recall.

'Not anymore. I gave up on all that whale song shit last year. I'm into direct action now.'

Bless her rainbow cotton socks. 'The night of Sunday, August fourth. Do you remember where you were?' Cato had cautioned her that she might be incriminating herself in relation to the vandalism but it didn't seem to be a problem.

'Writing "wanker" on a jet ski in Port Coogee.'

'Address? Time?' Ocean couldn't remember the exact address but her description matched the one round the corner from the murder scene. She reckoned it was around 11 p.m.

'How do you know?'

'My girlfriend rang me just as I was finishing. I noticed the time on the mobile.'

'Describe how you got there and left again, and what you noticed.'

She'd kayaked around from Coogee Jetty and pulled up in the marina like she always did. Hence the lack of trace of her on CCTV cameras elsewhere on the estate. She'd noticed nothing unusual on her way in – apart from the ridiculous cabin cruisers and some stupid boxy houses.

'And when you were leaving?'

That brilliant smile again. 'A car came round the corner, really fast, nearly ran me over.'

Cato checked which corner. It was coming from the direction of the murder scene. 'Can you describe it?'

'The headlights were off. It was probably going about seventy or eighty. Dark. Saloon. Good condition. Not a shitheap.'

Cato would get a minion to go through the car ID pics with her when they'd finished. 'Did you get a look at the driver?'

She nodded. She'd been giving him the finger as the car passed under a streetlight. The driver had returned the gesture. 'Looked a bit like you but maybe younger.'

'Chinese?' said Cato. A nod. 'How much younger do you reckon?'

She shrugged. 'Hard to say. You look anything from thirty to fifty. This guy? Maybe nearer thirty? Younger?' Another smile and shrug. 'Sorry.'

He'd link her up with the e-fit artist to see if they could get a better fix on the look of the guy. 'Where did he go?'

'He headed off north towards the old power station. There's a back road along there, Robb Road, so you don't have to go out onto the main drag. I bike it down there sometimes.'

They finished. 'You know I'm obliged to arrest and charge you for the vandalism don't you?' said Cato regretfully.

She held out her wrists in a cuff-me gesture and beamed. 'Great. I'm looking forward to my day in court.'

*

DI Hutchens was waiting for Cato. It was now mid-morning and the wind was whipping up again. Another front was forecast to hit tonight. Hutchens and Pavlou were hot-desking like everyone else, all part of the efficiency dividend. Pavlou had been summoned away mysteriously so he'd installed himself back behind his desk and reinstated Frau Hutchens to the front of the filing cabinet. He asked for an update on Ocean Mantra and Cato gave him one.

'Chinese? Matthew you reckon?'

'I don't think so. He has alibis for the time between leaving his parents at nine p.m. and around midnight when he and Lily left the pub and said goodbye to their mates.'

'They could all be lying.'

'He's also on the pub CCTV purchasing a round just before ten forty-five p.m.'

'Bugger. So who is it then? Does he have Chinese mates who fit the bill?'

'Haven't a clue, we'll be following it up. After going through the pics and jogging her memory, the witness has identified the car as a Mitsubishi Magna, black or dark blue. It had WA plates but she doesn't remember the number. We'll add it to the inquiry list and see where that gets us. We'll also go through the regos.'

Hutchens flicked open his laptop, a prelude to closing their meeting. 'There's a memorial service for the family tomorrow. You going?'

'Of course. We'll be out in numbers.'

'When are the bodies due for release?'

'No time soon. Too many loose ends. The actual funerals could be a few weeks off yet.'

'I'll let you get back to it then.' A few taps on the keyboard and Hutchens raised his head again, looking strangely vulnerable. 'We still on for tonight? That steak?'

'Sure,' said Cato, backing out with an encouraging smile on his face. He turned around to find Deb Hassan grabbing car keys from her desk and summoning him as she broke into a run for the door.

'Zac Harvey,' she said, zapping the pool Commodore locks as they hit the street. 'Somebody's just beaten the crap out of him.'

It mightn't have started too well but the day was picking up nicely.

*

Zac Harvey was in Rockingham General Hospital. He'd been attacked at Rockingham foreshore. Local police were in attendance but when Cato and Deb explained their interest they were, after a phone call or two, cleared for access. Zac was a sorry sight. It looked like his face had been in a blender, his neck was in a brace, and both his hands were heavily bandaged. Cato turned to one of the uniforms guarding the patient. He had ginger hair and a certain territorialism about him. The name badge said Burns.

'What happened?' said Cato.

'He was found under the dolphin statue. Two blokes in broad daylight jumped out of a car, stomped him, and drove away.'

'Descriptions? Regos?'

'Whatever there is, the local Ds will have it. Ask them.'

'I'm asking you.'

Burns bristled. 'Asian. Dunno where from. Young, in their twenties maybe. Driving a Holden ute, white and fast. That's all we have so far.'

Cato nodded at the patient. 'Has he said anything?'

'Asked for his mum.' Burns smirked. 'That looks like her coming now.'

The door flew open and Mrs Harvey stormed in.

'What have you done to him, you animals!'

Deb Hassan lifted her hands placatingly. 'Calm down, Mrs Harvey, nobody here has done anything to your son.'

'Don't fucking tell me what to do, wog.'

'Calm yourself or I'll have you removed. We're looking into the matter and this isn't helping anybody.'

'Fuck off.' Mrs Harvey pushed past Hassan on her way to her son's bedside. 'Sweetie, what happened. Tell me.'

There was a certain inevitability about what happened next. The Red Mist had descended on Deb Hassan but she was horribly calm as she unclipped her taser, marched up and stuck it into Mrs Harvey's shoulder.

'Mind your manners, bitch.'

*

By late afternoon there was an evil light in the sky. Out on High Street awnings flapped on shop fronts, signs toppled, cans and other debris rolled along the footpath. It didn't look like the sun-drenched historic port city of the tourist brochures, it was more like some Gothic rendition worthy of Bram Stoker. Cato returned his thoughts to the meeting. DI Pavlou had resumed her place behind the desk. Frau Hutchens was once again at the back of the filing cabinet and the Von Trapps were out front. DI Hutchens glowered in the only other spare chair while Cato and Lara stood beside their chosen bosses. Lara seemed to have a flushed frisson about her; Cato put it down to some exciting development on the case. First on the agenda, Pavlou wanted an update on Mrs Harvey.

'She's up and about again,' said Cato as brightly as he could muster.

'Official complaint likely?'

'Probably.'

An irritated shake of the head. 'What did Hassan think she was doing?'

'You probably need to ask her, boss.'

'I will, you first.'

'Mrs Harvey was being verbally and physically aggressive. She jostled Deb and ignored our warnings to calm down or be removed from the scene.'

'Jostled?'

'Jostled.' Cato looked suitably serious.

'Good enough for me,' said Pavlou. 'Jostling an officer of the law. Not on. Tell me about the boy.'

'Rockingham Ds are on the case. Witnesses say two "Asian" blokes jumped out of a ute, did the business and drove off. We're following up on the vehicle, we've half a rego to go on. Hope to have some news later today.'

Cato filled everybody in on Ocean Mantra's news too. It seemed to brighten Pavlou's day. 'So we've got lots of Asians in fast cars being either dangerous or violent in connection with the various threads of this case.'

'Nicely summarised, boss,' said Cato, grimly.

'Which plays into the latest intelligence from ACC.' Pavlou clicked on an email, squinted at it for a moment, then moved her head in and out until she found the right focal length. 'Li Tonggui – let's call him Tommy like his friends do – has apparently had previous connections with Guido Caletti.'

'No offence, Sandra,' said DI Hutchens, 'but I think you might find Guido is an Italian name.'

'Well spotted, Mick. But Guido also hoovered up the remnants of the Tran gang after they broke up.' She glanced up at Cato. 'Remember them?'

Of course he did, he was the one who shot Jimmy Tran into quadriplegia. And it was Jimmy's little brother Vincent who'd tried to kill Cato, and Cato's son, with a nail gun. 'So your theory is?' he said.

'Guido could have used his boys to do a favour for Tommy Li. Maybe we should be looking at them for the Tan murders.'

'Evidence?'

Pavlou smiled. 'I was hoping you and Lara might go and find some for me.'

Lightning flashed and the clouds opened. The storm was imminent.

*

'Do you get the impression she's making it up as she goes along?'

'Wouldn't be the first time.' Hutchens stabbed his scotch fillet and Cato picked at his chicken and mushroom penne. Hutchens had shaken his head in disgust at Cato's order. They were in the back room of the South Beach Hotel, or 'The Dav' as locals stubbornly still called it. The fire was on, so was the Friday night footy. Outside it was bucketing and blowing a gale. The smokers huddled grimly just outside the door. Cato was reminded of poor Bernice, the Harvey dog, scratching pitifully at the French windows.

'How do you mean?'

Hutchens finished a mouthful of chips and took a sip of Kilkenny. 'It's what Major Crime do all the time.'

That seemed rich, coming from him. It wasn't that long ago that they'd both been disciplined for fitting up a bloke on a high-profile murder case. And come close to doing it again down in Hopetoun.

Cato didn't need another Hutchens rant about Major Crime. He'd follow up on the Guido 'lead' tomorrow with Lara. 'So was there anything specific you wanted to catch up about?'

Hutchens looked pained. 'Steak with a mate, isn't that enough?' He flicked some salad out of the way and speared a few more chips. 'But now you mention it.'

He told Cato all about the hostel inquiry, the allegations of abuse against the warden Peter Sinclair, his disappearance, and the subsequent discovery of his burnt-out car in Guildford. Then there was Andy Crouch's diary. Cato had to smile, it sounded like the Crouch he'd got to know too.

'And you don't remember a thing?'

'Not a peep, Cato mate. I was looking at the world through the bottom of a whisky glass in those days.' He finished off the last of his dinner, salad notwithstanding. 'So, any suggestions?'

Cato took a gulp of Fifty Lashes. All these new beers with their funky hipster names increasingly tasted the same to him; he may as well be knocking back some cheap wallop. What advice could he possibly offer on a fifteen year old crime and a case of convenient drunken amnesia? 'Do *you* think you did it?'

'Killed Peter Sinclair?' Hutchens' voice had risen enough to attract the attention of neighbouring tables.

Cato nodded.

Hutchens eyes went glassy. 'I could have. I was capable of it back then. Once I knew what he'd done.'

'How did you know?'

'What?'

'You've told me the evidence at the inquiry is that you told everybody to forget it. So what changed between you not taking it seriously and you wanting to kill him?'

A slurp of Kilkenny. 'I don't remember that either.' He caught the expression on Cato's face. 'You don't believe me?'

'No.'

'Thanks.'

'If you were outside, looking in on this, what would you be thinking?'

'I'm guilty as sin and full of shit. Not to be trusted for a second.'

Cato lifted his glass in salute. 'Now we're on the same page.'

Hutchens' eyes narrowed. 'You're enjoying this a bit too much.'

'Perks of the job. Maybe you should start looking at this whole thing from the perspective that you're probably guilty and all you need to do is find the evidence.'

'The Major Crime approach?'

'If you like.'

'That's what I get in return for a sumptuous steak dinner?'

'I had the penne.'

'Yeah, I noticed. No wonder you don't make friends easily.'

11

Saturday, August 10th.

St Patrick's Basilica was about three-quarters full. Outside, the media contingent was healthy considering all the overnight storm damage news. It was a blustery day, a blue sky patterned with fluffy but still threatening white-grey cumulus. Propped on easels in front of the altar were large framed individual photographs of the deceased along with the family five-shot portrait from the staircase. In the front pews sat Matthew Tan with his girlfriend Lily, his lawyer Henry Hurley, and some people that Cato recognised as Matthew's uncles and aunts. There would be no grandparents. Genevieve's folks had died in a car accident when she was still in her twenties. Franco's mother was in an old people's home in East Fremantle, completely gaga. Today that would have been some kind of blessing. His father had died of throat cancer six years earlier. In the rows following there were more family, business associates, friends, a couple of politicians, friends and teachers of the children, and a smattering of police. Cato's own sisters were also there with their partners. Mandy signalled a need to talk to him when he had a moment.

It hadn't occurred to Cato that either Francis or Genevieve Tan were Catholic but now that he thought about it he recalled Genevieve sometimes wearing a crucifix and, let's face it, their given names were Catholic as. A man was giving the eulogy; he was stocky and middle-aged with a shock of red hair greying at the temples. His face was a mess of freckles and his nose had the hallmarks of a youth of rough sport, fighting and drinking.

Cato heard all sorts of new stuff he hadn't known about Francis. His support for country sports clubs, his charity work, how proud he was of all his children, how good a friend he could be. This version must have materialised in the ten years since they'd drifted apart. Cato felt vaguely regretful that he'd missed seeing his friend grow into this less cynical, seemingly softer and perhaps more mature Francis. Lara slid into the pew beside him.

'Dodgy gangster at eight o'clock,' she whispered.

Cato glanced over his left shoulder a couple of rows back and across the aisle. It was Guido Caletti and a young tattooed woman who looked sex-kittenish in a chunky roller derby kind of way. Both of them really suited black. Guido nodded gravely at Cato while the sex kitten curled up closer and fiddled with her nose stud. A few hymns and chants later and the goodbye music was playing, people were crying, reaching for cigarettes and phones, proceedings were drawing to a close.

'You intercept Guido, make an appointment for a chat.'

'What about you?' said Lara.

He nodded to the pews up front. 'I'd like to pay my respects to the family.'

The church emptied onto Adelaide Street and the steady stream of Saturday shopping and tourist traffic. Cato made his way through the crowd of well-wishers and waited his turn to condole with the family. Matthew Tan's handshake was limp and brief. He lit up a cigarette and eyed Cato through the smoke.

'Any progress?'

'We're exploring a number of avenues.'

'I'm not a fucking journalist, Uncle Phil. I'm the surviving son.' Speaking of which, the media pack were muscling their way towards them. Henry Hurley and a couple of uncles moved in to shepherd them away.

'Sorry Matt, it's still too early. We're doing our best.'

'Sure.' Lily leaned into Matt protectively.

Deb Hassan sidled up. As Family Liaison Officer it was her job to try to keep Matthew sweet. Given the distractions of the last few days, that wasn't going too well.

'We did have a couple of questions about somebody who was seen in the vicinity of your parents' house around eleven p.m,' said Cato. 'We'd like to show you a photofit, see if you know them.'

'Is this urgent?'

'No, of course not. I'll get Deb here to drop round at your convenience.'

Matthew turned his gaze onto Deb Hassan. 'I'll be at the Shelley place at five. Don't be late. I'm going out at five thirty.'

'No problem,' said Hassan with all due respect.

Matthew and Lily headed for his Beemer behind a protective phalanx of uncles and cousins.

Cato felt a tap on his shoulder. 'I don't think we've been introduced.'

It was the red-haired eulogist. Cato stuck out a hand. 'Philip.'

'Des. Des O'Neill.'

'Nice eulogy. You knew Francis well, I take it?'

'Very. Friends and business partners for the last ten years or so. We spent a lot of time together. Holidays, fishing trips, business junkets, you name it.' A woman of similar age to Des linked her arm into his. She was pale and gaunt and wore a scarf to cover her hair loss. Radio or chemotherapy, guessed Cato. Possibly both. 'Our wives were thick as thieves as well. That right, Joyce?' Joyce nodded sadly.

'I'm sorry for your loss,' said Cato, trying to picture Genevieve and Joyce as friends.

'So how about you?' said Des. 'Rellie?'

'Friend. We went to school and uni together.'

Des's smile broadened. 'You're the cop. Phil the cop, is that right?'

'That's right.'

Des leaned in. 'You make sure you catch the cunt that did this, you hear?'

'I'll try my best, Des.'

'Good to hear.' Des patted his wife's arm and she dabbed her red eyes. He handed a business card to Cato. 'Anything I can do, mate. Anything.'

*

Guido had changed into his winter woollies and had an electric fan heater blasting away at his feet beneath the cluttered desk. It was cosy but any moisture had been sucked out of the air and Cato was parched. On Guido's wall there was a team photo of Juventus FC and a calendar featuring the leaning tower of Pisa. The office was cramped and smelled of cigarettes and men. Lara and James Blond had a chair each and Cato leaned against the wall. From down the hallway came the hiss of an espresso machine and the murmur of café patrons.

'You guys need a drink of something?'

Cato nodded, over-eagerly, but Lara and James Blond declined. Guido hadn't noticed Cato, so that was the end of that.

Lara took an iPad mini out of her jacket pocket and fired it up. 'Mr Caletti do you know a Chinese national by the name of Li Tonggui or Tommy Li?'

'Got any games on that?' said Guido.

'Just answer the questions, Guido,' said James Blond, 'and we can be on our way.'

'Mr Caletti to you, son.'

Lara gave James a glare. 'We appreciate you slotting us in today, Mr Caletti. We'll try not to take up too much of your time.'

A grunt. 'Li, you say?'

'Yes.' She repeated the full name for him.

'Rings a bell, yeah. Tubby bloke, always smiling. Everybody's grandad.'

'That's the one. How would you describe your relationship to him?'

'Distant. He lives in China doesn't he?'

'Is it a business relationship?'

'Was. We had a joint venture going a couple of years ago.'

'What kind?'

'That's commercial, in confidence.'

'In general terms?'

'Property. He was interested in a new housing development in East Perth.'

'And?'

'And nothing. He pulled out. Found another partner, another block of flats somewhere.'

'But you stayed in touch?'

'Sure. Never close a door on any future opportunity, eh?'

'When were you last in touch?'

'Why? What's he done?'

'We're just trying to build a picture, Mr Caletti.'

He nodded towards Cato. 'Is that why he's here? Crossword Man. Is he your China expert, then?'

'When were you last in touch with Mr Li?'

'Fuck knows. Last year, maybe?'

'Our understanding is that it was more recent than that. Just over two weeks ago in fact.'

'And where did you get your "understanding" from?'

'Sorry, can't say right now. So what was the call about?'

'Sorry love, can't say right now.'

'Mr Caletti we're investigating the brutal murders of four people, two of them just kids. We'd appreciate your help in this matter as an upstanding member of the community.'

'If you think I'm so upstanding then why are you tapping my phone?' He snorted. 'Upstanding. Understanding. My arse.'

Lara shoved her iPad back into its cover. 'Thanks for your time. We'll be in touch.'

They were shown the door.

*

On his way back down the freeway, Cato took a call from Deb Hassan.

'I called in on Matt. He doesn't recognise Ocean's mystery driver or have any ideas about who he may have been.'

'Do you believe him?'

'We haven't got much choice right now. But I also showed him photofits of the guys who stomped Zac Harvey and that got more of a reaction.'

'He knew them?'

'Said not, but he was way twitchy. I don't think he likes Zakkie-boy.'

'Who would? His sister's dead and this prick takes it on himself to rubbish her.' Cato didn't want to be drawn into this sideshow. 'Pass it on to the Rockingham Ds, they can have it, we've got enough on our plates.'

'Tell me about it.'

'How's it going with you? You okay?'

A shake in the voice. 'Yeah, nothing a bottle of wine and a good root won't fix.'

'Chaz back from the mines is he?'

'Tonight. I'm on my way to pick him up now.'

'Have fun.' Cato signed off.

Cato nearly missed the Canning Highway turn-off, his mind had been on going straight home via South Street. Then he remembered – Applecross, another summons from his sister Mandy. Wind whipped the river and grey clouds scudded over the distant Perth skyline as he crossed Canning Bridge. By the time he got to Applecross it was raining again. Judging by the sounds emerging from behind numerous closed doors around the house, Mandy's kids were either practising piano or engrossed in computer games. Except for the youngest, Bao, a pudgy toddler who lived up to his family pet name – dumpling. He was absorbed in tormenting the family cat, grabbing handfuls of fur and tugging fiercely. The cat would occasionally swipe feebly at him with a paw and this would provoke gales of laughter and more tugging. It was a patient old tabby but Cato could see this ending in tears. Mandy poured them coffee from a fresh plunger and nodded towards the sofa where she could still keep half an eye on little Bao.

'Where's Dad?' said Cato.

'Asleep.'

'Ken?'

'Squash club.'

'You wanted a word?'

Mandy frowned and sipped her coffee. 'I don't know whether it's the tumour or what, but Dad's obsessing about you, he talks about you all the time.'

That was the thing about Mandy. She never really coped with

the idea that she might not always be the centre of her father's universe. Any unseemly interest in her siblings must be down to his Parkinson's or, in this case, the brain tumour. But then again, she was the one who was doing all the heavy lifting on the day-to-day caring stuff that really mattered. 'Really?' said Cato. 'In what way?'

'He keeps on talking about you, using your Chinese name. He's never used it since you were Bao's age.'

'Chinese name?'

'You don't remember? It was Qian Ping. You're Kwong Qian Ping.' She spelt it for him.

Qian Ping. Something was drifting back to him now. Those half-formed pre-memories of early childhood. A ride on his father's shoulders. Firecrackers and cymbals. A dancing dragon. Qian Ping. His father's seemingly nonsense words to him a few nights ago. *Champagne, champagne.* Qian Ping.

A rustle, a hiss, and a wail arose – the inevitable had happened. The cat scarpered and Bao lifted his hand to examine an ugly red weal. Tears streamed into the folds in his chins. Mandy rushed over to comfort him.

Cato mustered a sympathetic uncle-type look and poured himself some more coffee. Eventually Bao's tears subsided. 'So what's Dad saying about me?'

'He wants me to warn you. He made me promise.'

'Warn me?'

'He doesn't want you to go back there.'

'Where?'

'China. He thinks you're going to die there. In China.'

'Why would I go to China?'

'I dunno. I tried to tell him that.'

'China?' said Cato.

'I know. Silly old bugger. Must be the tumour.'

*

Hutchens wasn't having a good weekend. He'd hardly slept on Friday night. The extra pint of Kilkenny had woken him around

2 a.m., bursting to escape his bladder. The night was cactus from then. Marjorie had tutted at his tossing and turning and bolted to the spare room. He'd finally drifted off just as the birds started squawking in the gum tree outside the bedroom window. Awaking mid-morning he'd found a terse note on the kitchen table informing him that his beloved would be out for the day and that while she understood he was under the hammer she really hoped he'd have lifted his game by the time she got back. The house was his. With their oldest daughter now moved in with her boyfriend in Subiaco and the youngest overseas on her gap year, the place seemed cavernous. He'd wandered through the weekend papers, aware that his juniors would be assembled at the Tan family memorial service. Had any of the guests acted strangely, it would be noted and followed up. But what was 'strange' behaviour anyway? What was normal? Cato had been offered a good steak and chose to eat chicken and mushroom penne for fuck's sake.

Maybe you should start looking at this whole thing from the perspective that you're probably guilty and all you need to do is find the evidence.

Thanks a bunch.

Three weeks out from Election Day, the newspapers were full of people pre-judging the guilt of others. The outgoing government – and there was little doubt that they were outgoing – couldn't win a trick. Perhaps they didn't deserve to after the infighting and dysfunction of recent years. But you know that when intellect, reason and compassion are dismissed as weak, yappy, and well, a bit gay, that the country is in trouble. Hutchens threw some cornflakes into a bowl and drowned them in milk. He was no different. Wasn't that how he usually treated Cato's intellect, reason and compassion? God forgive him. But for all his anti-intellectual bluster Hutchens had a soft spot for what he saw as old-time conviction politics. Left or right, he just wanted people to believe in something and stick their necks out for it. And Hutchens admired that in Cato. The bloke was something of an intellectual who did reason things through and sometimes took a fucking age about it, but the bastard knew exactly where his moral compass pointed. He knew what he believed in.

... you're probably guilty and all you need to do is find the evidence...

Cato's question – what had changed between telling that kid Mundine to bugger off and deciding that Peter Sinclair needed sorting out? Hutchens had said he didn't remember but some neural pathway had unclogged at that point and a dribble of memory seeped through. David Mundine and his extended family had been a pain in the arse for years. Hutchens had come into contact with them early in his career while still in uniform. They were thieves, bullies, wife-beaters, druggies and drunks. Barely a week went by without some kind of call-out relating to them. When young David had walked through the door that day in the Mundaring nick it had been easy not to believe him. He was at Hillsview Hostel doing some anger-management-drug-rehabilitation wank, at the age of fourteen for fuck's sake. That day Hutchens had enough on his plate, and a hangover like a second Hiroshima. Who wouldn't have told the little tosser to take a walk? But later he had gone back through the files and taken a look at Peter Sinclair, anyway. The man had no record, not even a flag of interest. But something had rung a bell. What was it?

A suicide. Two years before that. Hutchens was still in Armed Robbery. The suicide was the teenage son of one of his regulars, an ex-army hard man who'd done a string of hold-ups out in the wheatbelt. He lived in Narrogin and that's where the suicide happened. It solved one problem anyway: no more hold-ups, the boy's father was a broken man after that – drinks all round in the Robbery Squad. The boy was thirteen and had just come back from a nine-month stint in a hostel in a neighbouring town. His dad was doing another spell in Casuarina and his mum had gone off somewhere. The hostel had been the idea of an over-stretched Child Protection Department. The warden was Peter Sinclair; he'd authored some welfare report on the boy. Dad was allowed out of prison for the day to attend his son's funeral, in handcuffs and flanked by guards. Hutchens had been in attendance on behalf of the Robbery Squad. He'd recalled Peter Sinclair in the pew a few rows ahead across the aisle. He had a space either side of him.

Maybe he gave off a smell. That's what the office manager Carol Ransley had said at the Inquiry – he smelled funny.

So why hadn't Hutchens come clean with Cato on this newly jogged memory? That's what worried him. While Cato's moral compass pointed true north, Hutchens often felt he was navigating by distant dim stars on a cloudy night.

12

Monday, August 12th.

Cato found out about the raid on Guido Caletti's place when he got to work on Monday morning. Major Crime, backed up by TRG and other assorted uniforms, had raided five properties early that morning: Guido's office and home and three other residences. Guido and two others were in custody for questioning. One was being examined at Royal Perth Hospital for a suspected broken nose, another for possible concussion and taser burns. Meanwhile Guido was ensconced with his lawyer. Hutchens was going ballistic at being kept out of the loop and was stalking around Freo cop shop with an angina spray lodged in his nostril. DI Pavlou radiated a Xena Warrior Princess aura as she summoned them all to a squad meeting. Lara Sumich would have been one of the main movers behind the raid – *Thanks for your time. We'll be in touch* – yet she seemed unreadable, like she was somewhere else that was far more captivating. She caught him looking at her and squared her shoulders, the professional was back from her brief sabbatical in Faraway Bay. Outside the weather had cleared nicely. It was a sunny if blustery day and would remain that way for the rest of the week. The remainder of Saturday and Sunday had been, for Cato, a muted rondella of chores, reading, eating, and watching crap TV. He hadn't expected Jake's absence to leave such a hole in his weekend but it did. He'd dwelled no further on the Qian Ping and China stuff.

With a teacherly clap of the hands, Pavlou brought the crowded room to attention.

'As a result of intelligence from ACC plus some corroborating phone records we brought Guido Caletti and two of his associates, Minh Do and Bobby Huang, in for questioning. Minh and Bobby are back from the hospital and right as rain for those of you who had concerns about their welfare.'

An ugly titter ran through the room. Cato didn't like it, especially when a few pairs of eyes slyly checked him out for a reaction. 'What was the intelligence?'

The same eyes returned to him. How come the 2IC on the investigation wasn't in the loop? Cato knew he probably should have kept quiet and saved face but he felt combative today, although buggered if he knew why. Maybe it was the smug grandstanding, or maybe it was his shit family life. Pavlou came back with the inevitable reply. Classified.

'How about the corroborating phone records? What did they say?'

'They say that there was phone traffic between Guido and Tommy Li in Shanghai, and between Guido and his friends, Minh and Bobby, in the forty-eight hours preceding the Tan murders and in the following twenty-four hours.'

'From which you deduce...?'

A freezing smile from Pavlou. 'From which I deduce nothing, Philip. But it's worth having a chat with these blokes, you reckon?'

Of course it was. So why did he feel so aggro? He caught Lara looking at him, a hint of warning in her gaze. Maybe there was something much bigger going on here. Pavlou dished out the rations. She and Lara would take Guido, James Blond and his twin would have Minh, and another team would question Bobby. Nothing in there for Cato or his mob. Hutchens crooked his finger and invited him into a side office.

'It's a fucking circus.'

A rare meeting of minds. 'Boss.'

'We need to take back control.'

'How?'

'Don't know yet. I'll keep you posted.'

That sounded ominous. 'Getting anywhere on your *predicament*?'

'Nah.' A shifty look. For a political operator with decades of workplace experience, Hutchens was a crap liar. 'But you did give me food for thought.'

'Did I?'

'Yeah. So cheers for that. Must do it again sometime.'

'No worries,' said Cato. They went their merry ways. Back in the open-plan, Deb Hassan sought him out. 'How's Chaz?' The FIFO hubby.

A satisfied smile. 'Gagging for it, bless him.'

'Lovely. No word from Mrs Harvey yet?'

'You or the boss will probably hear before I do.'

'Which boss?'

'Let's not go there.' She nodded in the direction of a departing Hutchens. 'How's he taking all this?'

'A bit out of sorts, for sure. But I think he's shaping up for a fightback.'

'Good. Not before time. Want a cuppa?'

He put his order in for tea with milk and none and asked her to meet him down in Duncan Goldflam's lair in five.

Goldflam had news for them. 'There was some semen on a set of sheets in the laundry basket. The sheets were from the master bedroom but the stains didn't belong to Francis.'

'Or one of the sons?' suggested Deb.

A wince from Goldflam, he could still be a bit prudish sometimes, even in this job. 'No, not them either.'

'So Mrs Tan had a boyfriend?' said Cato. He wasn't sure how he felt about that. Residual jealousy for a relationship over which he'd long since lost any claim? Misguided loyalty towards Francis? It was illogical and unreasonable but it was there all the same.

'Or a sad wanking tradesman, yeah, something like that.'

'Does it match the other rogue DNA and stuff you found in the master bedroom?'

'Yes.'

'And you've put it through the criminal records system for a match?'

'Think it's worth a go, boss?' Goldflam's sarcasm could be wearing at times.

'Nothing, huh?'

'So far. I'll keep you posted.' Cato turned to leave but Goldflam lifted a finger. 'One more thing.'

'Yep?'

'The lab confirmed Zac Harvey as the father of Emily Tan's kid.'

Cato nodded. Another box ticked.

＊

Cato decided Matthew Tan warranted another visit. Deb had received a tip-off from the geeks that the 'Zac Harvey is Innosent' Facebook page had an interesting new post, a photo of Zac under the dolphin statue in Rockingham with the caption 'U got yours, white trash'. It had provoked a few dozen howls of outrage and threats of retribution from Zac's mates but a similar number of 'likes' from the less committed. After a call on the mobile they found Matthew in North Fremantle, househunting at the Leighton Beach development. He would meet them in the cafe at Port Beach. He was there with Lily when they arrived. They'd taken a spot by the window, warm from the sunshine while the wind whipped up outside. The ocean was blue and frothy with whitecaps and a smudge of clouds darkened the horizon. Deb went to organise some coffees while Cato played nice.

'Find your dream home, then?'

'Maybe. Keeping my options open.'

'View?'

'All the way to Rotto.'

Deb returned with the coffees. Matthew and Lily stuck with their beers. Lily seemed hostile, avoiding eye contact and looking bored. Or maybe that was her default state.

'Not cheap,' noted Deb, catching sight of the real estate leaflets on the table.

'Not wrong,' said Matthew, stony-faced. 'What was it you wanted to see me about?'

Deb showed him the photofits of the Zac Harvey stompers. 'When I asked you about these guys over the weekend you claimed not to know them.'

'And?'

She dug out two new pictures, proper ones, of real people. 'Are these mates of yours?'

'Yeah.'

Deb gestured at the photofits. 'You don't see the resemblance?'

'No,' said Matt. 'You need a better computer program. Yours makes us all look alike.' Lily smirked and snuggled into him.

'Did you set them on Zac?' said Cato.

'Zac who?'

'Zac Harvey, your dead sister's boyfriend.'

'Why would I?'

'Because he said nasty things about her on Facebook.'

'Really? I wouldn't know, I don't waste my time with that shit.'

'Any idea where I might find these mates of yours?'

Matthew looked up and over Cato's shoulder. 'Yeah.'

Cato swung around in his seat. It was the Zac Harvey stompers. Deb Hassan was on her feet, hand hovering around the various implements on her utility belt. Gun. Taser. It was anyone's guess.

Cato stuck out a hand. 'G'day. I'm Matt's Uncle Phil. And you are?' The disjoint between the blue police bibs and firepower and the 'Uncle' bit put them off their stride. Cato recognised the shorter of the two, he was Matt's cousin on Genevieve's side, a boy who'd dropped out of the Gifted and Talented stream at Perth Mod and taken up kick-boxing instead. 'Alex, isn't it?'

Alex shook hands, confused. 'Yeah.'

'And?' Cato smiled at his mate.

'Wayne.'

'G'day Wayne,' said Cato. He showed them the recent Facebook photo of Zac Harvey under the sandstone dolphins. 'Would you guys know anything about this?'

Wayne laughed. He obviously couldn't help himself. He just broke up.

'I'll take that as a yes,' said Deb Hassan, slipping the cuffs off her belt.

That's when Alex did a balletic high kick that sent her sprawling, and reaching for her bloodied nose. The small handful of cafe patrons scattered and the hospitality staff disappeared as if by magic. Cato took out his pepper spray and turned it on Alex, point blank, into his eyes. Alex fell backwards over a chair. Wayne jumped in, wrestling the spray from Cato's grasp and turning it back on him. Cato's eyes burned. A blow to his head sent him crashing to the floor. He felt some kicks in his back, some stamping. He was going to get the Zac Harvey treatment.

'For fuck's sake, give it a rest, guys,' said Matt. 'This isn't helping.'

There was the sound of approaching sirens. Cato was on his knees, half-blinded, eyes streaming. Deb was back on her feet, cuffs out, approaching Wayne. He received a nod from Matt and acquiesced. Cato hauled himself to his feet, giving Alex a sly kick on the way up. Two patrol cars screeched to a halt and a batch of uniforms raced in.

'Sorry, Uncle Phil,' said Matt. 'No hard feelings?'

'None at all.' Cato sniffed and dabbed a wet serviette to his stinging eyes. 'Now turn around and bring your hands together. You're under arrest.'

*

Alex and Wayne were charged with various counts of assault, obstruction, and resisting arrest. They were deposited in the lock-up ahead of a Magistrate's Court appearance tomorrow. Matthew was released. He had taken no part in the violence and there was no evidence yet to link him to the assault on Zac Harvey. Alex and Wayne certainly weren't going to give him up. In Alex's words, 'You're arresting the poor bastard after what he's been through?'

Maybe phone records and an email trail might deliver something but maybe Alex had a point. Matthew's family had been slaughtered just over a week ago and, to add insult to injury, some little twerp had posted foul things about Matt's dead sister on the internet. There was only very circumstantial evidence pointing to Matt as a person of interest in the murders. That, and his unseemly haste to spend his inheritance on a luxury waterfront apartment. Oh, and the bocce ball thing.

Deb Hassan's nose wasn't broken but it was swollen and painful. She was sent home for the rest of the day to enjoy her FIFO husband.

It was just as well. Just before she left, an email came through from Professional Standards about the Mrs Harvey tasering. They recommended Hassan be stood down pending the outcome of an internal investigation. Deb had been expecting it and as far as she was concerned the timing was brilliant. Her husband wasn't due to go back up north for at least a week.

Cato's eyes had dried up. All that was left was a sensation of bearable stinging and some tenderness where he'd been kicked. Hutchens had texted him to say he was out with the Police Union lawyer discussing Inquiry matters, back tomorrow. Lara Sumich detached herself from a huddle with James Blond.

'In the wars?'

'Some friends of Matthew Tan's.'

She gestured at his red face. 'Armed with pepper spray were they?'

'After a fashion. How's it going with Guido and the gang?'

'We've taken swabs of Minh and Bobby for comparison with Duncan's rogue traces from the bedroom.'

'I doubt they'll match. Dunc's already gone through the database. Our man isn't in the system. He's a cleanskin. Minh and Bobby aren't.'

'I know.' Lara pursed her lips.

'But DI Pavlou's not interested?'

'She's a very driven woman.'

'The ACC intelligence. Is that what's driving her?'

'It's very compelling.'

'I wouldn't know, I'm not A-List. So where does Guido fit in?'

'He's part of the phone traffic with Tommy Li at the time.'

'I know that. They could have been talking property deals. Have you got actual transcripts?'

'Yes.'

'And?'

She frowned. 'Inconclusive. Li is asking Guido for some non-specific help on an urgent matter. A visiting friend. Some hospitality. Guido says no worries.'

'You're thinking code. They knew they were being monitored?'

'Maybe.'

'Or maybe there's less to this than meets the eye. Maybe it was just hospitality for a visiting friend.'

A shrug. James Blond was taking an interest in their conversation. Lara seemed uncomfortable. 'You didn't hear any of this from me, right?'

'You don't buy it, do you?'

'I'm keeping an open mind.'

'Good luck with that,' said Cato.

*

'What did he want?'

'Who?' Lara had been making a cup of herbal tea and thinking about those beautiful ultrasound images. Then she found James at her shoulder, his breath smelling of too much time indoors.

'Kwong.'

She should have told him to mind his own damn business but she sensed it might not end there. 'He didn't want anything. I wanted to know what went on with Matthew Tan. What's it to you?'

'The boss has made it clear she wants him kept out of the loop.'

'I know. I was there when she said it. What's your point?'

'You guys have a history. Maybe there's some residual loyalty.'

'Fuck off, Jim. Run to Mummy if you like. I know which side I'm on.'

He looked hurt. 'It's not that, Lara. This is a sensitive operation and Kwong's got a history of going his own way, he's not a team player.'

'Thanks for the reminder. Let's get back to work, eh?'

The interviews with Minh and Bobby had yielded nothing and Guido had maintained his persona of wronged respectable businessman.

'This isn't *Underbelly*,' he'd said. 'Grow up, stop being so lazy.'

The spit samples were with the labs but, as Cato had already pointed out, the rogue traces in the master bedroom were from a cleanskin and Minh and Bobby definitely weren't that. So the murderer didn't have a record, or at least not one in Australia. Should they be going for an international trace, maybe getting the Chinese to put the rogue DNA through their system? She'd suggested it to Pavlou.

'Already on it, mate. They'll get back to us.'

'Anything else you'd like me to run with?' Lara couldn't keep the flatness out of her voice.

'Do I detect a trace of apostasy here?'

'I don't know, I just feel like we're missing something. We've broken the picture up, half of us focusing on Li, and Kwong and the rest of the crew on the domestics. Maybe we should be looking for any connections or patterns across the whole thing.'

'Which is my job, Lara. I have all of Kwong's reports.'

Lara knew when she was being told to pull her head in. 'Boss.'

'You need an injection of faith.' Pavlou slid a file across the table. 'Read and digest. It's the life of Li, unexpurgated. Feast on the possibility of landing somebody like him.'

'Thanks.' Lara headed for the door.

'Lara?'

'Boss?'

'You've had a certain absent-mindedness about you of late. Like you're not really here. Anything I need to know?'

'No, boss.'

'This is a tight group, Lara. Outsiders are clamouring to get in, detractors dying to see us fail. We all need to be focused and looking after each other.'

'Boss.' This seemed like as good a time as any to nip off to the toilet for a quick spew.

*

Hutchens and the Police Union lawyer, Joan Peters, were in a conspiratorial huddle in a corner of Gino's on the coffee strip.

'You could just do what the politicians do, dear. Say "I don't recall" over and over, practice makes perfect.'

'But maybe I did do it,' said Hutchens.

The lawyer stuck her fingers in her ears. 'La, la, la. I can't hear you.'

'What about Crouchie's diary?'

'He's a silly old coot. Just because it's written d[...]
mean it's not hearsay. They need a body and they[...]
fingerprints on a murder weapon. They haven't got eithe[...]
fucked, dear.'

He was beginning to warm to her. A few years younger[...]
might have turned on the twinkle. In fact he wasn't entirel[...]
that she wasn't flirting with him now. 'So just blank them? T[...]
your advice?'

'That's right.'

'Get paid much for this work?'

'Shitloads, dear. I'm really good at it.'

She gathered her bags, gave him a wifely peck on the cheek, and
left him to pay for the coffees. Somebody slid into the vacant chair.
David Mundine, the grown-up version of the abused boy he told to
piss off all those years ago.

'Didn't know this was your neck of the woods, David.'

'It isn't. Just visiting.' Mundine tore open a sachet of sugar and
poured it into his mouth. Then he did it again.

'I'm not sure we should be talking, mate. Probably some rules
against it at the Inquiry.'

'Chance meeting, Mr H. What's your problem?'

'If you've got something to say, say it. Or ...' Hutchens chose his
words carefully. 'Piss off and stop wasting my time.'

A snort and a bitter chuckle. 'Fucking laugh a minute you are,
Hutchens.'

'Mister Hutchens. Say your piece.'

'I was there.'

'Where?'

'Mundaring. The hotel car park. That night.'

'This supposed to mean something to me?'

'I know what you did.'

'You've been watching too many films, son, and laying into the
wacky baccy.'

'You wish. I know where Sinclair's car went afterwards. There
was blood in it.' Mundine seemed distracted, hands fiddling under

he table. 'Look, I'm the last to complain. The dirty old bastard had it coming. You did us all a favour Mr H.'

Hutchens leaned forward and summoned Mundine closer. 'Is there a point to this, only I need to be somewhere.' His phone buzzed.

'That's me,' said Mundine. 'It's a pre-paid, so don't get excited. Let's stay in touch, eh?'

'How did you get my number?'

'Wouldn't you like to know.'

'You need to be careful, son. You're way out of your depth.'

'That right?' said Mundine. 'So how come you're the one sweating like a pig?'

A smile and a pat on the shoulder and he was gone. Hutchens reached for the angina spray. It was nearly empty.

*

The afternoon drifted by and Cato found himself wondering about Lara and her misgivings about the investigation. It was a side to her he hadn't seen much of. As if the job had become secondary, and so doubt and insecurity had crept in. He could understand that: doubt and insecurity were second nature to him. He could feel a headache coming on, the lingering effects of the pepper spray. Cato checked his desk drawers for Panadol and found a couple. He took them with a swig of water from his bottle. He also noticed Des O'Neill's business card lying there. The down-to-earth farm boy from the Tan memorial service. Cato clicked a few buttons on his computer screen and got in to the investigation database. He couldn't see Des O'Neill's name on any of the inquiry lists drawn up by DI Pavlou. This was a close business partner of Francis Tan's, so why weren't Major Crime following him up? Their focus was clearly Francis Tan's relationship with Li Tonggui. The Chinese connection was the only thing they were interested in, along with the Northbridge identity Guido Caletti. The very least Des could provide was a bit of background to perhaps corroborate their 'Yellow-Peril-meets-Mafioso' theory. Instead they seemed to be heavily reliant on so-called intelligence from the ACC spooks.

We need to take back control.

Hutchens' words. Cato prodded his phone. 'Des? Philip Kwong. Francis Tan's mate, we met the other day at the service.'

'Phil, how's it going?'

'Good. Thought we might have a chat about a few things?'

'Sure. Cop business is it?'

''Fraid so.'

'Not a problem. When?'

'How does today suit?'

A chuckle. 'You don't ask much. Beer in Clancy's work for you?'

They agreed to meet there in half an hour. Cato chose to walk to fill in some time and give his head a chance to clear. Crossing Market Street he had to pause at the kerb while an election billboard was towed past him. It listed the number of asylum boat arrivals over the last twelve months and a simple slogan about stopping any more. A couple of passers-by gave it the thumbs up. A couple more gave it the finger. Fremantle had been built on the movement of boats, of people, of trade. Generations of immigrants and refugees had landed here and made it their home. The *Tampa* had docked here before and since those shameful game-changing days when Australia had decided to greet a leaking boatful of wretched humanity with guns and soldiers. Was it just him or did everything feel meaner and uglier now? Those sly looks in the squad meeting, checking out his reaction to the implied race jibes. It wasn't like these people were new. They'd always been there and had never gone away but now they seemed cocky, emboldened, given permission for their bigotry. Their time was nigh.

Across the road from the squat redbrick that was Clancy's Fish Pub, skateboarders sought refuge from the bitter wind against the graffitied wall of the long-abandoned Woolstores. They checked Cato out, decided he wasn't of interest, and continued their rolling and flipping. Inside, Des O'Neill was surveying a blackboard with its array of boutique ales with absurd names. He settled on a stout called Black Plague. Cato, head still wobbly from the pepper spray, went for a pilsener. They also agreed a cone of hot chips would go down well, and retired to a table near a fire. After some harmless banter about the weather, the election and the footy, the chips arrived and they got down to business.

'So how did you and Franco come to be partners?'

'*Partners* is probably overstating it.' O'Neill dipped a chip in some aioli. 'It wasn't a formal thing at first, we just found ourselves working together on a number of projects. We enjoyed each other's company.'

'Yeah?' said Cato.

'You seem surprised. What would a cool, sophisticated Chinese yuppie have in common with the likes of me? Am I guessing right?'

'To be honest, yeah.'

'Tell you the truth I wondered the same myself at the start. Is he slumming? Is he taking the piss? It took a while to find the man behind the smirk.'

'And you did? Find him?'

'I think so.' O'Neill drew from his pint of stout and winced. 'Fucking liquorice.'

'You did well. I've known him for twenty-odd years and never got near.'

That drew a chuckle of recognition. 'Francis just wanted someone to take him seriously. To wait for his jokes to run out, see what he had left. Me, I had all the time in the world.'

'What did he have left?'

'He had a real passion for this country, for the land, it was deeper than anything I've come across before or since. He loved the place: the bush, the desert, the ocean, the people, the history.'

'Franco?'

'Yep. Your mate was a true-blue patriot.'

Cato shook his head. 'Bullshit. He was a cynic. He was having you on.'

'Well if he was, it was the longest, drawn-out, most boring joke in history. He kept it going for most of the ten years I knew him.'

'But all that time he was trying to sell this place he "loved" to his Chinese mates.'

'What's wrong with that? The land is turning to dust in front of our eyes, farms going down the dunny everywhere you look.

When Francis travelled around this state he saw opportunities for growth, for renewal, for partnership. The people he knew have bucketloads of cash and are crying out for wide-open spaces. They're after clean land to grow clean food because where they live is pretty much stuffed.'

'It all sounds very noble.'

'You're not convinced? Neither was I for a long time. As far as I was concerned it was just a profit grab, asset-stripping vulnerable cockies who had the bailiffs at the door and nowhere else to go.'

'Until?'

'Until nothing. I had no real problem with asset-stripping and profit-grabbing. I'm a businessman. I was happy to let him peddle his schtick if that's what sealed the deals. But one day I realised he actually believed in it.'

Cato's pilsener was slipping down surprisingly well, the headache had gone. 'Go on.'

'There was a farmer down south. A couple of thousand acres, god knows how many sheep. The wool and lamb prices had gone through the floor. The animals were starving, all rib, no meat. The bank was demanding the keys to the place. The next-door neighbour, a so-called mate for life, had his eyes on the farm and was trying to nail the poor fucker for a fraction of what it was worth. The bloke was past caring. Francis could have had it for a song. Instead he offered over the odds, more than his Chinese partners had budgeted, and found the difference himself by mortgaging his own house.'

Hence the move from the river view mansion on Preston Point Road to Port Coogee, guessed Cato. Saint Francis, who'd have thought it? 'And where did you fit in?'

'It was my job to soften up the cockies for takeover while Francis got the financial backing from China. Sweet as.'

'So mainly rural deals, then?'

'For the most part. Also did the odd block of luxury flats here and there.'

'Any enemies along the way?'

'People who might want to kill him, you mean?'

'Yes.'

A long thoughtful draw from the pint of liquorice. 'I could say no, nothing worth killing for, but people get topped for fuck-all these days, don't they?'

'Anything stand out, particularly over the last, say, twelve months? A ripped-off farmer or something?'

'As I said, Francis was a kindly soul. Maybe too kind. He tried not to rip off any poor cockies. Me? I'm not so sentimental.'

'You didn't do it, did you?' said Cato with half a smile. 'Kill him?'

'Now that would be a really stupid thing to do, wouldn't it? He was my cash cow.'

*

Lara had kicked off her shoes and her work gear, luxuriated under a hot shower, then slipped into her jimjams and thick woolly bedsocks. Not the most romantic and alluring of get-ups, she knew, but it was winter and she felt comfortable enough to do this with John. She was putting together some pasta when he came through the door. His face dropped. Had she miscalculated badly? Was the nanna gear a no-no?

'Everything okay?'

'You didn't get my message?'

No, she didn't.

'I'd booked our favourite restaurant.'

'Sorry sweetie. I'm stuffed,' she said. 'Besides, dinner's on now.' She was trying not to pout at being taken for granted and he was obviously putting on a brave face about something.

'No worries.' That smile of his warmed the room.

They ate, chatted about the day, and when it all threatened to slip into something too homely and domestic they retreated to the bedroom for a glorious fuck.

As the heat subsided he propped his head on an elbow, face deadly serious. 'I've got something I need to say to you.'

Uh-oh, here it comes, she thought. Maybe she'd been wrong all along. She'd thought John was different. With the odd exception she'd always chased the same kind of man: mad, bad and dangerous to know. A showman like her father. A showman like those buskers working the weekend crowds in Fremantle. A fire-breathing juggler to light up her night. But in the morning all that remained was singed sheets and a bleak aftertaste of stale paraffin. Then came John, leaving his tricks at the front door and bringing only his passion and sincerity into the bedroom. But now this.

'John?' she said, bracing herself.

And that's when he produced the engagement ring.

*

It didn't take Mundine long to follow through. Hutchens received a text as he was settling down with a glass of merlot to watch News 24 while Mrs Hutchens prodded the roast.

5K wd be a good start

Hutchens texted back.

fuck off

Another one came through. A photo this time. It was of the front of his house, with Mrs Hutchens doing some gardening. The bloke was asking for a slap. Hutchens would be happy to give him one.

OK lets meet

Another picture. A pornographic image and the caption: **Suck mine**

Little psycho. Hutchens turned his phone off and answered the cooing call to dinner. 'Coming, love.'

'Work?' she said, sliding a plate of lamb and vegies his way.

'What?'

'Your phone. Buzzing like billy-o.'

'Yeah, turned it off now, trivial stuff.'

She looked concerned. 'Any more chest pains?'

'Nothing to worry about, Marj. I've got the spray.'

'That's not the point. You used to only get them now and again. Now it's pretty much every day. You need to get to the doctor.'

He reached across and squeezed her hand. 'I will, love. Another week or two and this will all be out of the way.'

'Another week or two and you might be dead.'

'Okay, I'll call tomorrow and make an appointment.'

The home phone went. Marjorie picked it up. He could hear the yelling from where he was. She handed the phone to him, pale. 'It's for you.'

It was Mundine. 'You turned your phone off. Don't fucking ignore me again, fat man! Ever! You hear?'

13

Tuesday, August 13th.

Cato was called into DI Pavlou's office first thing. She must have heard about his chat with Des O'Neill and wanted to slap him down.

'Morning, Philip. Coffee?'

There was a plunger of freshly brewed on her desk and a spare couple of mugs. Was it some kind of trap? 'Sure, thanks.'

She poured him some and pointed at a plate of biscuits. 'Help yourself.'

There was a knock at the door, Lara joined them, flushed and happy, and dragged up a chair. She was offered coffee too but showed them all her herbal tea. Finally James Blond, hair still wet from the rain and a smell of recent lycra and bike oil about him.

'Something come up?' said Cato.

Pavlou was beaming. 'Indeed it has. Lara, tell him.'

'I'm engaged.' She flashed her ring.

'Lovely, congratulations,' said Pavlou. 'But I meant the ACC news.'

'Right.' Lara reddened. Cato found it cute, he smothered a smile. 'The passenger list from Mr Li's flight into Perth immediately preceding the Tan murders.' She dispensed copies to the assembled throng. 'The ACC ran a check on his fellow travellers and got a result.' She referred them to a name highlighted on the list. 'Yu Guangming is known to the Chinese authorities and has a violent criminal history, including murder.'

'Don't the Chinese normally execute people who've done that kind of thing?' said Cato.

'His history isn't formally on the record. He's never actually been caught and convicted of anything. It's what they believe he has been involved in. He also seems to have some kind of protection at a higher level.'

'And this is a Chinese government agency sharing this with you?'

'No. It's via our AFP liaison office in Beijing and their Chinese counterparts.'

'Friend of a friend of a friend.'

'Now, now.' Pavlou's happy face was slipping.

'Okay,' conceded Cato, 'let's assume this unofficial portrait of this guy has some substance. What's his connection to Li?'

And that's where it got interesting.

*

Cato retired to his office. He had to admit even he was beginning to buy the Major Crime line that Tommy Li had questions to answer about the Tan murders. Approaches would now be made through various diplomatic and other channels to set up an interview with him. Apparently they'd already sussed out his Perth office and, according to them, he wasn't due back in Australia anytime soon.

'But I thought he told us he was usually over here every few weeks?' Cato had reminded Pavlou.

'Change in plans, shifting priorities,' said Pavlou drily. His sudden unavailability added to their suspicions.

So why had Cato now been brought into the loop? Was Pavlou feeling confident and therefore more benevolent? Who knows? Chris Thornton popped his head around the door.

'Sarge? Got a moment?'

Cato followed Thornton to a workstation with two large video monitors with split screens. There were various angles and locations and frozen images of a car: Matthew Tan's BMW.

'Why the ongoing interest?' said Cato. 'I thought Matthew had alibis for that night, and his journey home had been corroborated by the cameras?'

'He has,' said Thornton. 'Half a dozen friends, happy to swear in court that he was with them during the relevant hours, plus CCTV in a couple of bars to back him up.'

'So?'

'So I got one of the civilians to run through Matthew's story one more time and cross-reference it to the supporting evidence. It was a paperwork housekeeping thing really, part of putting him on the backburner. Neatly boxed off until and unless something else comes up to put him back in the frame.'

Cato could only marvel at the anal qualities of Thornton's record-keeping but he really hoped the bloke would get to the point soon. 'And?'

'Look at this.' Thornton grabbed a mouse and clicked some keys. 'His car follows girlfriend Lily's through the lights on Hampton and South. They've gone past amber and Matt triggers the bad-boy camera. There's extra illumination from the big Shell servo on the corner.' He froze the frame.

Cato squinted at the blurred image. A small shadowy bump where there shouldn't have been anything. 'There's somebody in the back seat?'

'Looks like it.'

'And your theory is?'

'The murderer hitches a ride out of Port Coogee in Matt's Beemer. But is he a stowaway, or is Matt in on it?'

'Tell me,' said Cato.

Thornton zipped forward towards the end of Matt's journey back to his girlfriend's house in Shelley. CCTV in a servo on Leach Highway catches him buying some cigarettes. The cameras in the forecourt aren't directly on the car. It's half in and half out of shadow and small on the edge of a wide frame. 'It's like he knew where to park, isn't it?' said Thornton.

'You've got a suspicious mind.'

Thornton grinned. 'He makes sure he goes into the servo shop to buy something and the camera gives him an alibi. But look at this.' Thornton zoomed the picture in to the parked car in the distant background. On the blind side, away from the camera, the rear passenger door opens and a shadow hops out and merges with the rest of the darkness.

'So we still can't tell from that whether Matt is in on it.'

'No, sarge. But worth another chat you reckon?'

*

Hutchens had received notification from the Inquiry registrar that proceedings would reconvene on Monday week as the presiding judge had been called away on pressing family business. Could he confirm that he had received appropriate legal advice and would he be able to continue as per the said schedule? Yes, he just needed to kill David Mundine first. Hell, they were going to try and pin Sinclair's death on him, he may as well do Mundine too and get his money's worth. So he had about two weeks up his sleeve for dealing with the prick. He'd also fixed a doctor's appointment for later that day, there'd been a cancellation and he didn't have much else on – apart from a murder inquiry, a growing backlog of cases from assault through theft to a peculiar upskirting charge in a local department store. Oh, and being stalked and blackmailed by a sociopath. Things were closing in and his chest seemed tighter by the minute. Marjorie was right, he might not see the next two weeks out. But maybe a catastrophic heart attack was a better prospect than jail.

He needed to get a grip. The lawyer had said just blank them, they can't prove a thing. What's the worst that could happen? An adverse finding by the Inquiry and an administrative slap on the wrist? Cato and Major Crime were responsible for the Tan murder case. They could worry about that. The backlog? That never went away. Really the only urgent matters were his chest pains and David Mundine. He dropped by the office to see Cato.

'I hadn't realised I was so popular.'

'What?'

'Everybody wants to talk to me, today.'

'Enjoy it while it lasts,' Hutchens sniffed. 'What's happening with the general backlog?'

'I've farmed out most of the volume stuff to the neighbours over at Murdoch.'

'Good work. Happy are they?'

'Do we care?'

'Not really. What was the upskirting one about?'

'A bloke got stopped in some boutique on South Terrace taking photos up the skirts of the mannequins.'

'Is that illegal?'

'Dunno. Murdoch are on to it. They specialise in saddos.'

Cato updated Hutchens on the Matthew Tan line of inquiry and on Tommy Li and his mystery flying partner.

'When are you going to see Matthew?'

'Later today.'

'Good. Keep it to yourself. See if we can steal a march on Edna Average.'

'What do you think about the Li thing?'

'To be fair, if I was in Pavlou's shoes I'd be doing a little dance as well. So what's the plan? Invite Li in for a chat next time he graces these shores?'

'Far as I can tell they're aiming to pay him a visit.'

'She'll like that. Apparently the shopping in Shanghai is to die for.'

'That was cheap and unworthy, if I may say so, boss.'

'Sorry.' He wasn't.

'Any developments at your end?'

'No,' said Hutchens. He paused. 'What?'

'You don't look well. Everything okay?'

'Nothing to worry your pretty little head about.' Hutchens saw he'd gone too far. 'Thanks for the concern. All will be well in the fullness of time, Cato mate.' He mustered a reassuring smile.

He left Cato and retreated to a vacant workstation to check his emails. Two hours until his doctor's appointment.

*

When Cato and Chris Thornton pulled up at the Shelley house there was no sign of Matthew's BMW but Lily's i30 was in the driveway. Cato went to ring the bell and found the front door ajar.

'Hello?' There was a yap. The yellow-bowed poodle was home. 'Lily?'

No sound apart from the yapping dog. Cato pushed open the door and stepped across the threshold.

'Lily? It's me, Philip Kwong. Fremantle Detectives.'

The dog seemed unsure whether to yap, whine, or growl. It sounded like it was coming from upstairs. There was a trail of blood spots on the stair carpet.

Cato took out his gun and Thornton did the same.

'Lily?'

He edged up the stairs, hugging the wall, half-crouched, eyes straining for any sudden movement, every nerve jangling. Blood rushed through his ears, he wanted it to stop, he wanted to be able to hear anything, everything. There was a rustle and scrape, a patter of steps and the poodle was at the top of the stairs, yapping and growling. Its yellow bow was askew, teeth were bared. There was blood around the muzzle.

'Can we shoot it?' whispered Thornton.

'Not yet.'

There was a groan. Low, animalistic. It wasn't the dog.

Cato took the last few steps quickly and followed the blood trail into the bedroom. Lily was on the floor, kimono askew. She'd been badly beaten, punched and kicked. But she was alive and there were no signs of any other weapon being used. Her face was pulpy, hair matted with blood, some teeth were missing. Cato could see them on the carpet. Thornton was on his mobile summoning assistance.

'Who was it, Lily? Who did this?'

She reached a hand up to him, a varnished nail had split and torn away from the finger. Tears mingled with the blood on her face.

'Did Matt do this to you?'

No answer. The hand dropped back to the carpet. Cato put an alert out for Matt anyway as an ambulance siren wailed in the distance.

*

DI Pavlou wasn't best pleased by the turn of events. If nothing else, it took the shine off her Thomas Li theory which had been building nicely. Now it was reverting back to a sordid little domestic starring Matthew Tan – Bad Seed.

'So where is the little shit?'

'Don't know. We've got people out chasing him down. We're checking known associates, usual hangouts, et cetera. The geeks are monitoring his phone and bank cards. The airports have been alerted. Every mobile patrol will be looking for him. Short of that...' Cato shrugged.

'Media?'

'Along the hall, waiting for your word. Hannah's ready to brief you.'

She stood up and grabbed her phone and specs from the desk. 'Next time you get a juicy little lead I want to know first, not last. Right now I'm still tossing up whether or not to have you suspended.'

'The lead only came to light late this morning through Chris Thornton's diligence,' said Cato. 'You had made it clear that I was responsible for the Matthew Tan side of the inquiry. You've shown little interest in anything except Thomas Li.'

Pavlou was half out of her door. She stopped, came back, closed it. 'Pull your head in, Kwong.' She let out a ragged breath, gathering her thoughts. 'You know there's a bit of a pattern developing in your behaviour: sabotaging Lara's work, undermining mine. I thought you were better than that, Philip.'

'Boss?'

A curl of the lip. 'Blokes in the workplace. Over the years I've found they come in all shapes and sizes – buffoons, cavemen, gimps.' A locking of eyes with Cato. 'And passive-aggressives. They come. They go.' She opened her office door again. 'I'll let you front the media today, mate. Take one for the team.'

*

Hutchens heard the news on the radio as he drove to his rendezvous with David Mundine. He allowed himself a grim smile. So it looked like it was the Tan boy all along. It was sunny with a cold gusty wind shaking the trees and a harsh brightness to the winter daylight. Mundine wanted to meet him at J. B. O'Reilly's pub in West Leederville. Mid-afternoon, and the place was dark and dead. A couple of diehards grimaced into their pints. Mundine was sitting in a corner under a wall of Disneyfied Irish paraphernalia: street signs, shamrocks, sepia photos of rebels, diddle-eye fucking oh.

Mundine shook his nearly empty glass at Hutchens. 'Guinness.'

Hutchens ordered one and a Kilkenny for himself and returned to the table. 'You can't do that shit, mate.'

'What's that?'

'Phone my home and swear at my wife.'

'Sensitive is she? Well brought up?'

Hutchens looked around the room, measured up some consequences. 'If I killed Sinclair what's to stop me going that one step further?'

'Are you threatening me, Mr Hutchens?'

'You're a useless junkie waste of space. A fuck-up. No wonder Sinclair took you as a girlfriend. Some people are born victims.'

'That right?'

'You know it is. Now piss off and leave me and my family alone before you get badly hurt.'

Mundine flicked through his iPhone, found what he was looking for, a photo of Hutchens' oldest daughter. 'Melanie, isn't it? Lovely girl. Just moved into that nice place in Subiaco.'

'I'm going to kill you.'

'That bloke of hers goes away a lot doesn't he? Filmmaker or something. Always out ...' his fingers curled in air quotes, 'on location.'

Hutchens leaned across the table and grabbed Mundine's throat. Glasses went flying. The barman, an Irish backpacker, wanted them to cut it out. 'Fuck off,' Hutchens said to him over his shoulder. He was about to draw back his fist for a punch when he felt a prick of pain in his left side, level with his heart. He looked down. A long blade was poised to enter his rib cage. A trickle of blood spreading on his shirt.

'You're right, Mr Hutchens,' Mundine rasped. 'Some people are born victims.' Hutchens released his grip on Mundine's throat. The blade stayed there. 'You've just been owned by a junkie fuck-up, Mr H. What does that make you?' Mundine felt around for Hutchens' wallet. Found it, emptied it, kept the money and the family snapshots. 'My price just went up. You'll be hearing from me.'

And he was gone.

The barman put some more diddle-eye music on the CD and asked Hutchens if he wanted another drink while they waited for the police to arrive. 'On the house, sir.'

'Cancel the police,' said Hutchens, mopping his bloody shirt with a paper napkin. 'Just a misunderstanding.'

*

It was dark by the time Cato got home. Rain dotted the windows as he defrosted a tub of pesto in the microwave and set some pasta to boil. There was still no sign of Matthew Tan even though his face and description was now on all major news outlets. Cato was just sitting down to his pesto when the front doorbell rang.

It was Jake.

'Hi. Come in.' Cato tried to hug him but was rebuffed. His son was almost the same height as him now, his voice deeper, and there was an outcrop of acne at the corner of the mouth. It complimented the livid nail gun scar on his cheek. 'Everything okay?'

The boy slumped at the kitchen table as Cato flicked on the kettle. 'No.'

'What's up?'

'I want to come and live with you.'

This was news. Last week he couldn't even be bothered to come over for a visit at the weekend. 'Why?'

'Does there need to be a reason? You're my dad.'

'What's going on?'

'Nothing. Just sick of home that's all.'

Cato slid a mug of tea towards his son and plonked a bottle of milk beside it. He waited, not filling the silence.

'Simon's a dickhead. I hate him.'

'Why?'

'He just is. Always on my back. Sticking his nose in.'

'Jake, just get to the point. What is it that's really pissing you off?'

A glint and the hint of a smile hidden by the tea mug. 'He doesn't like my mates, wants to stop me seeing them.'

'Why would he do that?'

'He reckons they're a bad influence.'

'Are they?'

'No. They're just mates.'

'He must have his reasons.'

A flare in the eyes. 'Must he? Maybe he's just imagining shit. He just needs to get a life.'

'Imagining what?'

A shrug. 'Ask him.'

'I'm asking you.'

An exasperated sigh. 'He reckons we're doing drugs and stuff.'

'Are you?'

'No.'

This could take all night. 'I'll have a chat with your mum.'

'Good luck. She's in babyland, boring everybody with her pregnancy.'

'Feeling left out?'

'Yeah, Dad. Nobody's child. So can I move in here with you?'

'Like I said, I'll have a chat with your mum.'

'Don't bother.' Jake slurped from his mug and banged it back down on the table. 'I get the picture.'

14

Wednesday, August 14th.

DI Hutchens' door opened and Cato was summoned with a wave.

'How's your passport? Up to date?'

'Far as I know, yeah.'

'Nip home and bring it in. Urgent. We need to get you a visa.'

'Maybe you could start at the beginning?'

'You're Shanghai-bound my boy. Special invitation.'

'Li? He's Major Crime's job.'

'He is indeed but he's only agreed to be interviewed by them if you're along for the ride.' Hutchens allowed himself an evil chuckle. 'Pissed off Pavlou, no end.'

Cato wasn't aware he'd made much of an impression on Tommy Li that night at the airport. Or was that the point? Li had chosen him because he could; it was a way of putting DI Pavlou in her place. Cato's focus was Matthew Tan, he needed to find him. A pawn in somebody's power game? He didn't need this right now and said as much to his boss.

'Four or five days they reckon. Home by Tuesday at the latest. I'll keep things ticking over here, I'm not due back at the Inquiry until a week Monday.' Hutchens ushered Cato towards the door. 'Loosen up, mate. Sit in on the interview. Buy some souvenirs. Come home. Gig of the year.'

Hutchens seemed bright and unflappable. Almost manically so. 'Everything okay with you, boss?'

'Never better, mate.'

Cato didn't buy it. Hutchens' face was pink and tight. The voice was a half-note higher like air escaping from a balloon. 'You seem, I don't know, a bit wound up?'

Hutchens ushered him through the door. 'Off you go, now.'

Apparently there was no way out. Cato went home and found his passport. He'd tried a few times to reach Jake but the boy's mobile was turned off. He sent a text: **sorry if I was grumpy last night, lets talk more**. That afternoon, while he waited for compelling leads on Matthew Tan, he googled Shanghai and got the gist – Paris or Whore of the Orient – depending on your point of view. Early Christian missionaries had formed the opinion that if God didn't smite Shanghai then he owed Sodom and Gomorrah an apology. Population twenty-three million – the whole of Australia crammed into one city. In addition it often had smog to die for and sixteen thousand dead pigs had floated down the Huangpu River back in March. Oh, and a new strain of chicken flu had killed around forty people in the last few months. Great. Pollution and calamity on an Old Testament scale.

'Can't I just sit in on Skype?' he'd whined after handing over his passport and bringing Hutchens up to date.

'It's all about face, mate, you should know that. And Li wants your face, present, in the room. Look, flu-schmu, you've got more chance of catching mesothelioma with all the devil's dust they've been finding around the old office these last few months. Just stay clear of pork and chook and you'll be right.' A reassuring pat on the shoulder. 'Tofu. That's the gear.'

*

Hutchens would be glad to have Cato out of the way for a few days. He was torn between murdering David Mundine and capitulating to him. Either way, he didn't want Cato's saintly presence haunting him, judging either his evil intent or his vile weakness. Mundine was getting the better of him. What was happening?

You've just been owned by a junkie fuck-up, Mr H. What does that make you?

What precisely was the threat here? Mundine claimed to know what had happened between him and Peter Sinclair that night and wanted money to keep quiet. Further than that, he was displaying all the signs of being a stalking little control freak and had issued veiled threats to physically harm Hutchens' family. The two didn't seem to go together. Money for silence was a straightforward enough motive but the added antipathy towards Hutchens and his brood? That was crazy enough to derail the blackmail scheme. So which was most important to Mundine? If Hutchens paid up there was every reason to believe that the problem wouldn't go away.

He needed to separate the issues and deal with them differently. Mundine could stand up at the Inquiry and claim to have seen something that night but without corroborating evidence it surely counted for very little. So what did he have? What did he know?

On the matter of the personal menaces there were witnesses at J. B. O'Reilly's who would have seen Mundine threaten him with the blade. But they would also have seen Hutchens grab his throat first. Mundine, the victim of sexual abuse and a key witness at the Inquiry, versus Hutchens a thuggish corner-cutting cop with questions to answer. How would that look? At this stage there would be little mileage in making any official complaints about Mundine's actions. But Hutchens did know people, hard men who could have a quiet word. Was he prepared to go down that path? He recalled the pic of Melanie on Mundine's phone. Hell, yes.

His phone buzzed.

10K cash, leave with barman @ JBs by Friday

He texted back asking what he would get in return.

Peace of mind

PART 2

15

Thursday, August 15th – Friday, August 16th.

The Qantas flight touched down at Pudong International Airport just after 10 p.m. Cato had spent most of the long day and two flights sandwiched between Lara in the window seat and James Blond in the aisle – the seating arrangements were no doubt DI Pavlou's last-minute revenge. James Blond had played *Call of Duty* on his games console, twitching furiously with each kill and robbing Cato of any sleep. When she wasn't squeezing past for an excessive number of toilet visits, Lara had snapped on a blindfold, plugged in her earphones, and stayed AWOL. Cato had snuck a glance at her engagement ring while she dozed. Lara in love? Good luck to her, she was certainly less abrasive to be around. Cato wondered if the same could be said for him.

Tommy Li had specified the three underlings or nothing, and he got his way – he was under no obligation to return to Perth for interview. Of the three, Cato was the senior officer, so ostensibly he was the boss. Was that another one of Li's little games, arrange it so the Chinese guy is in charge of the visiting cops? Either way, it was still Lara who held the paperwork and Pavlou's list of questions.

An immigration officer had studied Cato's passport for longer than felt necessary before firing off a stream of Mandarin at him.

'What?' said Cato.

The official looked at him in disgust. 'Tourist or business?'

Cato assumed that the class of visa in his passport and the boxes he'd ticked on the form made it clear enough. The official was interrupted by a rap on his cubicle rear window and the appearance of a more senior-looking colleague accompanied by a tall Westerner in a Hawaiian shirt. More words exchanged, the Westerner seemed to be fluent in Chinese. They were waved through.

'Rory Driscoll.' The tall stranger stuck out a hand for shaking.

'Philip Kwong,' said Cato.

'AKA Cato?'

'Philip should do it – for now.'

Driscoll had the look of a footy player turned commentator: plenty of teeth and grooming but a mongrel never far from the surface. He shared a manly handshake with James Blond and upped the wattage on the smile for Lara. They jumped into Driscoll's car, Cato taking the spare front seat and the two juniors in the back.

'Perth? Sydney? Melbourne? Where do you call home?' said Cato, to make conversation.

'Warnambool. Gunditj mob. The wild west of Victoria,' said Driscoll. He broke into a chuckle. 'You've got to admit, mate, it *was* funny.'

'What?' said Cato.

'You weren't expecting an Aborigine to be the Chinese interpreter for a bloke called Kwong who can't speak a fucking word.' He slapped his thigh and roared.

Cato found himself grinning. Then laughing. A lot.

'Fluent in Mandarin. Impressive,' said Lara. 'It doesn't seem like an easy language to learn.'

Driscoll studied her in the rear-view. Looking for signs he was being patronised? 'I can also speak half a dozen Aboriginal languages, fluent Bahasa and Tagalog, passable Japanese, and you should hear my Pidgin. Awesome.'

No reply. Cato glanced over his shoulder. Lara looked deep in thought.

'I was brought up to believe that if you go through someone else's country you need to ask their permission, pay your dues, and try to learn a little of their language and culture. You never assume a divine right to be there.' Driscoll's gaze drifted over to James Blond in the other back seat. 'It's about respect. That right, brother?'

James yawned. 'Sure. Whatever.'

'I can see already you guys are going to go down a storm in Shanghai.' He closed the conversation by switching on some music. The Gipsy Kings.

Music aside, they drove in tired and companionable silence along an elevated expressway. It was bland, as most airport roads are, but still an improvement on the tawdry ribbon of fast-food barns and no-tell motels on the way out to Perth International. Lara had tried asking a few questions, like who the hell was Driscoll anyway, but was met with a smile and the promise of a full briefing first thing tomorrow.

'You guys are too stuffed and won't take anything in right now. As my nan used to say, "I never boil me cabbage twice."'

They crossed the Huangpu River but it was too dark for Cato to see if there were any dead pigs in it. *My name is Legion, for we are many.* They were dropped at a hotel in a city of a million brightly lit tower blocks. Cato noticed a bilingual street sign as he stepped out of the car into the humid night: Nanjing Road. According to Driscoll it was about ten minutes walk to the Bund – that way, he thumbed in the direction. He gave them his business card and wished them goodnight. They all had neighbouring rooms on the nineteenth floor. Cato went into his and fell straight asleep.

*

Cato woke early and went to find the Bund. The day was humid and a milky-white sun hung behind a jaundiced veil of ozone. In the street, the smell of cooking oil mingled with petrol fumes and something overripe. Along the way, Nanjing Road became a pedestrian mall. It was throbbing: huge department stores already opening their doors, office and shop workers on their way somewhere, old and middle-aged couples waltzing to Chinese love songs, and a handful of western tourists capturing everything on their cameras and phones, even the quiet, intimate moments of complete strangers. Then suddenly there it was, the Bund, wider and more open than he had imagined. It was Shanghai's iconic landmark, according to the travel guides he'd scanned in transit. The solid and grand nineteenth-century architecture of the old bank, shipping, and insurance buildings reminded him of visits to Liverpool, Manchester and other European cities from a bygone age. And along the wide, muddy brown swirl of the Huangpu huge industrial barges chugged, belching smoke as they must have done for a century or more. By contrast Pudong, across the river, definitely belonged to the future; the space-age architecture was right out of The Jetsons. So this is Shanghai, thought Cato, old meets new, east meets west – simple really. A clock atop one of the old buildings struck the hour, eight, tolling out a tune that was unmistakably Chinese and vaguely martial in tone. Cato strolled the length of the Bund and back without being bothered by any touts, as the anglo Westerners were. Descending the steps into Bund Park he passed the bronze statue of Chairman Mao beneath which tourists posed for happy snaps.

On his return to the hotel, Lara emerged from her room freshly showered and flushed from exercise.

'Run or gym?' said Cato.

'Both, they have a treadmill. Had breakfast yet?'

'No.'

'See you down there. If you're good I'll show you my file.'

'Whoopee,' said Cato. 'Where's 007? He invited too?'

'He's skypeing his mum. He'll meet us down there.'

*

Business or casual? Cato surveyed his open suitcase and opted for casual. It was muggy and he felt no great need to impress Driscoll, Lara, James Blond or anyone else today. Li? He'd think about it. At the breakfast table Lara was eating yoghurt and fresh fruit and JB was working his way through a fry-up. Cato found some cereal and coffee at the buffet and joined them.

'How's Mum?' he asked James.

'Good, thanks. Sends her regards.'

'Really?'

'No.'

Lara slid a file across the table to him. Inside was an enlarged passport photo of Tommy Li's fellow traveller, Yu Guangming: it was one of those chiselled faces, heroic and handsome from one angle, cruel and petulant from another. There was also one sheet of A4 and a photocopy of a press clipping. It was brief but still an advance on the thumbnail sketch they'd been given in Pavlou's office earlier in the week. Four years ago Charlotte Wen, a twenty-two year old Singaporean exchange student, had been raped, beaten, and left for dead in a Sydney hotel room. She'd survived and not only provided police with a description but also a name. She had met Yu Guangming in a bar in King's Cross but remembered little after that. Traces of the date rape drug Rohypnol had been found in her system. Yu was arrested and the trace samples taken from him backed up her story. Unaccountably he was released on bail and within a week had left the country.

'So?' said Cato.

'Read the other sheet,' said Lara. 'The ACC profile.'

Yu Guangming, and his handful of aliases, seemed to be anything from thirty-three to forty-two years old. Using various names he had criss-crossed the Asia Pacific regularly over the last few years: Australia, New Zealand, PNG, Nauru, Fiji, Indonesia. It seemed that everywhere he went he left bodies or maimed victims. Meanwhile the student, Charlotte Wen, had subsequently tried to retract her allegation and now suggested the sex had been consensual and that somebody else must have beaten the crap out of her. Sydney detectives were apparently keeping an open mind.

'If we know this guy's movements and his history why do we keep letting him go?'

Lara shrugged. 'Conspiracy or fuck-up, we haven't worked that one out yet.'

'But you believe he's here in Shanghai, connected to Li, and involved in the Tan murders?'

'Yes. The bodies in New Zealand, Indonesia, and PNG were of people who seemed to be either blocking or threatening projects in which Li has interests.'

'What about the other bodies in Fiji and Nauru?'

Lara shrugged again. 'Maybe some were business, others were pleasure.'

'Interesting,' Cato conceded, 'but still a bit circumstantial so far?'

'Enough to shake a few trees with though, eh?' Lara gathered up the folder and downed the rest of her orange juice. 'Driscoll's meeting us in the lobby in ten minutes.' She checked out Cato's T-shirt and shorts. 'You getting changed or what?'

*

The Australian Consulate was about a fifteen-minute drive west along Nanjing Road. It was on the twenty-second floor of a tower block surrounded by expensive-looking shops selling high-end Western brands. After passing through security scanners and being issued visitor passes, Driscoll ushered them into a boardroom with a view east towards the Bund. There was just one other person there, a Chinese woman. Her hair was cropped short, pixie-like; she had swimmer's shoulders and wore a slightly bored expression.

'Allow me to introduce Ms Wang, our AFP liaison from the Beijing office,' said Driscoll.

Cato had upped his sartorial game as per Lara's request. He stepped forward and played leader of the pack. 'Nee ha,' he said, bowing slightly and holding out his hand.

'G'day,' she said, shaking the hand. 'Sharon.'

Cato flushed. 'So you're not actually from Beijing then.'

'Bendigo.' She shook hands with Lara and JB then lifted her chin at Driscoll. 'Rory, got your Powerpoint ready to go?'

They spent the next ten minutes looking at a series of flowcharts showing how international police agencies communicated and cooperated while in China. Finally Driscoll sat down.

Sharon Wang frowned. 'I think a saw a typo in one of your cards, Rory. It's two m's in communication.'

'Very funny, Shaz. Maybe you could let them know the ground rules and we'll take it from there.'

'Cool. So which of you is really in charge here?'

'I'm the senior officer,' said Cato.

'So why did you look at Ms Sumich before you spoke?' Wang tilted her head towards Lara. 'You want to interview Mr Li then, do you?'

'Yes.'

'And Kwong here's your front man.'

'Yes.'

She snapped her fingers in a gimme gesture. 'List of questions?'

'There isn't one.'

'My arse. DI Pavlou would have given you a script and we need to see it.'

'Why?'

'Because that's what Mr Li, his lawyer, the mayor of Shanghai, the city police chief, and half the Politburo are expecting. It shows respect. It's pretty important over here.'

Lara fiddled with her iPhone and Driscoll's left pocket throbbed. 'It's a Word attachment.'

'Felt very nice, too,' said Driscoll, standing. 'I'll print it off.'

A few minutes later, after scanning Lara's list of questions, Wang sat back in her chair and twirled a pen. 'What are you hoping to achieve here, Sumich?'

'We're trying to establish whether Mr Li knows Yu Guangming.'

'What if he just says no?'

'Then we'll press him on the matter.'

'No, no, and no again. What then?'

'We'll go home and write a report.'

'You're not holding anything back, no cards up your sleeve, no ambushes?'

'No.'

'Good.' Wang appraised the three of them. 'So DS Kwong here is your question master. Hope you know how to kowtow properly, mate.' She switched her gaze to James Blond. 'And what's your job?'

James grinned. 'Muscle?'

Wang snorted. 'God help us.'

Lara put up her hand. 'While we're on the subject, we know what you are but what about him?' Driscoll. 'What's his job?'

'Iyam Koltural Attache!' he said, in a mock Boris-the-Russian voice. Nobody thought it was funny. 'I work for embassy. On special projects.'

Lara nodded slowly. 'Oh, a spook. How cool,' she said, without enthusiasm.

'Tonight I take you to ballet,' said Driscoll, resuming the accent. 'Then we drink plenty vodka.'

Wang gathered up her papers. 'Mr Li's agreed to see you at eleven a.m. for twenty minutes. Time for a cuppa then we'll drive you over.' She tapped Lara on the shoulder on the way out. 'No surprises, I'm deadly serious.'

*

Li Tonggui occupied the thirty-sixth floor of a Pudong tower with a panoramic view back over the river to the Bund and a building that looked like a kid's drawing of a space station down to his right. He welcomed them with a huge smile into a plush, thickly carpeted office with floor to ceiling windows. His lawyer was a young woman called Phoebe with killer heels and a stare to match.

Cato kicked off. 'Thank you for sparing us some time, Mr Li.'

'My pleasure. How do you like Shanghai?'

'Spectacular so far,' said Cato nodding at the view. 'I'm looking forward to seeing a bit more before we leave.'

'Oh, you must, you must. There's so much more to Shanghai than skyscrapers and light shows.'

'No doubt.' Cato unfolded his sheet of questions while Lara took out a notepad and James Blond laid an MP3 on the table.

'Not allowed,' snapped Phoebe, flicking her wrist at JB's gadget.

Sharon Wang glared at James and he put it away.

Cato smiled like nothing had happened. 'I understand you're aware of our line of questioning. Are you happy to proceed?'

'Of course, of course. Fire away!'

'Can you remind us of the purpose of your visit to Perth in the days preceding the murder of the Tan family?'

Li proceeded to reiterate what they already knew: various deals or prospective deals to be progressed, meetings, site visits, troubleshooting.

'Troubleshooting?' said Cato.

'The FIRB.' Foreign Investment Review Board, recalled Cato. 'I still had hopes to rescue that deal, to change their minds.'

'That's the one Francis Tan was part of, lost you a few million?'

'Eighty-seven in development costs to be precise.'

'You must have been angry. A sum like that?'

'In the scheme of things it was small change. I can write it off against tax. But the deal was worth saving. It would have been a big project.'

Cato showed interest. 'This is a departure from the script, Mr Li, but I'd love to know what it was. The big project.' He earned himself triple warning glares from Phoebe, Sharon and Lara.

Li outlined the project. Millions of acres of farmland were to be purchased in the Great Southern providing certainty for struggling Aussie farmers and clean and bountiful food security for increasingly affluent and choosy Chinese consumers. Huge profits for Li. Win-win-win. Cato thought about the pigs in the Huangpu, the chicken flu, and the pollution. He could see Li's point. He moved into more dangerous territory.

'And you travelled alone?'

'No, I had my personal assistant with me.'

'Nobody else?'

'No.'

'Yu Guangming. Do you know him?'

'No, sorry. Who is he?'

'He's a man with a history of violence. He was sitting a few rows behind you on your last flight into Perth.'

'Everybody was sitting behind me. I tend to travel first class.'

Cato read the list of aliases.

Li denied knowing those names too. He exchanged a glance with Phoebe the lawyer and checked his watch. 'Is he a person of interest in those dreadful murders?'

'We believe so,' said Cato.

'On what basis?'

'I'm sorry that's confidential.'

Li was smiling. It was a 'well, thanks for coming' smile. The body language said he was getting ready to wind the interview up and Cato knew he'd got precisely nowhere. Lara looked far from happy to leave it there.

'His DNA was at the murder scene, his sperm was inside Mr Tan's wife,' said Lara. She stood up and pointed a finger at him. 'You're a liar and no matter how big you think you are, we're going to have you.'

All hell broke loose. Phoebe pointed her finger back and yelled in Mandarin, Sharon Wang and Rory Driscoll rounded on Lara, and James looked unsure about what he was meant to do. Cato and Li sat in the maelstrom and regarded each other. Both knew this wasn't going to end well.

*

They were back in the boardroom at the consulate being chastised. Driscoll was jumpy and Sharon Wang was incandescent.

'What the fuck do you think you're playing at?'

The question was addressed to Lara.

'We've got four murders to solve, a family bludgeoned to a pulp in their own home. We're not here to piss about with diplomatic niceties or "inter-agency cooperation". We need to rattle that bastard's cage.'

Nice one, thought Cato. Lara was growing into the job.

'Those protocols are for everyone,' said Driscoll. 'They help keep the Chinese authorities reassured about working with us on much bigger issues like drug and people trafficking. Fact of life: your family murder isn't worth rocking the boat for.'

'Tell that to the Tans,' said Lara.

Wang shook her head. 'Oh grow up, Sumich. That little exchange might have made you feel better but it didn't progress your inquiry one jot. Li didn't even blink. His reach goes all the way to the top here. He could have you all sliced and diced in broad daylight and nobody would say a word, here or in Australia.' She twirled her biro. 'You've done nothing to help your case and you've probably stuffed up years of work for us. Thanks, now piss off back home.'

'Our flight leaves in two days,' said Lara.

'Good. Do some shopping and sightseeing and keep your heads pulled in. Expect a formal reprimand and hopefully a suspension on your return.'

'That goes for all of us, I assume?' said Cato.

'Ra-ra-ra, three bloody musketeers,' Wang muttered. 'Sure it does.'

Driscoll stopped pacing and slid into a chair, drumming his knuckles on the table absent-mindedly. 'Why the hard-on for Li? I've seen the files and reports. It's all circumstantial.'

Surprisingly, James Blond spoke up. 'He's bent, he's shipping truckloads of meth and heroin into Australia, and he's laundering his money by buying up great swathes of our country.'

'Whose country?' said Driscoll.

James hadn't finished. 'He's involved in the Tan murders, has to be.'

'Funny how people get uneasy about the Chinese buying the farm,' said Driscoll. 'We've already sold them half the topsoil in the Pilbara and everybody's cool with that but we can't hack them actually coming to town. Poms can come and blow up their nukes at Maralinga, the Yanks can set up military bases in the Top End, all good. But Chinese buying up a few acres? Nah. You're a hypocrite, Jimmy.'

Lara sat back and folded her arms. 'Nice speech, Rory.'

Driscoll shook his head contemptuously. 'Li, a drug runner and murderer? Evidence would be good, mate. The Yellow Peril stuff won't stand up in court.' He left the room, followed by Sharon Wang. Bollocking over.

Cato's phone vibrated in his pocket. A text. Sender unknown.

My apologies for this morning. Allow me to invite you to breakfast tomorrow. Royal Garden Restaurant, Zhongshan Park, 9.30. Take the westbound metro line 2 from near your hotel. Alone please. Thomas.

Cato wondered what Li wanted to apologise for. And how he had this mobile number? And how he knew which hotel they were in?

Lara was waiting. 'Anything we need to know about?'

'No,' he said.

16

Saturday, August 17th.

Cato arrived at Zhongshan Park station an hour early. It was several suburbs west of their hotel and the area, to his untrained eye, was indistinguishable from anywhere else he'd so far seen in Shanghai. Skyscrapers. Galore. He'd thought he could maybe recce the joint, spot any potential dangers, mark out escape routes, check if he was being stalked. He knew he didn't really have a hope but it seemed like a good and diligent idea. The park itself was a splash of green among the traffic, the concrete, glass and steel. But just a few steps in from the road, the noise and the fumes seemed to fade into a distant background to be replaced by birdsong, the perfumed rustle of cherry blossom trees and the gentle chatter of neighbours. A dozen men and women of varying ages practised tai chi under the guidance of a lithe woman in a black silk pyjama-type outfit. On a nearby bench a bookish middle-aged man sawed at a two-stringed Chinese violin. But it was the calligraphers who captivated Cato: ordinary-looking blokes with jars of oily water and brushes drawing Chinese characters on the flagstones with deft, graceful strokes only to see them evaporate within a few minutes. It seemed futile, existential, and so bloody beautiful all at the same time. Cato felt an urge to learn the names of these things, to understand the movements, to partake in the gossip. He felt both enchanted and lonely. As he ventured further into the park down narrow meandering paths, across ornate stone bridges, he came across more people waltzing, playing badminton or mahjong. The park wasn't just a splash of green in the midst of a mega-city, it felt to Cato like an oasis of calm and culture from another time and place altogether.

After yesterday's dressing-down at the consulate they'd all retreated to their hotel rooms to brood. Cato could hear Lara through the wall giving her report back to DI Pavlou. Through the wall on the other side, James Blond was watching a succession of action movies. By mid-afternoon Cato was getting cabin fever so he'd checked his guidebook and gone out shopping for souvenirs. South of the Bund, the City God Temple market had offered some manufactured old-world energy and charm. The temple itself was an antidote to the skyscrapers with its ancient open courtyard, smoking incense, and believers kowtowing to their ancestors. He'd sipped an expensive cuppa in a teahouse midway across a zigzag bridge over a lake festooned with water lilies, koi and turtles. Further south and west, the Dongtai Road Antiques Market offered all you could want in the form of tacky memorabilia: from Chairman Mao ashtrays to Cultural Revolution alarm clocks. Nostalgia knows no shame, reflected Cato. He bought his son a fur-lined army hat complete with red star and fold-down earmuffs. Jake was at an age when something that naff might be ironically cool. He hadn't got around to making that call to Jane to discuss their son's apparent unhappiness; maybe later, after this meeting with Li, he'd give it a go. Or in a few days when he returned.

He'd bought some tea for his sisters and felt guilty for not popping in to say goodbye to his father before he left. For all he knew the old man would cark it while he was gone. Cato Kwong – Family Man. Further meandering brought him to the Shanghai Street That Time Forgot. Old shambling terraced houses leaned drunkenly into their neighbours as if to help keep the other from falling. Winding sunless alleyways were crammed with people crouched on small plastic chairs eating from bowls of noodles. The street itself bustled in gentle chaos with peddlers hawking basins of wriggling eels, twitching crabs, and gasping fish. The gutters ran red with piscine blood and guts. There was room only for bikes, mopeds, and pedestrians in the narrow tree-lined road, no cars or trucks. All available space was utilised. Washing even hung from the low-slung powerlines. Cato had watched as a young mother, baby in one arm, used a steel pole to hook two metal hangers of laundry onto the line. From a health and safety perspective it gave him the heebie-jeebies, from another it was almost life affirming.

On his return mid-evening, Cato had sent a brief text to Hutchens – **shit, fan etc** – checked and answered a few emails, napped, watched CNN, and eaten a room service dinner. He'd failed to fall asleep and around 10.30 he'd rapped on Lara's door.

'That stuff about Yu Guangming and Genevieve Tan, is that real or made up?'

Lara looked ready to retire. 'Is this urgent?'

'Just tell me.'

'Yes. He was at the house and his sperm was inside the wife.'

'How come I'm the last to know?'

'Ask DI Pavlou.'

'Don't worry, I will.'

Slumber was a long time coming. He'd woken and showered and resolved to play his cards a little closer to his chest. The look that passed between him and Li yesterday: Li knew that it wasn't just him who had been ambushed by Lara; Cato too had been played. But it was clear that this was now between the two of them and, for that reason, he was keeping this morning tea rendezvous with Li a secret. That may or may not turn out to be a mistake, he would know soon enough. Kites skipped in the air and nightingales sang in their bamboo cages but Cato felt his sense of serenity slip away as he stepped over the threshold of the Royal Garden Restaurant.

Thomas Li had taken a window table. He was dressed in pastel casuals; perhaps he'd just been to, or was on his way to, a game of golf. He greeted Cato with a warm smile. 'Tea? It's Cloud and Mist from the Yellow Mountain. Or would you prefer coffee?'

'Tea's fine. Thanks.' Cato took a seat.

'Are you hungry?'

'No, I'm good. Cheers.' The tea had a sweet musky fragrance and a delicate taste.

'I love Zhongshan Park,' said Li wistfully. 'I used to play here as a child, fly my kite, run around. I grew up in an old overcrowded shikumen house near here, bulldozed now, to make way for a shopping mall. My family history, all dust.' Li fiddled with a pack of cigarettes before deciding against lighting up. 'Such is the march of progress. Fortunately, I now own the shopping mall.'

'That must help ease the pain,' said Cato.

A humourless nod. 'I would like to apologise for the ugly scene yesterday.'

'Why? It was not your doing.'

'Still, I was the host. It occurred while you were my guest. It was unpleasant.'

Cato doubted Li's sincerity. They both knew an apology was not needed. This was the overture for a completely different transaction. 'Thank you,' said Cato. 'Water under the bridge.'

A small smile tugged the corner of Li's mouth. He gestured out of the window at two men standing close up against each other, hand-sparring in slow motion. One would push with a hand or arm and the other would block and push back. Others nearby stood in clusters, doing the same.

'Tuishou,' said Li. 'Pushing hands. It's a form of taiji, or tai chi, as you may say. The idea is to maintain constant contact, pushing neither too much nor too little in a harmonious, natural and spontaneous flow.' Li sipped from his Cloud and Mist tea. 'The essence of tuishou is that you dissolve an oncoming force before striking a blow. Push too hard and too early and you will most likely lose your balance and fall.'

The flow of movement was hypnotic. With difficulty Cato returned his attention to the here and now. To Thomas Li.

'You should take it up,' said Li. 'I think you would be a natural.'

'Why?' said Cato.

'Instinctively you seem to understand the way of things here. Unlike your colleague, Ms Sumich, a beautiful woman but so angry and impetuous.'

Cato cleared his throat. 'Sorry, mate, you've got me wrong. I might look Chinese but I can play the barbarian too. The oriental mysticism thing doesn't cut it with me.'

'You think so? Many Overseas Chinese seem happy to lose their culture. You? I sense some kind of loss, of yearning. Maybe you don't even see it yourself.'

Outside, one of the sparring partners leaned too far forward and lost his balance. They broke contact, smiling, and drank some water before facing off again.

'Maybe you're right,' said Cato. 'And I do accept your apology for yesterday. Perhaps, as a favour, you might be able to put me in touch with Yu Guangming. He may not be personally known to you but I'm sure a man with your influence could find him.'

Li signalled for the bill. 'I'll see what I can do but you must understand once and for all that I had no part in those murders in your city. I will not say it again.' He gestured once again to the tuishou practitioners outside. 'In the meantime enjoy this city and all it has to offer. A walk every day through this park can teach you much about life.'

They shook hands and Li left.

Cato wandered back along the winding path that would take him out of the park to the Metro station. He replayed Li's words, looking for layers of meaning, looking for warnings.

The essence of tuishou is that you dissolve an oncoming force before striking a blow.

He stopped again to admire the graceful and seemingly futile strokes of the calligraphers, wishing he could grasp their essence before they evaporated.

A walk every day through this park can teach you much about life.

Another group practising taiji, this time with swords. There would be a special name for this and Cato wanted to learn it. Why? Because there was no reason why he couldn't or shouldn't. It needn't be a mystical yearning to belong, he reasoned, just a thirst for knowledge. The swords flashed in the filtered smoggy sunlight. Cato's shirt clung damply to his torso. Out of the corner of his eye he noticed someone detach themselves from the taiji group and fall into step just behind him, sword in hand.

He could have you all sliced and diced in broad daylight.

He braced himself for the slash and hack, knowing already he was powerless to stop it.

'G'day. How was brekky?'

It was Sharon Wang, blowing up from her bottom lip to cool her face. She handed her sword to a friend and waved goodbye as she slipped in beside Cato. He hadn't realised how short she was, her head just reaching his shoulder.

'Let me guess. This isn't a coincidence.'

'Not wrong. Nice chat with Mr Li?'

'You're monitoring my phone?'

'Jeez, you're not easy to get an answer out of. Li. What did he have to say for himself? Comprende?'

Cato couldn't help but notice the parts where her taiji outfit stuck to her. Only moments ago he was bracing for a bloody death. Now he was having impure thoughts about Sharon Wang. Maybe it was some life affirming yin and yang thing. 'We shared a nice pot of tea. Li explained the rules of tuishou. He apologised for yesterday.'

'*He* apologised?'

'Yup.'

'And?'

'I graciously accepted.'

'That's it?'

'That's it.'

'You didn't push the Yu Guangming thing?'

'Why would I?'

'You're a cop. And I thought I detected something a bit more personal in your reaction to Sumich's stunt. You weren't in on that, were you?'

Stunt, thought Cato. The revelation that Yu Guangming may have raped and murdered his former lover? Some stunt. 'No, I didn't push it with Li,' he lied.

They came to the park entrance. There was a car waiting for her, a Chinese police car.

'This is me,' she said. 'So, if I invite you to dinner to apologise for yesterday would you accept that invitation too?'

'At this rate I'm going to be well ahead on the per diems.'

'I'll take that as a yes. I'll pick you up at the hotel at eight.' She issued some stern-sounding Mandarin commands to the driver and hopped in the back. At the last minute two men jogged up and joined her in the car. Two of the tuishou sparring partners.

*

'So when are you coming home?'

'Soon, precious. Same flight as planned.' Lara fought her rising irritation. Yes, they missed each other. Sure, she'd rather be there with him. But this was her job. She checked her facial expression on the small screen in the bottom corner to make sure she wasn't giving anything away. John wasn't bothering to hide his feelings. It was written all over his out-of-focus, juddering skyped face.

'But if it's a dead end you may as well just get out of there.'

'You know how it is.'

'Yeah.' He dredged up a brave smile for her. 'So what do you think of Shanghai?'

Her face twisted. 'Makes me want to move to Manjimup, dig truffles, keep goats, fuck in the forest.'

'That could work,' he said. 'I could have the Officer In Charge down there sacked on some trumped-up charge. Create a vacancy.'

'Don't bother. I'll take a job at the IGA, or make my own jam and sell it. Life's too short to be a cop, clearing up other people's crap. Getting nowhere.'

'You, an Earth Mother? What kind of example is that to set for our daughter?'

Lara found herself caressing her tummy. 'A glorious one. She can skip around the paddock picking daffodils while Mummy and Daddy cover each other in jam and root in the mud. What do you think of Skye for a name?'

'We'll have Child Protection knocking at the door.'

'For calling her Skye? How about Tiger Lily?' Another call was beckoning on the skype screen. It was Mike from the ACC. 'Gotta go.' She kissed her fingertips and placed them over his lips on the screen. 'Love you.'

*

They were in a busy Japanese place near the consulate. Sharon Wang looked unnervingly attractive in a figure-hugging blue Mandarin dress. She finished stirring some wasabi into her soy sauce and prodded a piece of tuna with her chopsticks.

'You worry me.'

'Why?' said Cato.

'You do the Mr Inscrutability thing well. I can't predict what you're going to do next. Sumich, she's easy. She goes off like a firework in everything she does. She's the original cow in a china shop.'

'Give her a break. Lara believes in what she's doing and her heart is in the right place.'

'I suppose. But she did directly countermand my explicit instructions.'

'Is this the apology you were talking about?'

She grinned. 'Fair cop, I probably went a bit overboard, but she ...'

Cato held up his hand. 'Apology accepted.' He tried to change the subject. 'So what brought you to China?'

'A double degree in Mandarin and Law and a burning desire to do good.'

'Mandarin and Law? You could be riding the mining boom on that.'

'And climbing the walls with boredom. Also I was at a loose end, I had some aggro to work off. My first husband had just run off with one of his MBA students while I was on secondment in the Solomons.'

'First husband?'

'I haven't found a second. Yet.' She dabbed her lips with a napkin. 'What about you?'

'Bit sudden don't you think? I haven't really got to know you. Yet.'

'Dickhead. You married?'

'Divorced. Got a son, fourteen.'

'Snap. Except for the offspring bit.' She plucked something from another plate.

'Is that chicken?' said Cato.

'Yeah. Teriyaki.'

'Is that wise, with the bird flu and that?'

'That was about six months ago. You ever thought of being a Pom?'

Cato's chopsticks slipped and a piece of tuna slopped into the soy sauce dish sending a dark slash across the white tablecloth. 'Fuck. Sorry.' He retrieved his tuna. 'You worry me, too.'

She took a gulp of Tsingtao from a frosted tankard. 'Why?'

'I can't predict what you're going to do next.' She smiled enigmatically. 'And I wonder whether you're really a stickler for the rules of diplomatic protocol or whether you're gatekeeping for Li.'

'Don't hold back, mate, say what you mean.' Sharon stabbed another piece of raw fish. 'That's quite an accusation.'

Cato shrugged. 'Maybe it's not deliberate. Maybe it's just a by-product of the "inter-agency ground rules".' He mimed the parentheses. 'They help shield people like Li from any unpleasant surprises or scrutiny.'

'I know which side I'm on.' She gave him a stern look and ordered another round of beers. 'Look, here's my private email and non-work mobile.' Sharon took a business card out of her wallet, scrawled the new details on the back and slid it across the table. She also slid a mobile SIM card across, 'Use that when you're calling me. It's not being monitored. I can and will help.'

Her business card said 'Agent Sharon Wang Hongying – Australian Federal Police'.

'Hongying?' said Cato.

'My full Chinese name. It goes down well in certain Beijing circles. "Wang" means a few things depending on how you say it. In my case it means "King" although I prefer the possibility of it also meaning "Hope". Unfortunately "Hongying" is a bit out of favour these days – it means "Red Heroine".'

'Sharon Hope Red Heroine. Rolls off the tongue, doesn't it?'

'My dad's twisted little joke. He thought "Sharon" would help me fit in at Bendigo High and the "Hongying" would remind me who I really was. He used to be a Red Guard in this area during the Cultural Revolution. A real teenage ratbag, he waved the little red book, sang the patriotic songs, beat up the capitalist running dogs, all that.'

'How did he get from that to having you in Australia?'

'After a few years Mao decided the Red Guards were no longer any use to him. He packed them off to the countryside for re-education. They sent my dad down to Yunnan Province on the Burmese border. He just kept walking, all the way through Burma and into Thailand. He did something a bit dodgy for the Aussies in Bangkok during the Vietnam War and wangled a visa.' She thumbed at herself. 'The rest is history.'

'So he lives in Bendigo now?'

She shook her head. 'Semi-retired to Daylesford. He runs an adult retreat for Melbourne yuppies wanting a dirty weekend. Champers, choccies, spa, oils.' She licked some beer foam off her lips. 'You should try it sometime. You might like it.'

'I'd be terrified he'd come barging into the room in the middle of the night to denounce me.'

'Only if you've done something really bad,' she said with a look that made Cato's blood rush. Sharon Wang – Crouching Tiger, Hidden Vixen. 'So what's your history? Where do your family come from?'

'I don't know. My dad was never really into that family heritage stuff but his grandfather or great grandie or something lived in Bendigo I think, or was it Ballarat? Anyway something to do with the gold rush, I assume.' He hesitated, not sure whether to share this or not, feeling curiously vulnerable. 'When I was very young my father had a pet name for me: "Qian Ping".'

She smiled. 'It means powerful but gentle. It's a beautiful name for a man. Kwong Qian Ping.'

Cato felt himself blushing.

'If they've been around that long your family should be pretty established. Gold rush, that's blue-blood Chinese-Aussie. Do you want me to ask my mob? I mean "Kwong", how hard can that be?'

Twice in one day he'd been nudged towards his Chinese ancestry. He realised he too wanted to be able to recount a tale like the one he'd just heard from Sharon Wang. Something to pass on to Jake, something for the boy to find some pride in, instead of his stoner mates. Cato recalled that surge of emotion he'd felt watching the calligraphers in Zhongshan Park.

'Sure,' he said. 'Why not?'

17

Sunday, August 18th.

Cato woke early after an inappropriate dream about Sharon Wang. The night out had ended well enough, a goodbye and a little wave, like an old-fashioned first date or something. Cato wondered if he was reading too much into it. Probably. He'd tried a late night phone call to his sister in the vain hope of catching Dad awake.

'Do you know what time it is?' Mand had grumped at him.

'Sorry. Dad asleep then?'

'Yeah. Why?'

'How's he been?'

'Same as ever. Crap jokes. Forgets everything. Sleeps a lot. How's Shanghai?'

'Big, busy. So far, I like it.'

'I didn't think it would be your cup of tea.'

'Shanghai?'

'China in general.'

'Where were Dad's mob from, do you know?'

'Ballarat. Before that, who knows? Why?'

'Just curious.'

'Have you been drinking? You sound funny.'

Cato was aware of a surge of feeling, a hotness in his face. 'Yeah, a couple of Tsingtaos.'

'Don't forget the old man's warning. Look after yourself over there, okay?'

'Sure, no worries. G'night sis.'

He'd also tried Jane's and Jake's mobiles. Both were switched off.

The room was already hot with thick hazy sunlight spilling through his window. He zapped the aircon into action and pulled back the curtains. The sky was a muted gauzy pale blue with distant dark clouds holding the promise of an afternoon storm. He headed for the bathroom and spotted the note that had been shoved under his door.

Our phones are tapped. Meet me in the hotel gym ฉ 10. L

He found Lara on a treadmill jogging steadily, sweat beading her brow and darkening her singlet. She'd reserved the machine next to her by draping a towel over it. The gym was noisy, thumping music overflowed from an aerobics class in an adjoining room. Good choice for a clandestine meeting, thought Cato. He stepped on the treadmill and set off at a leisurely walking pace. Lara pushed up to a sprint for a minute or two then dropped down to join him on his gentle perambulations.

'My nanna walks faster than this,' she said, still looking straight ahead as if she didn't know him.

'Good for her. Why the cloak and dagger?'

'We fly out tomorrow night. We need to do more to provoke a result.'

'Like what?'

'I've been given the name of a lawyer. He's involved in a case against Li. Compensation for some tenants kicked out of their homes for a property development. He might help us shake things up a bit.'

'Relevance to our case?'

'At face value, zero. But he might give us an insight into Li's unofficial business methods. Some of those tenants were hospitalised and crippled for life. He may have even come across our Mr Yu Guangming.'

Even though it was only walking pace Cato was working up a sweat. 'Who's your source?'

'That weedy Fed bloke who hangs out with Pavlou.'

Mystery Mike. 'How did you get that info without it being tapped?'

'We skyped but these days they can hack into that too. Look, even if they're already onto us, we're showing them we're not stepping back. Fuck them.'

Fair enough, thought Cato. 'So have you contacted this lawyer?'

'Yep. Got supernerd to do it from over there to try and bypass the tapping.'

'And?'

'Midday today at the Big Bamboo Sports Bar in an area called Jing'an, not that far from here. Apparently they screen AFL, the beer's nice and cold, and the Dockers are playing.'

'Perfect. How do we lose our minders?'

'I've been thinking about that,' said Lara. She leaned over and pressed a few buttons on his console. Cato was being forced to run.

*

The lawyer's name was Richard Chan. His business card showed a head office in Hong Kong and, on the back, law qualifications obtained in England, Australia and Beijing. He was in his early thirties, medium height with a spreading waistline and a nervous countenance. He was casually dressed and spoke immaculate, precise English. Lara's basic plan to shake off any tail had been for the three of them to head off in different directions using different modes of transport and then meet up again. Hardly *Bourne Ultimatum* stuff but, so far, it seemed to have worked. Cato had deliberated on whether or not he should keep Sharon Wang in the loop but decided against it. They were meeting a lawyer in an expat sports bar in broad daylight. What could possibly go wrong?

Lara outlined their interest in Thomas Li while Chan listened, nodding and sipping from a glass of white wine. Chan's eyes widened at the description of the Tan killings. On the flat screens it was midway through the first quarter and the Dockers were two goals up against the Demons. As usual, Hayden Ballantyne was getting in the faces of the opposition. The bar was mainly haunted by pasty pudgy expats and, with the familiar VB and Guinness signs, it could have been suburban Perth. Except for a couple of local Chinese guys in a nearby alcove who stuck out like sore thumbs. One, the older, was wheelchair bound. The younger companion was scowling in Cato's general direction. Both wore thin, cheap clothes that suggested they weren't part of Shanghai's booming middle class and probably couldn't afford to be drinking at expat bar prices. They were sipping at Cokes and ignoring the footy – sacrilege. Lara wrapped up her preliminaries and sent James Blond off to the bar for some refills.

'Does that sound like the Li you know? Maybe you could fill us in on your dealings with him.'

Chan put down his glass and looked like he was settling in for a long session. 'Li Tonggui belongs to what we call "the bitter generation", born in the nineteen fifties. At the time they should have been getting an education, they got instead the chaos and destruction of Mao's Cultural Revolution. At the time they should have been embarking on a career and maybe starting a family, they were sent to the countryside for re-education. Ten, fifteen years later, at the time they might have been leaders in their chosen career, they were made redundant by Deng Xiaoping's free market economic reforms. And now, at the time when maybe they should be looking forward to retirement, they have to use up all of their savings to help their children buy an over-priced apartment in the new capitalistic economy.'

Apart from the Cultural Revolution bit it sounded like the lot of any baby boomer, reflected Cato. 'So?' he said, hoping for a nice short answer this time.

'So to survive those challenges intact is a major feat. To then flourish and prosper like Li has done, you need to be lucky, very smart, and a little bit ruthless.'

'Tell me about the case you're involved in now,' said Lara.

Chan shrugged. 'The same old story. An area of old laneway or longtang community housing demolished to make way for one of Li's skyscrapers. Agreements were signed with the local municipal government to compensate and re-house the tenants. The agreements, of course, were worthless.'

'This is an established part of Li's modus operandi?' said Lara.

'He's done this at least four other times, in China, to my knowledge.' Richard said something in Mandarin to the two locals in the nearby recess. They abandoned their Cokes and the younger one wheeled the older over to join them. Chan did the introductions.

'Zhou and Little Zhou.' They all shook hands. Chan said something to them and they nodded, the older man clearing his throat and about to spit on the floor until Chan shook his head. 'I've asked them to tell their story. I will translate.'

It was the son who spoke, evidently the father couldn't.

'We live in Songjiang district, further upriver: my father, my mother, me, my sister. My father was a sanitation worker, my mother cleaned the apartments of rich people, my sister and I went to school. Not rich but not so poor. We have a small house in a longtang, it is enough. We are honest people.'

A look passed between father and son.

'The local government came to us late in March to say we have to move to make way for an extension to the new housing development they built last year. The existing one is still empty, why would they want to build more?' Little Zhou's scowl deepened. 'We refused to move so they sent in the chengguan.'

'Chengguan?' said Cato.

'Local government law enforcement officials,' said Chan. 'Often little more than hired thugs. Several of the resisting tenants were hospitalised. Zhou here was crippled for life. They snapped his spine. Their belongings were thrown on the street and the bulldozers moved in.'

'No compensation?' said Lara. 'No alternative accommodation?'

Little Zhou snorted without waiting for the translation. Clearly he had some English. 'They put us in an overcrowded shikumen block, anything up to ten people to a room, one filthy toilet for the whole floor, hick migrant workers from the provinces gambling, drinking, fighting, and pissing in the hallway.' He nodded to his father while Chan finished interpreting. 'Our place is on the third floor, stairs only, we have to carry him up and down like a sack of rice.' He glared at the older man. 'Only not as useful.'

The father's eyes clouded over and he looked at the floor.

Chan chastised the younger man in their own language;

probably for his public harshness to his father. The boy glowered.

'Compensation?' he pressed on. 'The chengguan stole any cash that might have been coming. My sister was offered a job as a whore at the girlie bar around the corner from here.' His head twisted in the general direction.

'Did she take it?' said James Blond.

Little Zhou's face darkened even further. The kid was storing up some serious rage. He switched to English. 'My sister is not your business.'

Lara slid the photo of Yu Guangming over to him. 'Do you recognise this man? Is he one of those chengguan?'

He looked at the photo. 'No, I don't know him. Who is he?'

Lara started to tell him.

Chan intervened. 'He seems to be a bigger fish than those street thugs. But I'll ask around if you like. Can I keep this?'

'Sure,' said Lara.

Chan dismissed Zhou and Little Zhou with a smile and a folding of cash into the boy's palm. Suspicious and curious expat eyes followed them all the way off the premises.

'Do you expect to win your case?' said Cato.

'I never expect anything. But if you kick up enough fuss sometimes a settlement can be worked out.'

'If violence is part of Li's repertoire doesn't that worry you, personally?'

Chan nodded. 'To be honest, yes. Civil lawyers and compensation cases of this sort are still relatively new to China. But with a surging economy there's also a growth in predators and in victims. I live in hope that my high profile will protect me.' He laughed nervously and raised a toast. 'To justice.'

They clinked glasses. Quarter-time and the Dockers were still ahead.

*

The four left the Big Bamboo together, emerging into sweaty heat and glaring sunlight. Lara slipped on her shades and heard the incoming message tone on her phone. There was a chorus of beeps and buzzes; the others' phones were doing the same. As she reached into her pocket, someone barrelled into her from the left side knocking her to the ground. Lara was aware of something being very, very wrong. They were all around her, stomping and kicking. She curled up as tight as she could, protecting her head with one hand, her stomach with another. There were weapons too, sticks or rods. She felt her knuckles, fingers, and arms turn to fire. She absorbed the pain and waited for them to stop, or for her to die. My baby, she thought, my poor baby.

A command was issued in Mandarin and the beating ceased. Lara opened her eyes. One of them was sticky with blood. A few metres away she could see James, wild-eyed, struggling, bloodied. More words, and the men kneeling on James held out his arm, flat against the ground. The man who was doing the talking walked over and brought a kitchen cleaver down on the outstretched hand. James screamed. The man picked up the severed fingers, walked over to Lara and knelt down. He wore a mask, only the eyes were visible. Grey-brown pupils in a jaundiced jelly. A strong cigarette smell like a mishap in a tyre factory. He scrubbed the fingers in her face then let them fall.

'Fuck off home, lady,' he said.

It was all over. They left.

Lara slowly rose to her feet. Her blood, mixed with that of James, ran down her face and down the front of her shirt. James was clutching his hand and whimpering. A scabby puppy scampered out of a laneway and disappeared with one of the severed fingers. Lara collected up the two that remained. It was the middle of the day. A crowd had gathered and everybody just stood there looking at them, like this happened all the time.

'Ambulance. Hospital. Police. Somebody, please,' said Lara.

A young man finished a call on his mobile. 'They're coming now.'

Lara hurt all over, but in particular in her stomach where some hard kicks had connected. She tried not to think the worst. Failed. She looked around. Richard Chan was lying still and lifeless with a large gash in his neck.

And Cato was missing.

*

Cato was lying on his side on the floor of a van that moved slowly through Shanghai traffic. His hands were cable-tied behind his back. There was a cloth bag over his head. It was stifling hot and he was choking on a foul mix of petrol fumes, old food spillages, and cigarette smoke. And something else; moisturising cream? His fellow passengers were using him as a footrest, chuckling and chattering in Chinese and occasionally giving him a kick to remind him of his predicament.

It wasn't necessary.

His phone buzzed in his pocket. A hand reached in and removed it. Switched it off. His wallet was next. Some rustling and more sniggers. It was thrown back at him. It felt empty. He'd received a few kicks and punches as they dragged him to the van but it seemed nothing compared to what he saw being done to the others before the bag slipped over his head. Were they already dead? What was in store for Cato?

The essence of tuishou is that you dissolve an oncoming force before striking a blow.

If this was Li's doing, then he was making his point very well.

*

'He's not answering his phone,' said Sharon Wang.

'Probably in a meeting,' said Lara, dully.

'Look, how about we drop the tough girl act and work together on this. Okay?'

'Okay.'

Driscoll, meanwhile, was gabbling away on his mobile in urgent Mandarin. He and Wang had been summoned by the Shanghai police first on the scene as soon as they'd worked out where the foreigners were from. 'Ao-da-li-ya, ao-da-li-ya,' Lara had heard. Even she could work that out. Now she was in a hospital room with her left arm in a sling. She had two suspected fractured knuckles, a dislocated pinkie, and severe defensive bruising and abrasions all over her body. An ultrasound had given the all-clear on the baby. Only then had she allowed herself to cry. James was being operated on to try to reattach the severed fingers of his left hand. The middle one was still missing, probably in the belly of that ratty little mongrel somewhere in Jing'an. James would be medivaced out to Perth once the operation was complete and he'd stabilised; sometime in the next forty-eight hours. The lawyer, Richard Chan, was dead.

'Go through it again,' said Wang. 'What do you remember?'

Chaos, pain, blood and terror were the essence of her memories. But as she broke it down she also recalled the synchronised phone messages: coincidence or coordinated distraction to maximise the element of surprise? Two motorbikes, carrying two men each. A dark blue van with more men emerging. The one who did the talking was squat, wiry, scary. Masked, yet something familiar about the eyes. The strong cigarette smell. The cleaver. The fingers rubbing against her face, warm and wet. She fought the urge to gag.

Driscoll had finished his call. 'So they definitely took him, he didn't just leg it?'

'Fuck off,' said Lara, wondering who he'd been talking to.

'Did you get anything useful out of Chan before they topped him?' asked Driscoll.

'Nothing concrete.'

'Big surprise,' he said.

'What does that mean?'

'He's an ambulance-chaser, thrives on reasonable doubt and the balance of probabilities.'

'He must have been on to something,' said Lara. 'It got him killed.'

'Why do you think they've taken Kwong?' Wang addressed her question to Driscoll.

He shrugged. 'Maybe they want to do him slowly. Maybe they think he's worth something.'

'Money?' said Wang.

'Or influence.'

'So what do we do now?' said Lara to Driscoll. 'And who were you talking to?'

'Classified,' he smiled. 'We've got the locals interviewing witnesses and chasing down the bikes and van. We've got a GSM trace on Kwong's phone in case it gets switched on again.'

Wang bit her lower lip and summoned Driscoll out of the room for a private chat. They switched to Mandarin but Lara clearly heard the sounds of Driscoll giving her a bollocking. What was that about? They returned, Wang flushed, Driscoll back on his mobile.

'What's the score?' said Lara.

Wang shook her head sadly. 'God knows.'

*

The van stopped. Cato was dragged out, still hooded, and carried somewhere. There was a tang of motor oil. He was dumped on a hard, cold floor that felt grimy but, after the choking claustrophobia of the van, it was something of a relief. Then someone hit him on the side of the head. More blows followed, some with weapons, but mainly with feet, kicking and stomping. He tried to curl up into a ball. The pain was relentless, its application systematic. And that smell again – moisturising cream.

*

Lara was left alone in her hospital room to reflect upon the day and on how much of it had been her doing. Chan dead, James horribly maimed, and Cato missing. All down to her wanting to rattle Li's cage and get a result. Some result. Guards were stationed at her door but she had the impression that nobody was really expecting any follow up. The message had already been well and truly delivered. How close had she come to losing her baby and for what?

She called John and told him what had happened.

'Get the hell out of there. Next flight. Please.'

'I can't. Cato's missing. I've got to find him.'

'Can't you leave it to the AFP, the embassy guy, the locals?'

'Would you?'

Of course he wouldn't, and neither would she. They both knew it.

'What if you don't find him?'

'I will. One way or another. I have to.' They said their goodbyes. She detected a crack in John's voice. Defences crumbling. A vulnerability she never thought he was capable of. She wanted to be home with her lover and far away from this madness. She resolved to quit, or at least take long leave, when she got home and to focus on the things that mattered. In the meantime she needed to sort this mess out.

A nurse wheeled a trolley past Lara's door. Phones rang. Words floated up the corridor. Words she didn't understand. Lara felt totally helpless: she needed to find Cato. James was out of action, Driscoll was an untrustworthy prick. Sharon Wang? She clearly hated Lara's guts but she obviously had a soft spot for Cato and had been doing something wrong behind Driscoll's back. Lara found her mobile in a bedside drawer. She scrolled through to Wang's number and sent a text. Outside, there was a flash of lightning, some thunder, and then rain hitting her window.

*

Cato didn't know how long he'd been out. The hood was off and he was able to breathe more freely but he was scared to open his eyes in case it provoked more beating. The room was silent. They'd gone, for now. He decided to risk it. He found he was able to open one eye, the other was gummed shut. He looked across a floor covered in oil stains and splashed by his blood. He was in some kind of mechanic's workshop: moped parts, tyres, an oxy-acetylene burner, drills, spanners, screwdrivers, cans of oil and petrol, tyre levers, hammers. Enough playthings for the inventive torturer, if that's what was to come. He'd never known pain like this. It pulsed through his whole body. He now understood how people could beg for death. More of his senses kicked in: touch, hearing, smell. Cato had pissed himself during the beating. Outside he could hear the steady patter of rain and the occasional roll of thunder. Some flashes through the tiny gap beneath a buckled and rusty roller door. The clouds he'd seen at the start of the day had finally arrived. Should he shout for help or would that just alert them that he was awake and ready for round two? He kept quiet and closed his eyes again.

He must have drifted off. When he awoke there was a man crouching beside his head. Cato recognised him from a file photo. Yu Guangming.

'Hello,' he said.

'Hi,' rasped Cato.

Yu unscrewed a water bottle and held it to Cato's lips. Cato drank.

'Better?' said Yu.

With difficulty, Cato nodded.

Yu said something terse-sounding in Mandarin and stood up. Cato heard footsteps behind him and braced himself for more hurt. Instead he was hauled upright and dropped onto a flimsy plastic chair. They studied each other, Cato trying not to be too obvious in case it brought down more violence. Yu Guangming was a cut above his colleagues. He was better dressed, he smelt better, spoke English, and was halfway handsome. He could see how he might turn the head of an impressionable young woman in a Sydney bar. But then he thought about what Yu had done to her later, and to Genevieve Tan.

'Mr Kwong. The Chinaman who doesn't speak Chinese.' It didn't seem to invite a reply. 'A useless specimen, really. You've been looking for me, I hear.' He gave Cato another drink. 'So you've found me. How can I help?'

Cato didn't feel in the best shape to conduct a comprehensive professional interview so he got to the point. 'Did you kill the Tan family in Perth?'

'No. Next question.'

'Your DNA was at the crime scene. Your sperm was inside one of the victims.' Cato felt a tooth wobble, an exposed nerve seek his attention. 'Can you explain that?'

'Sure,' he said.

'Then please do.'

Yu smiled. 'I like your manners.'

Cato didn't like his. If the cable ties were cut, he felt just capable, injuries notwithstanding, of beating Yu to death.

'I've known Mrs Tan for some years, ever since her unlucky and lazy husband started to gamble other people's money on stupid business ventures.' Yu lit himself a cigarette from a packet proclaiming Double Happiness. 'A lonely woman with strong needs. We have come to a private arrangement on a number of occasions.

Each time it has bought her husband an extra few days to keep up his debt repayments. Man, that is one loyal wife.' He blew out a plume of pungent smoke and smiled. 'A hospitable family in general. Lovely people.'

'And on the day of the murders?'

'Same-same. I was there in the house. She seemed warmer towards me than usual. I think Mr Tan was maybe affected by his stressful business dealings. Not being a good husband, you know?'

There was a few moments silence. 'It's a good story,' said Cato. 'Is it true?'

'I say it is, yes.'

'How do you know Mr Li?'

'Who says I do?' he smiled.

'Me.'

'Ah, I see. You have me in the role of Mr Li's evil henchman. Yes?' Cato nodded.

'But I wanted to be the Master Villain, it's not fair!'

Cato grimaced. 'You're not doing too badly on that score.'

Yu chortled. 'A sense of humour in difficult times. I like that. Have you any more stereotypes you'd like to share with me?'

'So if you're not the evil henchman and you weren't collecting debts on behalf of Li, then who?'

'Maybe I do my own dirty work?'

'You? And all those trips to PNG and New Zealand and elsewhere? Your money, your business?'

'Boring now. Do your homework, policeman.' He stubbed his cigarette out. 'Mr Li is known to me primarily by reputation as a very successful businessman and a great contributor to the community. Sometimes we work together, sometimes not. We are like every other entrepreneur; we use our guanxi, connections. Okay?'

'Okay.'

A contemptuous snort. 'Uncle Li. He thinks he is a modern day Du Yusheng, have you heard of him?'

Cato shook his head.

'A famous Shanghai gangster from the nineteen thirties. "Big-eared Du" they called him, but not to his face, eh?'

Cato wondered where this was going.

'He ran the opium trade, the prostitutes, the protection rackets. He was a kind of Chinese Al Capone. Did you know that all those beautiful old buildings on the Bund were built by the British and French with opium money?'

Yes, Cato vaguely recalled it from the brief background he'd googled when Hutchens first put Shanghai on the agenda. When was that, three, four days ago? Yu was in full flow.

'Modern Shanghai grew out of the Opium Wars and Big-eared Du also built some nice Shanghai mansions with his own opium money. We learn quick, eh?' He lit himself another ciggie. 'But Du craved respectability. He financed the Kuomintang against the Commies, bad move. He was even unofficial Mayor of Shanghai for a while.' Yu laughed. 'And now Uncle Li is like Big-eared Du. He forgets where he came from and he wants everyone else to forget too. Soon he will retire, or die. Either way, he is finished.'

So there was no real love lost between Yu and Li.

Yu seemed to be winding down. 'Just over the road is a river, Suzhou Creek. It joins the Huangpu just up that way.' He gestured in the direction. 'Big-eared Du used to throw his enemies in the creek and watch them float away. If you like I'll take you down there tomorrow and show you.' He patted Cato's shoulder. 'It's been a big day. Sleep well, Mr Kwong.'

Hands grabbed him from behind, forced a rag into his mouth and ran some tape over it. Cato began to panic, he felt he was going to choke to death. Yu leaned down close to his ear.

'Relax. Breathe evenly, through your nose. You're going to be okay. You won't die tonight.'

The bag went back over Cato's head and he was pushed off the chair onto the floor. Outside there was a loud crack of thunder and the rain got heavier.

18

Monday, August 19th.

The first call came through just after 6 a.m. as arranged. Lara took a deep breath and hoped that what she was about to do wasn't going to seal Cato's fate. Last night Sharon Wang hadn't taken any convincing to come back to the hospital and talk. In fact she seemed relieved and energised by the idea. Lara hadn't beaten around the bush.

'Why's Driscoll pissed off at you?'

Wang told her about the unmonitored SIM card she'd given Cato, the one that now needed to be added to Driscoll's GSM trace list.

'Why did you do that? You obviously don't trust Driscoll either.'

Wang measured her words. 'It's not that. I just don't always share his priorities. Those guys play by different rules.'

'All that Mandarin on the mobile, what's he up to?'

'He seems to be as much concerned with managing it as a news story as he is about finding … Cato? Is that what you call him?'

'Yep.'

'So tomorrow everybody will read about a drunken brawl outside an expat bar during which a number of foreigners and local Chinese nationals were seriously injured with one later dying of his wounds.'

'Prick.' Lara shook her head.

'On one level I can see what he's doing. The truth would drive certain people into a corner, limit their options for stepping back, for walking away.'

'Face?' said Lara. Wang nodded. 'Do you think it will work?'

'No, not this time. I think we need to make a lot of noise, put the pressure on, seize the initiative.'

'How?'

'By doing the opposite of what Driscoll is doing.'

Their plan was to hijack Driscoll's spun headlines, get a heap of international media attention on the story, quickly, mentioning the names Li Tonggui and Yu Guangming as often as possible. There would be a flowdown to local media, and potentially a shitstorm that would either see Cato bargained for silence, or killed. Wang had been awake half the night revving up her contacts. First was the ABC's man in Beijing, an effusive chap who liked a bit of theatrics. He was booked on the first plane down and would be in Shanghai in a couple of hours with a crew. In the meantime he wanted to get the gist by phone. Lara gave it to him: a gruesome family murder in Perth, business connections to Li.

'Yes, that's right,' she said. 'Li Tonggui. Would you like me to spell it for you?' The correspondent, a fluent Mandarin speaker, declined the offer.

Another man wanted for questioning in relation to this and other murders and acts of violence.

'Yu Guangming,' said Lara. 'Got that?'

An Australian police officer badly wounded in an unprovoked attack, another abducted and still missing. And yet another man, a prominent Hong Kong-based lawyer involved in a case against Li, murdered. Finally, the bit that would probably bring a load of grief down on Sharon Wang.

'No, neither the consulate nor the Australian Federal Police seem to be taking this seriously.'

'But it was Sharon who called me,' said the man from Aunty.

'I guilt-tripped her into it. She'll probably get into trouble for this.'

'Not if I have anything to do with it,' he said.

More calls followed. Associated Press. Reuters. The BBC. It was showing on their news websites by now. *South China Morning Post* was particularly interested in the untimely and bloody death of one of their own – Richard Chan.

'Yes, Li Tonggui,' said Lara. 'Would you like me to spell it for you?'
Finally the *Shanghai Daily*.

'Yu Guangming,' said Lara. 'Got that?'

*

Cato awoke with a start, his heart racing, panic surging. He'd woken several times during the night with recurring dreams of suffocation, of drowning, of being buried alive. Each time it would take a moment for him to remember where he was. He wasn't sure which was worse: the nightmares or the reality. Was his father's premonition about to come true? Cato would die in China. He lay still, listening, trying to work out what was going on in the world beyond his hood. In an adjoining room people were speaking low in Mandarin. He recognised one voice as Yu Guangming's but the other sounded oddly familiar too. The door opened and somebody came in. By the footsteps, it was at least two people. Cato's hood was pulled off. The other voice had been Rory Driscoll's. They must have negotiated a release or ransom deal. Driscoll tutted at the state of Cato while he removed the tape and gag.

'Been in the wars, mate?' He gave Cato a sip of water from a bottle, wrinkling his nose. 'What's that smell?'

Cato had lost control of his bladder again during the night. He tried to sit up, gesturing at the cable ties. 'Get these off me.'

Driscoll shook his head. 'Not so fast, buddy.'

So that was it, realised Cato, with cold certainty. Driscoll and Yu were working together. It accounted for Yu's untouchability as he flew around the Asia Pacific wreaking mayhem.

'You know why Mr Li specifically requested your presence in Shanghai, don't you?' said Driscoll.

Cato's tongue probed a loose tooth. 'We connected meaningfully?'

'You could say that.' Driscoll crouched down and reached a hand towards Cato's face. Cato flinched, expecting a blow. Instead his hair was gently brushed from his forehead. 'Quiz time. List the Bali Nine.'

Cato played along. 'Renae Lawrence, Scott Rush ...' He ran out of names, quickly.

'Who were Barlow and Chambers?'

'The two Aussie drug traffickers that got hung in Malaysia in the eighties?'

'Van Nguyen?'

'Who?' said Cato. Then he remembered, a few years ago a Vietnamese-Australian had been executed in Singapore for drug trafficking.

'Schapelle Corby?'

'I get the picture.'

'Of course you do,' said Driscoll. 'The Great Australian Public couldn't give a toss about you. You're not one of them. You could be a bogan fuckwit with a record as long as your arm and we'll be rooting for you all the way. Or you could be as pure as the driven snow but if your face and name don't fit you're finished. Nothing. Your eyes are the wrong shape so nobody gives a damn and nobody will remember your name.'

Cato didn't want to believe that, he wanted to believe that when push came to shove he had more friends than Driscoll credited him for. 'What's your point?'

'People like you and me, when we're not sticking out like a sore thumb, we're invisible. Me? When I'm at the top of my game I can stop governments from toppling, but I can't stop a cab in King's Cross at the wrong time of night.' He leaned closer as if taking Cato into his confidence. His voice dropped a notch. 'They can bury us alive here. Sure we've got a handful of friends and colleagues who might look out for us but if it needs higher powers ...' Driscoll shrugged.

'So I'm Tommy Li's hostage?'

Driscoll shook his head in pity. 'To be a hostage you need to be worth something to someone.' A call came through on his mobile, in English this time.

'Yes sir,' said Driscoll with a frown. 'I'm onto it. I'll give you a ring in an hour with an update. Cheers.' He severed the connection and snapped something at Yu Guangming in Mandarin. Then he gave Cato a funny, almost sad look. 'Gotta go. Few spotfires to put out.' He replaced Cato's gag and tape and pulled the hood back down. 'Chin up, bro.'

A pat on the shoulder and he was gone.

*

'You're in a shitload of trouble now, aren't you?' said Lara.

Sharon Wang nodded. 'Probably. But some things are worth more than a job.'

'Like Cato?'

Wang blushed. 'I meant, like doing the right thing.' A pause and a smile. 'But now you come to mention it.'

Lara thought she was doing a good job of her poker face but Wang saw right through it.

'You've been there, haven't you?'

'Truth be told, he didn't have much to do with it.' Lara gave the lowdown on her encounter with Cato in a Hopetoun motel room. 'I've had worse,' she concluded.

Wang stifled a grin. 'You shameless trollop!' They were interrupted by a call on Wang's mobile. An exchange of Mandarin. More media? She covered the mouthpiece with her hand. 'It's Li, he'd like to talk to you.'

Lara frowned. 'In Pudong?'

'No, he's downstairs at reception.'

'Send him up,' said Lara.

Li came in with a big bunch of flowers and Phoebe. 'Number one daughter,' he said.

So now she was Phoebe the Daughter instead of Phoebe the Lawyer, a softer, more pliant and filial version. Lara wondered how many more there were. She thanked them both for the flowers.

'Terrible thing, this. Terrible.' Li looked troubled and Phoebe copied him. Lara wasn't sure whether he was referring to the violence and the abduction, or to the saturation media mention of his name in connection with something unsavoury.

No point wasting a meeting. 'Did you have Richard Chan killed?'

He looked mortified. 'Heavens, no!' Phoebe's stern lawyer face nearly returned but she stopped it just in time. Li unfolded a slip of paper from his pocket. 'You'll find Yu Guangming here,' he said. 'Hopefully we can bring this terrible business to an end and safely recover your colleague.'

Lara looked at the address, it meant nothing to her. She passed it over to Sharon Wang.

Li levelled his gaze at Lara. 'You are a remarkable young woman, Ms Sumich. I do not appreciate your methods but I certainly admire your tenacity and your decisiveness. I wish you success in your endeavours.' He turned to leave.

'One moment, Mr Li,' said Sharon Wang. 'I request that you and your daughter attend Police Headquarters this afternoon for an interview.'

'I believe I have some business appointments.'

'Cancel them. As you are aware, there is now a great deal of local and international scrutiny of these matters. It is important that we are seen to be diligent in our investigations, without fear or favour.'

Phoebe's lawyer face was well and truly back. Li was also having some difficulty holding his composure. 'As you wish, Ms Wang, these are turbulent times. Be we princes, satraps, or peasants, we all must learn to chart the stormy waters or be dashed upon the rocks.'

'Yeah thanks,' said Sharon. 'Two-thirty okay for you?' It was, but it earned her a dangerous look from Phoebe.

As Li and his daughter left, Driscoll returned. He too looked like he was struggling with his composure. 'Whose idea was it?'

'Mine,' they both said.

He shook his head at both of them. 'Do you realise how difficult you've made my job, now?'

'Tell me,' said Lara.

'I'm combing this city looking for your mate. I'm gradually getting people to talk. Suddenly it's all over the radio, the internet, the newspapers. Bingo. They clam up again. Meanwhile I've got the top brass here, in Beijing, and Canberra all wanting to know what the fuck's going on and why they are being asked to comment to the media on something they've never heard about.'

'Hmmm,' said Lara.

'You know this could sign his death warrant?' said Driscoll.

Wang showed him the piece of paper. 'It flushed somebody out. Li gave us this.'

Driscoll studied it. 'Interesting,' he said.

'So do we get a SWAT team in?' said Wang.

A call came through on Driscoll's mobile. 'Wei?' He listened for a few moments then spoke some Mandarin to the caller. He put the phone to his chest. 'This guy here reckons he's Yu Guangming and he knows where our man is.'

'So tell us,' said Lara, trying to stay cool.

More Mandarin. 'I'll put him on speakerphone, he reckons he's okay with English.'

'Hello?' said the man who called himself Yu Guangming.

'You have some information for us, Mr Yu?' said Driscoll.

'Yes, I know where your colleague is. He is safe and unharmed.'

'So release him,' said Lara.

'Who are you, lady?' said the voice.

Lara now recognised it, the same voice that told her to fuck off home as he scrubbed James Maloney's bloody fingers in her face. Those eyes above the mask, the same ones from the file photo of Yu Guangming. 'Lara Sumich, Western Australian police.'

'Okay, this is what must happen now. You, Miss Lara, and your colleague must leave Shanghai, then Mr Kwong will be free.'

Driscoll muted the speakerphone and looked at Lara. 'Not a huge ask,' he said. 'And less dangerous for Kwong than a Chinese SWAT team, believe me.'

'What's wrong with Chinese SWAT teams?'

'Don't get me wrong,' said Driscoll. 'They're great, very efficient, invariably get the job done. It's just that they operate under the political principle of the individual subsuming their needs to those of the greater good.'

'Meaning?'

'If the hostage survives that's a bonus.'

'No,' said Lara. 'We leave together or not at all.'

Driscoll unmuted the phone and reiterated Lara's view. There was a torrent of angry Mandarin. Driscoll picked up the phone and tried to calm Yu, stepping away into a corner and lowering his voice soothingly. Lara and Sharon exchanged a glance. Another nail in Cato's coffin?

'I have an idea,' said Driscoll after a moment. 'How about I go to where this guy is, vouch for Kwong's wellbeing, and when you're checked in at the airport I confirm that to Yu. Then I escort our boy out of there. You all catch the same plane and Yu gets what he wants. Deal?'

'Will he buy it?' said Lara, not wanting to push her luck.

'He already did,' said Driscoll with a grin.

A few details were finessed and the call concluded. Lara was uneasy. 'You're putting yourself into some danger there.'

'We'll still have a SWAT team nearby as back-up,' Driscoll reassured her.

'That's all he wants? Us gone?'

'Face. Never underestimate its potency.' He pulled up a chair and turned to Sharon Wang. 'You need to call your boss in Beijing. He'd like a word.'

'What about?'

Driscoll shrugged. 'Probably wants to know how much super, holiday pay and long-service you have owing and how soon you can clear your desk.'

*

Cato had been allowed a shower and provided with a change of clothes. Something bought from a nearby market: a pair of jeans that were a size too small and a Union Jack emblazoned T-shirt with the logo 'London Cool Boy'.

'Deadly threads,' said Driscoll with a grin. 'I know a few clubs where you could make yourself a dollar dressed like that.'

Everything still hurt but being clean was a bonus. It was early evening, already dark, and more afternoon storms had rolled in. Driscoll had outlined the plan and filled in some of the missing pieces. Cato hadn't been aware of Richard Chan's death or James Blond's disfigurement.

'What was the point of it all?' asked Cato.

'To get you guys to stop flashing Yu's picture around and asking nosy questions. It creates too many difficulties for him locally. He just wanted you gone. You were the leverage to make sure it happened.'

All of that was mind-blowing enough – the level of violence inflicted to achieve that aim. But Cato's main concern right now was Driscoll.

'I don't trust you,' he said.

'Don't blame you, mate. I'm a shifty bugger at the best of times, goes with the job.'

Cato nodded towards the doorway into an adjoining room, Yu Guangming, pacing nervously in the background and sucking on a cigarette. 'The two of you are in this together. You've got something up your sleeve.'

'You're not really in a position to trust or not trust. It's irrelevant, just do what you're told.'

Cato tried a different tack, playing with what little knowledge he had to see if he could unsettle Driscoll. 'If Yu and Li aren't working together, why did Yu arrange for Richard Chan to be killed? What's in it for him?'

'Yu doesn't have to be an employee or partner of Li's to do him favours. You've heard of guanxi by now? Connections, mutual obligations. Li now owes him one.'

'What about you and your guanxi?' said Cato. 'Who do you owe favours to?'

Driscoll sighed. 'Okay, in simple terms, Yu is our inside man on some major meth and people trafficking operations into Australia. He delivers good information which has helped us significantly frustrate their efforts.'

Cato recalled one of James Blond's outbursts. 'Is Li involved?'

'Nah, not directly anyway. Maybe ten arms lengths away he might have invested some petty cash in the occasional consignment but really he's playing for much bigger and far more legitimate stakes: land, property, minerals, industry. Drugs and prossies are so tacky.'

'But the ACC don't think so. They have Li flagged.'

'The ACC is wrong on this one.'

'Still Yu gets to make trouble for his rivals?' said Cato.

'It's called containment,' said Driscoll. 'Even small-town cops do it with the local brothels in Woop-Woop. Hardly rocket science.'

'And he gets away with rape and murder across the Asia-Pacific.'

'Yes, that has been morally unsettling at times but we try to keep our eyes on the big picture.'

'Big picture?' said Cato. 'The man is an animal. Give me a break.'

A call came through. The others were at the airport and checked in.

*

They were seated at a Starbuck's in the Departures hall: Lara, Sharon, and two Shanghai police minders. James had been wheeled straight through and on to the plane, heavily sedated, blitzed on painkillers, arm and hand swathed in bandages. A doctor and a paramedic would be flying with him, just in case. They were in Business Class which was a bonus. All they needed now was Cato and they'd just heard that he was free, safe and well, and on his way.

'Thanks for all you've done, Sharon,' said Lara. 'I hope I haven't completely stuffed up your career.'

Wang smiled and they clinked paper cups. 'All my own doing. Don't worry about it.'

Lara grinned wickedly. 'I reckon you'd be good for Cato. He needs a more regular seeing-to. Might cheer him up.'

They lifted their cups again. 'I'll drink to that,' said Sharon with a wink. She nodded towards Lara's stomach. 'When's it due?'

So she'd seen the ultrasound results at the hospital. Lara instinctively caressed her belly. 'End of February. It's a girl. Haven't thought of a name yet.' A mischievous smile. 'For a while there I was thinking "Sharon" but I decided no fucking chance.'

'Bitch. The dad a good bloke?'

'Yes,' said Lara. 'He is. I'm looking forward to getting back to him.'

'You look happy,' said Sharon.

'Yes I am.' Lara stood. 'Anyone seen a loo?'

Sharon pointed in the direction and Lara headed that way. There was a sudden surge of crowd, a big family send-off by the look of it. Lara edged her way through the throng. Somebody punched her hard in the chest. Lara gasped. 'Shit, watch where you're going!'

The crowd scattered, staring at her fearfully. She looked down, feeling wet, hearing splashes. There was a knife in her chest and blood pumping down her shirt.

'Oh no.' She slipped to the floor. 'Please, no.'

Sharon was beside her, trying to stem the flow. 'Somebody get help.' She repeated the cry in Mandarin. 'Ambulance! Now!'

Lara spoke in a small voice, clutching her stomach, cold spreading through her body. 'It won't stop, Sharon.'

Sharon was pressing on the wound but the blood kept coming. 'Help, somebody help, for fuck's sake!'

A long way off, Lara heard two shots somewhere down the terminal. The police minders had found their man and dealt with him. She looked at the blood draining from her body and at Sharon's pale, scared face. Not now. Not like this. Oh god, she thought. My baby.

*

They were in Driscoll's car on the elevated expressway to the airport when they heard. Lara was dead.

'Shit,' said Driscoll, turning off his speaker phone.

Cato had his eyes closed, head back against the seat rest; this was a nightmare.

'What do you want to do?' said Driscoll. 'We can keep heading to the airport and you can be with her.'

'Or?'

'Or we can go back and kill the fucker.'

Yu Guangming. It had to be.

Cato opened his eyes and stared straight ahead, unable to look Driscoll in the face. 'Let's go and find him.'

Driscoll took the next exit and headed back the way they came. 'I'm so sorry, mate.'

'Don't,' said Cato, grimly.

Yu Guangming wasn't at the address they'd vacated but some of his associates were. Driscoll stayed relaxed and chatty, so did Yu's men. They were either good actors or very cold, or they weren't in on Yu's plans to doublecross. Apparently he'd only just left about five minutes earlier. Heading on foot for the Bund, to his favourite bar.

They caught up with him at Waibaidu Bridge, a steel span structure perhaps fifty metres long, the last bridge before Suzhou Creek joined up with the main Huangpu River.

They parked up on a footpath twenty metres ahead and walked back.

'Waibaidu,' Driscoll informed him, 'means foreign white crossing, more or less.'

On the other side of the bridge was an old large white building flying the Russian flag. Their consulate, assumed Cato. Yu was leaning on the railings halfway across, smoking and gazing into the creek. Driscoll greeted him in Mandarin. He turned, puzzled, saw Cato and realised something was wrong. Driscoll produced a gun, put his arm around Cato's neck and poked the barrel into his ear. He continued speaking to Yu in Mandarin. Cato was no longer sure which side Driscoll was on. Was this part of the plan or was it the final betrayal?

'What's happening, Driscoll?'

'Shut up,' he said.

He edged Cato towards the railings, leant him over, poking the gun now into the back of his head. Passers-by were suddenly aware of something untoward. They were scattering, raising their voices in alarm. Two Chinese army guards from the Russian consulate had stepped away from their sentry posts to see what the fuss was about. They unslung their machine guns and edged towards them. Cato found himself staring at the black eddying waters of Suzhou Creek, the final resting place of Big-eared Du's victims. Shit, he thought, they're going to find me floating face down in the river wearing this crap London Cool Boy T-shirt. Driscoll was still speaking Mandarin, a note of urgency creeping into his voice. Yu must have decided everything was okay, he jogged up to them.

Driscoll turned and shot Yu at point-blank range. He hefted the body and dropped it over the railings into Suzhou Creek. It floated gently towards the Huangpu where the bright lights of Pudong beckoned. Then he threw his gun on the ground, knelt and put his hands behind his head, gesturing for Cato to do the same.

All the time, keeping up a reassuring stream of Mandarin for the approaching twitchy consulate sentries.

'What are you saying?' said Cato.

'I'm dropping the name of a well-known PLA General who'll chop their balls off if they harm us.'

'You really know him?'

'Sure, we're friends on Facebook. We've done some joint ventures together.'

Yu's corpse was still visible bobbing on the tide. 'You could have let me kill the bastard,' said Cato.

'Too much paperwork, mate. And it's not your style. You strike me as the type that would find it morally unsettling over the longer term.'

19

Tuesday, August 20th.

The next morning Cato parked himself at a spare desk at the Australian Consulate and dealt with a blizzard of emails, paperwork and phone calls to and from Perth, Canberra and Beijing. James Blond had been sent out on the same flight last night as intended. His medical condition was too fragile not to. There was an autopsy to be performed on Lara, her body to be repatriated, reports to be filed, questions to be answered. The bureaucracy and logistics were a welcome distraction for Cato. Sharon Wang cast the occasional concerned glance across the top of her computer. Her eyes were red and puffy, whether from grief or sleeplessness he didn't know. Probably both – maybe he looked the same. Wang had told him about Lara's pregnancy, about how happy she was, ready to settle down and build a family with the man he knew as Farmer John. That glow, the smiles, the engagement ring: all dust.

Driscoll was nowhere to be seen. Maybe he was keeping a low profile, maybe he was putting out more spot fires. How culpable was he in all this? Very. He'd allowed Yu Guangming too long a leash. The bastard should have been garrotted long ago. Cato copied DI Hutchens in on one of his summary reports and pressed send. His mobile buzzed. He didn't recognise the number.

'Yes?'

'Mr Kwong?' It was Thomas Li. 'I'm so sorry to hear about what happened to your colleague.'

'Thanks.'

'If there's anything I can do ...'

'I don't think so. Goodbye, Mr Li.'

'I feel I owe you ...'

'Forget it,' growled Cato.

'Don't you want to know who killed the Tans?'

'This isn't the time for games.'

'No games. There's something I think you should see.' Li told Cato what he needed to do. 'I'll send a car to pick you up. Is one hour from now okay?'

*

If they really wanted the authentic English town centre feel, thought Cato, a bit of graffiti and half of last night's kebab on the footpath would have done the trick. Li's chauffeur had just taken him on a drive-by tour of Thames Town – an enclave in Songjiang, south-west of Shanghai central. Songjiang, he recalled, was where the Zhous lived before they were brutally evicted from their home. Thames Town was a bizarre, slightly eerie interpretation of what a typical English village might look like. There were mock Tudor facades, red telephone and postboxes, and quaint Pommie names for the streets: 'Church Lane' and such – which unsurprisingly led to a cute little village-style church. If he'd known, he could have worn his London Cool Boy T-shirt. There was even a murky narrow river supposedly representing the Thames itself. It gave off an acrid aroma as if some sewerage had been added for Dickensian authenticity. Maybe the architect was a descendant of Samuel Coleridge, a bit too heavy-handed with the opium pipe, concocting his own little twisted Pommie Xanadu a few generations too late. The place was empty. Not a soul around. No Postman Pat. No twittering birds. Completely weird. But if you needed some peace and quiet away from the madding crowds of Shanghai, this was the spot.

Thomas Li was waiting for him on a park bench overlooking the Chinese Thames. Two ducks, real ones, quacked at his feet while he fed them some broken-up bread. Li looked up and greeted Cato, sweeping his arm to encompass the strange little ghost town. 'Build it and they will come.'

'So what happened here?' said Cato.

Li shrugged. 'Poor marketing, bad management, cynical speculators – who knows? There are homes here for ten thousand people just sitting empty. You'll find several thousand developments such as these all over China, some as big as a suburb, others are as big as Shanghai itself, ghost cities stretching from here to Mongolia. Meanwhile people sleep rough on the streets of Shanghai and Beijing. A terrible shame, don't you think?'

The scale might have been different but Cato could have said the same for Perth, Melbourne, Sydney, Port Hedland and Karratha. There was an oversupply of vacant homes for the haves, and blankets in doorways for the have-nots. It all depended which side of the boom you were on.

'And you want to go and build more, just over there.' Cato took a guess and pointed at the building site on the far side of the mock Thames. 'Where Mr Zhou and his family used to live?'

'Ah, Mr Zhou. You think I am responsible for his tragedy?'

'Aren't you?'

Li shook his head. 'The local government and their enforcement officers are responsible for rehousing and compensation of existing residents. All I do is buy land from willing city authorities and develop it for the good of all.'

'The good of all obviously doesn't include Zhou. It's a fine legalistic and semantic point you make but it doesn't absolve you, in my view.'

'That's a harsh judgement but it's your prerogative, Mr Kwong. I already have all of the lots on my site pre-sold. I'm a developer, not a speculator. I build real homes for real people paying real money.'

'Whatever. I didn't come to hear a justification of your business methods. You said you had something to show me relating to the Tan killings.'

Li stood up from the bench, his back seemed to be giving him trouble. Cato noticed for the first time that Li looked old, today anyway. 'Walk with me,' said Li.

Cato did as he was asked. Li's driver stepped out of the car and followed on foot. Cato saw that he was well built in that henchman kind of way with a smooth babyish face and bench press shoulders.

There was something vaguely familiar about him but Cato couldn't place it. So here they were: a ghost town, a ruthless entrepreneur, a potentially deadly sidekick, and a nosy and naïve Australian cop. Had Cato just handed himself over yet again as a walking loose end waiting to be snipped off? At times like this he missed Rory Driscoll.

'You and Mr Driscoll did me a very good favour last night.'

Speak of the devil, thought Cato. 'Are you talking about Yu Guangming?'

'Of course, who else?'

'I thought you'd never heard of him?'

'Did I say that? I'm old, forgetful.'

'So we've removed some of the competition for you?'

'Not competition exactly. Yu was a very volatile, unpredictable man. Sometimes that can be a hindrance to business confidence.' Li paused, as if they'd arrived somewhere meaningful.

They'd come to a sign on a fenced-off village green advertising properties for sale. The artist's impression was of nondescript anywhere-houses, not particularly English in style. The name of this proposed complex was Cambridge Gardens. It was an offshoot of the original Thames Town and, according to the plan on the billboard, an enclave bridging the old development with Li's much grander plan over the river. Cato had seen the like before on building sites from Hopetoun to Port Coogee, all over: promises of living the dream, sign here on the dotted line. Li's driver took out a pack of cigarettes and fired one up: Double Happiness – Yu Guangming's favourite brand. The driver blew smoke into the air, the very soul of nonchalance. He was looking everywhere but at Cato.

'Anyway,' said Li. 'One good turn deserves another.' He held his arm out in a revelatory tah-dah fashion.

The driver's foot scraped the ground. His hand went into his pocket. A gust of wind rustled the trees and sun broke through the clouds, glinting off the windscreen of Li's limousine.

With an angry quack the ducks flapped and rose and headed for an ungainly landing out on the river. Cato realised he was jumpy as hell. Everything seemed unreal, strange, and sinister yet at the same time there was some element of déjà vu. Then he saw it, saw what

Li was getting at. On the sign advertising the Cambridge Gardens development there was a name he recognised. Li nodded and smiled and proceeded to fill in some of the jigsaw for him.

Five minutes later Cato had a pretty good idea who might be behind the Tan killings and perhaps why. All he had to do now was prove it. He'd also realised what was familiar about the driver. The smell of moisturising cream. He strolled over, making a 'gimme a cigarette' gesture. The driver dug into his jacket pocket, retrieved the pack, and looked up to offer Cato one. Cato headbutted him then drove his fist deep and high into the man's gut.

'What the hell do you think you're doing?' said Li.

'Nearly finished,' said Cato.

The driver lay on the road torn between gasping for breath and stemming the blood from his nose. Cato kicked him in the kidneys. 'As a rule I tend not to kick a man while he's down.' He kicked him again. 'But mate, you started it.'

He turned to Li. 'Thanks for the tour and the tip. I'll make my own way back. I noticed a Metro not far from here.' He gestured at the man on the ground. 'Maybe you'd like to ask your employee why he's been moonlighting for Yu Guangming. Unless, of course, you already knew about that.'

20

Wednesday, August 21st.

The Shanghai sky was clear and blue and a fresh breeze kept everything comfortably cool. Under any other circumstances you might have called it a perfect day. Cato would accompany Lara Sumich's body home on a flight due to leave in about six hours. It went via Hong Kong and would arrive in Perth early the next morning. He would be seated next to Lara's father, the retired diplomat Oscar Sumich, who he'd met briefly the previous evening. On first impressions Sumich was a cold and aloof man but his stiff upper lip failed to mask the bewilderment and naked loss felt by any parent called upon to bury their own child. Early that morning Cato had caught a story in the English-language *Shanghai Daily*. Local billionaire Thomas Li Tonggui had reached an out-of-court settlement with the plaintiffs in the property development litigation, the late Richard Chan's clients. Li was quoted as saying that he hoped this sad misunderstanding was now at an end and that everybody could move on to embrace a prosperous future. Tick, sorted. All Cato had left to do was to collect his stored luggage then head to the airport and get on the plane. But first he needed to say goodbye to Sharon Wang.

He was by the number one entrance gate to Zhongshan Park. And there she was in her black pyjamas stepping through some taiji moves with a tasselled sword in her hand. She looked beautiful. After a few minutes the group completed the sequence and she took a break, walking over to join him.

'Nee ha,' he said.

'G'day.' She leaned in and gave him a long soft kiss on the lips. So the chemistry hadn't been all in his imagination. She smelled and felt wonderful.

He lightly touched her pyjama top. 'What do you call this anyway?'

'Taiji jimjams.'

'Taiji jimjams?'

A nod. She did a great poker face. It took Cato a moment to register he was being had.

'And this?' he pointed to her sword.

'Taijijian. It means...'

'Tai chi sword?'

She nodded, grinning.

'Taijijian,' said Cato.

'I love it when you talk Mandarin to me. Here let me show you something.' She took his hand and led him over to the calligraphers. She said a few words to one of them and he chuckled and nodded, drawing some symbols on the flagstones.

'What is it?' Cato asked.

'Your name: Kwong Qianping.'

The calligrapher went a step further, retrieving a bottle of ink and a sheet of paper from his backpack and drawing the symbols on it for Cato to keep.

'He says it's a gift.'

'Xie xie,' said Cato, deeply moved.

Sharon led him to an empty bench nearby. 'I got an email from my dad. He hasn't been able to find out anything about you Kwongs. He reckons your name is common as muck.'

Cato smiled and held up the calligraphy. 'This'll keep me going for now.'

'On the subject of names, something interesting came up on the bloke they shot at the airport.' Lara's assassin, a young man still in his teens. 'No apparent connections with Yu Guangming but it turns out he was the son of a man crippled by Li's chengguan thugs.'

'Jesus.' Cato shook his head. 'Little Zhou.'

'You know him?'

'We met briefly in the expat bar on the day of the attack. Chan introduced us.'

'The mother told us they'd been visited by a representative from the property development company, offering some serious compensation in return for a favour.'

'Was it Li?'

'No. A woman. The mum showed us a business card. It said "Li Xiaodao". The name means filial piety or obligation. In short, Li's dutiful daughter.'

'Phoebe.'

'Creepily "xiao dao" also means "little knife".'

The essence of tuishou is that you dissolve an oncoming force before striking a blow ...

Cato thought about his strange meeting with Li in Thames Town. He had believed that Li really was, in his own way, trying to do the right thing. Now this. 'Do you reckon Tommy Li knew, or was Phoebe going solo?'

'There's a Chinese tradition of blaming everything on evil bitches. If you believe some people, Mao's Cultural Revolution was all just an honest mistake and the real blame lay with Madame Mao. Complete bullshit of course.' Wang shook her head. 'Even if Li didn't know on this occasion, he created her.'

'We're never going to see justice for this, are we?' said Cato bitterly.

'The one thing I've learned during my time in China is to assume nothing. The prisons and cemeteries are full of high-flyers who thought they were untouchable. According to Rory, there's already rumblings in Beijing and talk of a move on the Lis.'

'I'll watch this space,' said Cato, unconvinced. 'Speaking of Driscoll, what's he up to?'

'Keeping his head down until you've gone, I think.'

'Good move,' said Cato. 'Do you think he already knew about Phoebe Li when he shot Yu Guangming?'

'Who knows what goes through that man's mind. Rumour has it that he's being headhunted for a clandestine job in Java for the next government's Stop the Boats campaign.'

God forgive us, thought Cato.

She stood up and led him by the hand. 'I'm sick of talking about work. Dance with me.'

They joined a group of people slow-waltzing to an old Chinese love song. Cato held Sharon close, not wanting to let her go. He tried to relax into the music, into the moment but there was a tightness in his chest. Everything blurred. He saw Sharon looking up at him, felt the tears on his cheeks.

She placed her hand on his chest. 'Don't let the manner of Lara's death define her life, or yours. Or this city.' She tilted her chin towards their dancing companions. 'Look at these people around you. Those older ones, they've witnessed, experienced, maybe even done, some terrible things during their time. But here they are every day, dancing, chatting, exercising. Living life, now.'

Cato looked at them. She was right but it didn't stem the flow of his tears.

And maybe that was not a bad thing.

PART 3

21

Thursday, August 22nd.

The atmosphere at Freo cop shop was as gloomy as the weather. DIs Pavlou and Hutchens invited Cato in for a chat. There seemed to be a rare air of party unity about them.

'How are you?' asked Pavlou, pouring him a coffee from the plunger. Did he detect traces of recent tears in her red-rimmed eyes?

'Okay.'

'Really?' said Hutchens. 'You don't look it.'

Cato could have said the same for Hutchens. He still seemed overly pink, tight and shiny. Like a blister ready to burst. Cato himself was covered in bruises and abrasions and he felt emotionally empty. But it was all relative. 'Yep,' he said.

'You want counselling, any of that shit?'

'I'm fine for now, boss. I'll let you know if I'm not.'

The coffee tasted bitter to Cato, then again, so did everything else. He'd been travelling all night but managed a few hours' sleep in the relative comfort of Business Class. Oscar Sumich's conversation had been limited to the occasional 'excuse me' as he went to the toilet. Each time he would return with his face freshly scrubbed of the tears he must have allowed himself in the privacy of the cramped cubicle. Cato wasn't tired. There was a nervous, angry energy that wouldn't let him rest.

Lara's funeral was set for the following Saturday, the day after tomorrow. Full bells and whistles and top brass. The results of the Chinese post-mortem and police investigation weren't going to be challenged by the family so there was no need for any further delay. They wanted the whole sorry matter expedited. That morning there'd been a two-page spread in the *West* with big colour pics of the photogenic Lara Sumich, a potted history of her career including the dramatic manhunt two years earlier when she'd collared Dieudonne, the former child soldier turned hit-man, along with his rogue cop handler. There were testimonials from her colleagues and family to the effect of what a warm-hearted and good person she was. It was a side of her Cato had rarely glimpsed, until recently. And a photo of her heartbroken fiancé, Farmer John.

'So,' said Pavlou. 'Li?'

'Like I said in my report, I really don't think he's behind it. He's too big for that stuff. The losses incurred by Francis Tan were small change to him.'

'Yu Guangming?'

'He said not but I don't believe him. He admitted to being on the scene, on the day.'

'So if it was him, he's dead. Case closed?'

'It would wrap things up pretty neatly,' agreed Cato, aware that any talk of Des O'Neill and the Wongan connection would be snuffed out unless and until he could offer more concrete supporting evidence.

'But?' said Pavlou.

'There's Matthew Tan's mystery stowaway. I take it we haven't found Matt or his passenger yet?'

'Nah,' said Hutchens.

'How's Lily?' said Cato.

'Recovering. Mum and Dad cut short their holiday in Mauritius to come back and look after her.'

'Let's make Matthew a priority then, shall we?' said Pavlou. 'His attack on Lily was probably just a domestic. And if he can explain the stowaway, or even just deny all knowledge, then we might be able to pin the Tan murders on Yu Guangming and file it away.'

Hutchens bristled. 'Finding Matthew Tan has never *not* been a priority, Sandra.'

A reassuring pat on the hand. 'Sure, Mick. But it would be good to give the Commissioner some good news ahead of Lara's funeral, eh?'

'Absolutely,' said Hutchens, playing nice.

Sandra. Mick. If the entente got any more cordiale Cato thought he might puke.

*

Cato had other thoughts. He was happy enough to see Yu Guangming in the frame for the murders but there were other people who had some explaining to do. Here and in China. He opened up his laptop and summoned Francis Tan's financial records from the investigation database. The folder included the Tan family's individual and business bank and credit card statements, the Tan business balance sheets plus a flowchart and timeline of business deals and associations over the last five years. It looked very thorough. The geeks at the ACC had been busy.

According to the financial profile, things had started to go wrong for Francis Tan between two and three years ago. Before that his star had been on the rise as a result of his lucrative partnerships with Thomas Li in China and Des O'Neill in Australia. Li had a shopping list of property assets he was interested in and O'Neill and Tan between them had a good eye for a bargain and a persuasive manner for unlocking the riches of both urban and rural Western Australia. At his zenith Francis Tan would have had a personal wealth of around twenty million dollars. Then it began slipping through his fingers. A string of bad luck and bad decisions that commenced about three years earlier sent his business into a tailspin. But was it really just bad luck or did somebody have a hand in his downfall?

In Thames Town, that confected English ghost city on the outskirts of Shanghai, Thomas Li had drawn his attention to a sign advertising the bland Cambridge Gardens sub-development. One of the partners was Wongan Holdings. Wongan, at first glance, looked like a Chinese company but Cato had seen the name before, in this ACC profile. Wongan, as in Wongan Hills, the birthplace and company name for Des O'Neill's business venture. According to Thomas Li, O'Neill had started spreading his wings about two years earlier, coincidentally the same time Francis Tan started his run of bad luck, and had taken an interest in property speculation in China. To do so O'Neill would have needed a Chinese partner but, according to Li, neither he nor Tan were involved. Cato had asked, so who then? Li had pointed to another partner on the hoarding, Suzhou Dragon Enterprises. Aka Yu Guangming.

Of course he only had Li's word for that last connection. He needed the ACC or somebody to look into and confirm Yu's connection to Suzhou Dragon. In the meantime Cato scanned the Tan financial profile once again looking for the hand of Des O'Neill and for a possible motive for murder.

*

Hutchens was sitting in the gloom of J. B. O'Reilly's with a half of Kilkenny and a bulging backpack at his feet, the second instalment of the ten K Mundine had demanded by last Friday. Hutchens had concocted a bullshit story about cash flow to try to limit his risk but he was still three thousand down so far. It was a 'good faith' investment which he aimed to recoup from the fucker in due course. The seven K balance was once again to be handed over to the middleman, the Irish backpacker barman. His name was Dermot apparently and he had caught Hutchens' eye meaningfully several times since handing over the drink. Once again, mid-afternoon, the place was as quiet as the proverbial. There were only two other patrons, the same two pissheads as last time. Mundine was taking a big risk letting a backpacker mind a bag full of cash for him. He either really trusted Dermot or he was a fucking idiot. So far, more's the pity, the idiot theory hadn't played out. But that made Dermot more interesting and potentially useful. A trawl of the files and public records and some words in the ear of local cops had failed to locate a home address for Mundine. The Inquiry paperwork had him as 'No Fixed Abode' and they seemed happy to work around that. Either way Hutchens wasn't going to press them for the address of a major witness; it wouldn't look too good. Dermot was the key and he had a shift break due in half an hour.

Mundine had slipped off the radar somewhat since last Friday. No more hysterical texts or threats. Maybe the first cash payment had restocked his medicine cabinet. For a while Hutchens harboured the faint hope that the prick had used the money to buy a bad batch of smack and OD'd in some filthy suburban hovel. No such luck. Just that morning a measured text had come through with a reminder and instructions for the next instalment. Hutchens downed his drink and made his move as per the agreed routine. He took his backpack up to the bar.

'Can you watch this for a moment, mate, while I take a piss?'

'No problemo,' said Dermot, hanging it on a hook behind the counter.

Hutchens went to the toilet, locked himself in a cubicle, and checked his Glock.

He came out, winked his farewell to Dermot, jangled his car keys and headed for the exit. Then he drove around the block and parked up just out of sight over and down the road, in the shade of a flowering flame tree dancing with rainbow lorikeets.

Dermot appeared about twenty minutes later with the backpack slung over his shoulder. He headed west down Cambridge Street and turned up a side road in the direction of West Leederville train station. Hutchens allowed some distance then followed in the car. He knew Dermot only had a half hour break so he wouldn't have time to go far. A train to somewhere and back in that time seemed a bit ambitious. Dermot didn't go up to the platform. Instead he headed for the pedestrian underpass. Hutchens cursed and slapped the driving wheel – Surveillance and Tailing 101 and he'd just failed. But Dermot didn't enter the underpass, he stood and waited at the northern end. A yellow moped drew up beside him, the rider took the backpack and rejoined the burgeoning after-school traffic. Hutchens followed.

It turned out Mundine lived in a block of flats in Jolimont. It might have been one of Perth's leafy green western suburbs but there was little sign of affluence in this run-down corner. The walls of the three-storey block were stained by the scum of bore water. There was a car on bricks under a rusting shelter. A grubby torn mattress leaned against a graffitied wall. Garbage skittered in the breeze. It was skanksville. That suited Hutchens because it was the type of place where neighbours kept their noses out of other people's business. He put in a call to a friend and passed on the address.

*

By the end of the afternoon Cato's eyes were blurring from a combination of travel fatigue and from reading and re-reading the Tan financial profile. Accountancy wasn't one of his strong points and he couldn't see anything that jumped out as a clear indicator of malfeasance on the part of Des O'Neill. The spreadsheets were as cryptic as any crossword. All that remained was the coincidence of timelines. During the same couple of years that Francis Tan started going downhill, Des O'Neill was heading up. And making friends with Yu Guangming, a violent man who had been at the crime scene on the day of the murders and left his semen inside Genevieve Tan.

It wasn't enough. Cato couldn't even begin to approach O'Neill without some concrete evidence of wrongdoing. First he would send Cato packing, second he would cover his tracks. As things stood, O'Neill may not have any idea that the police were interested in him and Cato intended to maintain that slight advantage. His phone went, it was Chris Thornton.

'We have a lead on Matthew Tan.'

'Go on.'

'His ATM card was used this afternoon in Scarborough.'

'By him?'

'No, the CCTV says it was a woman. I saw the print out and I agree. She is.'

'And?'

'According to the database he's got a friend, the girl kind, who lives up the road, just north of Trigg.'

'Doorbusters?'

'On the way, we'll meet them there. I'll pick you up out front in five.'

'Have you told Hutchens?'

'He's out. Phone turned off. I left a message; but Pavlou's in the loop.'

It was dark by the time they got there. Apartment 32 was on the third floor of a five-storey block just back from the beach with a view out over Mettam's Pool and the Marmion Marine Park. Cato, Jane and Jake had come snorkelling here in happier times. It was a calming protective reef just offshore with all variety of fish. Jake had been so excited he'd tried talking through his snorkel and took a big swallow of seawater. Now it was dark and chopped up, froth foaming the surface. A handful of uniforms were waiting, decked out in protective gear and wielding a battering ram. But first they had to get through the downstairs lobby door and the entryphone system. Cato pressed the relevant button and announced himself to the female occupant.

'What do you want?'

'Just open the door please, madam, and we can state our business face to face.'

The door buzzed and clicked and they all filed in. The uniforms took the stairs. Cato and Thornton hopped in the lift.

The young woman at the entrance to number 32 was the spitting image of Lily Soong, minus the bruises.

'Matilda,' she said, peering at Cato's ID and sniffing at the riot squad. 'Matilda Soong. Lily's sister,' she added, in case anybody hadn't worked it out yet.

'Is Matt here?' said Cato.

'Matt who?'

'Matthew Tan, the bloke who beat your sister up and put her in hospital.'

'Oh,' she said. 'Him.' She thumbed over her shoulder. 'Back bedroom. Help yourself.'

Matthew Tan was out cold. He looked terrible and smelled worse. The room reeked of Jim Beam or some other bogan spirit. One of the riot squad waved a hand across her face in disgust. 'Nobody light a match.'

'He's been a bit upset,' said Matilda leaning against the door frame. 'So how did you know to come here?'

'You were on the video at the ATM using Matt's card.' Chris

Thornton was finding it hard to tear his eyes away from Matilda's décolletage.

'Housekeeping. I needed some groceries.'

'Do you know that harbouring a fugitive is an offence?' said Thornton.

'Sorry,' she said. 'Finished looking at my chest, yet?'

Cato sat on the edge of the bed and shook the prone figure. 'Matt? Wake up.'

A grunt and expulsion of foul air from both ends.

Cato gestured to Thornton to help him bring Tan to a sitting position. 'C'mon, Matt. Wakey, wakey.'

Matt finally opened an eye. A tear came out of it.

'Do you know where you are, Matt?'

One of the uniforms brought a glass of water over. Cato held it to Tan's lips. 'Get this down, you'll feel better.'

Matthew sipped. Then he spewed all over their feet.

Matilda swore and went to get a sponge.

*

David Mundine was viewing some violent online porn when his doorbell sounded. He was almost glad of the interruption; the storyline was doing nothing for him, it lacked bite. He zipped himself up and shuffled to the front door, uggs flapping where the sole had split from the upper. He opened the door to two men in hoods. He tried to close the door on them but failed. They were over the threshold, gloved hands covering his face and mouth, an arm around his neck. Then everything went black.

When he awoke he could feel that he was taped to a chair and the floor was hard under his feet. His head hurt and one of the fingers of his left hand throbbed, maybe broken or dislocated. Something warm, blood or snot maybe, dribbled from his nose. Tape had been wound around his eyes but he knew he was still in his own kitchen. He could smell the meal he'd cooked earlier, a mushroom omelette.

A voice said, 'Davey you need to learn to stop bothering good people.' High-pitched and nervy, like a two-pot screamer. 'Stick to your own skanky circle.'

'What? I think you've got the wrong person. This is all a mistake. I've done nothing.'

'Where's the money?'

'What money?'

A slap around the back of the head. Oh, you bitch. That was so mean.

He put a shake in his voice. 'What do you want? I don't have money. I'm on a pension. My nerves.'

'The money. Don't fuck about.'

A drawer was opened followed by the sound of rummaging through the cutlery. 'This should do it.' The second voice was lower than the first. More manly. Must be the hubby.

'What are you doing? What do you want from me?'

'The money.'

'I don't have any money! Please stop.' He lifted the volume a notch. 'Jesus, somebody please. Help me!'

Tape went around his mouth. That was good. He didn't want them to see him laughing. That would ruin it. This was better than B-grade porn any day.

A more conciliatory tone from the deep-voiced hubby. 'Look, mate. We know you've got a backpack with lots of money in it. Just tell us where it is and we'll be out of here. Nobody gets hurt. Okay?'

Mundine shook his head, grunted into the gag.

A sharp pain in the top of his thigh. He squealed like a pig. He wondered what was being used. It didn't feel like a knife. The corkscrew? He did the squeal again, to convince them they were getting somewhere.

Hot breath beside his ear, some spittle. It was the two-pot screamer again. 'Your last chance, before things turn really bad.'

Delicious.

He nodded his head vigorously, he would tell them everything. Take the gag off. Release me from this terrible torment.

The tape gag came off, tugging at his hair and making it sting a bit. Ouch.

He took a steadying breath. Fixed them with a look. 'Tell Mr H. I've been hurt by experts. Tell him I'm coming for him. Now fuck off out of my home.' He couldn't help himself. He started laughing.

They didn't have the heart for it. He knew they didn't. They had goodness at their core. They left.

22

Friday, August 23rd.

Matthew Tan was still under the weather but had recovered enough for a little chat, on the record and under caution. His lawyer, Henry Hurley, was in attendance, as were Cato and Chris Thornton. By the time Cato had arrived home mid-evening, he was dead on his feet. The previous night's travel had well and truly caught up with him and the restless, raging energy that had fuelled his day had dissolved. He hadn't bothered eating and he'd once again neglected to call those members of his family who needed his attention. He collapsed on the bed and didn't wake until his alarm smacked him into submission.

Henry Hurley read out a statement. His client confessed to the assault on his girlfriend Lily Soong and he was genuinely remorseful for his actions. A domestic argument had got out of hand and, under the enormous mental strain of his recent bereavement, he had allowed his temper to get the better of him. Matthew was aware however that the slaughter of his family was no excuse for his atrocious behaviour and he was prepared to face whatever legal consequences may ensue. In addition, of his own volition, he would be signing up for the next available anger management program. Finally, his girlfriend, Ms Soong, had forgiven him, an email printout was appended as proof, and they hoped to be fully reconciled real soon.

'If you were so remorseful why didn't you come forward earlier? Why did we have to come and find you?'

'My client has been under enormous emotional pressure of late.

His actions, although erratic and, at times, reprehensible, can be attributed to his volatile mental state.'

Cato flicked his gaze away from the lawyer. 'Is that right, Matthew?'

'Yes.'

Time to move on. Cato placed two traffic and CCTV photos of Matthew's car on the desk. 'Can you identify these for me, please?'

Matthew confirmed it was him, driving his car, through those places, on the night of the murders. As per his previous statements.

Cato substituted two close-ups of the same images and prodded the blurry shadow of Matt's passenger. 'Who is this?'

Matt didn't know. He seemed genuinely surprised to have had a stowaway. 'Sorry, I haven't a clue.'

'You really weren't aware of a presence in the back of your car?'

'I was miles away. To be honest I might still have been a bit over the limit.'

'You didn't hear anything? Smell anything? Sense anything?'

'Sorry.'

'Any idea who it might be?'

'My client has explained his bewilderment at this turn of events. It is not up to him to speculate. It's up to you to do your job.'

'Thanks,' said Cato. 'But help us out here anyway, Matt. No ideas?'

'As I said, sorry, no.'

And that's all they could do, for now. Matthew Tan was returned to the cells for a magistrate's appearance later that morning on the assault and related charges. DI Pavlou would be pleased. It was shaping up nicely to load everything onto the conveniently deceased Yu Guangming and close the case. Cato put in a call to Hutchens to bring him up to date. Still no answer. He left a message.

*

Hutchens took the call from his special friend halfway through a breakfast of soft boiled eggs and toast soldiers.

'I thought you said he was piss weak?'

'Has to be,' said Hutchens, taking a slurp of instant coffee. 'He was Sinclair's plaything in the hostel for two years. He's been in and out of prison since and usually hooked on some shit or other. What happened?'

The friend told him.

'And you didn't hurt him anymore?'

'I'm not a sadist. This was a favour. You asked us to scare him. He doesn't scare. End of story.'

'Fuck's sake.'

'He asked us to pass on a message.'

'Yeah?'

'Words to the effect of he's been hurt by experts and he's coming to get you.'

'Thanks,' Hutchens muttered. 'I owe you one.'

'On the house. Sorry about the money, we looked around but couldn't find it. Watch yourself, Mick, this bloke is more than a bit troppo.'

So. He was ten grand down and he had a psycho stalker who knew no fear. He'd kept on taking Mundine for granted and getting him wrong. He needed to do his homework and he needed to start taking this seriously. Maybe the best thing was to get Marjorie and the kids out of town for a couple of weeks, hunker down and deal with whatever was coming. He poured himself another coffee and mooted the question with Mrs Hutchens.

'Ten thousand bucks? What the fuck were you thinking, love?'

'Right now the money is not so much of an issue, it's the fact that he's a nutter.'

'It's an issue for me, sweetie. Fucking hell.'

'Marj, maybe you could go and stay with your folks in Augusta for a week or two until this blows over?'

'What about my job? I've got half a dozen punters waiting for me to sort out their future nest eggs. Financial gurus don't work teachers' hours, Mick.'

'Tell them it's a personal family crisis. It's the truth, they'll understand.'

'Can't you just have the bastard killed?'

'No, pumpkin. It's not legal.'

'Shit.'

'Sorry.'

'S'pose you want me to take Melanie as well, do you?'

'If her bloke's out bush making another one of his poncy documentaries, yeah, you'd better.'

She sniffed. 'One week. Get it sorted.' She pecked him grumpily on the cheek. 'And take some more of your spray, you're looking pink again.'

*

'So do we have enough corroboration to sheet this over to the Yu fella and file it away?'

The question came from DI Pavlou. She'd called a Cabinet Meeting of the heads of various departments: Cato, Hutchens, forensics honcho Duncan Goldflam, Chris Thornton as data wrangler and statement checker, and Mystery Michael the ACC spook. And it seemed to Cato that Lara Sumich's ghost also haunted the room, restless and demanding. Demanding what? The ghost of the old Lara would have been a vengeful one. Cato suspected the new Lara was less strident, but still insistent to be heard.

'We can now put Yu's DNA in the master bedroom and in one of the victims on the day of the murder,' conceded Goldflam who was still smarting over the ACC and Pavlou holding back on him about the ID on the mystery traces.

'I showed Yu's photo to the graffiti girl, Ocean Mantra,' Thornton added. 'She's pretty confident it's the same guy she saw driving erratically near the scene that night.'

'And you can confirm Yu's admission to you of being on the premises that day?' Pavlou was looking at Cato expectantly.

'Yes. But we still haven't cleared up the matter of Matthew Tan's stowaway.'

'This wouldn't be the first case I've dealt with that's had its little ... anomalies.'

'Not wrong,' said Hutchens, half under his breath. But not half enough.

Pavlou turned to Hutchens. 'Nor you for that matter, Mick.' Back to Cato and the business at hand. 'Philip, can you oversee the boxing off? Take care of the paperwork and send the finished product off to the archives. In the meantime, a summary report in my inbox by day's end so I can give the top brass some good news. Doable?'

No, thought Cato. This is not right. 'Sure,' he said.

'Chuck any "loose ends" into your concluding paragraph if that makes you feel better.'

'Okay.' Count on it.

They were dismissed. Michael the ACC man hadn't said a single word in the whole meeting. Come to that he hadn't said a single word since Cato had first glimpsed him a few weeks ago. What was the point of him? Cato's inbox started to fill with the jigsaw of the Tans' final hours. He dutifully set to piecing them together, ignoring any holes in the picture and crafting his conclusions to fit Pavlou's needs. In effect, by day's end she should be able to ship out back to the Major Crime suites up in Perth. He didn't intend to hold her up.

*

Marjorie and Melanie would be en route to Augusta, three hundred or so kilometres south. Hutchens dragged Mundine's name out of the system. Know thine enemy. He'd already done a cursory printout on the charge sheet to prepare himself for the Inquiry but he hadn't realised then what he was dealing with. Now the matter certainly warranted closer inspection.

David Christopher Mundine was just past his twelfth birthday when he was sent to Hillsview Hostel late in 1995. His mother was in Bandyup on drugs and various dishonesty charges and his father was an unknown quantity. David was a troubled child, coming to the attention of successive juvenile justice teams for stealing, vandalism, drug, and alcohol offences. It was hoped that time away from his dropkick mother in an environment with rules might do him some good. The warden, Peter Sinclair, had a reputation for being 'tough but fair'. There was very little recidivism on his watch – none of the kids ever wanted to go back for more.

Soon after Sinclair's disappearance in late October 1997, Mundine returned to the family home. Mum had been out of Bandyup a good six months already but expressed an inability to cope and asked if the authorities could hold on to David a little while longer until she was ready. David, meanwhile, was completing an anger management course at the hostel. By early November, Hillsview had more than enough problems of its own and sent fourteen year old David home to Mum, ready or not. It took less than a month for the boy to reappear before yet another juvenile justice team. This time he'd used his recently acquired height and bulk to menace money out of a younger kid at school. Several times. The menaces had been not only violent but also sexual in nature and had involved inappropriate touching to illustrate his point. David was transferred to another school and ordered to attend yet another round of counselling sessions. He never showed up at the new school or the counselling sessions and, from what Hutchens could make of the records, nobody bothered to follow it up.

More charges. More recommendations for counselling. More absences. Some time in Banksia Hill Juvenile Detention Centre at the age of sixteen where he kept his nose clean and kept out of trouble. The next ten years or so were peppered with more petty drug and alcohol offences, dishonesty convictions, assaults and some vandalism, his charge sheet looking very similar to his mother's before him. Two years ago a violence restraining order had been taken out on him by a de facto, Lisa Gangemi. It had since expired.

Mundine presented as a Class-A pathetic fuck-up, more a victim than a perpetrator. But there were clues to his more proactive potential. The extortion with menaces at high school and the more recent VRO suggested a very different temperament from his Inquiry persona of Little Davey the Victim. Hutchens went through the database and put together a TO DO list.

*

Reviewing the evidence, Cato was satisfied that Yu Guangming played a central role in the murders of the Tan family and had almost convinced himself that the business connections to Des O'Neill were little more than a distracting 'look over there' from the wily Thomas Li. Almost. He was also pretty much satisfied that Matthew Tan was not in the frame, based on his convincing display on the news of the murders, on his alibis, and on the lack of any compelling forensic evidence. Pretty much. Maybe the stowaway was just some street kid messing about, or he'd found a nice warm spot for a sleep and wasn't expecting to wake up in transit somewhere. Maybe.

His phone rang. It was Jane.

'Is Jake with you?'

'No. Why?'

'I just found a message from the school on my phone. They say he didn't turn up today.'

'You've tried his phone?'

'Yes, of course I have. No answer.'

'How have things been?'

'How do you mean?'

'Before I went away, he came over. Said he wanted to come and live with me. Things didn't seem to be going too well.'

'When was this?'

'Over a week ago. I left messages but I was going to call you to talk about it properly. I forgot. Work and that.'

'Work and that,' she repeated icily. 'What else did he say?'

'Not much more. He said Simon had been getting at him about his mates. Do you know what that's about?'

'Simon reckons some of his mates are deadbeats, probably on the dope like a lot of kids their age. He's been around. He can spot them a mile off.'

'So, what do you think?'

'I think I'm doing the best I possibly can to hold some bloody family life together.' An exasperated sigh. 'Give me a call if or when your son gets in touch.' The line went dead.

Cato tried Jake's mobile. No answer. He sent him a text. **Call me. Dad.**

Call me Dad. After missing out on a huge chunk of Jake's formative years due to his obsession with work, Cato believed he had found some connection with his son. Now it seemed to be slipping away again. Was he to blame? Probably. Should he be worried? Worst case scenario, the boy was shooting up in a crack den and about to go and bludge a pensioner to death. Or he was at his mate's listening to rap music and doing a couple of bongs. Neither option appealed to Cato but he had to try and maintain some perspective. And short of suspending his day and sending out a search party, he had little choice.

Outside it had clouded over again but they didn't look like rain clouds. He ventured out for some late lunch, treating himself to a seafood laksa down the road at Café 55. On the way he tried phoning his sister to organise a Dad visit. No answer, so he left a message. Café 55 was crowded as usual but he found a perch on a stool facing a wall festooned with posters for upcoming cultural events around Fremantle. Nearby there was an abandoned *West* and a virgin cryptic. He clicked his biro in readiness.

Dishonest stock-taker. Six and seven. The laksa arrived and he made space for it on the narrow counter. *Cattle rustler.*

Imagine one less mix up to a mystery. *Enigma.*

Cato decided that he was sick of carrying passengers. Michael the mystery ACC man needed to start earning his keep. He put in a call then got stuck into his laksa. It was delicious.

*

Hutchens lifted all the virtual rocks in the database and peered beneath, but Lisa Gangemi was nowhere to be found. She'd dropped off the face of the earth, or at least the immediate public record. David Mundine's mum was easier. She was back in Bandyup. But it would still be highly irregular for Hutchens to approach her. Luck, however, moves in mysterious ways. Hutchens put in a call to Cato.

'Got anything on?'

There was hubbub in the background. 'The remains of a laksa and Pavlou's report so she can be on her merry way by day's end.'

'Amen to that,' said Hutchens. 'Got time for a trip to Bandyup?'

'Why?'

'The mannequin upskirter we pulled in week before last?'

'Yes?'

'Possibly part of a disturbing pattern.'

'Serious?'

'Am I ever not?'

They opted for South and Roe to take them out and around the urban sprawl and north to Bandyup Women's Prison. Hutchens filled Cato in en route.

'So our upskirter is a former de facto of this Tricia Mundine who's locked up?'

'Yeah,' said Hutchens. 'He was the love of her life for a few weeks earlier this year.'

'And she can attest that he was a bit weird back then?'

'Yeah, bound to.'

'And this warrants the attention of a detective inspector and a detective sergeant?'

'Acting,' Hutchens reminded him. 'Look it's a matter of public safety and wellbeing, mate.'

'It's bullshit. What's really going on?'

Hutchens told Cato everything. Except the bit about getting some pals to put the frighteners on Mundine.

'No wonder you've been looking like a walking cardiac arrest.'

'Thanks, mate.'

'What do you want to know from her?'

'Any more history on her darling son, although she doesn't seem to have been around much in his formative years.'

'Okay.'

'And anything I can use to neutralise him.'

'A taser's probably your best option.'

'It's on my list.' They pulled into Bandyup car park. Squat pale buildings, barbed wire, bleak-looking visitors, and some complaining crows to set the scene. 'Good luck,' said Hutchens. 'And thanks.'

As Cato strolled away towards reception, Hutchens felt another tightening in his chest and reached for his angina spray.

*

'Ian who?'

'Ian Rigby. Your former partner. You took a restraining order out against him back in February.'

'Did I?' Tricia Mundine was struggling to catch up. Cato could sympathise. A few months inside for unpaid fines had done little to purge her inner workings. She had a hacking smoker's cough and the complexion of a Rolling Stone. 'What for?'

Cato checked the paperwork. 'Violence, harassment, threats. It says here.'

'I put that on all of them.'

And so she did. She was a serial restrainer. For her the VRO system was a means of retaliating against people who had wronged her in any way: the next-door neighbour for complaining about the noise, an old boyfriend for leaving her, or not leaving her. Twenty-three and counting. And Tricia Mundine wasn't alone in using the system to score petty grudges. The VRO paper wastage in Perth could have fuelled Collie Power Station for decades. No wonder they were practically unpoliceable. It was a pity about those that were genuine and foreshadowed serious domestic violence or even murder. They never stood out from the mass until it was usually too late.

'But you also claimed that Ian was sexually aggressive.'

'Oh, *that* Ian.' She visibly brightened.

'What did he do, then?' asked Cato

Tricia scratched at a scab on her wrist. 'He was always taking pictures. Me during sex, from all angles. Surprised he could still concentrate on the deed. Then it got weirder. Me in the dunny snapping one off. Asleep, catching flies. That's okay if it's just for him but then he was selling the pictures.'

'Who to?'

'Some website in Russia that deals with all sorts of weird stuff? I mean who wants to pay to see me doing a dump? But they did. Ian showed me the webpage once. Click. There's me on all fours backing his way. Click. And another one of me when I had this bout of gastro.' She grimaced and shook her head. 'He had to go. He didn't even share the money with me.'

This was as good a time as any to change the subject. 'Heard from David recently?'

'Who?'

'Your son.'

'No. Why, what's he done?'

Cato filled her in on the hostel inquiry and his role in it. 'Do you remember if he mentioned anything at the time about the warden, about what was going on there?'

'Nothing. Some bloke fiddling with him, you say?'

'Yes.'

A shrug. 'Wouldn't have been the first time. I've made some poor choices in boyfriends over the years.' A vague look of regret. 'I had my suspicions about a couple of them. More interested in him than me, they were.'

'Any that stand out?'

She looked like she was trying to remember. 'Nah. Sorry. Why? I thought this was about Ian whatshisname and the shop dummies?'

He ignored the question. 'Did David ever seem capable of violence?'

'Oh yeah, he belted me once. Big time. Put me in hospital.'

'Do you remember when? The circumstances?'

'He must have been a bit older then, maybe sixteen. Can't remember why he did it though. I must have upset him or something.'

The interview wound to a close. Cato was running out of questions and Tricia was running out of answers and becoming increasingly insistent on wanting to know what this was all about. Cato said his farewells, reasonably confident that her shattered brain cells wouldn't hold the memory of this encounter for long.

*

Cato passed on the salient highlights of the encounter as Hutchens drove them home through the late afternoon traffic and the fading light.

'So you reckon there's a Russian website specialises in upskirted mannequin shots?'

'Nothing would surprise me,' said Cato. 'And if it's a crime then it's probably a victimless one.'

'Flickpass it back to Murdoch. Tell them they could be on to something big.' Hutchens braked sharply to allow a dickhead back into the traffic flow. They exchanged middle-finger salutes. 'So Mum says Davey has a propensity for violence and that Peter Sinclair might not have been his first love?'

'In a nutshell. But I can't see how any of this helps with your current problem.'

'No worries, Cato mate. Thanks for the favour, you're a legend.'

That sheen of sweat had returned to Hutchens' face.

'Have you seen a doctor at all lately?'

'Yep. Blood pressure's up a bit but he's got me on some tablets.'

'And you're okay for going back to the Inquiry on Monday?'

'Absolutely.'

'Maybe you should move into a hotel for a few days until this stuff with Mundine gets sorted?'

'Two hundred bucks a night? No way.'

'Maybe you should be going official with this. Get some help.'

'There's no evidence of him doing anything, yet.'

'What about the texts to you? The abusive phone call to your wife?'

'Unregistered phone. Unreliable witness. They'll send me packing. They'll say I've lost it.'

'There must be something.'

Hutchens turned and beamed at Cato. 'You've been a diamond, mate. Really.'

*

When Cato got home Jake was waiting for him on the weatherworn couch on the front verandah.

'Where've you been?' he said, accusingly.

'I might ask you the same thing. Why weren't you at school today?'

No reply. Jake followed his father into the house.

'So?' said Cato.

'So what?'

'School. Where were you?' He shepherded Jake to the kitchen table. Sat him down and put the kettle on. There was a sweaty fug about his son. None of the obvious smells of dope. Maybe it was just teenage funk. But something wasn't right. 'Answer the question.'

A smirk. 'Am I under arrest?'

'Stop being a smart-arse.' Cato phoned Jane to let her know what was going on. He said he'd keep Jake there for the night. Jane didn't object. Cato finished making a cuppa and slid one Jake's way. 'Once again. Where were you today?'

'Mates.'

'Who? Where?'

'Stef's. White Gum Valley.'

'Who else was there?'

'A few others. You wouldn't know them.'

'And Stef's parents. Where were they?'

'Working.'

'What did you do all day?'

'Hung out. Talked. Played music. Video games.'

'Any drugs involved?'

'Been talking to Mum and Simon, have you?'

The obfuscation, the attitude. He'd seen too much of it in his job not to recognise what probably lay behind it. Cato took a decision he hoped he wouldn't regret.

'Empty your school bag.'

'Are you serious?'

'Do it.'

'What happened to trust, here?' Cato took the bag from him and started rummaging through. 'You can't do that. That is just so wrong.'

'Watch me,' said Cato. 'If there's nothing there you've got nothing to worry about.'

He emptied the bag onto the kitchen table. Books. Files. Scraps of paper. Pens, pencils, a calculator, eraser. School lunch, untouched. Cato opened the lunchbox. Two halves of a ham salad sandwich in grainy brown bread. An apple, a bruised banana. And a pipe. And a lighter. And a small plastic bag of leafy material.

Cato shook his head. 'I'd thought you were better than this ...' he searched for words, 'bullcrap.'

'Sorry. Dad.' No apology at all. Just contempt and derision. Jake's phone started beeping.

'Hand it over.'

'No.'

Cato wrestled the phone out of his son's hand. It was from Stef – a photo of him with his pipe. And a message: **Duuuuude!**

'I hate you,' said Jake, red-faced, his eyes watering with anger.

'I don't hate you. But I don't think much of you right now.' Cato sent Stef's number to his own phone. 'Your mum and I will need to talk about some punishment for this.'

'What for? I've done nothing wrong. Everybody does dope.'

'You won't be doing it anymore. If there are no consequences then it won't stop.'

'You are so naïve. This is pathetic.'

'No, I'll tell you what's pathetic. A bunch of affluent western suburbs kids bunking off school, fucking up their studies and doing dope. That's what's pathetic. There's no noble rebellion in any of this because you've all got parents who'll dig you out of whatever hole you get yourself into.'

The phone buzzed. Stef again. **Wassup?**

'And you haven't got enough real rebellion or independence in you to go out and buy your own bloody gadgets. Meanwhile there are people crying out for the kind of privileges you have. Poor little rich boys. That's what's pathetic.'

'Don't hold back, Dad.'

'Cut the backchat.' Cato wrenched open the fridge door. 'Scrambled eggs for dinner. Okay?'

23

Saturday, August 24th.

Lara Sumich's funeral was a full-dress uniform affair at St George's Cathedral in the city. The Commissioner was there along with the Police Minister and other top brass. Farmer John was there, holding it together, just. Mr and Mrs Sumich and their entourage occupied the front rows. She was a porcelain figurine ready to crack, whereas Oscar Sumich had snapped into professional diplomat mode, pressing the flesh of dignitaries, putting on a show. It would have been nearer to the world he understood. Whatever it takes, mused Cato.

There was a large photo of Lara on an easel in front of the coffin. An earlier picture. In the last few weeks Cato had caught glimpses of a different Lara, one who seemed a whole lot more human, happy, in love. This photo showed no hint of any of that; it showed the self-assured, steely, ambitious Lara. Maybe that was the only Lara her parents got to know, or wanted to know. Certainly Oscar Sumich's eulogy stuck to that script.

She was buried in the family plot in Karrakatta. A kilted police bagpiper had led the funeral procession the last few hundred metres through the tombstones. Cato wasn't sure where the Scottish connection came in but it all sounded and looked quite impressive. The news media certainly got what they came for, including a statement from the Commissioner that the horrific Tan family murders had now been solved and attributed to a business feud involving a Chinese national, since deceased. High fives all round.

'She'll be missed.'

It was DI Pavlou, eyes red-rimmed. Cato wasn't expecting emotion from her. 'Yeah,' he said.

'It's good that you nailed the bastard responsible.'

'The kid? The locals took care of him.'

'Yu Guangming. He was behind it wasn't he? You and that Driscoll fella sorted him.'

Cato shook his head. 'Odds on it came from Thomas Li, or at least his daughter. We'll probably never know.'

'Unfinished business for you, then?'

'Story of my life,' said Cato. 'But I think Lara's death has to mean more than a bit of spin for the Commissioner.' Over Pavlou's shoulder, Cato could see Farmer John being gently led away by rellies. The man was an absolute wreck. 'Lara deserves to rest in peace, not be swept under the carpet.' Cato wondered if he'd gone too far.

Pavlou appraised him. 'You're a good man, Philip, and a good cop. We all know that. But you need to learn to let go of things. Not rock the boat.' She drew a pack of ciggies from her bag and offered him one. He declined. She lit up and blew a plume of smoke towards the heavens. 'Major Crime needs some balance, maybe an injection of integrity and heart. Not too much of course.' She spared him a wry smile. 'The careerists are taking over, they cut corners, give us a bad reputation.' She nodded towards the grave and the mourners drifting away. 'There's a vacancy. Think about it.'

*

Cato got home, changed back into civvies, and drove around to Jane's house in East Fremantle, the house they'd shared when they were still married. It was a large airy old place in King Street with polished wood, open-plan kitchen, lots of natural light. Tasteful art and photographs on the walls and expensive ethnic rugs. He'd dropped Jake there on his way to the funeral and agreed a catch-up time with Jane to discuss their wayward son. Simon, it was agreed, might exacerbate things and would be encouraged to head off to the Men's Shed for an hour or two to make some more cigar-box guitars.

Jane pecked him on the cheek and offered him a coffee. He felt her expanding bump brush his pelvis as she'd leaned into him.

'How was it?' she said.

'Grandiose.'

'You looked good in your uniform when you were dropping Jake.' A mischievous smile, like old times. 'Specially with your macho bruises.'

Cato enjoyed the rare intimacy. 'So, where is he?'

'In his room, sulking, playing some video massacre game, writing soulful poems. Who knows?'

They decided to ground him until the end of term, about four weeks, and confiscate his phone and laptop. No pocket money either.

'What about the parents of the other kids?' said Jane.

'Do you know them? Are you in touch?'

'I see them sometimes at basketball. Maybe I should have a quiet word?'

'Your call, but in the end their kids are their problem. We'll deal with ours, our way.'

'He won't like it.'

'He's not meant to.'

'What if he doesn't stick to it?'

Cato gave it some thought. 'Fingers crossed, he will. We'll cross that bridge if and when.' They discussed Jake's wish to live with Cato and agreed it was a bad idea, he'd be under even less supervision with Cato's erratic hours. But they'd both do their best to pay him a bit more attention. They summoned Jake from his room and gave him the news. He nodded and grunted and went back to his pit when they'd finished.

'Well, that went well,' said Cato.

*

David Mundine's yellow motor scooter was parked outside Hutchens' house when he returned from the funeral. The man himself was sitting on the verandah, messing with his phone.

'Mr H.! Nice threads.'

'You need to leave my property, now.'

'Or?'

'Or I'll make you.'

He wiggled his hands in mock fear. 'Oooh. Scary. Where's your mates today, then?'

'Which mates?'

'The ones you sent round to talk to me.'

'Dunno what you're on about.' Hutchens thumbed over his shoulder. 'Now piss off.'

'Nah. Happy here.'

Hutchens grabbed him by the throat and hauled him to his feet. Mundine went limp, became a dead weight. Hutchens found himself straining, brought in his other hand to share the burden. And felt a claw grip his crotch, digging in deep and twisting. He'd never experienced pain like it.

'Breathe through it, Mr H. Slow and steady. One, two, like that.'

Hutchens was blacking out. He could feel it. The hold he'd had on Mundine changed to a grasp for support.

'That money you sent over has already been banked. You won't find it.' Another twist. Another jolt of agony. 'I'll want more but you need to understand it's not the main game anymore.'

A slight easing of the pressure.

'Do you know what it's like to be alone in the world, Mr H.? To know that nobody is going to help you?' The grip turned into a caress of his groin. 'To come to love your tormentor because he's the only one who really understands you?' Mundine leaned into Hutchens and breathed in his ear. 'You will.'

*

Cato found himself daydreaming about Sharon Wang. He'd been pottering around: tidying up, doing chores, chopping wood for the pot-belly as the clear skies sent the night-time temperatures tumbling. He'd tried playing the piano but wasn't in the mood. It was the weight of Jane's pregnant bump against him that had triggered the thoughts. He missed, and craved, some physical intimacy. There was a kaleidoscope of emotions: at Lara's funeral he'd recalled their brief encounter in a Hopetoun motel room. Then Jane's casual pressing of her weight against him and her musk of motherhood and sexuality. Or was it just him? Dateless and desperate? Either way, it all came back to Sharon Wang.

They hadn't spoken since he'd left China. But that last day, dancing in the park, the lingering kiss. It was like they were already lovers. But they weren't. They were thousands of kilometres apart with no plans to reconnect. They led separate lives. So what was the point of thinking about her?

What was she doing now?

He lifted his mobile, scrolled through and found her number. His thumb hovered over the keypad. He dialled.

'Philip? You okay?'

'Yeah, I just wondered how you were going?'

A brief and, to Cato, awkward silence. 'Good, yeah. You?'

'It was Lara's funeral today.'

'How'd it go?'

'Oh, you know.'

'Yeah.' There were voices in the background. She had company. 'You okay?'

'Pretty much.' Cato heard the murmur of a male voice nearby, saying her name.

'Look, I'm sorry I have to go. You take care, right?'

'Sure,' said Cato. 'You too.'

*

Hutchens was losing it. He was old, fat, out of condition. Past it. And Mundine wasn't going to go away. The bastard had done nothing that warranted official intervention. Nobody was going to solve Hutchens' problem for him.

Do you know what it's like to be alone in the world, Mr H.? To know that nobody is going to help you?

His options were limited. He could take his family with him and run away. But where to? And what was to stop the mad fucker coming back into their lives sometime down the track? Or he could kill Mundine and accept the consequences: the rest of his life in jail.

But at least his family would be safe.

The pain in his chest was getting worse. It was almost constant now. Neither the angina spray nor the tablets could stop it. He was weak, he was useless. He couldn't rid himself of the sour taste of self-loathing.

He went to the bedroom, crawled under the doona and lay there staring at the wall. Gasping at the thin air.

24

Monday, August 26th.

Unfinished business. The Tan murders might have been consigned to the archives but Cato wasn't going to let go. As far as he was concerned the remaining matters were not loose threads or anomalies, they were valid questions that required an answer.

Top of the list: did Des O'Neill's partnership with Yu Guangming have anything to do with the Tan murders? He'd retained a copy of the ACC profile on Francis Tan's finances but while O'Neill's business entity warranted passing mention, his and Yu's dealings were not part of the picture. Wongan Holdings and Suzhou Dragon. Cato googled Wongan first, figuring much of the info on Yu's company would be on Chinese websites and probably in Mandarin.

Wongan Holdings.

Proprietors: Desmond John and Joyce Therese O'Neill. Registered office in Attadale, care of the accountant. No company website. It figured, Des didn't seem the type. News reports. Des shaking hands with cockies and sealing deals to save the family farm. Des with visiting Chinese delegations, one with Francis Tan incorrectly captioned as a potential foreign buyer. Des winning a rural business award. All good news. No sign of anything dodgy, so far.

On the sixth page of the google search it got a shade darker. A family tragedy in the Great Southern. Three years earlier a fourth-generation sheep farmer near Lake Grace, depressed by mounting debts and imminent foreclosure to the banks, had shot his wife and then himself. They left behind a twelve year old son who'd been away at boarding school at the time. Long-time family friend and respected rural businessman Des O'Neill had expressed his horror at the loss and would be administering the estate to ensure the best possible future for the little boy. Was this the same story Des had told him about Francis getting involved personally in a farmer's sorry tale and selling his own house to help fund the bailout? At the time Des had mentioned nothing about his personal link to the family or the scale of the tragedy – a murder-suicide, an orphaned child.

Nothing further. Cato switched over to Suzhou Dragon Enterprises. What little he found on English-language websites was, on the face of it, non-controversial and showed no hint that CEO Yu Guangming was in fact a violent and ruthless gangster. No surprise. The development projects linked to Suzhou Dragon meant nothing to Cato. Who knew what might have happened behind the business headlines? So still nothing from either search that pointed towards the Tan murders.

The next idea was a real forehead-slapper. Why hadn't he already thought of this? He made the call.

'Driscoll.'

'Philip Kwong. WA Police. Remember me?'

'Sure, mate. What can I do for you?'

'Where are you?'

'It's a secret. Why?'

'I was just wondering.'

'Oh, that's okay then. I'm in Canberra talking to some gubbas in suits.'

Best not to know, thought Cato. 'I need your help.'

'Go on.'

'Yu Guangming ran a company called Suzhou Dragon.'

'That's *Soo-joe*, not *Soo-zoo*, just so you know.'

'Thanks.' He laid out his interest in Yu Guangming's dealings, business partnerships, the type of projects plus any associated dirt, and anything on Wongan Holdings. 'That's *Won-gan*,' said Cato. 'Just so you know.'

'I'm a bit busy, mate. Can't your mate Sharon help you out on this?'

'She's got enough on her plate and it sounds like she's already in trouble because of me. I don't want to get her into more.'

'How sweet,' said Driscoll.

'Look Yu's dead, he was a bastard who probably slaughtered a whole family here. I'm not after any state secrets. I don't need any of your spook records unless you judge it to be germane. And you owe me.'

'Do I?'

'Deep inside, you know you do.'

A pause. Maybe he was searching for his conscience, must have left it somewhere. 'I'll get back to you.'

*

Hutchens was on the stand at the Inquiry. He and Joan Peters, the Police Union brief, had been summoned early morning before the retired judge to double-check they were ready for this. They were. Peters had gone first, leading Hutchens down the long and winding road of schtum and no recall. It hadn't taken too long. No, he had no recollection of making such a call to Andy Crouch late that night and no he couldn't explain why Crouch had a record of it in his diary. Maybe to spice up his memoirs which nobody seemed to be interested in? No, he did not know the whereabouts of Peter Sinclair. So, Joan Peters asked, why had Hutchens dismissed David Mundine's allegations?

'It was a different era. These things were often overlooked to our collective shame.' Hutchens lowered his eyes. 'If I knew then what I know now, of course I would have acted differently. As it was, I was an overworked and stressed-out cop with too much on my plate. David was a troubled kid.' He shot a glance towards Mundine in the public gallery. The young man had reverted to quivering victim mode – a remarkable piece of theatre. Hutchens added a little cameo of his own, he allowed his lower lip to tremble. 'I'm sorry.'

He thought he caught the ghost of a smile from Mundine. In the row behind, Crouchie was miming silent applause.

Joan Peters cast her eyes around the room, a throw-net trawling for sympathy and common sense.

Then she handed the floor over to Andrew Burke QC.

'You're a busy and important man, Detective Inspector. I think we all appreciate the demanding job of frontline policing.'

Hutchens didn't respond.

'But if you could bear with us for a while longer I'd like to go through the sequence of events leading up to that night in October nineteen ninety-seven.'

'Be my guest.'

So they trekked once again through the territory already covered by the testimony of David Mundine, the hostel office manager Carol Ransley, and retired police officer Andy Crouch. They were all there in the public gallery, they wouldn't miss this for the world.

'And you have no recollection of your whereabouts that evening of October twenty-first, nineteen ninety-seven?'

'The record shows that I attended a call-out to a disturbance at the Mundaring Weir Hotel but I have no personal recollection of that. I've attended lots of call-outs to pub fights over the years.'

'And you have no recollection of making that phone call to Mr Crouch?'

'No.'

'He indicated that he believed you might have been intoxicated at the time.'

'That's what he says in his journal, yes.'

'Did you have a problem with alcohol during that period?'

'I was a younger man, an occasional heavy drinker, in those days it went with the job.' Hutchens shrugged. 'We all get older, we grow up, leave behind the misdemeanours of youth.'

'Of course we do.' Burke checked his paperwork. 'And you must have been particularly motivated to do so, having received two cautions and a reprimand over the course of the preceding six months?'

'That's right,' said Hutchens.

'Your superiors have noted, on the record, quote, "that while DS Hutchens has an excellent track record for getting results, of late his excessive alcohol consumption has increasingly impaired his professionalism". Unquote. What did they mean by that?'

'Probably what it says. But if you're after details you'll need to ask them. To my knowledge there are no further such cautions or reprimands on my record.'

'Apart from the Beaton problem.'

He should have seen that coming, really. The wrongful conviction of a man for murder which had seen him transferred to Albany and Cato demoted into Stock Squad. For the benefit of the Inquiry and the public gallery and, of course, the news media, Burke replayed it in all its sordid detail.

Hutchens squared his shoulders. 'My recollection of the internal inquiry at the time noted a general cultural and systemic problem which contributed to the inappropriate procedures and processes. Problems which have since been addressed.'

'And you were at the heart of those cultural and systemic problems, were you not?'

At this point Joan Peters stood up and asked how relevant any of this was to the matter of an inquiry into sexual abuse at the Hillsview Hostel during the late 1990s.

The Inquiry chair concurred and asked Burke to get to the point.

'My point is that there was an officer with an ongoing record of alcoholism, unprofessionalism, and corrupt practices at the heart of both the inaction on the abuse allegations and the subsequent disappearance of Peter Sinclair.'

'That's a bit harsh,' said Hutchens. But he sensed victory, of sorts. It was all fluff and mudslinging but, without a body, they were fucked. They had nothing. He exchanged a look with Joan Peters. She knew it too, the twinkle said it all.

*

While he waited for Driscoll to get back to him, Cato delegated some jobs out to the minions. The weekend had thrown up the usual assaults, drug charges, thefts, and such – the volume crime that never went away and remained the essence of his job. Deb Hassan was back on duty, duly counselled about her people skills and awaiting the result of a professional standards inquiry into her tasering of Zac Harvey's mum. The likely outcome would be an official reprimand

and if that didn't suit Mrs Harvey, she'd have to take civil action to remedy the matter. Cato had a job for Deb.

'Can you line up the Soong sisters, Lily and Matilda? Separately. I'd like to hear precisely what triggered Matthew's recent hissy fit.' He brought her up to date with developments. 'Maybe it was just soggy toast or lukewarm coffee. Maybe there's something worth a look.'

'You haven't given up on him, then?'

'No, not yet. If they're wondering, just tell them we're tidying up the paperwork. Take Chris Thornton with you. Just in case.'

'Just in case what?'

'Occ Health and Safety. It's a toss-up. Matthew might hit you with a spanner or you might zap him with your ray gun. Just covering my back, I don't need the paperwork.'

'Thanks, sarge,' she muttered on the way out.

His desk phone went.

'Is there a guy called Kwong there?' The caller sounded about thirteen.

'That's me, who wants to know?'

Her name was Tracey and she was in fact a senior corrections officer from Bandyup. She'd gone through the visitors log and tracked him down. 'Patricia Mundine, one of our clients, remembered talking to some Chinese bloke last week, that'd be you I guess, and she wanted us to pass on a message.' All of Tracey's sentences ended on an upward questioning inflection.

'Go on.'

'She said the bloke's name was Paul.'

'Which bloke?'

'The old boyfriend. She said you'd know. Something to do with the son?'

'Paul what?'

'Just Paul.'

He thanked her, gave her his mobile contact as an alternative, and ended the call. One day another synapse might spark and Tricia would remember Paul's surname. Or maybe not. Cato got on with his life.

Hutchens had a celebratory lunch with Joan Peters. They found a Thai place in the city and got stuck into the massaman and the green chicken. He even stumped up for two glasses of SSB from Marlborough.

'Cheers,' he said.

'Cheers, dear.' They clinked.

'You were right. They had nothing.'

'I don't think you're out of the woods yet. They could still bring out an adverse finding against you.'

He grunted and forked some beef. 'Least of my worries.'

Peters looked concerned. 'Why's that, dear?'

Hutchens smiled reassuringly. 'Nothing. I think I'm on the home straight now.'

She didn't seem convinced. 'Maybe you should take a few days leave? You've been through a lot of stress lately.'

'I've been thinking the same thing myself,' he beamed. 'Few days in the country, do me the world of good.'

Peters lifted her glass again. 'I'll drink to that.'

Their phones buzzed simultaneously. They took their respective calls.

'Fuck,' said Hutchens after a moment.

'Shit,' said Peters, round about the same time.

*

Driscoll got back to Cato way earlier than expected.

'Nothing.'

'Nothing?'

'Yup.'

Cato didn't believe it and he told him so.

'Don't blame you, mate. I don't believe it either.'

'There has to be something, however banal or innocuous.'

'I know.'

'So?'

'It's piqued my interest. I've seen this kind of thing before. There's a black PR company based in Shanghai. Its name translated means something like "Born Free".'

Driscoll explained. Black PR companies offered a service probably only possible somewhere like China. Officials fearing an impending corruption inquiry could pay to have themselves deleted from the internet, to clear up their reputations and be reborn, free. But it wasn't cheap. Money was required to bribe webpage editors and if it happened to be a government site the fee would of course be higher. Censorship notices, real or fake, could be issued to give the deletion an official-seeming imprimatur. All for a hefty price. It could only work in a regime where there was strict control over the internet and over the population. Beautifully Orwellian. The Ministry of Truth. Turning yourself into an unperson. Neat.

'So you think Suzhou Dragon has had itself whitewashed?'

'I have my suspicions.'

'You'd have to be pretty worried about something to go to those lengths.'

'Yep.'

'Anything we can do to find out what?'

'Leave it with me. Are you around for a while? Not going away anywhere?'

'No. Why?'

'I've got to be in Perth by tomorrow night. A training course with the SAS at Swanbourne Barracks.'

'I won't ask.'

'Best not.' He severed the connection.

Cato felt the first stirrings of hope that he might finally be getting closer to the truth behind the Tan murders.

*

It was on the radio news as Hutchens headed back down the freeway. As a result of recent publicity surrounding the Hillsview Hostel Inquiry, police had received an anonymous tip-off in connection to a related missing persons case dating back to 1997. They were now scouring bushland in an area of John Forrest National Park near Mundaring.

'Mundine. Has to be,' he muttered to himself.

His phone buzzed. A text from the devil himself.

good show 2day

Hutchens didn't reply. Another followed.

wheres the family?

He didn't bite.

X marks the spot

So he did know what became of Sinclair. He hadn't been bluffing.

catch you later then

The bastard must be on one of those unlimited SMS plans. He resisted the temptation to text back – **get a fucking life, weirdo**. The way things were going, Mundine might just do that.

Things moved quickly after that. Within an hour of getting back to Fremantle he got a call from Major Crime. DI Pavlou no less.

'There's signs of old earth disturbance at the spot the tip-off gave us. We'll be bringing in the cadaver dogs and GPR.' Ground penetrating radar. He detected genuine sympathy in Pavlou's voice. 'We'll probably want to speak to you soon, Mick. Maybe tomorrow, on the record, to set the ball rolling.'

'No worries,' he said.

He felt the first jolt just after he put the phone down. He'd thought it might be static or something. Or indigestion from the Thai lunch. Another across his chest, his arm and shoulders numb, everything tight. He felt hot. Nauseous. He sank to his knees. Jesus, he thought. This is it.

25

Tuesday, August 27th.

Cato had heard the commotion from his office across the corridor. A uniform was giving Hutchens CPR while another yelled down the phone for an ambulance. All the time Cato was thinking that this was inevitable, he'd seen it coming and he'd done nothing about it. All attempts to contact Hutchens' wife and family had so far come to nothing. His boss had removed them from his phone and email contacts. What was that about? A falling out? The bloke had been under huge pressure lately so family tensions were not an impossibility. Cato suspected something else. Like the clients of Born Free, the black PR company in Shanghai, had Hutchens erased his family from the record? He feared something, and that something was very probably David Mundine.

Hutchens had tried to convince him that he could handle Mundine, and that everything was under control. But all he ever did was get pinker and tighter and shinier until he burst.

Hutchens was now in intensive care on the fifth floor of Fremantle Hospital. In the absence of family it was Cato who'd stayed at his bedside all night. According to the cardiologist, Hutchens had been lucky. What he'd had was a warning, something that could be mitigated with medication, stents and, down the track, a bypass operation. Hutchens' phone had buzzed in the small hours of the morning.

Why aren't you at home?

Cato had assumed it was Mrs Hutchens or one of the daughters.

He'd tried to phone the number but nobody had answered. So he'd texted instead.

In hospital. Heart scare

The reply. **LOL**

Mundine.

Cato now had a new project.

*

By breakfast time he was exhausted. Sleep in the armchair next to Hutchens' bed had been fitful at best. He grabbed a coffee and a chocolate bar from the machine along the hall and made some calls. According to the GPR results, DI Pavlou definitely had some human remains on her hands up at John Forrest so she was naturally sceptical about the turn of events and wondering if Hutchens was just trying it on. Cato put her straight, he tried explaining about the threats against Hutchens and his family. She definitely wasn't buying into that and saw no need to increase security at the hospital. They couldn't spare the manpower.

'Where's the evidence against Mundine? This is a victim of child sexual abuse. Do you realise what you're saying here? He's also a weedy little bloke who happens to be testifying against Hutchens at the Inquiry.' Pavlou was resolute. 'It's not a good look, mate. No way.'

Cato had to let it go.

Her parting shot. 'This might be a sign, Philip. I can't see Mick getting back to work any time soon. Maybe this is your opportunity to move on?'

That was another thing. They were left with a serious hole in the leadership team at Freo Detectives. Ordinarily Cato himself should have stepped into the breach but he might be the only thing standing between Mundine and the patient along the hall. He'd have to organise a protection roster – himself, Hassan and Thornton – and he'd need to juggle a few balls in the air to keep the office functioning. He was almost tempted to let Mundine get through and do his worst. Maybe that would convince the powers that be to take this seriously.

When he returned to the room there was a new vase of flowers. Daffodils. And a card with a message: **Get Well Soon, Mr H.**

*

David Mundine checked the fridge and found some cold meats, mustard and posh heart-tick marge. There was half a loaf of sliced wholegrain in the bread box. He got himself a plate and knife and put together a few ham sandwiches, flicking the kettle on while he worked. He settled at the kitchen table, dragging out a second chair to rest his feet, and sorted through Hutchens' mail.

The marigold gloves made the letter opening a bit fumbly. First, the credit card statement. He took a note of the details, number, expiry, et cetera. The list of purchases was pretty mundane: restaurants, weekly groceries, wine delivery, Bunnings. Boring. A letter from the Salvos asking for a donation for 'at risk' youth. Mundine felt generous. He gave them a thousand bucks, filled out Hutchens' credit card details and shoved the slip in the reply paid. He'd post it on his way home. Gas bill. Phone bill. He made a note of the second mobile, Mrs H.'s no doubt. He also noted some of the more commonly called numbers. Maybe one of them would be the lovely Melanie. He looked at her photo on the fridge door. Very tasty. No address book next to the phone like you usually see. Maybe Mr H. was being clever. Next to the photo of Melanie there was one of Mrs H. and some oldies, her folks no doubt. It was by a river. He recognised the place, it was the mouth of the Blackwood down at Augusta. Lovely spot. He'd been there a few times and always meant to go back.

He went through to the bedrooms. Nothing of real interest in the grown-ups' room. A glass on the bedside table. He sniffed it. Whisky. Mr H.'s nightcap. He checked the other rooms. A study for Mrs H., the ghost of some strong perfume. He wrinkled his nose. Next, Melanie's old bedroom perhaps, or the other younger daughter, some clothes still in the walk-in. And some undies in a drawer. He pressed them to his face. Contemplated a wank but decided against it. DNA.

Mundine returned to the kitchen, washed the dishes and

stacked them. Wiped down a few surfaces. He put Mr and Mrs H.'s laptops in his backpack and left. Then he had a thought. He doubled back, found the box of wine deliveries in the laundry and selected a nice shiraz.

*

Deb Hassan took over from Cato by late morning. She updated him on the Soong sisters along the way.

'Lily's not giving us anything. She's too scared of Matt, she has to keep living with him.'

'Why? She could just leave him.'

'For some women it's not that simple. Anyway, whatever her reasons, she's saying she doesn't remember anything. Matilda's a bit more interesting, though.'

'Yeah?'

'By the way have you seen those two in the same room together? Creepy. Like Dolly the Sheep.'

Cato was desperate for some sleep. He needed brevity. Hassan caught the look in his eyes.

'So, Matilda, yeah. She reckons Matt was running off at the mouth when he was drinking himself senseless at her place.'

Cato yawned. 'And?'

'He hates Lily. He wants to leave her, can't stand her materialism and neediness, apparently.'

'This is the same guy who drives a new BMW at the age of nineteen, doesn't seem to have a job, and bullies his mum for more money?'

'That's him. Matilda reckons little sister has a bit of a coke habit and Matthew is covering her debts. That's why he's getting into deeper shit.'

'So why doesn't he cast her adrift?'

'Matilda reckons he's too much of a softie.'

'Do I detect an agenda with Matilda?'

'Yeah, she's screwing Matt too. On an as-needs basis.'

'Keep me posted,' said Cato stifling another yawn. He gestured back at Hutchens, still out for the count. 'Nobody gets in here unless they're a doctor or a nurse.'

'What about the tea lady and the cleaners?'

'Check their IDs first.'

'Do we have any pictures of this Mundine character?'

'I'm working on it.'

Hassan checked her Glock and took a seat by the bed. 'Gives me the willies being back here, like this.'

Cato sympathised. Two years earlier Hassan had been one of two guards on a suspect requiring medical attention. A brief lapse in concentration and a visit to the coffee machine along the hall had allowed the suspect to escape. But not before doing enough damage to Hassan's colleague to see him invalided out of the job.

'Two hours and I'll be back.'

She gave him a reassuring smile. 'Take longer, Chris Thornton's all set for the next shift.'

Cato left. He felt anxious, he felt guilty, he felt very tired.

*

His mobile woke him. He felt like he'd only had about five minutes sleep but when he checked the time he realised it was a couple of hours. The number didn't register.

'Is that Kwong?'

'Yes.'

'It's Tracey from Bandyup.'

They exchanged brief pleasantries and Tracey got to the point.

'Patricia remembered the rest of that name. Morrison. Paul Morrison.'

'That's it?'

'No, mate, she's excelled herself. It's those healthy lifestyle classes we're putting on. She's detoxed and dynamite, today, bouncing around like the Duracell Bunny.'

'Go on,' said Cato, trying to mirror her positivity.

'Well,' she said, as if settling in for a long story. 'Tricia reckons this Morrison bloke died a nasty death.'

'Any details? When? Where?'

Tracey tutted. 'One day at a time, mate.'

*

David Mundine checked the news websites on Hutchens' laptop when he got home. Mrs H.'s was password-protected so he'd chucked hers in the bin. Breaking news on the ABC was that human remains had been confirmed at the John Forrest National Park and that the area was now a crime scene.

Of course it was.

Nothing in the news about Mr H. and his heart problems.

He opened up the desktop mail application. The emails were personal non-work stuff. Hutchens must keep all that in the office, a good sign of a healthy work–life balance, although that must have got out of kilter a bit lately. The emails were between him and various family members, some mates in the yacht club arranging a weekend out on the water, the wine website sending him special offers. The ones between family were all dated at least a month earlier, nothing since. Everything since then had been yachties and wine and other boring stuff. Mr H. had been tidying up after himself. He must have foreseen something like this, a loss of control over his personal life, his destiny. One way or another it comes to us all eventually. He was trying to shield his family from exposure to danger. So the more recent ones he'd deleted must have had useful information in them, like contact details, possible whereabouts. But people of Mr H.'s generation always make mistakes, too old and stupid to fully understand computers, the internet and stuff. Too lazy to completely cover their tracks. Too arrogant to believe anyone could bring them down.

Mundine found it not long after. An email chain between Hutchens and an old school friend of Mrs H. about a surprise birthday bash for his wife six months ago. The old friend expressing wonder at the passage of time and how the girl they'd all known as Marjorie Coucher had weathered the years well. Now that he had a maiden name, he ran a White Pages search and located a number and address for the Couchers in Augusta. He rang it. A woman answered.

'Marjorie?' he said.

'No, this is her mother. She's out at the moment. Can I take a message?'

'No worries. I'll call again, later.' He put the phone down.

*

Cato took over from Chris Thornton mid-afternoon. Nothing to report, he'd said, apart from the fact that he might have fallen in love with one of the nurses on the afternoon shift. Keisha from Warnbro.

Cato didn't encourage him. 'Any sign of life from the boss?'

'He woke up an hour or so ago, gave me a funny look and went back to sleep. Deb said he'd had some food and liquid late morning and they changed his drip. Seems to be zonked out on something or other.'

Before they parted company Cato asked Thornton to run a check on any murder, manslaughter, or otherwise suspicious death cases involving a Paul Morrison.

'How far back and where?'

'Let's assume metro area for now and widen it if nothing turns up.' He did some mental arithmetic and plumped for the last fifteen years.

'That's quite a stretch. What's it related to?'

Cato told him. 'And we need a discrete look at Mundine himself. Not just his charge sheet but also his movements over the same period: jobs, education, training et cetera. But we've got to be careful. So far he's done nothing, so us digging dirt on him on the boss's behalf won't look good at the Inquiry.'

'I'll see what I can do.'

'Finally,' Cato held up a finger. 'Peter Sinclair: a résumé of his misdeeds.'

'The hostel pervo?' Cato confirmed as much. 'Anything else?'

'Not for now.'

With Thornton gone Cato settled into the bedside chair. His boss's face had changed over the last forty-eight hours. The pink tightness had been replaced by grey slackness. Hutchens looked old. Cato wondered if his boss would return to work after an ordeal like this – assuming the issues of the Inquiry and Mundine were successfully resolved.

The passivity of the situation was getting to Cato. He needed to be out hunting Mundine down, not waiting here for something that may or may not happen.

Hutchens stirred, opening one eye then the other. 'Every time I look up it's a new face. Is this a test or something?'

Cato smiled. It was a relief to hear shades of the old Hutchens. He offered him a drink of water.

'I don't think there's any need for this.'

'The water?' said Cato.

'The guardian-angel thing. That's not the way Mundine works. This is too public, too direct.'

'Better safe than sorry.'

'Yeah, thanks, but there's an office to run.'

'We've got it covered. And they're sending a relief DI to cover from tomorrow.'

'Who? Not Pavlou?'

'No, she's a bit busy.' On the body in John Forrest park, no doubt. 'A bloke from Midland. Jimmy Spittle?'

'Wanker,' said Hutchens.

'I don't know him,' shrugged Cato.

'What's the latest on the body?'

'Digging it up as we speak. I think Pavlou's hoping to have all the bits in place by day's end and then they'll start running the tests.' Cato lifted his chin at Hutchens and the beeping machines. 'Have the doctors spoken to you yet?'

'Yeah, they'll keep me in for a day or two more, gradually wean me off the jungle juice and send me home with some tablets and an appointment to get some plumbing done on the arteries.'

'We've tried contacting Marjorie and the kids but we couldn't find the numbers.'

'They've been changed.'

Cato told him about the text message that he believed had been from Marjorie and was in fact from Mundine. 'And he probably sent those flowers.' Cato waved at the daffodils.

'Bin them.'

Cato did. Hutchens located his wallet and dug out a slip of paper. 'Marjorie's number. Tell her I'm okay and to stay where she is.'

'Where is she?'

'Augusta, with her folks. Melanie's there as well.'

Cato tried to remember the name of the other daughter. Hutchens saved him the trouble. 'Don't worry. She's in Europe on her gap year. Not due back for months.'

Cato told him about the calls from Bandyup, about Tricia's old boyfriend Paul Morrison.

'And?'

'I've got Thornton looking at it.'

'How's everything else?'

'In hand,' said Cato.

Hutchens' lower lip trembled. 'You're a good bloke, you know that?' He took a shaky sip of water. 'Times like this, you really need someone to rely on.'

*

Deb Hassan resumed the seat late afternoon as the sun dropped, clouds gathered, and a wicked wind kicked in. Heading back to the office, bracing against sudden strong gusts, Cato phoned Marjorie Hutchens. She took some convincing not to drop everything and drive right back to Fremantle that instant.

'Was that you trying to ring earlier?' she asked.

'I don't think so.'

'Never mind. My mum said someone called and would ring back later.'

'On this number? The mobile?'

'No, the landline.' A pause. 'Why? Do you think it could be that weirdo?'

Cato sought to reassure her. 'I can't see how he would have got the number. It's probably nothing.'

'Well if it is that bastard, he'd better be fucking sure of himself, my dad's got a .303 and he'll use it on the arsehole.'

They say that if you live with someone long enough you begin to take on their characteristics. It was certainly so with Mrs Hutchens. He wished her well and rang off.

Thornton had done a trawl on dead Paul Morrisons and left the results in Cato's inbox. There were three: two in the metro area and one in Albany on the south coast. The first was a one-punch killing in a brawl in Leederville twelve years earlier. The victim, twenty-nine, cracked his skull when he landed on the footpath. Cato did the maths and decided he was probably too young. The second was a Paul Scott Morrison, aged forty-nine, who'd died in a suspected arson attack in Bassendean nine years ago. Finally Paul Joseph Morrison, fifty-three, had been beaten to death in his caravan at a semi-permanent site on the outskirts of Albany four years earlier. The last two showed promise, in terms of age group and timing and the nastiness of their deaths. Cato asked for more on each. There was nothing so far on Mundine's or Peter Sinclair's respective histories. That would have to wait until tomorrow.

He made a call to Deb Hassan. 'How's he looking?'

'He's eating his dinner, giving the nurse a hard time, and not far from his old self.' Some words exchanged over a hand-muffled phone. 'He wants to speak to you.'

The phone was passed over to Hutchens.

'Let the poor woman go home to her family, Cato. This is a waste of time.'

They discussed it further for a minute or two then Cato relented. 'Put me back on to Deb.'

'Yeah?' she said after the rustling.

'Go home. The boss is right, we can't sustain this.'

'Are you sure? It's no problem at all for me to stay. I've already made arrangements on the domestics.'

'It's fine. But leave him your gun just in case.'

'Is that allowed?'

'Do we care?'

Cato felt a presence at his shoulder. Hot breath in his ear. 'Well hello,' the voice said.

*

'Geez, you're jumpy,' said Rory Driscoll.

He was right, Cato's pulse was taking a while to steady. 'How did you get past reception?'

'Winning smile and a get-into-jail free card. Any chance of a coffee?'

Driscoll looked different. He'd swapped the Hawaiian shirt and boardies for smart winter casual and had a haircut and a shave. They adjourned to the departmental kitchen. It was less poky than the one in the old offices, this place did once belong to a bank after all. Cato put the kettle on. 'So, any news?'

'Our friend Yu and your friend Des were involved in a luxury housing development near Shanghai.'

'Yep, near a place called Songjiang, an extension of Thames Town, I knew that already.'

'The site they chose was not part of the original Thames Town.'

'Right.' Cato couldn't hide his impatience. 'Cambridge Gardens.'

'Sounds classy, doesn't it? Saw the photos on the website.'

'The reality was somewhat less shiny.'

'Did you know a fair chunk of the surrounding area had been bought up by Thomas Li?'

'Yes, he pointed it out to me. He was having trouble with a bunch of stubborn residents whose homes were being demolished. They brought some thugs in to move them on. A few people got badly hurt. The son of one of those victims killed Lara.'

'You're better informed than I thought. Sharon kept you in the loop, did she?'

'Until I left Shanghai.' Cato dished out the coffee.

Driscoll took a thoughtful sip from his mug. 'Stubborn residents weren't Li's only problem. Cambridge Gardens got in the way of Li's grand plans for a major development: a mini city, homes for something like half a million people. All spoilt by Yu's little enclave.'

'And?'

'Yu and O'Neill were set to make a killing. Li had agreed to their hugely inflated buy-out price. We're talking gazillions here. But the deal stalled.'

'Why?'

'Don't know yet. But if your mate Tan was involved it might be worth murdering for.'

*

That evening Cato popped around to his sister's in the hope of catching the old man. He'd taken a quick detour along the coast and dropped Driscoll at a house in Cottesloe. Ocean views and the stench of money. And it didn't look like it had been lived in for a long time.

'Yours?' said Cato.

'Friend. Thanks for the lift. Catchya later.'

The ocean foamed and the usual evidence of shipping lights, the navigation channels, and the Rottnest lighthouses had disappeared behind a curtain of rain. Once again he found himself stamping his feet on Mandy's welcome mat to shake off the excess drops.

'Dad's asleep.'

'At seven?'

'He's a free spirit, not constrained by the same things that hold us fast.'

'How's that creative writing course of yours going?'

'Piss off. Want some wine?'

They adjourned to the kitchen where Kenneth was trying to supervise the children's chores. It seemed even putting stuff in the dishwasher was way too much effort for their pre-pubescent oldest boy. The girl was showing unusually great interest in world events on ABC news while little Bao bashed an upturned pan with a wooden spoon. Kenneth mimed shooting himself in the temple and took a swig of wine.

Mand led Cato over to a less chaotic sitting area and handed him a shiraz.

'How was China?'

Cato told her about Lara.

'That job of yours. I don't know how you do it.' She touched his still bruised face. 'Are you okay?'

'On the mend.' He took a sip of wine. 'Any developments with Dad?'

'I had him at the doctor's yesterday. He wanted to know whether we'd made any decisions about keeping him at home or putting him in a hospice.'

'We didn't really settle anything on that, did we?'

'No. Any strong views?'

Cato shook his head. 'I suppose I'd want him to be close to family. But I know that in reality that means business as usual for you. What do you think?'

'Same. I want him here. Kenneth is with us on that.' She raised her glass and blew a kiss in his direction. 'That right, love?'

Kenneth was lying on the kitchen floor playing with Bao. A momentary lapse of concentration while he responded to Mandy cost him his wine as Bao's wooden spoon found its target. The explosion of glass was loud but luckily no casualties. Kenneth plopped a tearful Bao on Mandy's lap, smiled, and went off to get the dustpan and brush.

'It's settled then,' said Mand, chuckling Bao's chins.

'What about Susie?' said Cato.

'She'll think what we tell her.'

As Mand refocused her formidable determination back onto her immediate brood Cato felt a pang of pity for Susie. He could see why she sometimes kept her distance. The yin and yang of family. Strength and support one day, claustrophobia and control the next.

229

26

Wednesday, August 28th.

Cato got to the office early, parking down near the Roundhouse a few hundred metres away and hurrying back through the drizzle. Chris Thornton was already there and directed him to his email inbox.

'The gen on Mundine and Sinclair.' He grimaced. 'Not pretty.'

Cato grabbed himself a mug of tea and logged on. In fact a few other emails had crept ahead of the queue. DI James Spittle would be joining them from mid-morning following a briefing with Area Command at HQ and with DI Pavlou about the current shared caseload. He then wanted a meeting with Cato at 10.30. Cato let him know he'd be there.

He checked into the overnight incident log to make sure there were no surprises ahead of the meeting with the new DI. Luckily the rain had kept people indoors. There were fewer street incidents but an increase in domestics and a couple of burglaries, nothing out of the ordinary. He returned to his emails. Another from Pavlou asking if he'd seen the Major Crime vacancy list: there were two now with Lara gone and James Maloney not coming back. The deadline for an expression of interest was a week Friday. Cato studied the email. She was pushy. So why hadn't he already turned her down? He was fine where he was. He didn't need the politics and compromises that would come with such a job. His boss was in a hospital bed, he'd come close to death. Loyalty had to still count for something.

Times like this, you really need someone to rely on.

Cato closed the email. But he didn't delete it.

Chris Thornton's homework.

Peter Sinclair first. Sinclair was a cleanskin. No criminal record or police interest right up to and including the Hillsview Hostel scandal. No red flags from any social workers. The allegations at Hillsview were appalling: rape, torture, degradation. His victims as young as nine and as old as fifteen. Control had been maintained with tried and trusted methods: violence, threats and intimidation on the one hand, alcohol and drugs on the other. Some boys, now men, requiring a colostomy bag as a result of the anal tearing. There were six known victims who had lodged complaints – all ignored at the time – and were now appearing before the Inquiry. Among them was David Mundine.

As Cato had already gleaned, David Mundine had a troubled childhood. It can't have been easy growing up with Tricia Mundine as your mother. Chris Thornton, courtesy of a mole in the Child Protection Department, had pieced together what he could of the Mundine jigsaw. After he left Hillsview Hostel to return to the bosom of his family, David had continued petty offending, mixing drugs and alcohol to destructive effect. He'd had a couple of spells in the mental hospital at Graylands and at the Alma Street psych unit attached to Freo Hospital. He hadn't managed to hold down any jobs or education and was now claiming some kind of invalid pension after persuading a succession of doctors and psychs to sign the appropriate paperwork. A de facto, Lisa Gangemi, had taken a restraining order out on him a few years previously. She'd disappeared but Chris Thornton was following her up.

On paper, Mundine was the classic victim and the typical screw-up. Society was rife with such people, dysfunctional families crossing paths with dysfunctional organisations and each in the line of sight of determined predators. Result: yet another lost generation. Some folded up, turning the destruction wrought on them inwards. And some, like Mundine, turned the rage outwards wreaking new havoc. Somehow Mundine had bested Mick Hutchens, a seasoned police veteran with a tough reputation. How come? Where did he acquire the social and people skills and the street smarts to pull all this off? Maybe Hutchens was simply past it. Cato didn't think so. He reread Mundine's career highlights. After Hillsview he never returned to school, segueing seamlessly onto unemployment benefit and a whole bunch of life skills courses that he failed to turn up to. Except one: an IT course where he hung in there for the full week and was even issued a certificate of attendance. There was a scan of it attached. The signature on the certificate was an illegible scrawl with no printed name included. The course was called 'Let's Get Digital!' and had been held at a community centre in Maylands early in 2003 by which time David would have been about twenty. There were no further details but obviously it was enough to light a spark in Mundine. Completing the course was a rare upward blip in his curriculum vitae of ongoing failure. Cato tapped out a note to Thornton to see if he could find out more. A year or so later, he'd had another success. Mundine managed to pass his driving test. After that he pretty much reverted to character.

Deb Hassan stood in his doorway.

'Busy?'

'What is it?'

'One of the burglaries in the overnight log?'

Cato lifted his head and didn't like the look on Hassan's face.

'The boss's house.'

*

Cato and Hassan did a walk through. There was very little damage; indeed Cato got the distinct impression the burglar had actually tidied up. The place was cleaner than his own home.

'A neighbour found the back door ajar. She's used to going down the side if nobody hears her. Saw the damage around the lock and called us.'

'Anything obviously missing?'

'There's no laptops anywhere.' She pointed at the flashing box beside the landline phone. 'But there's a wireless modem.' She led him to the kitchen table, to the small stack of opened mail. 'And there's this. The postmark is yesterday, when the boss was in hospital.' And his family already in Augusta, thought Cato. 'Otherwise plenty of valuables, jewellery et cetera, even some cash, all untouched.'

'Mundine.'

'Do we tell the boss?'

Cato was torn. The bloke didn't need the added stress but he did need to know that Mundine had been through his house and may have found whatever it was he was looking for.

'I'll do it.'

She nodded. 'One more thing.' She led him into a bedroom off the hallway that seemed to serve more as a temporary storage room. In a walk-in wardrobe some clothes hung on hangers. A cupboard drawer was left open. It contained underwear, untidily rummaged through and hanging half out of the drawer. A pair of panties lay on the carpet.

*

Hutchens wanted to unplug himself there and then and hit the streets. Cato persuaded him to wait for the all-clear from the specialist due later that morning.

'I've sent Deb Hassan and a couple of cars round to that Jolimont address you gave me. We've got enough to bring him in, now.'

Hutchens eyed Deb Hassan's Glock on his bedside cabinet. 'Not good enough. He has to be stopped.'

Cato laid a reassuring hand on Hutchens shoulder. 'We're on it, boss.'

Cato took a call on his mobile from Deb Hassan.

'He's not there. A neighbour saw him go off on his scooter a couple of hours ago.'

'Put out an alert,' said Cato.

'Do we have grounds? According to Duncan Goldflam he left no significant traces at the burglary. Maybe some drool on the undies but it's low on the lab priority list. If it is him we'll probably not know until next month.'

Cato cut her off. 'If I'm wrong, I'll wear it.'

'No worries. There is one positive. We found a laptop in his wheelie bin. Could be the boss's.'

Cato passed it on.

'What make?' said Hutchens.

A short delay and a rustle. 'Toshiba.'

'That's Marjorie's. He must still have mine. An HP.'

'Anything on there to worry about?' asked Cato.

'It's not got a password, they give me the shits. But I did clear off anything about Augusta or about Marjorie's contact details.'

'Sure?'

Hutchens looked doubtful. 'That stuff's never been my strong point.'

Cato was aware he had a meeting in half an hour with the new DI; acting, he had to keep reminding himself. He farewelled Hassan and extracted a promise from Hutchens not to leave the hospital without the doctor's okay. A phone rang, this time it belonged to Hutchens. A typically terse conversation ensued. Hutchens' contribution was two 'yep's and a 'right'.

The call ended and Cato raised his eyebrows in query.

'Pavlou wants to talk to me.' He chucked his phone back on the bedside cabinet. 'The bones in the bush are Peter Sinclair.'

*

'How's Mick?'

DI Jimmy Spittle was tall and lean with a greying buzz cut. He was the same vintage as Hutchens, pushing fifty, but looked ten years younger. A product of regular sport and careful diet. He was a genial enough bloke and didn't seem to warrant Hutchens' unkind assessment of 'wanker'. Maybe that was Hutchens' default position on humanity in general and why he was in so much trouble right now.

'Bearing up,' said Cato.

'Good to hear. So what do you need from me?'

A helpful manager who showed concern for his colleagues. It was a good start.

'We offloaded some jobs to Murdoch last week. Not a lot has come in since then. I think the bad weather helps.'

'So?'

'Some leeway on the reporting and stats timetable.' If Hutchens' crop of misfortunes served as an excuse to lift the administrative burden that dogged modern policing then it would all have been worthwhile.

'No worries,' said Spittle.

'Can I speak to you in confidence, boss?'

'Sure.'

Cato told him about Hutchens, the Inquiry, and about David Mundine. While it wasn't exactly part of his caseload, he wanted to be able to do whatever it took to watch his boss's back. A free-ish rein would be nice.

Spittle appraised him, resting his chin on steepled hands. 'Keep me in the picture,' he said. 'If it becomes too much of a problem I'll jerk your leash.' Cato thanked him and stood to go. 'Sandra Pavlou tells me she's got her eye on you. I can see why, now. That kind of loyalty and honesty is in short supply these days.'

Cato found himself unaccountably blushing.

Spittle smiled. 'Does Mick know you're contemplating pastures new?'

*

David Mundine hadn't driven in over a year. His mum's Datsun stank of her cigarettes and old woman pong. It whined like a needy junkie whenever he put his foot down. At this rate he wouldn't make Augusta before dark. Then he'd have fucking kangaroos to worry about. He'd avoided the freeway and Forrest Highway and stuck to the old coast road for as long as possible, figuring any police interest would focus first on the fastest road south. He was just past the Dawesville Cut, south of Canalsville, and he knew there was a roadhouse not far away. He remembered the first time he'd gone there. He was eight and his mum had gone to pay for the petrol and buy some Chiko rolls and choc milk. Paulie had snatched the opportunity while she was away to make David rub his dick. Mundine felt himself get hard at the memory. He'd learned to control his self-disgust.

He pulled into Dawesville roadhouse, in the same parking space they always used. The one Paulie liked, just around the corner out of sight. He didn't need fuel, he'd filled up back in the metro area and was good now until at least Margaret River. He pulled the peak of his baseball cap down low, ducked his head and entered the shop. The place was empty, struggling for business with all the traffic now going down the new road. He knew where the cameras were, high on the wall, and made sure they wouldn't get a good look at him. He bought a Chiko roll and a choc chill for old time's sake and gave the old slapper a wink on the way out. His hard-on wouldn't go away.

He went into the toilets and jerked it off.

*

By mid-afternoon they located Mundine's scooter. It was parked near East Perth railway station. From there you could take buses or trains down south to Bunbury and then connections on to Augusta. Thornton and Hassan checked with the various ticket sellers and took a look at the CCTV footage. Two hours later they still had no fix on him. Colleagues down south had been alerted to wait at bus and train stops along the way to intercept arriving passengers or, if he'd already arrived earlier, to try and pick up his trail. The Augusta desk sergeant said that day's bus had already arrived and the passengers dispersed. If Mundine was on it they weren't any the wiser, so far. Cato asked them to park a car outside the Couchers' home.

'That's not as simple as it sounds, mate.'

'Why?'

'They're in East Augusta, over the river. The road in there is a big detour back through the bush. It's a couple of hundred metres swim but we're talking fifty-odd kilometres by road.'

'So do it anyway,' said Cato. 'Please.'

'Sure, but it's bucketing down here. If your mate's on public transport he's going to have a long wet walk unless he knows somebody with a boat or can hitch a ride.'

'I'm sure it wouldn't be beyond him.'

The sergeant blew out a breath and said okay. 'By the sound of it he'll fit right in over in East Augusta. Real duelling banjos country, it is.'

Hutchens had checked out of hospital by noon and phoned a yachting mate. He still felt pretty shaky and was warned by the doctor to try to relax and avoid stress over the coming week ahead of further tests. The stents were still settling in and he was on heavy-duty blood-thinning medication to minimise the chance of clotting. Don't bleed, they'd said. You might never stop.

'Absolutely!' He'd beamed at the specialist on his way out, feeling the weight of Deb Hassan's Glock in his jacket pocket.

The yachting mate had more money than sense. He also had a Cessna. They were on the approach to the Augusta airstrip now, south of the town on the way to the Cape Leeuwin lighthouse. The weather was atrocious and the plane was bobbing around like a paper kite in the gale. It was a white-knuckle landing and Hutchens thought he felt his stents popping. Huge black clouds had robbed the place of any remaining daylight.

'I owe you one, Baz.' They shook hands and the plane taxied and took off again. By arrangement with another yachting mate who kept a holiday mansion down here at Flinders Bay, a car had been left at the airstrip for him. It was a Prado and the keys were in the ignition. It was that kind of town.

He tried phoning Marjorie but there was no answer. Odds on, she couldn't get a signal. He also tried the landline but all he heard was crackles and hisses. The storm must have brought the lines down. Why did her bloody folks have to live on the wrong side of the river? And the wrong side of the century come to that. There was a missed call and a message from Cato. He ignored them. The rain was almost horizontal and the streets empty as he drove through town. On the far side of the Blackwood a few lights twinkled from the East Augusta settlement. Marjorie and Melanie were over there. Maybe Mundine was too.

*

Cato realised as soon as he got Chris Thornton's update that things had just got a whole lot worse. A series of phone calls and emails had tracked down a name for the tutor on the 'Let's Get Digital!' IT course that David Mundine signed up for back in 2003: Paul Scott

Morrison, who had now firmed as the most likely candidate for Tricia Mundine's abusive and predatory ex-boyfriend. The helpful course coordinator at Maylands community centre had even dug out the original brochure, with Morrison's photo on it. The one David Mundine must have seen. Within eighteen months Morrison would die in a house fire in Bassendean, just up the road from Maylands. They now had the post-mortem report on that incident too. Morrison's charred body showed signs of significant pre-fire injuries. It was evident that he had been tortured first.

Hutchens had discharged himself from hospital and wasn't returning Cato's calls. He wasn't at home, they'd checked. All the signs were that he too, like Mundine, was headed south to Augusta. It was now early evening. The wind had picked up. The weather from down south was coming this way. Cato feared the worst, and dealing with the worst was a significant resource issue. He phoned DI Spittle and brought him up to speed.

'You're thinking Tactical Response Group?'

Cato was.

'Unless we put them on a plane now they're not going to get down there for at least three hours, maybe four in these conditions.'

Cato didn't fill the silence.

'We'll look like complete fuckwits if this is a false alarm.'

'And worse if it isn't,' said Cato.

A few long moments more. 'I'll fix it,' said Spittle. 'Get this wrong and there'll be no hiding place for you, not even Stock Squad.' There was the sound of directives being issued behind a muffled mouthpiece. 'I assume you'll be hitching a ride with the Ninjas?'

Cato confirmed he would.

*

Mundine had seen the paddy wagon a mile off. The dozy bastard hadn't made any attempt to be discrete, or maybe that was the point. He'd doused the Datsun headlights and rolled into the driveway of an empty holiday home a few hundred metres up the lane. Rain pounded the roof. He reclined the seat and watched and waited.

He checked his phone. No signal. No surprise, he was with

fucking Vodaphone and they didn't service Swampsville. Mundine rummaged through his backpack and felt the satisfying clank and weight of the tools. He disentangled the bottle of shiraz from the rope and dragged it out for a swig.

Some headlights appeared, turning off the main road and into the settlement. Mundine slid lower in his seat as the car, one of those big rich-dick 4WDs rocked past through the puddles. It rolled up to the police car and stopped. The driver got out. It was Mr H.

Mundine smiled. This was going to be even more fun than he thought.

*

Hutchens was relieved to see the paddy wagon parked outside. The occupant was a young bloke fresh out of the Academy, alert, awake, and keen. His name was Jason. After Jason had checked Hutchens' ID they exchanged pleasantries and left each other to it. The neighbour's dog barked at the rain; useless mongrel. Hutchens rapped lightly on the front door and went on in. Marjorie was pleased and puzzled to see him.

'How did you get here? I thought you were in hospital?'

'Baz brought me in his Cessna. The doctor gave me the all-clear.' He went round everyone giving them hugs, except the old bloke, he was a handshakes only type. Melanie seemed cool. 'Sorry about all this, love.'

'No worries,' she said. 'Good to see Nanna and Pops again.'

'Ryan out on a film?'

'Bush south of Norseman, the life and times of a professional dog shooter. Some Serb ex-paramilitary.'

'Lovely,' said Hutchens. 'SBS is it?'

'Have you eaten, dear?' said Nanna.

'No Anne, I haven't. What you got?' He rustled up his hungry face, the one they all knew, like this was just another day.

She headed off to the kitchen to find something. Pops settled back into his favourite chair in front of the fire and resumed the crossword. He and Cato would get on well – they didn't speak much, both lived in their heads. Wind and rain lashed the windows and a dog barked in the distance. Marjorie wrapped an arm around his waist.

'Cato said you had a heart scare?'

'Nothing love, all good.' This wasn't the time to go into detail.

'Did they give you tablets or something?'

He patted his pocket reassuringly, feeling the weight of the Glock there. 'Shake, rattle and roll.'

'Do you really think this bloke is going to try something?'

Pops was listening in. His pen hovered over the cryptic. Hutchens noticed the .303 propped in the corner beside the firewood basket. 'Not with Bill and me on the case, he won't.' He winked at Pops. 'That right, Bill?'

'Yep.'

The dog from a few doors down barked again. Louder this time.

*

Cato was climbing into the plane at Jandakot when his phone went. The ten-man Ninja team were already in their seats, hardware stowed. Two were snoozing, others checking their phones or listening to iPods. There was a spare seat beside their leader, a bloke called Dave who Cato had encountered before. Cato's phone buzzed again.

'That'll be for you,' said Dave, not looking up from his iPad.

It was a text from Thornton.

Call me

He did. 'We need to make it quick, mate, the plane's about to start up.'

'Lisa Gangemi.' Mundine's former de facto who'd taken out a restraining order against him a few years back. 'She skipped the state and went to Townsville not long after the VRO. Changed her name.'

'How'd you find her?'

'Ways and means. Thing is, she's now a missing person in Queensland under her new name.'

'Missing how long?'

'Since about a year ago.'

The propellers started up. 'Nothing?'

'Not a trace.'

They finished the call.

'Santa?' TRG Dave's nickname for Cato. One night, two years earlier, Dave had found Cato wandering in bushland with a sack over his shoulder. Cato had been doing some Method Detecting, searching for a missing body, the sack meant to replicate the weight of a corpse. Dave tapped the screen of his iPad which held the operational briefing. 'This bloke dangerous, you reckon?'

Paul Scott Morrison. Peter Sinclair. Perhaps Lisa Gangemi too.

'Yes,' said Cato. 'I think he is.'

*

Hutchens polished off a cheese toastie and a piece of carrot cake. They'd already eaten. Bill liked his dinner at 5.30. On the dot. They settled in to watch the seven o'clock news and Hutchens went around the house checking doors and windows. What was the likely outcome here? Fuckface comes through the door like Norman Bates on meth, and he and Bill mow the bastard down in a hail of gunfire? Sweet. That would solve a few problems. But was it really going to happen? Maybe Mundine had just sloped off to a mate's to do a few bongs and jerk off and they were all getting excited about nothing. How long was he supposed to wait here to find out? Maybe they should all just pack up and hightail it back to Perth. Check into a hotel and put some guards on the door.

No.

That way the problem didn't go away. Something told him that one way or another they were obliged to sit it out here in Footrot Flats until the bitter end.

The doors and windows all seemed secure enough. Bill was like that. Handy. Reliable. Always fixing things. Sometimes when they were in Perth on a visit Bill would pop around while Hutchens was at work and fix some tap that had been dripping for the last nine months and Marjorie would give him her disappointed look when he got home that night.

The dog down the road was going berko. They should bring it in out of the rain.

Then the lights went out.

27

Cato and the Ninjas landed in Augusta just after 8 p.m. The pilot had struggled to bring the twelve-seater in through bouncing gusts. Cato noticed a few seasoned hard men gripping their armrests on the way down. Two minibuses, commandeered from local schools, were waiting at the airstrip with their Augusta police drivers. The pilot was happy to decamp to the town motel until the weather passed and they were all ready to go home. The local OIC confirmed that he had a bloke in place at the property in East Augusta but hadn't communicated directly with the occupants as the phone lines were down.

'Jason popped his head around the door half an hour ago and everything seemed to be fine. He said your colleague Mr Hutchens has arrived.' The OIC smiled reassuringly like that must have been good news and all part of the plan. Cato thanked him and they moved off.

The two-bus convoy was joined by a couple of extra paddy wagons from Margaret River and Nannup. All in all, a police contingent of eighteen including Cato – two more if you counted Hutchens and Jason, the solitary guard over in East Augusta. A cast of thousands. If this was just a false alarm then Cato's job was on the line.

Dave and half of his crew suited up in transit as the buses sped through the Augusta township, north up Bussell Highway then out east along Brockman Highway and around to East Augusta. Night-vision goggles slid into place and machine guns ratcheted. Meanwhile the other half of the TRG squad plus the four officers from Margaret River and Nannup drove down to the Augusta town jetty and took the short cut by boat across the river.

Cato tried both the Hutchens' mobiles but there was no reply.

*

Hutchens took the Glock out of his jacket pocket and went into the sitting room. The fire was still alive in the grate and gave off its flickering orange glow. Bill had also located a couple of torches and drawn everyone into a huddle in the centre of the room, ever the boy scout, but on this occasion Hutchens could have hugged him.

'Everyone okay?' said Hutchens.

Melanie's lower lip wobbled but she nodded.

'It's probably just the storm,' said Bill. 'It's happened before, more than once.'

Hutchens flicked his eyes towards Bill's .303 parked in the corner. Bill got the message and went to retrieve it.

'I'll pop out and check with Jason. See what he knows.' Hutchens took a spare torch from Bill and ventured outside.

The rain was still driving hard and the wind tugged at his jacket. Twigs, dust and leaves flew through the air, stinging his exposed skin. It was black dark. The power was out on neighbouring properties. Perhaps Bill was right and it was a storm outage, nothing more. Hutchens swung the torch and its beam found the paddy wagon still in place with Jason in the driving seat, his head resting against the side window. The bastard was having a snooze. As Hutchens stepped forward, his foot sank into a pothole and his ankle twisted. Pain shot through his leg and he lost balance. He dropped the torch as he tried to right himself. The torch rolled into a water-filled ditch and the light died.

Jason would have one. Hutchens limped up to the driver's window and tapped. He'd framed some choice expletives in his mind for the bollocking he was about to dish out. Jason didn't respond. Hutchens grabbed the door handle and yanked. Jason fell out. Lifeless and limp. Despite the rain and blackness Hutchens could see that Jason's shirt front was covered in dark liquid that could only have been blood. Hutchens heard a scrape behind him.

'Mr H.'

He ducked and felt a glancing blow off the side of his neck. Mundine was using a hammer. Ducking again, another one came to the shoulder. He lifted his arms to fend off the attack, felt a burning sensation along the bottom of his forearm. He bowed his head, aware he was already losing it. He could see his blood mixing with the rain on the ground, lots of it, flowing freely with the thinning medication.

Don't bleed. You might never stop.

The sound of footsteps and voices approaching through the bush. Flashlights, several of them, a few hundred metres away.

The blows stopped. A whisper in his ear and Mundine's familiar sour-milk breath smell. 'We're not finished yet, Mr H. Let's be getting you back inside. Quiet now, think of that lovely family of yours.'

Hutchens was lifted by his collar, his own Glock pressed into his neck.

Bill was waiting at the front door. There was momentary confusion as he tried to register the changed situation. It was all the time Mundine needed to shoot him.

*

'Shot fired.'

With those words over Dave's UHF, the siege began. By the time Cato and the remaining contingent arrived, the house was surrounded and a cordon had been established a hundred metres either way. The nearest house was empty. The one beyond that, with a yapping labradoodle, was just beyond the cordon. Dave summoned the owner, a young woman in a zebra-patterned onesie.

'What's its name?'

She bent down to hug the animal. 'His name is Jezza.'

'Quieten Jezza or he dies.'

Jezza was taken inside.

A tarpaulin, pilfered from the shed of the empty house, had been placed over the body of the young Augusta officer. His colleagues, angry and upset, were channelling their emotions into practical activities – driving, or chugging across river, back to town to get help. Already, across the Blackwood, the flashing lights of the ambulance and fire truck illuminated the night. Here at the scene any spare vehicles, except for Jason's which would be needed for forensic testing, had been placed strategically with headlights blazing to light up as much of the property as possible.

TRG Dave's mood was in a downward spiral. 'This is fucking hopeless. A siege, in a storm, in a power outage, on an isolated property with no mobile coverage. Is somebody taking the piss?'

The usual hi-tech siege paraphernalia – communications, monitoring equipment, sniper rifles et cetera – were all in a storeroom in Perth. They did have their UHF radios, guns, some stun and gas grenades, and a plan of the property had been downloaded to Dave's iPad before the signal loss. All they could do, for now, was lock it down and wait for help to arrive. Unless of course something kicked off in the house before that.

'What then?' said Cato.

'You come up with a plan, Santa.' Dave issued orders to some underlings. 'And I'll take it into consideration.'

'Do we have a megaphone?'

'No. You could try shouting when the wind drops a bit.'

Cato gave in. He took to fretting about Hutchens and his family instead.

*

Hutchens wouldn't stop bleeding. The stain was spreading out over the rug. Bill lay slumped by the front door. As far as Hutchens could tell, he was dead, or not far from it. The room was no longer in darkness with the fire in the grate and the headlights blazing through the windows.

'Party time,' said Mundine, thumbing out the window. 'Your mates are here.'

After being ordered to draw the curtains, Marjorie, Melanie and Anne crowded together on the couch. Melanie sobbed while the other two looked fearful and murderous at the same time.

Mundine occupied the armchair, Bill's favourite, by the fire

and prodded the flames with a poker, the end glowing red. The
Glock was resting on his lap and he'd brought out a bottle of red and
offered it around. No takers. 'I love it down here.'

'David, this has to end.' Hutchens was faint from the beating and
from blood loss.

'It will, Mr H. Soon enough.' Mundine took a swig from the bottle
and wiped his mouth. 'We used to come here when I was a kid. Me,
Mum, Paulie. Paulie had a caravan in that park just over the river.'

'Yeah?' said Hutchens, not particularly interested. Trying to keep
from passing out. Trying to see some way of changing the situation.
'Uncle Paulie was it? One of your mum's boyfriends?'

'One time we stayed in the caravan and this possum was thumping
around on the roof, all night.' A lazy, contented smile. 'We didn't
sleep a wink. Paulie went mad, grumping around all the next day.
He wanted to kill the possum, set a trap or something. I wouldn't let
him. He gave me a real belting.'

'Mum didn't mind?'

'Mum wasn't there.'

Hutchens started concentrating.

Mundine was rummaging in his backpack. 'I met Paulie again
a few years later. He took a while to recognise me. I wasn't the
same little kid he remembered.' A coil of rope came out of the bag,
followed by a knife, a screwdriver, and a roll of electrician's tape. He
lined them up on the floor next to the blood-soaked hammer. 'We
had a nice little reunion, chatted about old times.' He hummed. 'Like
yesterday once more.'

Hutchens lifted his chin towards the display of goodies. 'Got
some renos in mind, Davey?'

'Of sorts.' He pulled out a chisel and added it to his collection on
the floor. 'By the time I got to Hillsview I knew the drill. Mr S. liked
that. He spotted me straight away, knew where I'd been. He knew I
was the one for him.'

'This is all about you and me, isn't it, Davey?' Hutchens nodded
towards his family on the sofa. 'They're not part of this. Send them
away, then you can get down to business.'

A soft whimper from that part of the room.

'Do you know what it took for me to come and ask for your help that day?'

'I do now.'

'It was my fourteenth birthday. I'd decided enough was enough. It had to stop. Mum had never stopped Paulie. The other staff at Hillsview had never stopped Mr S. But that day I would end it. With your help, Mr H.'

'I'm sorry, David. I really am.'

'That's how society's meant to work, isn't it? The strong protect the weak from evil. That's right isn't it?'

'Sounds like a good idea.'

'When I got back he knew where I'd been. He knew nothing was going to happen to him. He knew I was all alone.' A tear rolled down Mundine's face. 'He'd always known. That's why he picked me in the first place.' Mundine wiped his eyes. 'He hurt me really bad that day. Made me bleed.'

He picked up the gun, strode over to Hutchens and pistol-whipped him. Then he took the tape and wrapped it around Hutchens' mouth. He kicked him in the head before going back to get the rope.

*

'We have to go in.'

They'd all heard one of the women scream. TRG Dave shook his head at Cato. 'He's armed and he's nuts. We have no idea what's going on in there. It was a one-off yelp. He probably just hit or threatened someone. Unless we hear more evidence of it really turning to shit we need to hold our nerve.'

'It could be hours before the techs arrive. We can't just sit here.'

'We have to.' Dave tossed a look at a muscled geek sitting under a flapping tarp. He was nursing a laptop and muttering expletives at the heavens. 'Tristran's trying to tap into the emergency band so we can talk to them on the mobiles. Meantime, sit tight. I promise you, if it really goes off we'll be in there.'

'Show me the property plan.'

'Magic word?'

'Please.'

Dave brought it up on his iPad. The living room, where smoke curled from a chimney and where the yelp had come from, was at the front of the house. It and the kitchen dining area were connected in an open-plan layout. A short central corridor led towards the back of the house with bedrooms coming off either side. At the back, the bathroom and laundry. Vehicle headlights illuminated the front and sides of the property but the rear was inaccessible to vehicles and still in gloom. Cato knew Dave had stationed four of his squad plus the two uniforms from Nannup around the back. They would each have their flashlights trained on the rear doors and windows.

'The occupants can't come out without being seen.' Dave powered down his tablet. 'We've got it covered.'

'And if it does go pear-shaped?'

'Doors down, guns blazing, fingers crossed.'

Cato gave a terse nod of thanks and stepped back out into the rain. He knew Dave was probably right but that didn't make it any easier.

There was another yelp from inside.

*

'Shush,' said Mundine.

The women were now trussed up together, the rope wound around them all and tape covering their mouths. Anne Coucher had used her remaining tape-free seconds well.

'You're a cowardly piece of shit and you're going to die by morning.'

She'd received a punch in reply. The outraged yelp had come from Marjorie on her mum's behalf.

'There,' he'd said, once he finished tying them together. 'Like a bunch of flowers. Lovely.'

Hutchens felt dizzy and very tired. Blood continued to drain from his various cuts and abrasions, and, as the doctors had warned, it just wouldn't stop. Would he bleed out and die? He didn't know how long he had left.

'When you're alone in the world you get plenty of time to think about stuff,' said Mundine. 'I worked a lot of things out. I worked out what that stink was coming off Mr S. It was leaking shit. Somebody must have been up him too when he was a kid. Gone at him so hard it stuffed up the plumbing.'

A second coil of rope came out of the bag and was wound around Hutchens' arms and legs until he was hogtied. Utterly helpless, just the way Mundine intended it. Hutchens made a gagging noise. Mundine pulled the tape away.

'What's that, Mr H.?'

'I can't breathe. I'm dying.'

'And?'

'You know you're not walking away from this, don't you?'

'I know that. None of us will be walking out of here. That's the point.'

Hutchens saw his daughter's eyes fill with terror. It was heartbreaking. He shook his head sadly. 'Here's me thinking for a while you were smarter than you looked.'

'Yeah? Hostage situations 101: this the wind-up is it?'

'A nice little bit of blackmail money from yours truly. Some compo from the Inquiry. And as a bonus you get to load me with Sinclair's murder. Sweet as. Now you've blown it all with that temper of yours.'

Mundine snorted. 'Money? What do I need that for? You reckon when I was lying there covered in Sinclair's stink I was thinking jeez this'll be a good little earner some day? Fucking idiot.' He picked up the hammer. 'As for the Inquiry – bit of a laugh, nothing more. You were the last on my list. My job's just about done. Who cares after that? I've already had the worst happen to me.'

Out of the corner of his eye Hutchens could see movement on the couch. The rope was unravelling. Marjorie twisting and stretching her hands and arms. Keep mad boy talking.

'What happened at the Mundaring pub that night?'

'I was in Sinclair's car. He gave me a packet of chips and a Coke and told me to wait while he had a beer or two. I was fine with that. Happy to sit there and bleed my arse out on the seat.' He grabbed the bottle of red and took a swig. 'Later on you took a swing at him in the car park. Pissed as but you landed a couple and put him down.

Nice work. Then you got in your car and left. I took my chance and finished the cunt off with a brick from the builder's skip.'

'How did he end up at John Forrest?'

'I nicked a shovel from the tradies' stash and drove him up. I was fourteen, Mr S. used to take me for "driving lessons" up there if he wanted a bit of privacy and the romance of the open air. Torched his car back in Guildford later, burned a treat.' He shifted the hammer to his right hand, took the chisel in his left and crouched down beside Hutchens. 'So now you know everything, Mr H. You can die happy.'

Marjorie smacked him full force across the side of the head with the poker. 'You talk too much, fuckwit,' she said.

28

Thursday, August 29th.

The storm had passed. Sun flickered on the still waters of the Blackwood and a pod of dolphins broke the surface, their spray hanging in the air. By the river's edge, half a dozen pelicans waited patiently for the remnants as an angler gutted his catch on a wooden bench.

By dawn the scene had been pretty much cleared and left to forensics. Both Hutchens and Bill Coucher had been medivaced by the Flying Doctor Service up to Royal Perth. Bill's gunshot wound to the stomach was life-threatening and the next twenty-four hours would be critical. Hutchens' blood loss had been stemmed and would be carefully replenished in a fine balancing act between the specific need to avoid clotting around his angioplasty and the general need of his body to have some blood in it. Cato left the details to the docs and hoped for the best. Hutchens' family were being put up in the Augusta Motel ahead of some questioning by detectives brought down from Bunbury. The young Augusta cop, Jason, would have his post-mortem later that day.

David Mundine was under observation and armed guard in Margaret River hospital and would be transferred back to Perth at the earliest opportunity. His ear had taken the brunt of the blow and that may have helped avert catastrophic brain damage, but the hot poker had left an ugly mushy wound badly in need of plastic surgery. From the little Cato had gleaned from Hutchens during the ambulance ride to the airstrip, Major Crime would hopefully be enjoying a conversation with Mundine about the remains in John Forrest National Park.

TRG Dave and his crew had already been summoned back to Perth for another crisis and the plane would be leaving the airstrip in half an hour if Cato wanted a lift. He did, although a few days holiday in Augusta seemed very appealing right now. The river had a hypnotic, calming quality and the air was clean and crisp. The dolphin pod surfaced again and the baby did a little leap. For no good reason, it seemed, except that maybe it was just good to be alive.

*

After landing at Jandakot, Cato was dropped off at home. He caught up on sleep for the rest of the morning, surfacing around 1 p.m. There were some missed calls on his phone: Deb Hassan, Chris Thornton, Rory Driscoll, and Jane. He spooned some bircher muesli into a bowl, added milk and called Jane.

'Jake broke his grounding.'

'How?'

'He went to Stef's house after school yesterday. Didn't get home until nearly seven.'

'What did you say to him?'

'I asked him his reasons. He gave none. I said I'd be talking to you.'

'What did he say about that?'

'Nothing. Shrugs. Who cares. That kind of stuff.'

'So we extend the grounding and withdraw more privileges.'

'Like?'

'I don't know. Guitar lessons? Weekend basketball? Take them away from him.'

'The only positive things he does with his spare time. Is that a good idea?'

'Good point.' Cato didn't have any magic solutions, neither did Jane. 'How about two weeks added on to the grounding and I'll talk to him again over the weekend.'

'What about?'

'Dunno. I'll try to find out what he values in life so I can snatch it away from him.'

Jane laughed. 'Don't forget it's Father's Day next week. You might want to be careful or you won't get any new socks.'

They signed off. He finished his muesli, downed a coffee, and caught the CAT bus into work. He didn't need parking hassles or anything else challenging today. He intended to tread water for the afternoon and have an early night tonight.

*

At the office his first port of call was DI Spittle to update him on the events of the last twenty-four hours.

'You made the right decision, even if the TRG weren't needed in the end.' Spittle spun his chair away from his laptop to give full attention. 'Is Mick okay?'

'They seem pretty confident he will be. His father-in-law's a different matter. His guts got pretty messed up by the bullet apparently. We'll know soon enough.'

'How about you?'

'Tired. Got a couple of hours this morning.'

'Everything's pretty much under control here. Usual stuff overnight plus a cabbie got robbed and bashed. Tamil bloke, he'd just finished a twelve-hour shift. But we've got the likely culprits on cab-cam and we're picking them up this arvo.'

'How bad is he?'

'The driver? In hospital, may lose an eye. That's what you get for working hard and trying to provide for your family. The ones who did it have a history, white trash scumbags from way back.'

'Judging by the polls, their day is at hand, apparently.'

Spittle smiled grimly. 'That's politics, son. None of my business.'

They parted ways and got on with their respective days. Chris Thornton was hovering by Cato's desk. Yes, said Cato, the boss is going to be okay. And me too. Thornton was glad to hear it. He had more good news.

'Lisa Gangemi is alive and well and living in Sydney.'

'How did you find her?'

'She found us. She phoned in after she heard from family that we were looking for her.'

Lisa Gangemi was petrified of David Mundine and had kept

moving and changing her identity even though, as far as could be ascertained from his travel movements, he hadn't tried very hard to find her. But she badly missed her home and family and had ABC WA news bookmarked on her computer. That morning's report of Mundine's arrest was the best news she'd had in years.

'Anything else new?' said Cato.

'Guido Caletti would like a word.'

'Urgent?'

'At your convenience.'

Cato took that as a no.

'And there was a call this morning.' Thornton waved his pen at a post-it note on Cato's computer. 'Left a number and a name but didn't say what it was about.'

Cato peered at the note. Driscoll.

He tried the number but it rang out. Rory was probably out on the assault course yomping it with the SAS. Cato made himself a coffee, sat down at his desk and logged on: circulars, statistics, budgets, timesheets, training courses. He'd been a sergeant before, a long time ago, and didn't recall the job being quite this bureaucratic. He deleted as much of it as he could. He returned Caletti's call and they agreed that Guido would do the commute to Fremantle this arvo, the coffees were on him.

'So what's it about?' Cato wanted to know.

'Chinese whispers,' said Caletti, with a gravelly chuckle.

That reminded Cato. He needed to call in and see his dad sometime today.

Cato was beginning to feel antsy. The serenity he felt overlooking the Blackwood that morning had evaporated. Maybe that had all just been relief at a not too bloody end to the siege. He'd returned to a diminished workload: Mundine was in custody, the Tan murders had been archived on DI Pavlou's instructions, and the daily caseload had been delegated away courtesy of DI Spittle. He had what he'd been hoping for, the opportunity to tread water for the afternoon and get an early night. He should have known he was kidding himself. He needed purpose.

The Tan case had been put to bed but he needed to wake it up and give it a good shake. For Francis. For Genevieve. For those kids. And for Lara too. He went into the database and extracted the files he needed onto a thumb drive. He did likewise with the information on Suzhou Dragon and Wongan Enterprises, Yu's and O'Neill's business entities. For the sake of spin and expediency, some of those ill-fitting pieces in the Tan jigsaw had been hammered into place and any remaining gaps ignored. The result was Mona Lisa in the hands of Picasso. Cato intended to take it all apart and put it back together again. Maybe he would make an enemy of Pavlou and she would be a powerful, vengeful person to cross. But it was purposeful. He was beginning to feel good again.

*

Cato met Guido Caletti at Gino's on the Cappuccino Strip later that afternoon. The minders were nowhere in sight and he'd toned down his 'gangsta' wardrobe to blend in with the South Terrace crowd. Maybe the Northbridge underworld identity thing was all just for show. Was this genial middle-aged man the real Guido? They shook hands and there was little of the handgrip gameplay in evidence. The smile seemed genuine. What was going on?

'I heard about what happened to Officer Sumich. Terrible thing, a real shame.'

'Yes,' said Cato. 'It was.' Guido had secured a table under the pergola and out of the wind. Cato's flat white was waiting for him. He removed the saucer lid which had been holding the heat in. Took a sip. Perfect.

'And that stuff overnight, down south. Was that you?'

Cato nodded. 'You wanted to tell me something?'

Guido leaned forward, lowering his voice, taking Cato into his confidence. 'I was talking to Matthew Tan yesterday.'

'Yeah?'

'We've sorted out a new repayment schedule on the loans. All sweet.'

'Glad to hear it.'

'He's been through a lot, I didn't want to add to his burden.'

'That must have set his mind at ease. So Lily's cocaine debts are in hand?'

'You don't like me, do you?'

'Should I?'

'No.' Caletti shook his head. 'I don't need you to. But you should know that her habit is not my doing. I don't know or care where she gets her shit from. Matthew's debts weren't for drugs, they were to cover his lifestyle. Champagne tastes, a winding back of parental support, and the little prick too lazy and useless to get a job. People like him are the backbone of my business.'

'So why are we here?'

'Matthew told me that the case has now been closed. You know who did his family. This Yu bloke. Dead now. That right?'

'That's right.'

'And Tommy Li is out of the frame?'

'We have no evidence to keep him in it.'

Caletti took a sip of his coffee. 'What did you think of Shanghai?'

'Big. Busy. Murders and beatings aside, a nice place to visit. Not sure I could live there.'

'Yeah, same with me. I was there a couple of years back. Couldn't wait to get out.'

'Was that when you and Li were still friends?'

Guido sniffed. 'Ever meet that daughter of his? Tasty, if you like a good back scratch.'

Guido and Phoebe. The mind boggled. 'Was that why you and Li fell out? Fingers in the till?'

A rueful smile. 'Partly. I'd like to be able to say she was worth it but she was a bit like you say about Shanghai. Nice to visit but you wouldn't want to hang around.'

'And that's what you wanted to tell me?'

Guido shook his head. 'Phoebe had someone else on the scene. Possessive, jealous type, he came to warn me off in my hotel the next day. He played the part well.'

'Yu Guangming?'

'That's right.' He grinned. 'How'd you guess?' He lifted his eyes to someone standing behind Cato. 'Can I help you, mate?'

It was Driscoll. He stuck out a hand. 'Rory.'

'Guido.'

'Have we met before? You seem familiar.'

'Always possible,' Guido smiled. 'I get around.' He made his excuses and left, but not so quickly that it looked personal.

'Is this a coincidence?' said Cato.

'I'm tracking your phone.' Driscoll winked. 'I know exactly where you are at all times.'

Cato's face darkened.

'Joke,' said Driscoll. 'I phoned your office. They told me.' He gestured at Cato's empty cup. 'Another?'

The answer was yes. Driscoll went to the counter to order while Cato thought about the pairing of Yu Guangming and Phoebe Li. Did Daddy know anything about his darling daughter having it away with his, his what? Rival, business associate as needs be, occasional ally. Here again was the complex and shifting world of guanxi, connections. Maybe it was an arranged pairing to shore up alliances. Or maybe Phoebe was not as filial as she presented. So was Guido suggesting that Phoebe might have something to do with the Tan murders, independent of her father?

Driscoll returned with two coffees and a plate of Florentines. 'It's that time of day. Sugar hit or nanna nap, it could go either way.'

Cato wondered how much Driscoll knew. His facial expression suggested everything. 'Do you know Guido, then?'

'I can't think where from.' He tapped his head. 'It'll come to me. Help yourself to the Florentines. They're ace.'

'How's the training course going?'

Driscoll swallowed the rest of his biscuit. 'Not as fit as I used to be.'

'So,' said Cato. 'You found me.'

'Nothing new to report on the nefarious deals in Thames Town, I'm afraid.'

'But?'

'But somebody knows you're digging.' You, not we, Cato noted. 'Serious people, with a long reach.'

'You're passing on a warning?'

'Just offering wise counsel. You have your murderer. Time to tilt at new windmills, maybe?'

Cato chewed on a Florentine. Driscoll was right, they were ace. 'I'm not interested in the Chinese, they're beyond my reach. But if there's any collars I can feel at this end, I'll do it.'

'And in so doing you might still cause more problems than you really want. Take somebody down here and it might send out ripples.'

'Guanxi?' said Cato.

'Your pronunciation's improving.'

*

Mandy had invited him for dinner but warned that they ate early. Both little Bao and old Jack were usually cactus by 7 p.m. so dinner was 6.30 prompt. That suited Cato, he'd probably be cactus by seven too.

When he arrived, Kenneth was taking care of Bao's bathtime, the other kids were doing homework or music practice, Mandy was draining the rice, and Dad was snoozing in front of the six o'clock news. Mandy slid a bottle of red and a glass across the kitchen counter.

'Help yourself.'

'Thanks,' said Cato. 'How's Dad been?'

'He fell over yesterday. Big bruise down his side. The Silver Chain woman reckons we should strap him to the bed.'

'Yeah, she'd love that.' It seemed Jack Kwong was awake. 'Misery loves company.'

Cato went over and gave him a hug. 'How's tricks?'

'I'm still dying.'

'What's the bad news?' said Cato.

Dad grinned. That was more like it. 'He touched one of the faded bruises on Cato's face. 'Did you win?'

'Should see the other bloke.'

'Good onya. Where've you been?'

'China.'

'What'd you want to go there for?'

'Find some new rellies. The ones here are not much cop.'

'Huh,' Dad and Mandy said in unison, enjoying the banter.

'Find any?' said Dad.

'Coupla million Kwongs. The name is common as muck over there.'

'That right?' said Dad. 'Ever heard of Kong Fu Tzu?'

'No,' said Cato.

'Otherwise known as Confucius, the renowned Chinese scholar. Kwong is derived from Kong so he's your great, great, great second cousin or something.'

'That's good. I'll let Sharon know.'

'Sharon?' said Dad and Mandy.

'A colleague. In Beijing.'

'Haven't seen you blush in ages, little brother. When do we get to meet her?'

No time soon, thought Cato, surprised at the depth of his regret.

They had dinner and the banter resumed. It was a great evening, even with the toddler chucking a fatigue tantie and the older kids pouting and squabbling, one of them with his head buried in his laptop – at the dinner table for goodness sake – it was a great evening. It felt like old times.

'See, Dad?' said Mandy, squeezing Cato's arm. 'You were wrong. Nothing bad happened to Phil in China. He came home safe.'

Dad paused with a forkful of food halfway to his mouth. 'Why wouldn't he?'

'You had a premonition of doom,' said Mandy. 'Don't you remember?'

Dad finished his chewing. 'That'll teach you to listen to a silly old bugger like me.'

*

His mobile woke him. He checked the time, 2.26 a.m. A call out?

'Hello?'

Nothing except for the hum of dead air, like you hear before a Delhi call centre connects you to that guy from the computer security department.

'Hello?' If it was a cold caller trying to wheedle his password out of him, blood would be spilt. Or he'd learn to just turn his phone off at night. Except that he wasn't allowed to, it went with the job.

There were voices. Laughter. Children there too. Then he recognised what it was: a recording of the dinner-time conversation at Mandy's earlier that evening.

See, Dad? You were wrong. Nothing bad happened to Phil in China. He came home safe.

Why wouldn't he?

You had a premonition of doom. Don't you remember?

That'll teach you to listen to a silly old bugger like me.

29

Friday, August 30th.

Cato hadn't slept well. He looked out of the window at the early morning sun brushing the top of the olive tree, the wind rippling the leaves. He stepped under the shower and absorbed the heat. Somebody was giving him a warning. That somebody had managed to obtain a recording of a private, domestic dinner table gathering. The content was well-chosen and the message was clear: his loved ones were at risk.

Cato towelled himself dry and checked his old knife scar – yes, manly as ever. He padded through the kitchen naked, flicking the kettle on and dropping bread in the toaster. He picked up a remote and the radio sputtered to life. A week out from Election Day and the pundits were in full swing. They all agreed that the government was heading for a wipeout by a tsunami of antipathy against foreigners, do-gooders and indecisive wimps. You had two choices: enjoy the ride or take cover.

Driscoll was one who had elected to enjoy the ride, mused Cato. He was gearing up for the new order and the adventures to be had for men of his calibre and loose morality. Their time was nigh. Driscoll had let Cato know that he was treading on toes and that someone was looking to stomp back at him. Driscoll was a spook who could make jokes about stalking people but could also just as easily turn it into a reality. Was he behind the phone call?

Cato threw some clothes on, made a plunger of coffee and spread some marmalade on his toast. He zapped the radio and the poll pundits back into silence and put a CD on instead. It was a soothing

Mozart andante that had been sitting in the tray, waiting to go. That was better.

He called Driscoll. 'You busy?'

'Got an appointment with Q this arvo but otherwise I'm just reading some boring statistics.'

They agreed to meet.

*

He wanted her to leave. Couldn't she see he was crook? Hutchens' head hurt like a bastard after the pistol-whipping and he was daubed in huge ugly black bruises. And there were the drips and the wires and the beeps and the lights. He looked and felt like the evil blob inside a Dalek.

'It's a shame Marjorie hit him so hard with that poker,' said DI Pavlou. 'He just dribbles and pretends he can't remember a thing.'

'He killed Sinclair. He admitted it.' Hutchens squinted against a sudden stab of pain in his skull. 'You've got four witnesses to what he said.'

'Not entirely objective though, are they?'

'Whose side are you on?'

'Truth and justice, Mick.'

'Fuck off.'

'The Inquiry has put your matter to one side and is pushing on with submissions from other former hostel residents and staff and associated agencies.' She leaned over from the bedside chair and patted his arm reassuringly. Just a little closer and he could wrap the drip tube around her neck and squeeze. 'Between you and me I think they'll be dropping the idea of pursuing you on Sinclair. Too-hard basket.'

'Not good enough. Mud sticks. I want Mundine charged.'

She frowned. 'Investigations are ongoing, Mick. We'll keep you posted.'

'Finished?'

'Have you thought about whether or not you'll be coming back to work?'

'Nothing to think about. I'll be back on Monday.'

'I hear Jimmy Spittle is standing in for you. The troops seem to like him.'

'Great,' said Hutchens, stony-faced.

She pursed her lips as if making a decision about something. 'I think I need to be up front with you, Mick. I've invited Cato to apply for one of the vacancies in Major Crime.'

'And?'

'The deadline is next Friday. He's thinking about it.' Pavlou gathered her notebook and phone and stood to leave. 'Don't hurry back to work. You've been through the wringer and the older we get the harder it is to bounce back.' She nodded towards the flowers, the cards, a basket of fruit, even a teddy. It was like a shrine at a crime scene. 'You're well regarded, Mick. People care about you. That's the stuff of life.'

*

Canary in the mine, frog in the cesspit: Cato wasn't quite sure what he was but something he'd done or said had triggered a response. First a quiet word in the ear and then the more sinister follow up, just to make sure he got it. It was Driscoll who'd been looking into the Thames Town land deal on his behalf. Suzhou Dragon and Wongan Enterprises would be the big winners in that deal. With Yu dead, then Des O'Neill would be the sole benefactor. Was that it? If so, then the threats had to come from O'Neill. Cato found that hard to imagine. O'Neill presented as a farm boy on the make. He might drive a hard bargain and be a ruthless deal-maker and you'd find his like in any stockyard in outback Australia, but murder and threats seemed a step way beyond. And Cato couldn't see Des having the resources or technical know-how to bug people's conversations, or was that just a country bumpkin stereotype he'd formed?

Alternatively, Thomas Li's much bigger development, which necessitated the buyout of Yu and O'Neill, was playing for even bigger stakes, 'gazillions' Driscoll had said. To Cato's mind two people were at the centre of all this dark economics: Driscoll the spook and possibly freelance fixer, and Phoebe Li the dutiful daughter who shared her bed with her father's rival Yu. Now dead.

Both Phoebe and Driscoll were killers and Cato had seen what they were capable of. Was he willing to provoke either of them further?

Driscoll returned from the counter with an orange juice for Cato and a bright green drink for himself. 'Kale smoothie,' he grimaced. 'The fitness instructor threatened to fail me this morning. He said I was a fat Canberra bastard and past it.'

'Harsh,' said Cato. They were in some new food dude warehouse in the West End: bricks, pipes, thick old-growth wood, and pierced hipster chefs – all of them with sleeve tatts and big Ned Kelly beards. The prices were daylight robbery too – the Kelly Gang should have just waited one hundred and forty years and opened a bistro in Freo and avoided all that heavy armour.

'Your focaccia's on its way. I'm having a fucking salad.' Driscoll slurped on his green drink. 'So what can I do for you?'

Cato told him about the overnight phone call. Driscoll's face betrayed no hint of any prior knowledge. He seemed surprised and concerned. But then he was probably trained in that kind of stuff.

'They mean business, then.'

'Who's they? Who precisely pushed you my way?'

'How do you mean?'

'You felt obliged to drop a word in my ear. What inspired you?'

Driscoll shrugged. 'Jungle drums. A friend of a friend of a friend of an enemy. You know how it works.'

'Phoebe Li?'

'Phoebe?' The nonchalance was a bit too nonchalant. 'What makes you think she's involved?'

'She had Lara killed. She's daddy's little girl and daddy has a lot of money at stake in that development.' Cato's focaccia and Driscoll's salad arrived. Cato took a bite, savouring the grilled eggplant, pesto and activated almonds. He had a Mars bar waiting in his desk drawer as back-up. 'And she was having it away with Yu Guangming. All in all, I'd say she's an ethically challenged individual.'

'Yeah,' conceded Driscoll. 'She's a dangerous bitch, all right.'

'So?'

'So you're better informed than I thought and here's me thinking

I was the one and true font. Your mate from yesterday, Guido, is he your new oracle?'

'Classified.' Cato had wanted to be able to say that to Driscoll.

'Touché. I did remember him a few hours later. I'd met him at a nightclub in Shanghai some time back. He was on the arm of the lovely Phoebe.'

'So *is* Phoebe behind all this?'

'Dunno, mate.' Driscoll prodded his salad despondently. 'But if you're thinking of rattling anyone's cage, it may as well be hers.'

Cato studied him. The guy would ace it in a poker game.

*

'How are you today, David?'

David Mundine kept his eyes closed and pretended he hadn't heard.

'David?'

His ear throbbed. He hadn't seen it yet, it was covered by a protective gauze. But he had seen the faces of the nurses whenever they changed the dressings. Disgust.

'David?'

He opened an eye but he already knew who it was. It was the lady detective wanting to know about the collection of bones from John Forrest. She had somebody with her. A young bloke, dark curls and big lashes. Peter's type.

'Umm?'

'DI Pavlou, we spoke briefly yesterday.'

He nodded weakly and asked for some water. Adonis did the honours.

'Are you up to a few more questions today, David?'

He gave them a brave wan smile.

'This is Detective Constable Fernandez. I'll leave you in his hands.'

'Sure,' said Mundine.

She left. Fernandez stuck out a hand. 'Joe.'

'David,' said David.

*

Cato wanted to know what it was that he'd done recently that had changed the game. He tried to plot out a timeline. It was only just over a week since his return from China. It seemed so much more. During that time they'd buried Lara Sumich and faced Hutchens' nemesis in the swampy lowlands of East Augusta. What else? On the instructions of DI Pavlou they'd sheeted the Tan murders away to Yu Guangming and archived the case. But Cato had kept digging. He'd dug into Wongan Holdings and Suzhou Dragon. Who knew he had? Driscoll for sure, otherwise it had been internet searches and the ACC profile. ACC. He'd asked Mystery Mike to earn his keep and look into O'Neill and Yu. The bloke hadn't got back to him and, in the distraction of the Mundine business, Cato had let it slide. He picked up the phone and dialled.

'That you, Michael?'

'Who's this?'

'Philip Kwong. Have you had a chance to follow up on that stuff I requested?'

'No.'

'Busy?'

'Not especially.'

'So?'

'So I ran it past both Sandra Pavlou and my supervisors and they confirmed that your request wasn't authorised.'

'No help forthcoming then?'

'Sorry.'

He ended the call and added Michael to his list of suspects.

He'd also had a visit from Guido Caletti who'd tipped him off about Phoebe Li and Yu Guangming. Almost immediately after that, he'd received the warning from Driscoll. Coincidence?

What else?

Matthew Tan? Cato still wasn't convinced about the stowaway but, as yet, he could see no link between that and somebody in China wanting to pass on a warning via Driscoll.

In Cato's view it had to be the Yu, Phoebe, and O'Neill nexus.

No further forward.

Reverse angle and rewind. Back to the basic question of the

murder. What could Francis Tan have known, or said, or done, that warranted the slaughter of him and his family?

Cato dragged Francis Tan's phone records out of the database once more.

This part of the investigation had fallen under the remit of Major Crime. The analysis of the phone data had been done by Detective Constable J. Fernandez with supervision from a Detective Sergeant P. MacMahon and sign-off by DI Pavlou. Calls and texts made and received had been itemised by date, time, duration and whether the person at the other end fitted into certain categories such as family, business, friend/associate, personal or other. Any anomalies such as extended duration or unusual times like middle of the night, or patterns such as repeated calls over a short period had been marked for follow up. Thomas Li and Guido Caletti came under the pink highlighter treatment as did Des O'Neill. In time, Guido and Des dropped off as Li became the focus. Email trails had been similarly analysed but these seemed a lot more carefully worded as if in anticipation that someday someone might come looking.

Cato made himself a cuppa and settled in for the afternoon.

*

Mundine reckoned he had DC Joe Fernandez wrapped around his little finger. He was back to his twitchy victim persona. No, he couldn't remember much of what happened. He was in this house down south with Mr H. and his lovely family and then the lights went out. No, he couldn't explain how he got there or why. He'd taken this blow to the head with a red-hot poker. Lucky to be alive really. A dead cop called Jason? Don't remember that. Peter Sinclair? Yes, he remembered Peter Sinclair, he was the dirty old man who had ruined his life. No, he didn't know anything about John Forrest National Park. Mr H. said that? Really? Paul Morrison's death in the Bassendean house fire? Who? Oh Paulie, Mum's old boyfriend. Really? Shame.

'So what happens next?'

'That's up to the boss, mate. But I'd expect some charges might follow and then you'll get your day in court.'

'Charges?'

'There's a lot of explaining to do. Mr H. ... I mean DI Hutchens and his family didn't get tied up or injured all by themselves, did they?'

'S'pose not.' Mundine rattled his handcuffed hand. 'So this stays on, yeah?'

'Yep.'

'I should probably get a lawyer, eh?'

'Might be an idea.'

'Know any?'

'Try Legal Aid.' Fernandez gathered his things.

'Is Mr H. okay?'

'He will be.'

'Good. That's good.'

*

It was in studying the week preceding the murders that Cato picked up on a pattern of calls and corresponding emails that, on paper, were explicable and seemingly innocuous. In hindsight they were anything but. It was late afternoon. Outside the light was dying and punters strode purposefully towards the pubs to launch their weekend. Jake would be dropped off tomorrow and Cato's guts churned a little at the prospect of more domestic angst. But this was parenting, he told himself, the good and the bad. You had to nip this stuff in the bud or ... what? Your offspring became the child of Satan, a little Matthew Tan bouncing bocce balls off the heads of innocent babes, a self-absorbed Zac Harvey trolling a dead girlfriend, a vengeful and murderous David Mundine stalking the night, or a vicious Phoebe Li erasing her enemies from existence. Maybe Cato was projecting a little too much here. Jake was a teenage boy who'd tried a bit of dope and bunked off school occasionally. Stop the presses. Anyway, that was tomorrow, this was now.

There were a number of calls on Tuesday 30th July between Francis Tan and Des O'Neill, and between Francis Tan and Thomas Li. It was forty-eight hours before Li and Yu Guangming would board that same flight to Perth. Just six days before the massacre of the Tan family in Port Coogee. There were four calls between Tan and O'Neill: the first from Tan lasted just over six minutes, the second from O'Neill just under three minutes, the third from O'Neill less than a minute, and the last from O'Neill just fifteen seconds. All within a twenty-minute block commencing at breakfast time that morning. Almost immediately after the last of those calls from O'Neill, Tan had called Thomas Li. There were three calls between them over the remainder of that day, short ones, about the length of a left message. After that last phone message Tan had followed up with a short email to Li.

Looking forward to catching up with you on Monday. We have much to discuss.

And the reply from Li.

Indeed. Your proposal could save us all a lot of money. Onward and upward good friend!

Finally, at day's end, an SMS from Des O'Neill to Tan. Initially erased but since retrieved by the techs.

Good luck, mate, you'll need it

In the follow-up interview O'Neill had explained this as being about Tan's upcoming fraught meeting with Li after the debacle of the FIRB decision against them. But the email exchange between Tan and Li did not seem especially fraught. If anything it was upbeat and optimistic.

Onward and upward good friend!

But what was it they were so upbeat about?

Cato's reverie was interrupted by his mobile. It was his sister Mandy sounding flustered, at the end of her tether.

'Dad wants a word. I'll put him on.'

There was the inevitable faffing about as Mand explained the phone to her dad and helped him put it the right way up.

'That you Philip? You there? Hello?'

'What can I do for you, Dad?'

'Fancy a nice walk?'

'Sure, when suits?'

'I'm ready now.'

Cato checked the time, late arvo, a howling wind outside. 'No worries. Where do you want to go?'

'My dad's old vegie patch.'

Here we go. Cato found a smile and put it in his voice. 'Give me half an hour, mate. Be right there.'

*

They were on the South Perth foreshore, Jack in his wheelchair, Cato pushing. Both were rugged up against the biting cold and threatening clouds. Across the wind-slapped Swan, the Perth city skyline was lighting up for the night and the ferry churned out through the foam towards Barrack Street jetty.

'Just over there.' Jack pointed and Cato pushed.

Mandy had been trying to juggle a screaming Bao, his recalcitrant siblings, and an insistent Jack. She was glad to see the back of at least one of them. 'Don't keep him out long. Just enough to catch his death.'

'South Perth?' said Cato, bewildered.

'Try living with this nonsense twenty-four-seven,' she'd muttered. Then guilt struck and she softened. She'd pecked Jack on the cheek. 'Have a good time, Dad. See you for dinner.'

They parked up near a gum tree that gave some flimsy shelter from the wind. Cato sat on a bench using himself as an additional windbreak for the old man. Jack seemed to be turning blue but the light in his eyes and the energy in his voice said 'Cold? What cold?'

'My dad's vegie patch was just here, about the size of Amanda's backyard.'

'What did Grandad grow then?'

'Spinach, cabbage, lettuces, tomatoes, you name it. I used to help him out, dig some holes, pop the seeds in, do the watering.'

'When was this?' Cato was trying to picture it, a sea of market gardens, before the skyscrapers and mansions arrived. Grandad was dead before Cato was born, he'd never known him.

'Long time ago. I was just a little kid. They called him Jack too, you know that?'

'Grandad?'

'Yeah. They called nearly all the Chinamen "Jack". Easier for them, I suppose. They didn't have to think, didn't have to try and pronounce the real names.'

'Jack,' said Cato, squeezing his old man's frozen hand.

'His real name was Xiaolong. Little Dragon.'

'Kwong Xiaolong,' said Cato. 'What about you, what was yours?'

Jack Kwong seemed not to have heard him. 'Dad loved this place, he spent every spare minute down here. He used to supply the vegie markets, made a good living from it, too. No choice, there was no other work going. They didn't like the Chinese, not for a job, but happy to buy from us, if the price was right.'

The old man was shivering. Cato needed to get him somewhere warm. 'What do you reckon, Dad? Time for tea? Watch the news?'

'They took the vegie patch off him, you know. Off all the Chinese. Some new government policy, "Whites Only". They gave it to some Slav. No compensation, no nothing.'

'What'd he do?'

A shake of the old man's head. 'He drank, cried, belted us all. Then one night he filled his pockets with rocks and walked into the river.'

'Jesus,' said Cato.

'Not interested in my Chinese name after that. Just Jack, that's me.'

Cato clicked the brakes off the old man's wheelchair and took him in out of the cold.

30

Saturday, August 31st.

Cato got the call just after 6 a.m. It was from Kenneth, Mandy was too upset. Little Bao had gone for one of his early morning wanders and tried to do a 'boo scare' on Pops. But Pops wouldn't wake up. Kenneth, an orthodontist, had some basic medical training, enough to confirm the obvious. The GP had been summoned to do the official business of pronouncement. Younger sister Susan was also on her way and Mandy was steeling herself for the day to come. Would Cato like to join them and say his farewells?

Yes.

Old Jack. Gone.

He showered and called Jane and they agreed Jake was probably best off staying with her for the weekend. The big father–son talk could wait.

'If he wants to say his goodbyes to Pops I can take him over if you like. Or we could all meet up?' Jane's voice cracked. Cato recalled she'd got on well with her father-in-law in the good days. The old man was an incurable flirt and she enjoyed his silly jokes and the twinkle in his eye.

'Sure,' said Cato. 'We'll play it by ear.'

When he arrived at his sister's house, the doctor was just leaving.

'Heart failure. He died in his sleep.' The doc zapped the locks on her Prius. 'I hope I go the same way when the time comes.' An empathetic half-smile and she was gone.

Had last night's antarctic stroll on the South Perth foreshore killed the old man off? Cato went inside. He did the hugs and kisses.

Mandy had come over slightly regal, the undisputed matriarch now. Susan had a cry into his shoulder. Kenneth put the kettle on again. The kids, even little Bao, were watching *Video Hits* with the sound respectfully low. Gangstas strutted and their harems twerked while the grown-ups discussed funeral arrangements. Cato went down the hallway to look in on the old man.

In death Jack Kwong seemed slightly grey and caved in. Cato kissed him on the forehead and laid a hand on his chest. His eyes blurred.

Just Jack, that's me.

Cato sat with his father for a while. It was peaceful in there, the room dimmed by the drawn curtains, the murmurs from the kitchen. A sudden jolt. Was the recording device still in place? Was someone, even now, listening in to the discussions of the funeral arrangements or had the bugging the other night been a one-off done by remote? He hadn't told Mandy about it and he didn't fancy the idea now. Sweeping the house for bugs, at a time like this. It could wait. If the bastards wanted to play today back to him in the small hours they could. He was coming after them.

He tried to recapture the serenity of the moment but it had flown. His final communion with his dad had been poisoned.

*

The rest of the weekend would be a numb blur of phone calls and arrangements, hugs and tears, endless pots of tea and coffee, and memories, some shared, others private. At some point the wine came out and Mandy got maudlin.

'I didn't mean it about hoping he'd catch his death,' she sobbed. 'You know that, don't you, Pip?'

'I hadn't realised you and Ken were in such a hurry for the inheritance. Kids school fees gone up again?'

She giggled through her tears and punched Cato's arm. They toasted the old man once again.

The funeral was set for Wednesday morning at Karrakatta and the wake would be held at Mandy's. Jane and Jake had called round later on Saturday to pay their respects. Cato was pleased to see his son turn on the charm and respect for the rellies and for the occasion. It was a good sign that the kid had enough social skills to still take others into consideration and reserve the shittiness just for his folks. That was fine. It was the kids who failed to moderate their behaviour for anyone that were the worry.

*

On that same Saturday, David Mundine was released from hospital, appeared briefly before a magistrate, and was then remanded to Hakea Prison ahead of a further court appearance on Tuesday. At Hakea he was put into the hospital block to continue monitoring of his burnt ear and possible concussion. His Legal Aid brief had been useless. A stuttering nervous limp-dick fresh out of uni. The tosser had failed to argue the case for bail, had been playing constant catch-up on his notes and his case load, trying to give all of his weekend clients the full benefit of his two-minute consultations. The prick had failed to realise that Mundine was the most important and that all the other low-life losers could get fucked. David knew now he should have refused to go to Legal Aid. All they did was shunt you along the conveyor belt. It wasn't as if he was short on cash, Mr H.'s money was still pretty much untouched.

So here he was. Hakea. A con. Just like his mum. The hell with that.

He needed to get himself a proper lawyer. One who would see him released at that next court session on Tuesday. He had some unfinished business to attend to.

31

Monday, September 2nd.

Cato looked in on Hutchens in Freo Hospital on his way to work. He passed on the news about his father going aloft.

'Sorry to hear that, mate.'

Hutchens was looking better. His skin was a healthier colour and his bruises were past their worst.

'What's the prognosis?' said Cato, maintaining some levity in his voice. He didn't want to drag the poor bugger down with tales of bereavement.

'Should be out of here tomorrow. There'll be a bit of to-ing and fro-ing at the outpatients while they check the blood thing and make sure there's no clotting.' Hutchens seemed to be avoiding eye contact. 'I had been hoping to be back at work by today, but ...' he trailed off.

'You okay?'

'Just told you, didn't I?'

'Anything else worrying you?'

'Nah, mate. Nothing.' He smiled up at Cato, sadness in his eyes. 'When's your old man's funeral? I'd like to try and make it.'

'Wednesday. Ten. Fremantle. But look after yourself first. Okay?'

'No worries.'

They parted. Cato was rattled by the exchange. Something was bubbling under the surface, a deeper malaise. Had Hutchens finally had enough? He'd been through enormous stress and trauma of late. Maybe DI Pavlou was right, maybe his boss was finally on his way out. The deadline for the Major Crime job was Friday. He dismissed the thought. If she and ACC Michael were swapping notes then odds on he was already cactus.

He dropped by DI Spittle's office and told him he'd like Wednesday off for the funeral.

'Sure. Whatever you need.'

Spittle updated Cato on the weekend's tally of stabbings, assaults, break-ins, drug busts and car thefts.

'Nothing special, then,' said Cato.

'You up to resuming a bit of the load, now the Hutchens stalker thing is sorted?'

'Yep.'

'And DI Pavlou tells me the Tan case is definitely closed as far as she's concerned.' Spittle met his eye. 'That right?'

'I understand that's her position on the matter, yes boss.'

'So you have a bit more time on your hands, funerals notwithstanding.'

'Yep.'

'Great,' said Spittle. 'Maybe have a chat with Hassan and Thornton. Divvy up the workload as you see fit. Keep me in the picture, eh?'

Cato asked if that was all. It was. Except.

'DI Pavlou mentioned she's looking forward to hearing from you before Friday.'

'Sir?'

'The vacancy? She seems very keen on you. You've obviously impressed her. You'd be a shoo-in, I reckon.'

Cato frowned. 'The timing's not real good. Flattered as I am.'

Spittle smiled. 'Don't worry about the loyalty thing. Apparently she's told Mick Hutchens everything.'

'Everything?' said Cato. 'Like what?'

'Dunno, but he's definitely in the loop on your career plans.'

Cato knew now what had been gnawing at Hutchens at the hospital. Betrayal and treachery. Pavlou had him believing that Cato was about to jump ship. He kept his face as neutral as possible. 'Did DI Pavlou drop by earlier?'

'No, she phoned.'

So he'd learned two things. First, Pavlou was playing silly cruel power games with the job vacancies. Why? Who knows. Second, she had phoned that morning with yet another message. Case closed on the Tans. Got it? Perhaps she and ACC Mike had indeed been comparing notes. Driscoll too, maybe.

*

Deb Hassan and Chris Thornton invited him over the road for a coffee and a catch-up, Thornton's round. It was mid-morning and Gram Parsons wailed from the gloom of The Record Finder next door, an Old Testament dirge about Satan, booze and women. It pretty well reflected the weekend crime tally.

'I'm doing the domestic stabbing,' said Hassan, licking froth from her upper lip. 'Chris is doing the boy racers and the drug busts. They're linked. We're sharing the break-ins.'

'What do you need from me?' Cato could already feel his attention wandering.

'Clarity of thought and decisive leadership.'

Uh-oh, thought Cato.

'Just kidding,' said Hassan, catching the look on his face. 'Take care of the home front, we've got it covered here.'

'Yeah,' said Thornton. 'Sorry about your dad.'

'Thanks.'

Cato's phone buzzed. Driscoll. 'Where are you?'

Cato told him.

'Don't move. See you in ten.'

'Something come up?'

'Yeah.'

They finished their coffees while Gram Parsons warned them about a fiery hell just around the corner if they didn't change their ways. According to him the whole town was insane and no amount of wealth would protect them from the Lord's burning rain. Another cavalcade of election billboards rolled by with a large evangelical image of the man whose moment cometh. Be careful what you wish for, mused Cato.

Driscoll rocked up soon after and immediately impressed Deb

Hassan. He flashed her one of his smiles and she went all girlish, a revelation to Cato. She and Thornton made their excuses and left, ruefully it seemed on her part. Driscoll got down to business.

He hummed a tune. 'Born Free'. The black PR company in Shanghai.

'What about them?'

'They don't just clean up your CV and your Facebook misdemeanours.'

'Go on.'

Apparently Born Free occupied a suite of rooms in a twelve-storey block in Shanghai's Pudong district. The rest of the building was made up of all manner of high-tech outfits involved in IT support, research and development, marketing, security, financial planning and analysis. Everyone in the building providing a lucrative and sought-after service and everyone in the building interconnected in some way.

'How do you mean?'

'Ownership, boards of directors, joint ventures; you name it.'

Cato still didn't see the point, and said so.

'That twelve-storey block is just part of a whole complex, a mini-suburb if you like, under the control of a specialist cyber wing of the People's Liberation Army. Unit 61398 it's called. From there they control the Great Firewall of China and what people can and can't see on the internet. They can also do their cyber attacks on enemies and business rivals as well as monitoring the phones, emails, social media accounts, and internet browsing habits of their citizens.'

'So?'

'So I think you're being hacked and bugged and stitched up. Not necessarily by that specific unit but certainly by somebody with a similar capability, perhaps a freelancer moonlighting from the day job. I hear the pay's not that flash for most of the drones. Anyway, like I said, Li has powerful friends and some of them might have a personal stake in some of his bigger property deals. His Aussie ventures would be particularly attractive to them; a good way of laundering ill-gotten gains. And these people are able to watch you all the way from Shanghai.'

'Where did you get this tip-off from?'

'Some of it is freely available on news websites. Other stuff is from friends and contacts.'

'Your PLA General friend?'

'Among others.'

'What can I do about it?'

Driscoll shifted in his seat. 'These folks give me the heebie-jeebies. If it was me I'd stay offline and hole up in South America for a few decades.'

Which wasn't entirely practical. But in some ways it was liberating. You were up against people so powerful that your fate was out of your hands. It was like being told you've got terminal cancer and your days are numbered, nothing you can do about it except try and enjoy what little time you had left. Then his father's premonition came back to him. The one about dying in China. In China, from China, because of China: what's a preposition between friends?

'Did your contacts tell you who precisely I'm pissing off and why?'

'No. But my bet is on Phoebe Li and her circle. Being a privileged rich kid herself she went to school and uni with all the other such kids – the high cadres' children, HCCs. These are the offspring of high party officials, army generals, and they've become untouchable. There was a road rage incident in Beijing recently. One of the HCCs, a seventeen year old kid, pranged his Porsche into a delivery truck. His fault entirely, according to the witnesses, but that didn't stop him and his mates dragging the truck driver out of his cab and beating him into a coma. They walked away laughing and nobody said a thing.' Driscoll shivered against a gust sweeping up High Street. 'Phoebe's crowd believe they have an absolute entitlement to wealth and power and they can do what they like without any consequences.'

And these were the same people who were probably behind the threats to him and his family. A daunting prospect. But he could sit and wait for them to come, or he could take the initiative. Cato smiled. 'We had a saying in Stock Squad, "may as well be hung for a sheep as a lamb". So if I wanted to rattle Phoebe's cage, how might I go about it?'

'I suspect her cage has already been rattled. You want to go further?'

'Yes.'

They considered their options while Gram Parsons continued his miserable bleating.

*

Back in the office Cato got to work. Driscoll had returned to the SAS barracks in Swanbourne to do his spook schtick. Maybe Rory's implacable unseen foreign enemy scenario was pure bulldust, a Yellow Peril scare for the twenty-first century with Cato, of all people, buying into it. It was convincing though: land deals, high cadres' children, cyber dragons in their twelve-storey lair in a mysterious Shanghai suburb. You'd almost want to believe it because it was so exotic and dangerous. Maybe the truth was more humdrum, low-rent, and closer to home. Yet Cato had decided to trust Driscoll and it was based on little more than gut instinct. So, if the cyber dragons were hacking him did that mean the whole Western Australian police computer network was compromised or was it just his personal laptop that had been targeted? His approach was not dissimilar to his Chinese Whispers tactic in Hopetoun. He tried not to think about how much trouble that had got him into. He would lay one trail of rumours with his personal laptop and a different trail with his work desktop. That would tell him which, at least, was the compromised machine, or even if it was both. After that things were likely to get trickier.

Cato laid his trail then spent the rest of the day dealing with the bureaucratic detritus of the job, drifting now and then into nostalgic reveries about his father. A failed attempt to get them both interested in footy when he was ten, Jack's excruciating jokes when Cato brought home his first girlfriend at fourteen, his mother playing the piano one evening and Jack bending down to kiss the back of her neck.

*

Guido Caletti had sent the boys home early, except for Bruno, his nephew. He knew Bruno wouldn't go. The lad watched his boss like a hawk, took his job too seriously. He needed to get a life, get a girlfriend. If the lad had been this diligent at uni he'd be a fucking professor by now, life tenure and all that. A small flock of night owls haunted the café, keeping Bruno from closing up. An alcoholic public servant from one of those ugly communist-style blocks in East Perth, the Department of Nothing Worth a Fuck, who hated his wife and kids so much he didn't want to go home to them. A tipsy couple who couldn't keep their hands off each other and should have been in a motel going at it instead of sipping sambuccas and playing footsie in his café. And the sad, lonely carrot cruncher in the Driza vest and beanie who looked like he'd taken the wrong turn at Wagin. Maybe he was hoping somebody would tell him where the brothel was.

Guido summoned up his Joe Dolce voice and laid on the accent to charm them out of there. 'Time please, ladies and gentlemen. You got no homes to go to, eh?'

The public servant muttered something worth stabbing him for, scraped back his chair and lurched out the door. The couple gave each other a last lingering tonguey and a wave to Guido and his nephew as they tiptoed off to bed. Bruno was busy washing and wiping the sambucca glasses. The carrot cruncher wasn't there. Obviously out the back in the dunny. Christ, give me strength, Guido said to himself.

'Leave the rest 'til morning, Bruno. Off you go. I'll shepherd the sad bastard out and close up.'

'You sure, boss?'

'Yep. See you tomorrow, son.'

Bruno grabbed his phone, ciggies and sunnies and left. Guido cleared the last of the cups and glasses from the tables and deposited them in the sink. Still no sign of sad sack. He went out back to find him. He edged his way past the boxes of Chinotto stacked in the passage and the mop and bucket outside the gents. He pushed open the door and spoke from the threshold.

'Sir? You in here? We're closing up now, mate.'

No answer.

He sighed and stepped in towards the closed door of the cubicle. Knuckles raised to do the rap.

A wire went around his neck.

32

Tuesday, September 3rd.

Cato heard about it on the news as he was driving away from the funeral parlour. He'd been tasked by Mandy to double-check last minute arrangements and confirm the choice of music. Mandy favoured Chopin but Cato knew his dad would also like to have slipped in a bit of Dean Martin. According to the radio report, prominent Northbridge identity Guido Caletti had been found dead that morning in his coffee shop. Major Crime were investigating and Organised Crime were also involved given the man's reputation. According to police spokesperson DI Sandra Pavlou, foul play had not been ruled out.

The call from Driscoll came just after the weather. 'Garrotted.' That probably would point towards foul play then. 'Did we do that?'

'We' meaning Cato. He didn't want to dwell on the notion of lightning striking twice. Chinese Whispers really was the deadliest game he'd come across, except maybe Russian Roulette. 'He wouldn't have been without pre-existing enemies,' Cato said.

'No,' conceded Driscoll. 'But it's a bit of a coincidence, eh?'

'It is,' Cato agreed. He felt sick.

Late yesterday, on his personal laptop, Cato had done a few google searches of Phoebe Li and put together a Word document of thoughts and queries which he'd emailed to himself marking it 'Personal – Safety'. The document had speculated on Guido's tip-off about Phoebe and Yu Guangming and possible involvement in the tangled Shanghai land deal. Was she in with Yu and looking to secretly profit from her father's vastly over-priced buyout of

Cambridge Gardens? In the Word document he'd included a note to himself to follow up with Guido on a few more details. So was Cato now next in line?

Meanwhile on his office desktop computer he'd sent a query to Chris Thornton asking him to look into Des O'Neill and, in particular, the story of the Lake Grace farmer who'd killed himself and his wife in a murder-suicide. It seemed plausible. Of course Cato would be interested in angles where blood had been spilt. But he had his answer now. His personal laptop was the one that was hacked and Guido Caletti had paid the price.

'Omelettes and eggs, mate,' said Driscoll. 'Don't fret on it. He's bound to have done bad things in his life to have earned his reputation. It's karma.'

'Thanks,' said Cato. 'I feel better. So, what now?'

'You know those big plastic neck braces they use when you've got whiplash? Maybe you should invest?'

They agreed not to talk any further on the phone now. Odds on, the hacking capacity extended to that too so they'd have to keep it brief and vague from here on in. They'd meet at the end of the day, after Driscoll had finished his training course. He was due to fly out on an early morning red-eye the next day. He couldn't say where.

Cato ended the call and parked near the Roundhouse for the walk back down High Street to the office. He looked up at Lara Sumich's apartment, the For Sale sign in the window. The world moves on. What did any of this prove? Yes, his personal laptop was probably in the grip of the cyber dragons and their evil mistress must be Phoebe Li but unless they could entice Phoebe over here none of this was worthwhile. Even then she'd probably pull a few strings and skip the country. He recalled a quote, often cited by his father, when he was encouraging Cato in his school studies, particularly the dreaded Maths. It was by the cellist, Pablo Casals, to the effect of 'the situation is hopeless, we must now take the next step'.

First things first, maybe that plastic neck brace.

*

Hutchens was having his drip changed when Marjorie phoned him. David Mundine didn't get bail as they'd feared but he'd walked free anyway. The private contractor providing prisoner escort duties managed to lose him in transit between Hakea and the magistrate's court on the fourth floor of the Murray Street justice complex. The relaxed and diffident young driver, a recent recruit on a starting wage of just over seventeen dollars an hour after tax, was pretty confident they had him when they entered the court building. But then it all got a bit crowded and busy, and confusing. Sorry.

'Fuck,' said Hutchens.

Marjorie agreed.

It wasn't the first time this mob had mislaid their charges and it probably wouldn't be the last. This was the same company earmarked to provide security at the reopened refugee detention facilities in the resurrected Pacific Solution gulag. At this rate the little munchkins would be scurrying all over Nauru like rabbits in a carrot patch. That at least offered some chink of light to those blighted souls who would come across the seas, our boundless plains to share. But it had put a real damper on Mick Hutchens' day.

'Enough is enough.' He turned to the nurse changing his drip. 'Can you get that tube out of the back of my hand? I need to be away.'

'Not without a doctor's say-so.'

'Get the doctor, get the paperwork. Now please.'

He wasn't being rude, just assertive.

It took a bit more wrangling and humming and hah-ing but an hour later Marjorie picked him up in the Kia and they were gone.

He dragged a clean T-shirt over his bruised head while she drove. 'How's Bill?'

'He'll make it. The bullet missed most of the important bits and they'll give him a colostomy bag to replace the rest. He's always been a fit old thing. Strong as an ox.'

'That's great, angel. You got Melanie sorted?'

'Yep. I put her on a plane to Cairns.'

'Good one, love. Got the gun?'

'Glovebox.'

'Right, let's go and find the bastard.'

They wouldn't have to look far. Mundine was two cars behind them on his scooter.

*

Cato had just made himself a coffee when Chris Thornton swung by.

'Got you that stuff.'

'What?'

Thornton flicked his fingers towards Cato's computer. 'That O'Neill bloke. I sent you an email.'

'Cheers, thanks for that.'

'Not going to open it then?'

How could Cato tell him it was most likely a waste of time, an experiment, and Thornton's task had been the placebo. O'Neill wasn't the person-of-interest, Phoebe was. 'I'll get on to it soon. Got a couple of urgent matters.'

'No worries.'

Cato thanked him again.

'You already did that.' He skulked off.

Cato rang DI Pavlou.

'Bit busy right now, Philip. Is it about the job?'

'Yes,' he lied. No point in having the phone put down on him immediately.

'Chuck me an email and your name's in the hat. I understand you've got a funeral. Sorry to hear it. This Caletti thing is going to run and run so don't hold your breath on a quick recruitment process. Could take a few weeks.'

He assured her that was no problem. 'Any ideas who's behind it?' The interest wasn't feigned, it was deadly serious.

'The garrotte was a bit special. We're thinking Eastern States.'

Cato whistled appreciatively. 'Nice. Underbelly stuff then, you reckon?'

'Open mind. As ever.'

'CCTV?'

She indulged him further, she must really want him on her team. 'A drunk, a canoodling couple, a young bloke we've identified as a staff member, and a Johnny No-Mates who went in the brothel down the road. The young staffer is in for questioning and the others are being followed up.' Muffled voices in the background. 'Gotta go. Bang that email through.'

Cato was happy to leave it at that.

*

First they drove past Mundine's Jolimont flat. Police were already there looking for him. They parked up the street and watched for a while. Nothing doing. They went along to J. B. O'Reilly's. Marjorie stayed behind the wheel ready for a quick getaway while Hutchens looked inside. Dermot the barman was there.

'Sure and you've been in the wars. What can I be doing for ye, sir?'

'Your mate been in?' growled Hutchens.

'Last I heard he was in the slammer and good riddance. Never paid me a cent, the bastard.'

'It was my fucking money.'

Dermot turned to the optics. 'A Jamesons, sir. On the house.'

Hutchens necked it. 'If you see him, tell him I'm looking for him.' He slammed the glass on the counter and departed.

'You're welcome,' muttered Dermot.

Mundine emerged from the toilets as the Kia screeched out of the car park. He slapped a wad of notes on the counter. 'Here's your damn money.'

'Looks like everyone forgot to take their happy pills this morning.' Dermot folded the money and put it in his wallet. 'Give the grumpy old tosser a kick from me.'

*

Cato needed to settle down. So Guido was dead; the man courted danger by his chosen lifestyle, he kept bad company. His death may or may not be coincidence, may or may not be Cato's fault. Either way he had embarked on a strategy and stage one seemed to have produced results; it seemed he was probably being monitored via his personal laptop. He and Driscoll had agreed that stage two was about upping the ante. Given that stage one had possibly elicited a murder it was difficult to see how you could up the ante without upping the body count. The phone call, the bugged dinner conversation.

See, Dad? You were wrong. Nothing bad happened to Phil in China. He came home safe.

Why wouldn't he?

Something tugged at his memory. One of Mandy's older kids, being antisocial and playing on his laptop at the dinner table. If it was possible for pervs to hack into people's laptop cameras and watch them getting undressed, presumably it was also feasible to monitor a distant conversation that way? Particularly some cyber super-nerd from Unit blah-blah of the People's Liberation Army.

You had a premonition of doom. Don't you remember?

That'll teach you to listen to a silly old bugger like me.

Was that what upping the ante entailed? They'd slaughtered a whole family before. No reason why they wouldn't do it again.

He scrolled through his mobile contact list, located the number, then used his office phone to make the call.

'Hi, it's me.'

'This is a nice surprise.' Sharon Wang's voice curled around his senses like a cat around his ankles after a long day of solitude.

'What's new?'

'Um, let me see. I'm back in Beijing and the smog is at factor five today. That means don't go out without a lead suit and scuba breathing tanks. I've got a ton of reports to read and statistics to digest. And a disciplinary hearing this arvo at two.'

'Ah.'

'How about you, when are you coming to visit me in China? There's a plane from Perth every day at eight thirty. I've checked. There's also afternoon and evening flights.'

Things were looking up. Maybe the seemingly aloof Sharon of the previous phone call had been an aberration.

'You wouldn't believe how tempting that is, right now.'

'Sweet-talking bastard. What are you really after?'

He told her.

'You realise you're drawing me into your international web of deceit and intrigue, don't you?'

'Yeah, sorry.'

'It'll cost you. I don't come cheap and I always exact my price.'

'Fair enough.'

'Leave it with me.'

She put the phone down.

Cato fantasised momentarily about that afternoon flight to Beijing.

*

After an afternoon of driving around and failed attempts to reach Mundine by call and text, Mr and Mrs Hutchens reached the inevitable conclusion and went home.

'He'll be coming to find us. We may as well make ourselves comfortable.'

'I'll put the kettle on,' said Marjorie.

'Good idea, pumpkin. Got any biscuits or cake or anything?'

'You're too fat, that's why you had the heart attack.'

'So?'

'There's lemon slice in the fridge. Cut me a bit while you're on.'

They settled down with their tea and cake and Hutchens flicked on News 24. Election coverage: lots of tossers in high-viz and hard hats looking uncomfortable with shovels. On the hour they recapped the headlines. The murder of Guido Caletti was a nice break from the election. DI Pavlou fronted the cameras.

'Is she the one you were talking about?'

'Yeah,' he muttered.

'I can see why she got you sparked up. I can just imagine her in stilletos and a bit of lace.'

'Love, can we just leave it?'

Marjorie wiped some crumbs down her blouse. 'No way,

sweetie. She got you so riled that was the best bonk we'd had for ages. Come to that, it was the only bonk we've had for ages. All power to her, I reckon.'

Hutchens slurped on his tea. Eyed the Glock on the couch beside him.

The news showed CCTV stills of the persons of interest. As usual they were blurred and murky and could have been anyone. They returned to the rolling election coverage. The polls looked catastrophic for the government. The opposition looked smug.

Then the TV went off. Power cut.

*

Cato got the emails and background info from Sharon Wang by the end of the afternoon. He wondered how her disciplinary hearing had gone. She'd put herself on the line for him and Lara. In a posting where political sensitivities were paramount, there would be little room for forgiveness. While he waited for the monitored emails to take effect, for the wire to go around his neck, he busied himself with loose administrative ends. He read reports, deleted circulars, inputted stats, returned calls, allocated budget codes. Another hour passed. No wire.

He opened up the email from Chris Thornton: the background on the Lake Grace murder-suicide. The lure to test who was listening in to what. Charlie Strickland's family had held their thousand acres just east of Lake Grace for three generations. He had been looking forward to passing it on to a fourth, his son Benjamin. But four years of drought, bad luck and poor health had taken the family farm to the abyss. Late in June three years ago, with still no sign of the rain he desperately needed, Charlie snapped. He blew his wife's head off while she was pegging out the washing, then, sitting in his favourite chair in the kitchen, put the shotgun to his chin and used his toes to press the trigger.

Benji Strickland was twelve at the time and at boarding school in Esperance. Not yet a teenager and already, it seemed, he was an orphan, an heir, and a bankrupt. Up steps family friend and benefactor Des O'Neill. Des organised for a mystery buyer for the farm, a foreign consortium. By some miracle or charitable sleight of hand he'd managed to raise far more than the farm was worth. Nobody was asking too many questions. The net result was debts paid off, the balance in a trust fund for young Benji who would continue his schooling and be looked after by his mum's sister's family. Was this another one of those deals where Francis Tan's reputed generous heart and love of country had loosened the purse strings for the greater good? It seemed so. Out of tragedy, a new beginning.

Thornton had appended the police and pathology reports on the murder-suicide and they concurred with the scenario as outlined by the investigating officers. News reports of the time added little. There was however a footnote of one further tragedy. Young Benji had died eighteen months later in a hit and run driving accident one early morning on his way from the residential accommodation to a music practice session at his Esperance boarding school. Apparently he'd been a very promising oboeist. The car and driver had never been found.

*

Hutchens bundled Marjorie into the bathroom and got her to lock the door. He handed her a claw hammer.

'If he comes through, use this. But make sure it's him first, not me.'

'Have you phoned the cops?'

'They're on their way. We just need to hold the fort for about five minutes.'

'It wasn't just a power cut was it?'

'No.'

Marjorie bolted the door on him and he turned to check if there had been any breach of the perimeter. He thought he'd locked all doors and windows before they sat down to their tea and cake. He hadn't heard any breakages since the power went out. Was he just getting jittery over nothing? Maybe he shouldn't have summoned the cavalry. He was going to look a complete idiot.

Mundine came at him from the old downstairs laundry that they now used as a wine cellar. No, he hadn't breached the perimeter. He'd been inside all along, waiting for them.

Hutchens felt a blow across the bridge of his nose. It blinded him. He dropped the Glock. He was on his knees, Mundine bludgeoning him with a cricket bat. Hutchens' old cricket bat, the one he'd once scored a century with for the under sixteens. He tried lifting his arms to defend himself but he couldn't summon the energy. He was very tired. Everything hurt so much. He was blinded by his own blood. That chemically thinned blood that couldn't stop sluicing out. He slumped sideways to the kitchen floor, the tiles cool and slippery on his skin. The blows kept coming. Mundine raising the bat with both hands in a chopping motion, the bat edge on.

Goodbye, Hutchens thought. Christ, this really is it.

The explosion was deafening. Mundine was lying on top of him. Warm, wet, a stink of the abattoir. In the distance the wailing of sirens. And Marjorie weeping, stroking his head with one hand, still cradling the Glock with the other.

'Don't die, love. Don't you fucking dare.'

*

Cato arrived as Hutchens was being carried out to the ambulance. There was a mask, a drip, and so much blood. He tried to get a prognosis out of the paramedics but all they would give him was a shake of the head. Marjorie was being comforted by a uniformed police officer. The radios chattered. A second ambulance was on its way and there was a body inside the house. Cato didn't know why Mundine was back on the streets or why Hutchens wasn't still recuperating in Freo Hospital from his last lot of injuries. It was like Groundhog Day. He glimpsed one of Pavlou's stooges, a young bloke called Fernandez.

'How did this happen?'

Fernandez told him about the private security bungle allowing Mundine to escape.

Cato growled. 'Where's Mundine now?'

'In the kitchen with a bullet between his shoulders.'

'Dead?'

'I fucking hope so.'

'What did the medics say about Mick?'

'Not much. Doesn't look too good.'

Cato felt his eyes swimming. He couldn't do this anymore. The Tans, Lara, now Hutchens. Too many good people being snuffed out. His dad.

Fernandez reached a hand out to him. 'You gonna be okay?'

Cato shook his head and walked away.

33

Tuesday, September 3rd – Wednesday, September 4th.

Cato sat at home with a bottle of shiraz two-thirds empty and a plate of chicken curry going cold on the coffee table in front of him. He knew he shouldn't be necking the wine. He would be burying his father tomorrow and he owed the old man a eulogy without the hangover. The news from the hospital was not good. Hutchens was on life support, in an induced coma. The head injuries were severe and the blood loss traumatic. Outside, the wind had whipped up again and one more cold front was approaching. Maybe the last. It was officially spring after all. New life. New beginnings. Rebirth.

Cato woke to the sound of knocking on his door. He checked the time on his phone: it was ten minutes to midnight and he'd had three missed calls and messages. His tongue was furry, his head thick. The wine bottle was empty. The late night noise had triggered some barking from Madge, next door's Jack Russell. There was a tattoo of rain on his tin roof. It was dark, it was late, it was raining and there was somebody at his front door. He decided to answer it.

He could see a shape through the door glass, back lit by the orange glow of the streetlamp. Big, indistinct. Dark clothing.

He couldn't remember whether or not he'd snicked the security screen door. He pressed the wall switch for the porchlight. It flooded the front verandah. The figure tensed, shifted uncertainly, reached a hand up for the screen door handle.

Tested it.

'Who's there?' said Cato.

'Me.' Rory Driscoll.

Cato invited him across the threshold, relieved and irritated in equal measure.

'You smell like a brewery, mate. Been hittin' it?'

'What do you want?' said Cato. 'And how do you know where I live?' He saw the enigmatic arching of the eyebrow. 'On second thoughts don't bother with the second question. I don't give a stuff.'

Driscoll shifted over to serious. 'So what's new? You weren't answering my calls. I got to thinking about garrottes.'

Cato told him about Hutchens.

'Jesus. That's bad. Sorry.'

'And on top of that I'm burying my father in the morning.' Cato filled a glass with water and took a long gulp. 'So this better be good.'

'Phoebe is on the move.'

'Headed this way?'

A nod. 'So I'm told. With two companions – a bloke who calls himself a lawyer, and another who seems to be her father's driver-cum-bodyguard.'

Skin moisturiser.

Driscoll filled Cato's kettle and dragged some mugs and tea bags out of a cupboard. 'So what transpired between you and Shazza?'

No way. Sharon Wang was already in enough trouble.

'She wasn't too enthusiastic. I've already caused her enough grief.'

'But?'

'But she copied and pasted those relevant sections of the extradition treaty between China and Australia, as requested, and gave me some contacts in the Feds offices in Perth and Canberra.' He drained his glass of water. 'Made a point of mentioning Phoebe three or four times.'

'It seems to have worked.'

'If Phoebe really does think we're looking at extradition then hopping on a plane to Perth isn't the smartest move. Killing me wouldn't solve her problems.'

'Hell hath no fury, mate.'

Cato shook his head. 'I don't buy it.' He accepted the mug of tea Driscoll slid his way. 'You on your way to the airport, then?'

'I rescheduled.' He grinned. 'Phoebe in Perth? I wouldn't miss this for the world.'

*

It was a godless service at Fremantle Cemetery. The way Jack would have wanted it. A solid turnout as well. Cato hadn't realised how many friends the old man had. There were colleagues from Curtin, and alumni old and young. Was it really less than ten years since Jack Kwong had left the job? He'd always claimed they'd have to carry him off campus in a box, he loved the place so. Instead, two years short of official retirement, the Parkinson's got the better of him and he'd sadly stumbled off to the car park with an armful of cards and gifts and a skinful of sauvignon blanc.

There were the tributes and the handshakes. The memories and the laughs. The tears. Cato choked a little during his eulogy, signing off as 'Qianping'. Jane and Jake were there. They hugged him, watched over him, shed a tear for Pops. The mourners drifted out of the ceremony to the strains of 'Volare'.

At the graveside rain spat through the sunshine and occasional gusts tugged at hats and skirt hems.

Jake sidled up to him. 'You okay, Dad?'

The temptation was to say yep, and give his son a brave and reassuring smile. But his eyes were swimming and bravery was beyond him. 'I'll miss him.'

'Yeah,' said Jake. 'Sorry.' A pause. 'About everything.'

*

It wasn't until Cato rolled home from the wake, late afternoon and a little tipsy, that he switched on his phone and was reminded of his three missed calls from last night plus a couple of new ones. Of the three from last night, two had been from Driscoll. The last had been from Sharon Wang.

'Bummer. You're not there. Hope you got the emails. I'm not sure what you're up to but the office seems extra tense all of a sudden. I had my hearing. Ugly. They pass sentence later in the week. I'll let you know how I go.'

The new ones were from Thornton. He'd dug up a bit more on Des O'Neill if he was interested, then ending up on an apology; he'd forgotten about the funeral. And Bandyup had called. Tricia Mundine wanted to speak to him. That could wait. You could only take so much of dropkick parents and their homicidal offspring. Speaking of which, he wondered if Phoebe had landed yet.

Cato dozed off. It was mid-evening when he woke. The drinks at the wake, on top of his late night with Driscoll, on top of a bottle of Shiraz before that, all in all, not a good look. But at least he hadn't been garrotted yet. He downed a large glass of water and called Driscoll.

'Any news?'

'They're staying at the Duxton. Phoebe's got a river-view suite and the henchmen are across the corridor, facing the city. They've had dinner, steak for Phoebe, bloody and rare. The boys had fish.'

'How do you get to know this shit?'

'I was with them, I had the pasta. They want to meet.'

'When?' Cato said, wearily.

'Now. You up for it?'

*

The Lobby Bar at the Duxton was furnished in retro green and purple stripes and flock patterned armchairs. For such an apparently classy place it was an assault on the eyes, particularly after Cato's recent indulgences. Phoebe unfolded her long legs and stood to greet him with a warm smile.

'Philip. So glad you could join us.'

Skin Moisturiser was there too. Cato was pleased to see he still carried faint traces of the bruising he'd given him in Thames Town. The handshake was brief. No warm smile. Finally the lawyer.

'Peter Tien, very pleased to meet you.'

Cato figured if the garrotte was going to come from anywhere it would be from Skin Moisturiser. He gave himself some space in the seating arrangements.

'Driscoll?' he enquired.

'Had to make a few phone calls. He'll be back soon.' Phoebe

summoned a waiter and asked Cato what he wanted to drink.

Mineral water would be fine. Yes, bubbles would be nice too.

'I feel I owe you an explanation, Philip. And perhaps an apology.'

For having Lara killed? For bugging his laptop and threatening his family? Or for slaughtering the Tans? 'I'm all ears.'

She explained that her less than hospitable, perhaps even hostile, behaviour during his recent visit to Shanghai was regrettable and she apologised. She could sometimes be overzealous in her protectiveness towards her father. 'I strive to be a loyal daughter,' she smiled.

Xiaodao: filial daughter, little knife.

'Did you pay Zhou's son to murder Lara Sumich?'

'Heavens, no!' Her hand clutched her chest, what a terrible thing to suggest. 'The boy apparently took offence at something one of your colleagues said when you all met in that expat bar. Chinese male pride can be deadly.'

Skin Moisturiser nodded in agreement. So his English was passable.

'Your visit to the family to offer them money?'

'Was purely coincidental. My father wanted to make reparation for the injuries Mr Zhou received during the evictions. Mr and Mrs Zhou will attest that there was no inducement.'

I'm sure they will, thought Cato.

'And your partnership with Yu Guangming and Des O'Neill on the Cambridge Gardens venture. How does that sit with your father?'

The perfect brows knitted together in a frown. 'There is no partnership. Any such suggestion is insulting and defamatory.' She took Peter Tien's hand in hers and for the first time Cato noticed the engagement ring. 'My reputation is paramount.'

At this point Peter the Lawyer handed Cato a sheet of paper.

'What's this?'

'We've been consulting with a local law firm. They have agreed to act on our behalf. This is a letter instructing you to cease and desist your allegations and enquiries into Ms Li.' His finger prodded a dotted line at the bottom of the page. 'You need to sign there.'

Cato studied the letter for a moment. Defamation, slander, libel, harassment, blah, blah. The threat was to take him to the cleaners if he didn't pull his head in. He crumpled the paper into a ball and bounced it off Peter Tien's nose. Skin Moisturiser stood up and leaned over Cato.

Driscoll returned with a middie. 'Jeez, the price of a fucking beer in this place, makes you weep.' He gifted them a grin. 'So how's it going with you mob? All good?'

34

Thursday, September 5th.

'I don't think they like you,' said Driscoll.

Cato had to agree. It was only a matter of time before they came for him. Phoebe's snarl of fury last night said it all.

'You will regret that.'

Skin Moisturiser looked happy. Game on. Return bout.

So Driscoll had elected to stay at Cato's overnight. He'd bedded down on the couch but the night was uneventful and, for Cato, sleep came surprisingly easy. Now they were sat at the kitchen table over a breakfast of coffee and toast.

'Like Ma and Pa Kettle,' Driscoll observed.

The radio was on. Two days out from Election Day and nothing had changed. Thought-bubbles, three-word slogans, squabbles over budget black holes, and the consensus: oblivion for the government and a new world order come Sunday. The opposition leader was giving out last-minute reassurances. The sky was not going to fall in if they gave him power. Promise.

'How can you work for that mob?' said Cato.

Driscoll smeared some marmalade on his toast. 'Who says I do?'

'A little bird tells me you're headed for the pointy end.'

Driscoll crunched and wiped some crumbs off his shirt. 'I have no problem with stopping the boats, mate. Shoulda done it two hundred years ago.'

If Cato had an argument for that he couldn't think of one right now. 'So you're a secret agent. ASIS? ASIO? Who?'

'Freelance.'

'Freelance?'

'Like Jim's Mowing – no job too big or small.' He took a mouthful of coffee. 'So what's your plans for today?' he asked, like it was a choice between visiting a winery or doing a swim.

'Thought I might buy one of those neck braces you were talking about.'

'Maybe a nice day at the office is the safest place to be?'

'Probably right. Pity I can't just arrest them.'

'For what?'

'Mmm,' said Cato. 'What about you?'

'Consider me your guardian angel, watching in the wings so to speak.'

'Why? Haven't you got a proper job to go to?'

'I have a strong sense of duty and obligation.' He poured himself more coffee from the plunger. 'And you're it. Until Sunday anyway.'

*

Cato received the post-funeral good wishes and condolences of his colleagues. The office was struck numb. Everyone's thoughts would be drifting towards Hutchens and the life support mechanisms anchoring him in this world. DI Spittle invited Cato in for a chat.

'How are you?'

'Hanging in there.'

'Good send-off?'

'Yeah,' said Cato. 'It was.'

'I've had some rumblings from above.'

'Yeah?'

'Some Chinese nationals. Highly influential. They claim you're running some kind of campaign of harassment and defamation. What's that about?'

Cato told him. 'You might want to take notes. It can get a bit convoluted.'

'You're not kidding,' said Spittle at the end. 'So you suspect them of involvement in the Caletti homicide?'

'Yes.'

'Don't you think it's worth mentioning this to Pavlou?'

'It's a bit loose, evidentially.'

'Not wrong. The whole story's a bit loose evidentially.'

Cato conceded that it was.

'I'll keep the top brass at bay. Maybe you need a break, somewhere nice and warm and far away. Let this all blow over. Recharge the batteries. What do you reckon?'

Cato said he'd give it some thought.

Back at his desk he found Chris Thornton and Deb Hassan hovering. All good, he reassured them. No, he hadn't been to see Hutchens, yet. He'd probably drop by later today.

'There was another call from Bandyup,' said Thornton. 'The mum's really keen to talk to you. Threatening self-harm if it doesn't happen soon.'

'Is that a problem?' said Cato.

'Your call, sarge.'

'Anything else I need to know?'

Hassan sniffed. 'I did a conciliation meeting with Mrs Harvey, yesterday.' Zac's mum, the one Deb tasered.

'How'd it go?'

'Terrible. I just can't bring myself to say sorry to the bitch.'

'What was the outcome?'

'She's considering her options. A civil action could be on the cards.'

'Sorry might not be the hardest word if she tries taking your house off you.' Cato thought of the letter from the Perth law firm threatening the very same to him. Physician, heal thyself.

'She did say something that made me think.'

'Yeah?' Cato felt his concentration slip its moorings.

'Yeah, her precise words were, "Zakkie was right. You lot can't see what's in front of your own noses". Unquote.'

'What do you think she meant?'

'Don't know. Maybe we should ask her?'

*

Taking Deb along to see Mrs Harvey might not have been the best idea but the antipathy between the two women could also prove creative. The suburb still didn't feature on the UBD or satnav. Deb had tried typing in *Trollsville, WA* but nothing came up.

'That Wikileaks bloke could hide out here,' she said. 'They'd never find him.'

Endeavour Boulevard was as bleak and windswept as ever and the doorbell still went ding-dong. Zakkie answered.

'What d'you want?' He was rugged up in a hoodie and trackies and uggs and seemed to have a sniffle. Something buzzed in Cato's rear cortex, probably a wine ricochet.

'Just the man,' said Deb, brightly. 'Can we come in?'

'No.' He twisted his head. 'Mum!'

There was the swish and static of lycra striding down a synthetic carpet. 'You have a nerve.'

Cato stepped forward. 'Mrs Harvey, I'd like a word with you and your son.'

'Piss off.'

Cato knew now what had tugged at his memory. Zakkie's hoodie. Same shade of green. The servo CCTV, a blurry figure hopping out of Matthew Tan's car and disappearing into the shadows.

Cato insisted on a word

They settled in the kitchen. No nice cuppas on offer. Bernice the tan staffie was outside again, eyeing them morosely from the shelter of a rusty bike. Mrs Harvey was late for the gym and not happy.

'Do you know how much a personal trainer costs?' she snapped.

'Sounds like we'd best get a move on,' said Cato. He turned to Zac. 'What were you doing in Matthew Tan's car on the night of the murders?'

The boy went very pale. 'What?'

'We've got you on CCTV. It is you, isn't it?'

'But you're not sure,' said Mrs Harvey.

'We will be when we link the green fibres we found in the car with Zac's hoodie,' lied Cato. 'So, Zac?'

'Maybe we should have our lawyer present,' said Mum.

'No.' Zac grabbed a box of tissues from the kitchen bench and blew his nose. 'Let's get on with it.'

Deb Hassan gave him the formal caution, took out her notebook and clicked her iPhone on to record. She announced the preliminaries and Cato repeated the question.

'I'd called around to see Em.' The Tan daughter, pregnant with his child. 'It was around ten-ish.' He knew the time because he'd received a text from her ten minutes earlier. He'd been waiting in the bus shelter up on Cockburn Road. The coast was clear, said the text.

'Why were you there if the relationship had finished some days earlier?'

His head went down. 'I was trying to get her back. I didn't want it to be over.'

'So you went in the house?'

'Yeah, the folks were still up. Clearing up and stuff.'

'What did "the coast is clear" mean then?'

'Matt was gone, he hates my guts.'

'Where did you and Emily go to talk?'

'Her bedroom. Her folks were cool with that.'

'And did you talk?'

'Yeah, for a while.'

'How long?'

A shrug. 'Half an hour? An hour?'

'Then what?'

A smirk. 'We went to the bathroom.'

'What for?'

'Really is this necessary?' said Mrs Harvey.

'Yes,' said Cato. 'What for?'

'A farewell fuck.'

The bathroom. Hence fewer traces of him than might otherwise have been. A goodbye shag, very accommodating.

'Farewell. She didn't want you back?'

'No.'

'Didn't that make you angry? Want to show her who was boss? The folks too? The kid brother?'

'No. She was trying to be nice. Wanted us to stay friends and that.'

304

'The coast is clear. Why did you wipe that text from your phone?'

'Because of what happened after.'

They'd never found Emily's phone. 'What did you do with her phone? It would have had that message on. Incriminated you.'

The boy looked scared. 'I never took it. I never.'

'Let's assume, for the moment, you're not lying. You and Em had your final encounter. What then? You left?' A nod. 'What time was that?'

'Eleven-ish.'

'Matthew didn't come back for his car until after midnight. What did you do until then?'

'I was pissed off. I wanted to do some damage to his BMW. There was a set of keys in a basket by the door. I took them. I was just going to scratch the paintwork.'

'Go on.'

'The zapper worked. I opened the car up, had a look inside. Thought there might be something I could rob.'

'Was there?'

More discomfort. 'Some pills. I tried one.'

'Oh, Zakkie.' Mum tutted.

'What happened?'

'Don't remember much. Felt good at first then all sorts of weird shit: lights, screams, doors slamming, cars revving. Powerful stuff. I climbed in the back and fell asleep. When I woke up Matt was walking towards the car, his chick had just dropped him off. He had another set of keys with him and zapped the locks.'

'He didn't notice you?'

'Bit pissed, I reckon, he smelled it for sure.'

'But you didn't let him know you were there?'

'You joking? He would have killed me.'

The rest of the story fitted the CCTV. He'd risked a look out the window to see where they were going. That had been caught by the Hampton Road camera. He'd taken his chance when Matt pulled into the servo on Leach Highway.

'So,' said Cato turning to Mrs Harvey. 'What did you mean by your words yesterday to Ms Hassan, quote, you can't see what's under your noses?'

A look of disgust from Zac. 'Oh, Mum. Did you have to?'

*

When the white Pajero made its third circuit Driscoll decided it was no longer a coincidence. He was parked in someone's driveway just up the street from the house Cato and his colleague were visiting. He'd been trailing them all morning, with or without Cato's knowledge, it didn't matter. Now the Pajero had turned up. It had heavily tinted windows so he wasn't sure how many were inside. He couldn't imagine Phoebe demeaning herself in such a way, or for that matter putting herself at such risk. But she was becoming less predictable by the day.

The Pajero parked up in the dusty windswept bays of a half-built primary school directly opposite Driscoll. Nobody got out. The driver's window was half-open and cigarette smoke drifted through the gap. Driscoll slid across to the passenger side of his Honda and slipped out the blind side. He reached the Pajero in a dozen strides and yanked open the passenger door.

'Mind if I join you?' Phoebe's bodyguard was alone. Driscoll switched to Mandarin. 'Feng, isn't it?'

'Feng Xilai.' He offered a drooping hand for a desultory shake.

'Mind if I open this window too? Double Happiness make me choke.'

'What do you want?'

'I want to know why you are following Kwong.'

'I was told to. It's my job.'

'Where are your companions?'

'That is none of your business.'

'Do you intend to hurt Kwong?'

'If I am asked to, I will do my job.'

'Do they pay you well?'

'Yes.'

'What if someone pays you more?'

'That would test my loyalty. The Li family does not like disloyalty.'

'They were happy to let you work with Yu Guangming?'

'It was Old Man's idea.'

'You have an obligation to him?'

'Yes.'

Driscoll took out a business card. A different one from those he had dispensed last night in the Duxton. 'We can pay you more. Call me if you are interested.'

Feng barely spared it a glance. He chucked it onto the dashboard. 'And if I don't?'

Driscoll switched back to English. 'No problem, my friend.' He went back to his Honda.

*

'So what is it we're missing? What's under our noses?'

Zac shook his head. He didn't want to play.

'Go on, tell him,' urged Mrs Harvey.

'Na.'

Cato didn't attempt to fill the silence. Mrs Harvey couldn't contain herself.

'She was having an affair.' A sly smirk. 'And they had the nerve to look down on us.'

'How do you know?' Cato focused on the boy. 'Zac?'

No response.

'Emily told you?'

Zac snorted, looked away.

Cato saw something in the boy's eyes he hadn't seen before. Vulnerability. Hurt. Was this what was behind his Facebook vitriol? Cato took a photo out of his folder. 'Was it this guy?'

The boy's face flushed. 'How did you know?'

'More important, how do you know? Where have you seen his photo before?'

'On Em's phone. She showed me. The slut was seeing the dirty old bastard.'

Emily and Yu Guangming? 'Are you sure?

'Yes. She was boasting about it.' Zac screwed up his face in a petulant imitation of Emily. 'Made her feel like a woman, she reckons. He was so cool and mature and sophisticated. Tosspot.'

'And her mother?'

'What about her?'

'Did she know?'

'I don't know. I don't think so. Why?'

Cato didn't offer an answer. 'So Emily was seeing this bloke. What about it?'

'She said he was coming round later that night. She was going to sneak him into the house. She'd got a text from him, making the arrangement.'

'Why didn't you tell us any of this before?' said Deb.

'Who's going to believe a story like that? Oh yeah I was in the murder house that night but it wasn't me, some mystery Chinese bloke came round later and did it. Honest.'

'And you probably didn't want the world to know she'd dumped you for somebody else,' said Deb Hassan. 'That right, Zac?'

His eyes welled up. 'Fuck you.'

*

Deb drove and Cato took a call from Driscoll.

'You've got company, the white Pajero.'

Cato had picked it up as they were leaving Trollsville. He recognised Driscoll's black Honda but the white 4WD travelling in the same convoy from such a deserted place was a bit obvious. Cato said as much.

'I don't think subtlety is the point,' said Driscoll.

'Should I be worried?'

'Not yet. I'll keep an eye on him.'

'Just the one? Who?'

Driscoll told him.

No surprise to Cato that it was Skin Moisturiser. 'What about the others?'

'Out buying garrottes, probably.'

'Cheers.' Cato told Deb Hassan where he wanted to go next.

'Bandyup?'

'May as well make a day of it,' said Cato.

*

Tricia Mundine was pink-eyed and slightly sedated as Cato took the seat opposite her. Deb Hassan had elected to wait in the car. On the drive up to the Swan Valley she got the strong impression that this was more of a social work visit. Deb didn't see the need to get involved.

'Not after what her little bastard did to the boss. No way.'

Cato sympathised. He was tempted to take the same stance. But something compelled him to hear Tricia out. Maybe it was just a rounding off, a balancing of the books. The karmic accountant in him.

'Were you there when they shot him?' Her voice was slurred, sleepy. They'd definitely given her something for the pain.

'No,' said Cato.

'Why did they have to do that?'

'Tricia, he was a killer. A violent man. He's left my boss in a coma. Killed a young cop down in Augusta. The bloke had a family, a little toddler.'

'Shame,' said Tricia.

'What do you want from me, what was so urgent?'

'My boy's dead. I don't suppose it's urgent though.' She looked around the interview room. The dull scratched walls painted and repainted. The smells: chemicals, cigarettes, misery. 'This is my ninth time in here. Home from home now.'

'It would be,' conceded Cato. He felt like telling her to do something about it, stop feeling sorry for herself, stop failing, stop breeding new generations of psychos and fuck-ups. Just die, he wanted to say. But he didn't.

She sniffed, a horrible mucousy rattle of institutional germs. 'I knew what Paulie was doing to him, you know.'

'Yeah?' Cato wasn't surprised. 'And you let it happen.'

'Paulie took him on holiday to the caravan in Augusta. I was back in here by then. Non-payment of fines.'

'And?'

'Next time they visited, I knew.' A tear rolled down her cheek. 'Davey just looked at me. He was eight or something. That look of his. Not angry or sad or anything. Just right through me, like I wasn't there.'

Cato already knew the answer to the next question. 'And you dropped Paulie once you knew?'

Tricia shook her head. 'I couldn't, could I? I didn't have anybody else to look after Davey. They'd have taken him off me.'

Cato cleared his throat, checked the time on his mobile.

'The next time, I thought he'd be better off in that hostel. Ward of the state, they'd take care of him there wouldn't they? Keep him away from the likes of Paulie.'

Wrong again, thought Cato.

'We do terrible things to our babies don't we? You don't even mean to, it just happens. We make monsters of them. And then they grow up and do terrible things to their babies, or other people.' Tears rolled freely down her face now. 'If your boss ever wakes up, tell him I'm sorry. Will you?'

'Sure,' said Cato. He stood up and they shook hands, a strange and awkward gesture under the circumstances. But a hug wouldn't have been right either. 'Take care.'

*

The white Pajero trailed them back from the Swan Valley. And behind the Pajero was Driscoll's Honda. Cato studied them in the wing mirror. Rain had blown in while Cato was inside the prison. Now it bounced off the windscreen and Deb Hassan had the wipers on full bore.

'Where to now?' she enquired. 'Geraldton?'

'The office.'

'Did she say sorry?'

'Yep.'

'That's all right, then.'

Cato wasn't in the mood for Deb's sarcasm right now. He switched on the radio. Election news. He fiddled with the tuner button until he found the golden oldies channel. The Easybeats, 'Sorry'. Cato turned it off again and phoned Driscoll.

'Any developments?'

'Feng called in to Hungry Jacks in Midland while you were visiting the prison.' A pause. 'Anybody interesting?'

'No,' said Cato.

'And according to the radio news you lot have somebody in the frame for the Guido garrotting.'

'Really? Did they give a name?'

'Nobody I recognised. Some dude from over east.'

Cato called Pavlou. 'You got somebody for Caletti?'

'Nabbed him on the Nullarbor just outside Eucla. The brothel-visiting Johnny-No-Mates we saw on the CCTV. He's an ex-mill worker from Tasmania, freelances for some Eastern States gangs. He puts on this slow-witted village cretin act and it works a treat. The Feds credit him with over thirty hits in the last three years.'

From *Day of the Jackal* to *Day of the Yokel*, mused Cato. 'So it was just some old grudge against Guido finally got paid off.'

'Yep.'

'You sure?'

A drop in the temperature. 'Yes, I'm sure. What's your interest?'

'I just wondered if, given his business interests, Guido had possibly crossed the Chinese.'

'No, it doesn't look like it. You and your Yellow Peril fixation.' Pavlou chuckled. 'Who'd have thought?'

Who indeed? So Guido's death was not a result of a hacking exercise run out of Shanghai. It was a humdrum domestic gang feud. 'Congratulations,' said Cato.

'No email from you, yet,' said Pavlou. 'Are you interested in that job or not?'

Hutchens on life support, hovering between two worlds. If he didn't make it would Cato still be happy in the Fremantle office? It depended on his boss. DI Spittle seemed a good sort but he was just a stand-in. Could Cato work for Pavlou? Right now, no. But he was too cowardly and perhaps too mercenary to take a position, yet.

'Been busy,' he said.

'Tick tock.'

Cato got back to Driscoll and told him about Caletti.

'The garrotte doesn't have your name on it then. You can breathe easy.'

'That secret hacking unit in Shanghai. Is that bullshit or what?'

'No, it's not. Phoebe is in town right now because she believes you're a threat. And she can only believe that from monitoring your communications.'

Or being tipped off by a friend closer to home, thought Cato.

He studied his wing mirror again. The white Pajero. The black Honda. He wondered which was the most dangerous.

*

Deb dropped Cato at the hospital. When he got to the room Marjorie was there, reading a book in the chair by Hutchens' bed, *Fifty Shades Darker*. She closed it and gave him a weak, tired smile.

'I'll leave you blokes in peace and go and get a coffee. You'll have a bit of catching up to do.'

'How is he?'

'Fucked,' she whispered. 'I think I've lost him.' Her eyes filled. She gave Cato a hug and a peck on the cheek on the way out.

Cato took his place in the vacated chair and studied the paraphernalia of life support around his boss. Tubes, wires, heart monitor, ventilator. What he could see of Hutchens' head and face that wasn't bandaged or gauzed looked hideous. He was barely recognisable.

'I've just been up to see Tricia Mundine.' It felt strange talking to a man in a coma, like talking to himself. 'She says she's sorry.' He waved a hand at the lights and beeps. 'For all this.'

He didn't want to talk work but, after racking his brain for an alternative, he had nothing else to offer. 'DI Pavlou has offered me a job with the Armani Brigade. Can you see me in one of those suits? Matching ties?' He shook his head. 'No, me neither.' He patted his boss's hand. 'You need to get yourself sorted and out of here before she drags me away. I thought you were a pain in the arse to work for, but she makes you look like a pussy.' He could hear Marjorie in the corridor, chatting with the nurse. 'Come back, mate.' Cato wiped his eyes with the back of his hand as Marjorie walked in.

She leaned over and kissed her husband.

'Jeez love, hurry up and get well or this bastard's going to start blubbing on me, or get the poetry books out or something.' She settled back into her chair, found her page in *Fifty Shades* and winked at Cato. 'You're a good sort, Phil. A real mate.' She squeezed her husband's hand. 'We're right here, pumpkin. Like it or not.'

*

On his way back to the office Cato grabbed some late lunch at the cafe over the road. He opted for a chicken salad roll and an apple juice and slid into a spare booth just inside the door. It was still raining and the sky, gunmetal grey, held the promise of plenty more to come. Next door, Roy Orbison drifted out of The Record Finder – 'Love Hurts'. Zac Harvey, the broken-hearted troll. Sixteen year old Emily and the Shanghai gangster Yu Guangming? Cato didn't want to believe it. Emily had once been like a niece to him. His main memory of her was of a four-year-old in pink, another Suzuki-trained piano prodigy bashing out tunes for him on their baby grand in the Preston Point mansion. But it wouldn't be the first time such an inter-generational matching came to pass. Yu had the looks and the predatory skills that could be mistaken for charm. If there was a history of communication between them then it would have been in his interests to take her phone with him. Her phone records hadn't been examined as thoroughly as her parents' and her older brother, Matt's. The focus had been Francis and his business connections, and then Matt and his history of bad behaviour. But what of it? Whether the motive was business-related or a crime of passion the result was the same. Yu had slaughtered the Tan family. Maybe DI Pavlou was right, maybe it really was time to bury the matter and move on. Several birds, one stone. If he stopped digging then probably the threats to him and his family would also recede.

In the office DI Spittle wanted a word. His role as acting boss had been extended indefinitely, he told Cato. And he had some good news: Cato's acting sergeant's position had been confirmed as permanent, he'd find the details in his inbox. Something in Spittle's manner gave Cato the distinct impression that the powers-that-be saw the attack on Hutchens as a blessing in disguise. The adverse publicity he'd generated at the Inquiry, added to his colourful history, could now be put to rest with a tragic yet heroic retirement and invalid pension. And if Hutchens died that would make things even easier. Spittle had brought his own family photos in – him and his lovely wife somewhere tropical plus another of his son collecting a footy trophy. He was settling in.

'How's Mick?' asked Spittle.

'Half-dead,' said Cato. 'That holiday you mentioned?'

'Yes?'

'How does two weeks from Monday work for you?'

A flicker of the eyelids, a hint of insult. He'd been the bearer of what he believed was good news. 'I'm sure we'll manage.'

'Cheers,' said Cato.

Loose ends. He called Driscoll.

'Pass the word along. I'm giving up on the Chinese connection. I'll even sign their "cease and desist" letter. Just tell them to piss off home and leave me and my family alone.'

'What's happened?'

'A dose of common sense.'

'That's not like you.'

'The times they are a changing. It's a new world order come Monday. Survival of the fittest.'

'Jeez, you are in a bad mood aren't you?' A pause. 'So I don't suppose I can appeal to your strong moral compass and sense of justice one last time?'

'Alright then,' muttered Cato, shoulders slumping. 'Let's hear it.'

Driscoll outlined his plan. 'Go on,' he said at the end. 'You know you want to.'

*

Driscoll was right. Cato did want in. He left instructions for Chris Thornton and Deb Hassan to review the Tan family phone records and, in particular, to look at those other family members who had previously received only cursory attention.

'I'm after any connections with Yu Guangming or any other such persons of interest.'

'Why?' said Thornton.

'Deb will brief you. It's about confirming a witness story – or not, as the case may be.'

'Fair enough. Did you get a chance to look at that latest Des O'Neill stuff I sent through?'

'No, give me the gist.'

'He was the executor of Benjamin's trust fund. Guess who stood to gain when the poor little bugger got run over?'

'Invite Des in for a chat in the morning. No hurry, no hint of drama. We'll see what he's got to say for himself. Meanwhile keep digging if you get any free time.'

'You due back any time today, sarge?'

'Can't say. I'm doing important work for the government.'

'Good luck with that. They're history after the weekend.'

'I'd better get my skates on then.'

*

He'd arranged to meet Driscoll in the lobby of the Duxton. It was late afternoon by the time he got there. Black clouds boiled over the Swan River and wind tore at the surface of the water. St Georges Terrace was clogged. Those who'd started their commute home early already had headlights on. Inside, the Duxton was an oasis of warmth, light and luxury. Driscoll was there with Phoebe Li and Peter Tien.

'No Feng?' enquired Cato.

'No,' said Phoebe. She snapped her fingers. 'Peter, give him the letter.'

The lawyer looked irritated but did as he was told. It was another copy of the cease and desist order. Cato read it through once more, out loud. How he must withdraw the allegation that Phoebe Li was in a business and personal relationship with Yu Guangming and further that she was involved in a conspiracy with said person to defraud her father's company and the Chinese people. And he was to stop harassing the Li family with his defamatory investigations. Blah, blah, and blah again.

'Remind me,' said Cato. 'What do I get in return?'

'Peace of mind,' said Phoebe.

'Not enough. My family and I have been threatened.'

Peter smiled reassuringly. 'You have our word that any such threat you perceive is henceforth vanquished.'

'Henceforth vanquished,' said Cato. 'I like the sound of that. But I also have other concerns. My career is in jeopardy, my financial security.'

Peter and Phoebe exchanged a look. 'Our understanding is that your career is flourishing.'

'You're well informed,' conceded Cato.

'But we do understand the need for financial security,' said Peter, entering the game. 'What level of jeopardy are we talking about?'

They agreed a level and a method of payment. Cato signed on the dotted line, two copies, one for him to have and hold. 'Happy now?'

'Thank you,' said Peter, graciously.

Phoebe was less forgiving. 'You have caused us a great deal of time and expense, Mr Kwong.'

'Sorry.'

Peter waved down a waiter and they ordered drinks to seal the moment.

'So when are you headed back to China?' wondered Cato, sipping a pricey Pinot Noir that carried a perfume redolent of fox piss.

'When we are ready,' said Phoebe.

'Checking out the sights?'

'Unfinished business.'

Cato took a punt, and deviated from Driscoll's script. 'That would be Des O'Neill?'

'Who?' said Phoebe.

Driscoll was shaking his head. Trying to warn him off. Cato ignored him. 'Wongan Holdings. With Yu Guangming out of the way, he's the only one standing between you and the Cambridge Gardens site.'

Peter Tien stood and offered his hand. 'Well, we have a few

matters to attend to. Thank you for your cooperation Detective *Sergeant* Kwong.'

'Pity. I was hoping to be able to say a proper goodbye to Mr Feng.'

'I'll pass your good wishes on to him.'

Phoebe didn't bother with the handshake. She hooked her arm in Peter Tien's and they left.

'Why couldn't you just stick to the plan?' hissed Driscoll.

'Another drink? Let's shove it on their tab, I'm sure they won't mind.' Cato resumed his seat. 'And then you can tell me where Feng is.'

Cato had switched to beer, a boutique IPA from a local brewer. It still tasted not much different to wallop, except for the price.

'They've been monitoring my work computer too.'

'How do you know?'

'They're full bottle on my career trajectory.' Cato explained: Tien's rebuttal that Cato's career was flourishing, his emphasis on Detective *Sergeant* Kwong at the end. 'All the recent developments on that are on my work emails.'

'That's it?'

'It also means they're interested in my musings on O'Neill. All of that stuff was also on my work computer.' Cato took a swig. 'That's where Feng is now, isn't he? With Des?'

'Yes.'

'Does he mean harm to him?'

'I doubt it. He's probably just making him an offer he can't refuse. Spilling blood in someone else's country is impolite and bad for business.'

'You knew that's where he'd be. Why no sharesies?'

'I didn't want to worry you.'

'Thanks. So did you get what you want?'

'I did.' Driscoll patted his jacket pocket, where the voice recorder was. 'Plus the phone on the table for back-up.' He nodded towards a first floor balcony. 'And pictures courtesy of our AFP colleagues.'

'Enough?'

'In an Australian court, probably not. In China, with the authorities ready to make an example of them, it should be more than adequate. The conviction rate in Chinese courts is ninety-nine point nine three per cent. Impressive, huh?'

'What about the remaining point zero seven?'

'I think they might be accounted for by deaths in custody before trial.'

'And what's to stop you turning all this against me? The corrupt cop, soliciting bribes and agreeing to drop an investigation in return. All signed on the dotted line and recorded on video and MP3 for posterity.'

'Trust me?'

'No, not really.'

'But?'

'I like living dangerously. So who's behind all this? Your General mate in the PLA?'

Driscoll smiled. 'I think we're about even now.'

'What will happen to them?'

'Show trial and firing squad. Tommy Li, Phoebe, Feng and poor Peter. Six weeks to live, if they're lucky.' Driscoll downed the last of his beer. 'Feeling guilty?'

Cato thought about Lara Sumich. 'No.' But he knew his face betrayed him.

'Maybe just a little, eh?' He patted Cato's shoulder. 'It's a good result. Believe me.'

*

Des O'Neill wasn't playing whatever game it was that Feng had in mind.

'No,' he said.

'It's a very good offer, Mr O'Neill.'

They were in O'Neill's favourite pub, Clancy's in Freo. It was pissing down outside and the place was rapidly filling with after-work drinkers. The fires were burning and steam rose from those recently caught in the rain. O'Neill had a stout, the Chinaman had a coke.

'It's less than half the previous offer. And that wasn't enough either. It's an insult, mate.'

Feng looked uncomfortable. They really should have sent somebody with the gift of the gab. This bloke was muscle, nothing more. What were they thinking?

'It is the last offer, Mr O'Neill. Take it or leave it.'

'I'll leave it.' He shook his glass at Feng and smiled. 'Another?'

'No. Thank you.'

'Fair enough.'

'We know about the Strickland boy,' said Feng.

Here it comes. 'Excuse me?' he said, cupping his hand to his ear.

'The boy. The farmer boy.'

O'Neill shook his head in exasperation and smiled apologetically, an old man, going deaf. 'This place is too noisy. Let's step outside, continue the conversation there.'

Feng studied the rain through the windows, shrugged and followed O'Neill. Outside O'Neill took a small canvas drawstring bag out of his briefcase and shook free a waterproof jacket, the one he used on his Bibbulmun walks. He zipped it up and raised the hood. They both took the opportunity to have a cigarette. O'Neill leaned in, seeking a light from Feng. 'Too windy, son. Just over here, there's a bit more shelter.'

They shuffled a few steps into shelter, out of the wind and rain, and out of view of the pub revellers. They bent once again to light the cigarettes. O'Neill drove the knife into Feng's heart then out again and across his throat. Let him slip to the ground, gurgling. He took hold of his ankles and dragged him under some bushes. In this weather the body wouldn't be found until the morning. He took the Chinaman's wallet and phone. Scrolled through the contacts list and sent a text to Peter Tien as he walked to his car.

He says no

A reply came straight back.

30, final

O'Neill sent one more so there'd be no further misunderstanding.

He says 50, final

Then he took the battery and SIM card out, stamped on the phone a few times and dropped the bits and pieces into bins and drains along the way home. Under a streaming downpipe he rinsed

Feng's blood from the waterproof jacket and shoved it into a rubbish bin a few kilometres along Canning Highway. He'd noticed a name in Feng's address list that gave him cause for concern.

Philip Kwong.

So the invitation for a chat in the morning was no coincidence.

35

Friday, September 6th.

Deb Hassan called him out of bed just after 6 a.m.

'Body in Princess May Park near Clancy's. Stabbing.'

Cato was there by 6.30. The perimeter tape and tent was up and Duncan Goldflam's crew were sifting and filming. It was light but the sun was yet to make its appearance. Either way the forensics crew had erected their own bright daylight over the scene.

'Any ID or description for me?' he asked Hassan.

'Male, Chinese, thirties. Medium build.'

Cato was getting a bad feeling. 'Who found him?'

'Some woman, a cleaner working at the offices over the road. She parks up behind the Film and TV Institute next door. That's her over there.'

Cato looked at the woman, an African, talking to Chris Thornton.

'Let's see the body,' he said.

It was Feng.

'Somebody made a real mess of him,' said Duncan Goldflam. He wasn't wrong. From the neck down Feng was drenched in dark blood. 'No ID.'

'His name is Feng,' said Cato. 'Chinese national. Staying with two associates at the Duxton.' Cato scrolled through his phone. 'Here's a contact number.'

'Friend of yours?' asked Goldflam.

'No.'

He left them to it and wandered over to Thornton. 'Did you book Des O'Neill in for a chat today?'

'Nine thirty at the office.'

'Thanks.'

*

Cato handed Des O'Neill a coffee and took a seat opposite.

'How you been then?'

'Busy,' said Cato. 'You?'

'Flat chat.' O'Neill sipped his coffee, a cappuccino from over the road. 'Nice.' He smacked his lips appreciatively. 'You wanted a word?'

'Yeah, thanks for dropping in. I did have a few loose ends to clear up but then something else cropped up overnight.'

'Yeah?'

'Yeah. Did you hear about the body in the park beside Clancy's?'

'It was on the radio when I was driving in.'

'You might know the bloke. A Chinese national named Feng.'

'Christ, really?' A shocked shake of the head. 'What happened?'

'Stabbed.'

'Jesus.'

'So you do know him?'

'Yes, well not really. I had a meeting with him in Clancy's last night. Some business. When I left him he was in fine form.'

Cato interrupted to do the caution and check it was okay to record from here on in. No problem according to O'Neill. Legal advice? Nah, what for? Cato invited Chris Thornton in to join them. Sure, that's cool. How did you know I was acquainted with Feng? I'm a detective, said Cato.

He pressed on. 'What time was it when you left him?'

'Eight-ish? It was pissing down.'

'Did you see anyone hanging around? Anything suspicious?'

'Not really. Couple of homeless blokes taking shelter in the Point Street Car Park. Poor bastards.' A pause. 'Shit, you don't think it might have been them, do you?'

'Describe them,' said Cato.

O'Neill did. One was young, skinny, and Aboriginal. The other was a bit older but otherwise the same.

They went through the story. The meeting with Feng was to

discuss a proposition for a business venture in China but O'Neill wasn't interested in the deal being offered. They stepped outside for a smoke, said their goodbyes and O'Neill went home. It was a wet, slow drive up to Glen Forrest in the Hills but he must have got there by about 9 to 9.30-ish. Joyce was waiting up for him, had some dinner in the oven bless her. Roast chook.

They'd check pub and car park CCTV, traffic cameras along the way, talk to patrons. O'Neill probably knew that and knew they'd back up his story. The best lies contain elements of truth. They'd need the clothes he was wearing last night for forensic testing.

'You think it was me?'

'We can't rule you out.'

'Fair enough.' He'd give Joyce a call and let her know to expect a visit?

No need. They'd all go up there together later.

'So,' said Cato. 'Moving right along. Benjamin Strickland. You know him?'

O'Neill's face went all sad. 'Poor little bugger. Very tragic life.'

'Tell me about it.'

O'Neill did. The Stricklands were old family friends. He'd gone to boarding school in Perth with Charlie Strickland, been best man at his wedding, and godfather to Benji. It had been a tragedy watching the family farm go into a downward spiral, taking Charlie with it. The man had low resilience and the Black Dog had descended. Des's only regret was that he hadn't stepped in earlier to help. After the tragedy that left Benji orphaned, Des had persuaded Francis Tan and his Chinese backers to buy the place out and the balance, once debts had been repaid, went into Benji's trust fund. Around a million, all told.

'A guardian angel,' said Cato.

'Francis was the main mover. He talked up the property to his mainland backers, way up, and even dug into the Tan family savings, mortgaged his place in Bicton, moved into that box in Port Coogee. I told him it wasn't necessary but the man wouldn't listen. Heart of gold, brain of mud.'

'How do you mean?'

'Charity begins at home. Get that wrong and you're up shit creek.'

'The family were unhappy?'

'Understatement of the year. Matt left home not long after, the girl Emily went off the rails, and the missus started lookin' elsewhere.'

'How do you know this?'

'Friend and confidante. Francis had a tendency to over-share after a good bottle of red.'

Cato stored that away. 'And you were the executor of the boy's trust fund?'

'Yes.'

'And then the boy himself died a year or so later. Hit and run.'

'Eighteen months. Yes. Shit, you learn to count your blessings, don't you?'

'What happened to the trust fund?'

'It covered funeral expenses and the remainder was handed over to the boy's auntie who'd been looking after him.'

'Are the accounts available?'

'Sure. Why?'

'Loose ends.'

'That it, then? Want to go and pick up those clothes?'

'Why not?' smiled Cato. 'Oh, one thing. How much did Francis talk the Strickland property up to? How far over its value?'

'A couple of mill?'

'And what did his backers say when they found out he'd been bullshitting?'

'Who knows?' O'Neill shook his head. 'Not best pleased I would have thought.'

'Do you know who the backers were?'

'No, he played his cards pretty close to his chest on that one.'

'Thomas Li?'

'Probably. Among others.'

*

O'Neill's clothes were ready for collection, freshly laundered, ironed, and folded by Joyce. Duncan Goldflam accepted them with a grim smile but took the washing machine draining filter with him too.

O'Neill gave them a copy of the Strickland trust fund accounts on a thumb drive. He was the very soul of cooperation and, with nothing concrete to link him to any wrongdoing, he was free to go about his business.

He and Joyce waved Cato and his team off the pretty Glen Forrest property, arms around each other's waists. In the bushes a willy-wagtail chittered merrily.

'What do you reckon, sarge?' said Thornton eyeing them in the rear view as he bumped down the gravel driveway.

'I reckon you've got a whole lot of CCTV to be checking this arvo.'

'Lovely.'

Cato's phone buzzed. Driscoll.

'Feng. Didn't see that one coming did we?'

'Have you talked to Phoebe and Peter yet?'

'Yeah, they're a bit upset. They aim to hop on this arvo's plane.'

'That might be a bit difficult. We'll need to talk to them about Feng.'

'That might be even more difficult. They're having morning tea at the Chinese consulate. I suspect they'll be staying put until the plane leaves.'

'Can they do that?'

'I think you'll find there's not much you can do about it. They think they're under the care and protection of the diplomats. In fact there'll be a white van waiting for them on the tarmac at Pudong and it's bye-bye happiness.'

'And you?'

'Job done. See you around.'

And he was gone. 'Who was that masked man?' murmured Cato.

'What?' said Thornton.

'Nothing.'

*

They spent the afternoon rounding up witnesses, mainly fellow patrons and pub staff, and checking CCTV and traffic cameras. O'Neill's story so far checked out: there'd been a reasonably amicable meeting between him and the Chinaman, stepping outside for a smoke, a parting of ways. The witnesses and pub cameras didn't contradict that, and nor did the car park and street traffic cameras contradict O'Neill's homeward trajectory in his white Toyota Corolla during the time frame he'd offered. There was, however, no sign of any vagrants taking shelter from the rain in the Point Street Car Park. Forensic tests on O'Neill's clothing and shoes would take longer to process and nothing was expected before next week. A cursory glance at the trust fund accounts suggested nothing untoward. Late afternoon, Feng's empty wallet was found in a rubbish bin about two hundred metres from the crime scene. Could it have just been a robbery gone way too far? Attacks and robberies on foreigners were statistically on the increase and the xenophobic election climate wasn't helping.

Cato wasn't having it. Des O'Neill was his man, and he increasingly believed that O'Neill was in some way tied into the Tan murders. How and why, he didn't yet know but the evidence wasn't there and without any they'd be unlikely to get warrants to dig further. He could just sit it out until the labs came back hopefully next week. Patience. It never had been his strong point.

Thornton popped his head around Cato's door. 'That analysis of the rest of the Tan family phone records you asked for? It's in your inbox now.'

'Ta. Anything else pending?'

'Nah. The Feng post-mortem won't happen until next week now. And the lab stuff on O'Neill likewise.'

It was nearly 6. 'Go and get yourself a weekend,' said Cato. 'See you Monday unless anything comes up.'

'Cool. Don't forget to vote.'

'Which way do you swing, or is that too personal?'

'The man in the budgie-smugglers, absolutely. Fit, good-looking, not a wimp or a talky smart-arse. If I was gay I'd have his picture on my wall. The ultimate Aussie. You?'

'Tree-hugger from way back.'

'Democracy's a wonderful thing. Have a good one.'

China was beginning to look more and more attractive. And it wasn't just because Sharon Wang was there.

He opened up the email and dug out the phone records. Thornton had helpfully transferred everything onto an excel spreadsheet and colour coded the fonts: Francis was blue, Genevieve red, Emily pink, little brother Joshua green, and big brother Matthew was orange. Other persons of interest had been added since: Yu Guangming, Des O'Neill, Guido Caletti, Thomas Li, Phoebe Li, Peter Tien. They retained standard black font but had been bolded and highlighted in yellow.

Charity begins at home. Get that wrong and you're up shit creek.

At first sight it was just a chaotic kaleidoscope of colours and Cato was beginning to think Thornton's font code had made things murkier rather than clearer. But then patterns did begin to emerge. Francis and Genevieve communicated with each other on average two or three times a day, as did the kids with their mum. There were no or very few calls between kids and father, little too between the siblings. Matthew was on to his mum even more than the younger kids, anything up to half-a-dozen times a day in the week preceding the murders. And both mother and daughter were in touch with Yu Guangming. That backed up Zac Harvey's tale of love and loss.

Francis Tan and Des O'Neill were in contact in the week preceding the murders. Cato already knew that – Des's text to Francis in the days immediately preceding Thomas Li's visit to Perth.

Good luck, mate, you'll need it

What they didn't yet have access to was O'Neill's independent phone traffic between say him and Yu Guangming, or Phoebe Li and her associates. Another for the warrants as and when.

But one connection did catch his eye. He made a call.

'Yes?'

'Matthew? It's Philip Kwong.'

'Uncle Phil. What can I do for you?'

'Wondered if we might have a chat?'

'Go ahead.'

'Face to face. Where are you?'

'Round at the Coogee place. Finalising a few details with the agent before the house goes on the market tomorrow.'

'Maybe we could catch up there. Give me twenty minutes or so?'

'Sure. No worries. Everything okay?'

'Absolutely,' said Cato.

*

A black bank of cloud hung out over the ocean as Cato signalled his turn right off Cockburn Road into the Port Coogee estate. Raindrops spattered the windscreen and wind buffeted the side of the Volvo. The seven o'clock news continued the last minute election reassurances: everything was going to be okay, really. The boats would be stopped and there would be no cuts to anything that middle Australia held dear. Vote 1 above the line for the Big Fluffy Bunny Party. Speaking of promises, promises, it occurred to Cato that he'd missed the deadline for the Major Crime job. So be it.

Leonidas Road was dark. Two of the streetlights were out or had never commenced operation. The pools of light from the remaining two were sickly and stagnant. Sand whipped across the road and tarpaulins flapped on the half-built shells of middle Australian dreams. Cato saw Matthew's BMW parked in the driveway and pulled in across the back, blocking it in. Three doors down there was a car pulled up on the verge, a nondescript white sedan. Otherwise the street was deserted. The tradies had gone home, blinds had been drawn on those few scattered houses that were occupied. The rain was coming down steady and heavy. It must have been a night such as this when the Tans were dispatched from this life, mused Cato. The For Sale sign was already up. The front verge had been swept clean and there was no trace of the flowers and teddy bear shrine. Lights were on in the house. Cato knocked. No answer. He knocked again.

'Matt?'

Nothing.

He pushed against the door. It was locked. He took out his mobile and rang Matt's number. It went to Messagebank. But not before he heard two trills from inside, and then silence.

'Matt?'

He knocked again, louder, slamming his hand on the woodwork. Nothing.

Rain ran down his face and the back of his neck. He shivered. There was a tall gate leading down a side path. Cato reached over and unlatched the gate, pushed it open and walked through. The movement triggered a sensor light. Cato decided it was time to bring out his gun. The wind caught the side gate behind him and banged it back onto its latch. The wind swirled, changing direction briefly and bringing with it the tang of cigarette smoke.

'Matt? It's Philip. I tried the front door and your phone. You there?'

'Round here, mate. Out the back.'

Cato rounded the corner onto the back patio. There was Matt sitting at a table, sheltered from the wind and rain by roll-down transparent plastic screens. He was sharing a bottle of whisky and a smoke with Des O'Neill.

Des lifted a glass. 'Join us, we're celebrating.' He noticed Cato's gun. 'Is that really necessary?'

Cato took in the scene. He relaxed and holstered his Glock.

'That's better,' said O'Neill. 'Pull up a chair.'

'I didn't realise you knew each other so well?'

'Why wouldn't we?' said Des. 'I've been a friend of the family for quite a few years now.'

'That's right,' said Matt. 'Round about the time you and Dad started going your separate ways, Des filled the gap. Sort of like a godfather to me since then, eh Des?'

'Cheers to that,' said Des.

Matt offered Cato a whisky. Feeling dangerous, he accepted. 'So what's the occasion?'

'Me and Lily got engaged. We put an offer on the apartment at Leighton Beach, view to die for.' They clinked glasses. Matt swept an arm taking in the property. 'And Uncle Des here reckons he can get me a quick sale on this place.'

Uncle Des, Uncle Phil. One big happy family.

'Let me guess,' said Cato. 'A mystery Chinese buyer?'

'Spot on,' said Des, meeting Cato's eye. 'Queuing up, they are. Thing is, we look at these places with our snob glasses on and we see an overpriced shoebox in an overheated market. But it's all relative.

In Shanghai you can pay over a million for a twentieth floor one-bedroom garret that I wouldn't put an asylum seeker into. This, my friend, is a steal, the height of luxury. Ocean views, marina, paradise.'

'Busted,' said Cato, grinning. 'I'm one of those snobs.'

'Here's to you then, you old snob.'

They clinked glasses again. The whisky was going down well, an old, smooth expensive one by the look and taste of it.

'What about you?' said Cato to Des. 'You celebrating too?'

'Yep,' interrupted Matt, exuberance and alcohol getting the better of him. 'Big offer from China this arvo. Everyone's a winner, eh, Uncle Des?'

Des smiled benevolently but Cato noticed a tightening of the knuckles around the whisky glass.

'Cambridge Gardens?' said Cato.

A nod. The temperature seemed to have dropped, and it was already pretty cold.

Matt noticed it too, he exchanged a glance with Des O'Neill. 'So what was it you wanted to talk to me about, Philip?'

No more Uncle Phil.

Wind tore at the drop screen and rain hammered on the colorbond pagoda roof.

'I was wondering about a couple of phone calls between you and Des here in the forty-eight hours preceding the murders of your parents and siblings.'

'What about them?'

'Well, according to the records, you don't appear to have much phone contact with Uncle Des usually. There's nothing in the whole month preceding. Then two on the Saturday, the day before the murders.'

Matt turned to Des with a quizzical look. 'Ring a bell with you?'

'Yeah, sure it does. I had some tickets to the footy, wondered if you could use them.'

'That's right.' Matt nodded. 'But footy's not my thing.'

'And the second call?'

'That would have been me ringing Des back to say no thanks.'

'No. The second call was also from Des to you. Late afternoon. After the footy.'

Matt shook his head. 'Sorry, can't remember. Why the interest?'

In for a penny.

'After the first call from Des, you then made four calls over the next few hours to your mum. After the second one from Des, you called your mum again, three more times, the last one just before midnight.' Cato chose his words carefully. 'I always knew you were a bit of a mummy's boy but seven calls, that's a bit keen isn't it?'

A frown. 'Nasty. That's not like you, Uncle Phil. Mum was a bit crook that weekend. I was checking how she was going. Des's other call? I must have mentioned Mum being crook. He was showing concern. That do you?'

Good answer. Time to crank things up a notch.

'Are you getting a cut from Uncle Des's Chinese deal?'

Matt couldn't help himself. 'Sure am. That right, Des?'

Cato smiled. 'Des O'Neill. The Orphan's Friend.'

'You stupid little bastard.'

'What?' said Matt.

Cato had his eyes on Matt when Des grabbed the whisky bottle and swung it into Cato's face. There was an explosion of glass and pain and his eyes filled with blood. He wondered if he'd been blinded. He felt a powerful hand grip the back of his neck and force his head down to the table. Another hand slipped the Glock out of its holster.

Cato felt the muzzle press into the base of his skull. 'It's all going wrong, isn't it, Des?' said Cato.

'Does this guy ever shut up?'

'Des, mate? What are you doing?' Matt was out of his depth.

'Matt doesn't know, does he, Des?'

The gun barrel nudged in tighter.

'Know what?' said Matt.

'Nothing, he's just trying to wind us up. Drive a wedge. Don't fall for it.'

'So Des didn't mention his business partnership with the bloke who murdered your family?'

The gun barrel whipped across the back of his head. Cato nearly blacked out. He wanted to. Knew he couldn't. Mustn't.

'It's over, Des. The killing has to stop. You have to give it away. Joyce wouldn't want this, she's going to need you over these coming months. She's not long for this world is she?'

'What would you know?'

'You were part of it?' Matt shook his head, stepping closer to Des. 'You knew that was going to happen?'

'Kwong's stirring. Don't listen to him, Matt. Please.'

'What's Des giving you, Matt? Ten per cent, twenty?'

'Kwong, shut it. I'll kill you if I have to.'

'You will have to, Des. And that won't save you. It's finished.'

'At least I won't have to listen to your fucking know-it-all whine.'

'It's less, isn't it Matt. What? Five per cent? But it doesn't matter anyway because it's five per cent of nothing. The deal is dead.'

'Bullshit. He got a text. He showed it to me.'

'Three, four weeks. The Lis will be in front of a firing squad. The Chinese authorities have decided enough is enough: assets confiscated, business empire broken up. They're history.' Cato felt a relaxing of the grip on his neck. Des O'Neill listening. 'I'm sorry, Matt. No mystery Chinese buyer for this place. No nest egg to help set you and Lily up. Nothing.'

There was a stillness. The wind seemed to drop. The rain eased.

Cato heard his gun go click.

36

Saturday, September 7th.

Des O'Neill was content to be represented by the Legal Aid lawyer. She was an old acquaintance of Cato's: Amrita Gupta, seven months pregnant and radiantly happy about it.

'November,' she beamed.

'Congratulations,' said Cato.

He meant it. Outside the wind still snapped and the rain spat but spring really had sprung. Birth, rebirth, life, all worth celebrating. The click he'd heard last night was Des O'Neill putting the Glock into safety before laying it on the table.

Des necked the remains of his whisky. 'Fuck it, I've had enough.'

'Des?' Cato had said, rubbing his neck in relief.

'I can't do this to Joyce. Leave her drowning in other people's blood.'

Des and Matt had a cup of tea while they waited for the paddy wagons to come and take them away.

'Pity about that whisky,' said Matt.

Cato had used a towel in the bathroom to mop the gash on his forehead where the bottle had connected.

Now Matt was having breakfast a few doors down and consulting with his lawyer Henry Hurley. He could wait. Des was the one with most of the jigsaw pieces in his pocket. They were lawyered up, announced on the tapes and ready to roll. Des and Amrita on one side of the table, Chris Thornton and Cato on the other.

'Where do you want to start?' said Des amicably.

'How about the beginning?'

'That depends on what you think I've done and when.'

They could only now begin the forensic accountancy on what might have happened with young Benji Strickland's trust fund but Cato suspected it was being milked by Des to help fund his dealings with Yu Guangming. But while it remained guesswork he couldn't go there, yet.

'Tell me about you and Yu Guangming.'

'By the time I met Yu, Francis was already in trouble. He'd been skimming, overpricing the deals to help out the poor cockies. His Chinese mates knew, thought he was an idiot, but it was small change to them. Usually ten to fifty grand here and there so they indulged him. Until Strickland.'

'That was three years ago, right?'

'Thereabouts.'

They'd nail the details along the way in subsequent repeat interviews. Cato was happy to go for an open account for now, to maintain flow. 'Why was the Strickland deal different?'

'He overloaded it big time. Valued the farm more than double what it was worth. His backers went ape when they found out. Thought it lacked respect.'

'You told them?'

'Had to, otherwise they would have come after me as his partner.'

'So?'

'Yu Guangming was working for Li at the time. Chief headkicker. He was sent over to have a discrete word with Francis. Old Li wanted a bit of distance from doing the nasties.'

'And you became acquainted?'

'He was a charmer. I was at a barbie at the Tans, they were still in Bicton at the time, and he was all over Genevieve like a rash. She didn't seem to mind too much either. Yu let Francis know he'd have to either reimburse them from the newly set-up Strickland trust fund or make up the difference himself.'

'But he didn't want to touch the trust fund? He downsized, sold Bicton and moved to Coogee instead.'

'Yep, and he told Yu Guangming that was his plan. Maybe that's what gave the bloke ideas above his station, or maybe not. He seemed cocky and ambitious anyway.'

'Go on.'

'He invited me to lunch. He told me about this development opportunity in Shanghai. Worth zillions for relatively small outlay.'

'Cambridge Gardens?'

O'Neill snorted bitterly. 'First rule of commerce. If something seems too good to be true, it probably is.'

'You wanted in and borrowed from the trust fund to make it happen?'

'No doubt your bean counters will dig it all out in time. The trust fund was a small part of it, yeah, but only in passing to help with cashflow. I did repay the loan when I disbursed the fund after the boy died.'

Cato could only ask. 'Did you have anything to do with the boy's death?'

'No. Why would I?' A shake of the head, how could Cato think such a thing? 'It served no purpose. The deal was on by then and I was able to repay the loan. No dramas.'

So the Strickland boy's death would remain an unsolved hit and run. Maybe just some bloke with two much grog still in his system after a big night out. Guilty, scared, waiting for a knock on the door. Over the following few years Yu Guangming established his own business empire, with the help of his then girlfriend Phoebe Li, and fed deals to O'Neill while sabotaging Francis's work with Old Man Li. Phoebe was the main saboteur.

'Motive?' said Cato.

'She didn't like the strong bond between her dad and Francis. And I think she was going through her rebellious phase. Flirting with dad's rival, doing deals behind Daddy's back. She was in on Cambridge Gardens for a while, part-funding our purchase of it and jacking up the pressure on Daddy for a big buyout to save his bigger deal.'

'But she finally came down on the side of the family business?'

'No choice. Filial daughter and all that. Besides there were big names attached to the main deal, party figures, military brass. They got wind of what she was doing. Quietly brought her into line.'

Unit 61398, or a freelance offshoot.

'You and Yu Guangming were out in the cold?'

A rueful smile. 'But holding on. We had too much invested by then and Joyce's cancer was back with a vengeance.' O'Neill's eyes clouded over. 'I couldn't back out, I needed the money too much. No super or shit like that. We dug our heels in.'

'Meantime, what was happening with Francis?'

In a tailspin. Phoebe's sabotages, culminating in the disastrous FIRB ruling that cost her father many millions, piled business pressure on Francis. Domestically the impact was huge. With the exception of young Joshua, the whole family turned on Francis for selling Bicton and taking them to Port Coogee and a generally less lavish lifestyle than they had become used to. Matthew moved out and kept on nagging his parents for money because he was too useless to organise his own life. Genevieve lost interest in her husband and began to look elsewhere, particularly at Yu Guangming who was in town more frequently on his own business these days. And sixteen year old Emily used her raging hormones and bitter teenage rebellion to maximum effect. Moving on from her bogan boyfriend Zac and turning her attentions full beam on her mother's lover.

'Yu was just playing her, though. Incurable flirt. Still he must have thought all his Christmases had come at once.' O'Neill grinned. 'Dirty old bastard.'

Amrita Gupta was finding it hard to hide her distaste.

'And then things took a turn for the worse,' said Cato.

'Much worse,' conceded O'Neill.

*

Marjorie Hutchens was eating a hedgehog slice while she worked through another gruelling *Fifty Shades* sex scene. Puh-lease she thought to herself, flicking crumbs off her chest, just smack him back.

'You still reading that? I thought you'd be finished.'

'Fuck me,' she said. 'You're awake.'

Hutchens smiled weakly through the bandages. 'Maybe later, love. Can I have a drink of water first?'

*

'They were trying to find a way around having to pay us for Cambridge Gardens. They'd even coopted Francis, told him I was working behind his back. Told him I was the saboteur instead of Phoebe. He believed it, things were a bit fraught between us by then.' O'Neill sipped some water from a bottle. 'We wanted two hundred million: dollars that is. We'd dropped it down to a hundred by the time the crunch came. True it was still three times its real value but it was still just tea money to the Lis.' He picked at a gouge in the desk top. 'I think Old Man Li would have gone for it but Phoebe was digging her stilettos in. She'd got word about Yu's dalliances with the Tan girls. The green-eyed monster had reared.'

'Stalemate,' said Cato. 'So what changed?'

'Francis had been going through some old papers. Trying to work out what went wrong with the FIRB decision on the Great Southern property, trying to redeem himself with Li. He must have come across the old documentation on the Strickland trust fund. He worked out I'd temporarily milked it. It offended his sense of propriety.'

'He was going to tell Li?'

A nod, which became a yes under Chris Thornton's instructions.

'But it was small change. Why would that be a threat to the Cambridge Gardens deal?'

'They could claim it was fraudulently obtained. A nod and a wink here. An envelope there. The local city officials could be persuaded to void their original sale of the land to us and blame the dodgy foreigner. And Francis now had the documentation to prove it.'

'Did Francis want anything to stop him blabbing and handing over the paperwork?'

'Nothing. He just thought it was the right thing to do.'

'All those calls and emails around that time. You tried to dissuade him.'

'He wouldn't listen to reason.'

'What reason?'

'I offered him a cut of the Cambridge deal. It would have solved all of his problems. Got him out of debt, out of Port Coogee. Maybe even got his wife and family back.'

'No deal?'

'No.'

'Why didn't he just scan the documents and email it all through?'

A shrug. 'Maybe a face-to-face with Li was his insurance, his bargaining chip, a way back into Li's confidence.'

'So you brought Matthew in. What was his part in it?'

'He was Mummy's boy. Mummy wasn't interested in communicating with me. She'd made that clear over the years. But through Matt, I made her the same offer. Get Francis to hold his tongue and they'd all be in clover.'

'And?'

'She tried, she failed. By then Yu Guangming was already in transit. He'd given me a chance to try and sort it out my way. Otherwise he would do it his way instead.'

'You knew his intentions?'

'Yes, I had a pretty good idea of what he was capable of.'

Good luck, mate, you'll need it

'You didn't warn the Tans?'

'No, it had to be resolved one way or another. Francis was scheduled to meet Li on the Monday and hand over whatever he had. Too much riding on it.'

Conspiracy to murder. But could Cato make it stick in court? 'Did Matthew know what was coming?'

'No.'

'But he must have guessed afterwards?'

'Must have,' Des said, grimly.

There'd been nothing about the Strickland trust fund at the crime scene so Yu must have found it, taken it, destroyed it.

'So mission accomplished,' said Cato. 'Francis was killed before he got to speak to Thomas Li.'

'So it seems.'

'Did you expect him to wipe out the whole family?'

O'Neill shrugged. 'No witnesses. He was in, job done, and out back to China. And for a while you guys were none the wiser.'

Something occurred to Cato. 'Once Yu Guangming was killed in Shanghai, that must have changed the game. Weakened your position?'

'It did a bit. The final offer on the land was pretty near to the true market value. I think Old Man Li was trying to play fair even though he didn't need to. By the time I had the meeting with Feng they'd somehow got word of the trust fund milking anyway, even with Francis dead.'

The cyber dragons, monitoring Cato's musings.

'You know we'll get the evidence to link you to Feng's death, don't you?'

A shrug. 'Let me know how you go with that.'

Cato had already had heartening news from Duncan Goldflam on that score. The washing machine filter contained suspicious blood traces that promised a result.

'What could be gained from killing Feng?'

O'Neill smiled. 'Hypothetically you mean?'

'If you like,' said Cato.

'I've been up to Shanghai, even met Old Man Li a couple of times. Funny old coot isn't he? Very formal and polite, but hard as fucking nails.'

'That sounds like him.'

'Did he do that "pushing hands" bullshit with you too? Toyshow, I think they call it.' Tuishou. O'Neill closed his eyes and brought his hands together in a mock prayer. 'So, grasshopper, you must dissolve the incoming force before striking the fatal blow.' O'Neill shook his head. 'Threats dressed up as mysticism. Silly old drama queen.'

'So,' said Cato. 'Feng. Hypothetically?'

'Hypothetically it sends a message that you're not finished yet.'

They wrapped up the formalities and turned off the recording equipment. 'What's going to happen to Joyce?' said Cato.

O'Neill shrugged sadly. 'God knows.'

*

Henry Hurley made a point of checking his watch as Cato walked through the door. The man didn't like to be kept waiting. Deb Hassan made all the announcements for the recording. Thornton was busy charging O'Neill with whatever they could, pending further enquiries. So far the main one was a murder conspiracy charge relating to the Tans plus the assault on Cato but they hoped, in time, to link him to Feng's death plus some financial impropriety. Enough to put him inside for a long while, leaving his wife to fade away from that cancer.

Matthew was a different kettle of fish, as they say. According to O'Neill, the boy had no prior knowledge of Yu's intentions to murder the Tans. So what could he be charged with: hindering the investigation by not revealing what he knew, or suspected, after the fact? By the looks on their faces both Matthew and his lawyer had already worked that out for themselves.

'Is Mr Tan charged, or likely to be charged with anything?' said Hurley.

'As yet, no. But we're hoping he may be able to help us clear up a few matters in relation to the horrific murders of his family.'

'Possibly. But he is also free to leave at any time?'

'Yes.'

'Then we'll play this by ear, shall we? Mr Tan has indicated to me that he is happy to help in whatever way he can.'

'Great,' said Cato. 'So, Matthew you stood to gain a lot if your father could be persuaded to not tell Mr Li what he knew about Des O'Neill?'

'I don't know what Uncle Des has been saying, nor do I know the details of his business but he did ask me to mediate on a sensitive matter between him and my dad.'

Henry Hurley had coached the lad well, he was a ventriloquist's dummy: a gottle o' geer, a gottle o' geer.

'Mediate in what way?' said Cato.

'Primarily by encouraging him to talk to Des about whatever concerns he had.'

'The phone records indicate that you weren't talking to your father much either. How could you mediate?'

'Through Mum.'

'And Mr O'Neill offered you some money in return?'

'We discussed a mediation consultancy fee, yes.'

'How much?'

'A million dollars.'

'That's a lot of money.'

'Yes.'

'Was that dependent on success? Because you failed to change your father's mind.'

'Best endeavours.'

'Did you know Yu Guangming?'

'I'd met him previously. Family functions. I saw him around the house on some occasions.'

'Yet you've previously been shown a photo of him and denied you knew him.'

'Did I? Must have been at the height of my grief phase.'

'What did you know about him?'

'He worked for some of my father's business associates in China.'

'Anything else?'

'Bit of a sleazebag. Mum seemed to like his company. Even Em had a crush on him. Yuk.'

'Did you know he was in a business partnership with Des O'Neill?'

'Not until you mentioned it last night.'

'And you didn't know that he was the one who killed your family?'

'Not at the time, no.'

'Later?'

'When you told me, it came as no huge surprise.'

'But in the days following the murders you must have had your suspicions, at least about Mr O'Neill. Yet you said nothing?'

'No.'

'Why not?'

'I was grief-stricken. Nothing would bring them back.'

'And if Des O'Neill was arrested, you wouldn't see your million bucks, right?'

'That's an outrageous and heartless allegation,' fumed Henry Hurley.

Cato ignored him. 'Matt?'

'I can't help it if you want to see the world that way, Uncle Phil. You've never really liked me since I chucked that bocce ball at your son. It was an accident, you know. Not my fault if he can't catch.'

Cato didn't rise to it. 'But either way, the million is down the dunny.'

Matt shrugged. 'The house sale, a few other inherited assets, I'll get by. Times like this you don't think about the money, you focus on the stuff of life. Love. Family. All that.'

Cato wrapped things up. He warned them that he would be pursuing a charge of hindering the investigation and he'd be in touch.

On the way out Matt shook Cato's hand like they were friends.

'Oh, did I mention? Lily's pregnant. I'm going to be a dad!'

*

It was mid-afternoon by the time Cato had completed the necessary paperwork and could head home for what remained of his weekend. First of all he voted. It was with a heavier heart than usual. There was an ugliness and tightness in the air, a feeling of scores about to be settled, blood about to be let. He'd received a text from Driscoll just after lunch.

Li dynasty in chokey

It was accompanied by a smiley face. Sign of the times. Would the impending apocalypse be texted to us all with a sad emoticon?

He decided to call in on Hutchens at the hospital. He was surprised and mightily relieved to find him awake.

'G'day,' croaked Hutchens.

Marjorie gave Cato her chair and nipped out for a toilet break and a cuppa. Come to think of it, she said, she should probably go and vote too.

'Lazarus with a triple bypass. Good to see you on the mend, boss.'

'So I am still your boss? You didn't go with the Velvet Hammer?'

'I don't think I'd have lasted long.'

'I'm stuck with you?'

'Yeah.'

'Fuck's sake.' Hutchens studied Cato's latest battle scars. 'Been in the wars?'

'Thin blue line, all that stands between decent folk and chaos.'

Hutchens lifted a hand at the spaghetti of tubes and wires keeping him in existence. 'You and me both.'

'I'm off on holiday for two weeks, come Monday.'

'Anywhere nice?'

'Dunno yet.'

'I'll see you when you get back. I aim to be out of here by then.'

'No hurry,' said Cato.

'Mundine gone yet?'

'Cremation next week.'

'Thank Christ for that. Thought I was going to have to buy a crucifix and some fucking garlic.'

'The Inquiry?'

'Can say what they like, I don't care. I got a text from that cunt Andy Crouch. Some local publisher wants to print his memoirs. Can you believe that?'

'You'll be famous.'

'I'll be rich. I'll sue the fucker.'

They parried and jabbed for a few minutes more but Cato could see the old bugger was tiring. 'I'd better make tracks. Don't suppose you're voting today, then?'

'I'm excused, I've got brain damage.'

'It's not stopping anybody else,' said Cato.

EPILOGUE

Zhou sat in his wheelchair and gazed out of the window at the sun melting in the smoky western sky. They were on the tenth floor of a twenty-storey apartment block not so far from where they lived before the pigs came floating in. A block with an elevator! The property development company had been true to their word and now he was installed in the skyscraper of his dreams.

From here he could see the muddy twist of river, the scavengers on the banks, the stallholders still scratching an existence, and the earthmovers once again bullying the ground into shape. His wife was downstairs cleaning one of the apartments of their richer neighbours. None of those neighbours spoke to them. Perhaps our clothes are too shabby, he thought, maybe I still have the stink of the communal bins about me. But they now had a living and that was something. The girl had one more year left at school. A better one now, private, also paid for by the property company. She had a good brain and a good future. No more talk of nightclubs and massage parlours. Had Little Zhou's sacrifice been worth it? He'd known that what he was being asked to do was wrong. He'd also known that they would most likely kill him for it. But that look they shared when the boy made his decision. All of that anger seemed to dissolve, like an evil spirit driven out. And so here they were, in the skyscraper of their dreams.

It was a pity about that foreign woman. The Australian. But one life in China? It was the swat of a single mosquito on the long road to a cure for malaria. Zhou wiped away a stray tear and lit himself a Double Happiness.

*

The election was all over by early evening WA time but the pundits were obliged to drone on until the loser officially capitulated and the incumbent claimed victory. In time he did and the choreography was hardly subtle. The flags, the rapturous triumphant audience, even the family wardrobe choice underlined the new order: White Australia was well and truly back.

Cato's mobile buzzed. He muted the TV.

It was Sharon Wang. 'Are you watching it?'

'Yeah,' said Cato. 'You?'

'Online. Turn it off and devote all your attention to me.'

Cato was happy to oblige. 'Where are you?'

'Beijing. Packing my bags.'

'The meeting with the bosses didn't go too well?'

'I'm a disgrace. I'm insubordinate, disobedient and unreliable. Not a team player. Et cetera.'

'The sack?' said Cato. 'Far out.'

'Worse. Demoted and transferred.'

'Shit. Where to?'

'Some hick airport at the arse end of the planet. hands up the bums of drug mules, escorting drunks off planes. Crap like that. I'll just get my papers and have a look.' There was a rustle and she was back. 'Perth? Where the hell's that?'

Cato found himself smiling. 'God, that sucks.'

'What am I supposed to do in a place like Perth?' she grumbled.

'I can think of a few things,' said Cato.

'Yeah?' she murmured. 'Tell me.'

ACKNOWLEDGEMENTS

All characters appearing this work are fictitious. Any resemblance to real persons, living or dead, is purely coincidental. While Port Coogee, WA, is an actual location, the defining characteristics of this housing development in this novel are the work of the author's imagination. In fact, some of the author's best friends live there.

I'd like to thank the Asialink Foundation for supporting my two-month residency in Shanghai and enabling me to get a glimpse of daily life in such an amazing city. Thanks to my hosts, the Shanghai Writers Association, for their hospitality, advice, and network of fabulous contacts. Thanks also, as ever, to Dr Isaac Harvey for his ongoing medical expertise and no, he's not really an internet troll and does not have a frullet. Alain Otto is to thank/blame for supplying me with the 'yesterdie' joke. Thanks also to the team at Fremantle Press for all their support and efforts on behalf of Cato and myself. In particular my editor, Georgia Richter, who continues to keep me grammatically honest and is generous with her editorial wisdom and guidance. Thank you too to my agent Clive Newman for working to ensure Cato has a few more adventures in him yet. Finally my beautiful wife Kath and son Liam who continue to support me in my literary endeavours and put up with those long periods when I stare into space and conjure up terrible things.

Bad Seed is an Asialink Arts Residency Project supported by the Department of Culture and the Arts, WA.

Government of **Western Australia**
Department of **Culture and the Arts**

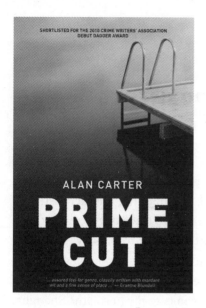
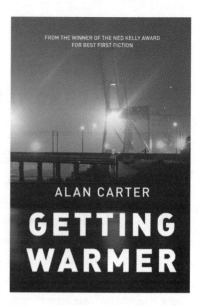